VICTOR

VICTOR

ANIMUS™ BOOK TWELVE

JOSHUA ANDERLE

MICHAEL ANDERLE

DISRUPTIVE IMAGINATION®

Copyright © 2020 Joshua Anderle & Michael Anderle
Cover Art by Jake @ J Caleb Design
http://jcalebdesign.com / jcalebdesign@gmail.com
Cover copyright © LMBPN Publishing
A Michael Anderle Production

LMBPN Publishing
PMB 196, 2540 South Maryland Pkwy
Las Vegas, NV 89109

First US edition, June 2020
eBook ISBN: 978-1-64202-980-2
Print ISBN: 978-1-64202-981-9

THE VICTOR TEAM

Thanks to the JIT Readers

Dave Hicks
Kerry Mortimer
Jeff Eaton
John Ashmore
Kelly O'Donnell
Diane L. Smith

If I've missed anyone, please let me know!

Editor
The Skyhunter Editing Team

DEDICATION

To Family, Friends and
Those Who Love
to Read.
May We All Enjoy Grace
to Live the Life We Are
Called.

CHAPTER ONE

"They've blown the gate!" one of the mercs yelled over the comms. His report was followed quickly by the sounds of laser fire and a pained yelp before his vital signs flat-lined.

"Shit, we need to get you to the pad asap," one of the team said and turned to the leader.

The man nodded to his employer. "Mr. Solos, we have to go now."

"Is it safe?" the CEO asked but immediately grimaced. "No, of course not. I can tell simply by hearing those blasted noises outside." He sighed as he stood and straightened his jacket. "I should have stayed on the station. I hear Pocock and Liu are only being kept under guard, but the rest of us—Hell, 'rest of us' might mean I could be the last one left on this damn planet."

The group of Red Sun mercs exchanged glances. The leader shook his head and rested a hand on the AO council member's arm. "Sir, moving at once would be—"

"Don't touch me," Oliver commanded and straightened to his full height. "We shall go, but I will not be dragged around my own manor."

The man nodded as one of the other mercs opened the door out of the safe room. They led Solos hastily up the stairs. Four took point and checked each corner as more blasts and the sounds of battle raged above. "I should have double-checked the sound-proofing down here," the CEO grumbled.

"We're about to enter the first floor," the Red Sun leader told him brusquely. "Keep your head down and we'll take care of things."

Oliver wanted to make a snide remark but instead, kept it to himself and muttered a low, "See that you do." As he crouched a little, the leader held a hand up and pointed forward. The troops in front opened the door and filed out quickly to check the large living area.

"It's clean, but I see fighting through the windows," one reported.

The leader ran to check and peered through the outside window. Figures in dark-red armor—his troops—battled other mercs in black-and-crimson. The Omega Horde was backed up by a growing number of droids in white and sterling silver. "Then let's get up there in a hurry so we're not caught. How long until evac?"

"They are on the perimeter, sir, trying to keep out of the battle zone until we are ready."

He motioned behind him for the others to bring Solos up. "Tell them to head this way. It's not like it'll take us long to go up four stories."

"Right." One of the team activated his commlink. "We're heading up and will be there in—" His words were cut short when the windows were blown out. An explosion had detonated near the front of the living room and laser fire and kinetic rounds swept the room.

"Shit—move!" the Red Sun leader ordered and grabbed Solos. Despite his earlier protests, the CEO said nothing as the leader and two other mercs forced him to the stairway while the rest of the team returned fire. At least three cried out and fell as the escapees rounded the corner.

The group raced up the stairs, but two Arbiter droids appeared from the opposite hall and fired at them. One of the mercs stopped to return fire and was able to eliminate both mechanicals before an Omega lobbed a grenade up the stairs as he turned to catch up. The thermal exploded, killed the man, and destroyed the first-floor stairs. It didn't seem to slow the invading force, however, as more droids filed in and tried quickly to climb the walls to reach their prey.

After a muttered expletive, the leader gritted his teeth in growing frustration. When they had been hired, he'd thought the number of creds they had been paid upfront was almost too good to be true—a fortune for babysitting a businessman who claimed he was targeted by a powerful organization. He had heard of contracts like that and most were caused by paranoia and overinflated ego. Still, he'd brought way more troops than most missions required. But when the first shots were fired and he saw the approaching army, he realized they were not only under-staffed but grossly underpaid.

"In here!" Solos yelled. He hauled a small painting off the wall to reveal a scanner that he placed his hand on. It blinked green and a doorway in the wall opened. He and the leader ran through, but the last remaining fighter remained behind. The man retrieved all his explosives before he fired at the scanner to deactivate it and shut the door as the bombs detonated.

The merc, now alone, began to fire, although the clouds kicked up by the grenades obscured his vision. What sounded like the searing of metal told him he was making contact at least. A bright blue glow appeared amongst the smoke. He turned to fire and heard a metallic whine as the blast was launched and he threw himself to the side to dodge the attack.

Clicks from above made him look up to where three droids were poised above him, having climbed along the ceiling. He aimed, ready to fire, but his gun was too hot and he had no time to vent. With a curse, he dropped it and tried to draw his pistol, but his enemy simply fell upon him as their blades extended.

The two other men sprinted up the last two flights of stairs tucked out of sight and which could only be accessed through the secret room. Solos panted, obviously unused to the exertion, but he made no complaint and seemed determined to endure despite his lack of physical fitness. They reached the top of the stairs and the Red Sun leader kicked the door to the roof out. He fired at a group of bots that surged over the edge and lobbed a shock grenade to his left when several made an appearance. The grenade slowed them, but none deactivated so he finished the job and vented his machine gun quickly.

Solos joined him as he closed the vent. "Sir, you should wait inside until—"

"And if I need to get away? Where would I go at this point?" the man demanded. His protector had to admit—when he looked around at the fighting below, the three Omega assault ships in the distance, and the fighting force they attempted to escape from—the CEO had a point.

"Is that the shuttle?" Solos pointed at the horizon and a grey ship that seemed on a direct trajectory toward them.

"It is. Let's get to the landing pad so we can leave as soon as it—" A rocket was fired from the ground below and it immediately locked onto the shuttle. The transport took the strike on its side and the damage blew one of its thrusters. It pulled away and missed the manor but plummeted earthward, where it plunged into a group of troops engaged in a heated battle.

The CEO lowered his hands. No anger was visible on his face and instead, simple recognition and dejection settled over his features. "Honestly, that was closer than I would have hoped at this point."

"Dammit. We called for a group of shuttles in case of a situation like this," the leader protested, although he constantly made sure to remain aware of their surroundings. "Where the hell are the others?"

"I believe you can guess as well as I can what happened to them—if they came at all." Solos muttered and folded his arms. "I must apologize to you. It seems all I paid you for was to commit suicide."

Both men turned when something made impact with the roof. More droids had arrived and the Red Sun leader could see several grappling hooks attached to the edge. He pushed his principle back as he aimed, but before he could fire, the advancing mechanicals were mowed down by shots fired from above. He looked up as several fighter ships descended. The aircraft spread out and began to fire on the battle zone below, seemingly taking care to fire only on the droids and Omega troops.

"Are those yours?" Solos asked in confusion.

"No. We don't have a ship station anywhere nearby and those aren't our colors." The leader sounded puzzled and zoomed in with his visor. "Those are military."

"Military?" The man sounded almost amused. "It's not exactly good for me but better, I suppose. I don't think they are here to kill me outright."

More fighters as well as bombers appeared and flew directly to the assault ships that had begun to close in. The bombers made quick runs along the tops of the vessels and set them ablaze with their payloads. A group of about six shuttles followed. Five of them descended to the combat zone and military troops dropped out, along with over a dozen other soldiers in non-military garb. Their armor and weapons, however, were too high-grade for them to simply be gang members or anything like that.

"Resistance," the Red Sun leader remarked and studied the new arrivals who defeated the surprised Omegas in rapid succession. He turned to his companion. "Those are mostly Ark Academy people, yeah? Do you think they will want you dead?"

Solos nodded slowly. "Assuming they know of my involvement, I would think so. I suppose I'll have to hope they want information from me more than my life."

The remaining shuttle circled to the roof and the side-door opened. The leader raised his weapon as several figures stepped out. A few were obviously military but two of them appeared to be Tsuna, he realized when he noted the infusers on the armor. The last man walked up to the two fugitives with a pistol in his hand. He wore dark armor with an armored jacket around it, and he stared at the CEO through a red visor, seemingly uninterested in his protector. Given how many other weapons were trained on him, though, it wasn't like he could do much to resist.

"Are you Oliver Solos?" the man asked. "One of the council members of the Arbiter Organization?"

Solos nodded wearily, a small smirk on his face. "Are you here to kill me?"

"I'd like to," he admitted and held a pair of cuffs up. "But you are more use to us alive for now. All your other friends on Earth are dead."

"I had come to that conclusion," the CEO stated as he nodded to the leader to put his weapon down and held his arms out. "Very well. It would appear that my value to Merrick is lost, at least in his eyes. Perhaps I could still prove valuable to some—" The words died in his throat when he felt a sudden pressure in his chest, followed by immense pain. He staggered as the Red Sun leader spun, followed by the troops behind the figure in black who rushed forward.

"Kaiden, sniper!" one of the Tsuna shouted as Kaiden caught the wounded man and flung them both to the ground. The other troops fired at the attacker, but Solos' hearing had begun to dull. He moved his hand over his chest and felt the blood from his wound.

Surprisingly calm, he looked at the resistance soldier. "I suppose I haven't much to give at this point."

Kaiden shook his head and glared at the councilman. "Are you gonna be like the others? Start spouting about how Merrick is doing this for the good of all and how we have no chance?"

"Not…exactly." The CEO chuckled and it ended in a slight cough. "I do think your chances are grim but I didn't follow him out of devotion. It was business."

"Your business killed millions." The ace growled with restrained emotion.

"And would have made me trillions." He sighed while his gaze drifted over the soldiers fighting to where the Omega assault ships began to crash. "There isn't much business without those to sell to, however. I can see that this…may end differently than…how I expected…guess it…already has."

"Do you want your last words to be your regrets? You still have a chance to help," Kaiden reminded him.

Solos refocused on him and smiled to reveal a smear of blood on his teeth. "Anything I have left…I had hoped it could be a …bargaining chip in case something like this happened… I won't get…any use out of it now." He tapped the metal of the roof. "The safe room… There is a vault… card to open it is…in my coat pocket."

Kaiden removed one hand from his back, slid it inside the coat, and withdrew a folded handkerchief. He unwrapped it to find a white card with a silver ouroboros emblem.

"So… How will this… end?" the wounded man asked.

The ace looked at him. "With Merrick dead. I haven't thought much beyond that."

Solos' smile widened as his eyes closed. "That would have...infuriated me a...couple of months ago..." He dragged in one last deep breath. "Now...I think it sounds... rather promising."

CHAPTER TWO

Haldt eliminated the droid under his boot with two shots from his pistol as Silas and a soldier ran up. "Is that all of them?" he asked.

"We're sweeping now," the military trooper responded. "Some escaped and left the droids to hold us back. But the assault ships are down and unless they can sneak shuttles in, they shouldn't be able to get far."

"Unless they all have bombs in their head," Silas countered and earned confused looks from the others. "Weren't you guys there during the assault on their factory? Ah, okay, but when the factory blew up, all the remaining scientists and techies were found dead in the hills. Apparently, a remote device detonated and left no survivors."

"Oh, yeah, I remember being filled in." Haldt sighed. "Well, that is a possibility at this point. Merrick doesn't seem to be playing whatever his version of chess is. He's made our work of killing his forces easier."

"I don't get this guy's plan," the enforcer admitted. "He's recalled most troops to the embassy and he's sent teams from what few strongholds he still has here to kill his board members? Doesn't he need their expertise or something? Why have them in the first place?"

"From what we know, they helped build and maintain the AO over the last couple of decades," the military man explained. "But at this point in the fight, I don't think he has much use for them. We've been able to freeze most of their accounts and have the various corporations on lockdown. They are more use to us for information than they are for Merrick's games."

"Oliver Solos was the last one we know of who is down here." Haldt looked at the roof. "They should have recovered him by now, right?"

The door to the manor—or rather what remained of it —was kicked out and Kaiden stood in the doorway, his arms folded. "Get in here. Solos is dead."

The three men looked at each other and Silas' eyes widened in surprise. "Well...shit." The military trooper ran to help with the search for survivors and Haldt and Silas joined the ace. "What happened up there?" the enforcer asked as they walked into the mostly destroyed first floor.

"It was a sniper shot but not a complete loss." He held up the key card he had taken from the victim as they walked into the living room. "He said any info he has is down in the safe room in a vault. The door to the room is on lockout but Genos said he has a way in."

"Indeed I do," the Tsuna announced. He held his gauntlet up and it took the form of a claw. His expression smug, he drove it into a panel, grasped a number of wires that he pulled out and sorted through, then touched three together. Bolts on the inside of the door clicked loudly. "There, that should do it."

"So you don't even try for subtle anymore, Genos?" Silas asked as Kaiden walked to the door and took hold of the lever.

"Given our surroundings, I don't think it is much of a problem to destroy one more thing." As if to accentuate his point, a few pieces of glass still stuck in the frame gave way and spilled onto the floor.

The ace slid the door open and the group descended cautiously. When they reached the bottom, they scanned the lavish chairs, a stocked liquor cabinet, several monitors, and even a few paintings. Clearly, Solos had intended to ride through any tragedy in luxury, at least while he could.

"There, Kaiden—in the corner." Jaxon pointed to a large standing vault in the rear of the room. They hurried toward it and Haldt and Genos checked for traps as they drew closer. Kaiden saw a small, thin hole where the handle should be. When he knelt and slid the card in, three red lights appeared. Each took a second to turn green before they blinked in unison and the door opened with a sharp pop.

At the bottom of the vault were several paintings, antiques, and other items of immense value. The way they had been carefully packed left little doubt about that. Above them on the next shelf stood several containers, all silver boxes. Kaiden took one and examined it carefully. They simply had numbers engraved on them so he passed it to Jaxon and retrieved the rest. There were six in total, which left him holding two and his teammates one each.

"Do you think they're safe?" Haldt asked.

Genos examined his box. "I don't see anything that would suggest a trap. There are no triggers or odd protrusions. I would have to run a scan to see if there are—"

Kaiden interrupted his train of thought when he flung a box across the room. It thudded into the wall and opened, and three items fell out.

"They seem fine," he stated as he wandered forward to pick it up. His teammates looked at each other and shrugged as they opened their containers. The ace retrieved his, along with the three sticks that had fallen out. They were storage devices, probably filled with information on the AO, but how much use it was at this point was debatable. Solos had been one of the credit managers, as far as they could tell, so most of this could simply be receipts and spreadsheets.

"I have a video device," Genos alerted them and held up a small stick with a circular indentation on it.

"Most of these seem to be only storage," Silas muttered as he glanced at their haul. "I guess we can search through them when we get back."

Kaiden looked at one of the monitors and saw a slot on the console beneath. "Genos, pop it in," he ordered and pointed at the insertion point.

The mechanist nodded and hurried forward to insert the device. The group waited as dozens of video files appeared. When they scanned through them, most seemed to be personal logs or records of meetings. The ace stretched over his teammate and pressed a second tab to reveal another page of videos, these marked with more unique names. *Interrogation_IS* and *Colossus_Found* caught his interest, but the one that captured his attention was marked, *M_Confession*.

"M?" He frowned thoughtfully. "Do you think that could be Merrick?"

The group members glanced at each other. "It could be. We should still have enough time before we depart," Jaxon told him.

Haldt nodded to the screen. "Load it up."

Kaiden tapped on the file and a video player appeared on the screen. The footage displayed a somewhat hazy video of a man seated in shadow while a hand moved away from the camera, possibly having activated a secret recorder on their lapel.

"I can't say I understand, sir," Solos said. "I thought our objective was to continue the evolution of humanity and push it forward. But you wish to go to war?"

"I'm saying it may come to that, Oliver," the man said, his voice grim and low in tone. He looked up and the ace recognized him as Merrick, although he was much younger. There were fewer lines on his face and his arched brow and set jaw were less pronounced than he remembered, so this must have been recorded years before. "When they gave me the serum, it not only increased my physical ability, it opened my mind like never before."

"And it gave you…what? A vision?"

"A premonition. Or something contacted me. Something is coming for us, our planet, and our galaxy. We have to be prepared. That is why I've sought you and the others out."

"I see. But I was enticed by the potential profits as they were explained to me," Solos stated and sounded irritated.

"It is rather easy to profit from war but from extinction? The ramifications of what you are saying this could lead to—"

"Are inconsequential compared to there being nothing," Merrick snapped and pushed from his chair in an abrupt movement. "You'll get your pay and you'll get a title when this is all over. But if you want it to mean anything, you'll need to live to see it. We all will be indebted to those who brought about our salvation and our evolution. That should help bolster your records, shouldn't it?"

Oliver shifted in his seat and the hand he'd rested on the table tensed. "It certainly would. Even simple thought on the matter confirms that this could result in a tidy sum for me. But if this 'premonition' of yours is true and you are able to force your hand to get humanity to your side, what can be done against this being you talk about?"

The Arbiter leader drew a deep breath. "Our focus will be to prepare for a war the likes of which this galaxy has never seen. We will start with the Ark soldiers and give them the same gift I was given." Kaiden, Genos, Silas, and Jaxon looked at one another. "They will see what I have seen and will know and convince the rest of what needs to be done. They will all be my students once again."

Kaiden's fist balled and he struck the screen to shatter it as he yanked the drive out. He shoved it against Genos' chest as he picked his cases up and walked to the stairs. "Like hell."

CHAPTER THREE

Sasha Chevalier and General Hartman walked through the halls of the temporary WCM military HQ in London. "Team Alpha reported in before you called," Sasha stated. "They said Solos was killed during the rescue attempt but they were able to retrieve a number of storage units from a vault in his safe room."

"Then it means any remaining AO council members are on the stations." The military man sighed. "They'll return soon, correct?"

"They said they are already on their way," the Nexus chancellor confirmed and adjusted the cuffs of his jacket. "Team Bravo, on the other hand, are still preparing, but they should begin their strike in only a few minutes."

"That's good to know. We'll need those access codes for the next stage," Hartman noted as they entered the war room. A large circular table stood in the middle surrounded by many holoscreens and monitors, each showing feed from different campaigns and stations. He walked to the table's console and activated it, and it displayed a holographic recreation of an Omega Horde encampment. "They will need to work quickly. We are already preparing to strike the stations. The codes they retrieve won't be active for more than another three days according to the report. We'll need to capture the Icarus base by that time and upload them to command the station."

"That's understood. They'll get it done," he promised.

The general nodded. "And you made sure they understood that they had permission to do this as viciously as they pleased? There's no need for stealth maneuvers at this time."

Sasha allowed himself a small smile. "I did one better. I chose my team based on those who wouldn't bother with stealth anyway."

"Team three reporting. Still fucking nothing," an Omega merc muttered into his comm. He sighed and turned to look at his two teammates. "When the hell are we leaving? We've been on this station for three months now, doing the same boring shit while everyone else is taking off. What about us?"

"Quit your bitching," another responded and flipped through videos on his tablet. "I'm glad to have a little break. I was at Nexus Academy during the fight a couple of months back and barely made it out. If we have plans to take it to the military, I'm fine with waiting to live to see it."

"Agreed, but he has a point too," the third man interjected. "More of the Horde are being called back. The longer we stick around, the more we'll become a target. We should get into the stars with the others."

"We'll be out soon enough," the lazy one grumbled. "I heard shuttles and a transport carrier will be coming in a few days. Until then—" His sentence cut short when all three heard a couple of loud bangs, not like a gun but rather something heavy detonating. He put his tablet down and snatched his shotgun up as they looked down from their tower. "What the hell was that?"

"I don't know. An animal maybe?" one reasoned.

"It sounded mechanical. One of our generators?" the other responded.

"We don't have one in that direction," the third reminded them and his gaze shifted to scrutinize the jungle. "We should check with the techies to see if anything is picked up on the—"

The roof of their tower caved in as two heavies powered through. One was aglow with energy and the other wielded a large hammer. The merc with the shotgun turned to fire but was hurled out of the tower by a blast from the vanguard. The titan raised his hammer and pounded it onto the floor, and a portion of it collapsed. The two guards plummeted through the hole and banged off the spiraling stairs below during their painful descent.

"Our tower is clear," Luke announced as he and Mack leapt off the tall building to the ground below. The rear gate to the Omega base was obliterated and a team of Nexus soldiers rushed in. Marlo vented his cannon as he jogged with the party.

"So is ours," Cameron announced as the fourth member

of the defenders was felled by a shot from Flynn. "Indre, Otto, how are the internal defenses?'"

"They are down so there's no need to worry," Otto replied as he closed his holoscreen.

"I doubt they were," Indre replied as she launched three drones. "Let's join the fun, huh?"

An Omega tried to man one of the stationary turrets but was knocked over the head by a tracker drone. Raul grinned smugly as Izzy slid under an enemy heavy and vaulted onto her opponent's back. She pressed her pistol against his armor's power unit and fired to cripple the heavy until the gun overheated. As she vaulted clear, Luke raced forward and swung his hammer into the side of the merc's chest and the force of the impact hurled him against the wall of one of the buildings.

"Is anyone wounded?" Julius asked as he lobbed a grenade at a group of oncoming mercs. It erupted and filled the area with purple smoke. The enemy began to choke and staggered out of the gas but within moments, they fell and began to curl where they landed.

"I don't think anyone will ask for help from the man with chemical weapons," Amber told him as she finished attending to an arm injury for one of the soldiers and turned to fire her pistol at a merc who tried to sneak up behind them. She forced him back until a shot from Flynn from a higher vantage killed him.

"Chemicals can be used for life and death," Julius explained. "And what of your actions?"

"I'm a battle medic. Kindness and aggression both have value on the battlefield," she retorted as the two medics returned to the field.

"We're here for those codes, right?" Mack asked. He formed a barrier around a couple of enemy grenades to seal their blast off as several other soldiers ran past. "Maybe we should get on that before these jackasses try to get away with them."

"It doesn't work like that but it is nice to see you being the voice of reason for once." Otto's compliment held an undertone of amusement.

"Right. Otto, Indre, Raul, and Izzy, you guys are with me," Cameron stated. He used his grappling hook to snag the underside of one of the towers and swung down. "The rest of you...well, keep it up."

"Did we vote him as leader?" Flynn asked as he shot an enemy demolitionist's launcher out of his hands. Marlo turned and fired a blast from his cannon. It exploded beneath the enemy's feet and launched him into a nearby group of mercs. "Because I don't remember that."

"Do you wanna argue or work on your score?" the bounty hunter retorted as his group gathered. "Besides, you're still rusty from your nap, Rapunzel."

"That was Rip Van Winkle, you dumbass," the marksman told him as he moved from his current position when an Omega sniper tried to take shots at him.

"Ah...right. Shit," Cameron muttered. He located the hostile sniper, eliminated him with two shots of his rifle, and opened the vent. "Whatever. You'll have your turn when we spin the wheel. Let's go." As the group hurried to the main building, one of the docks opened its massive doors and several heavies emerged.

"Big guys coming out the main door," Izzy shouted and the team took aim.

"Be right there," Marlo bellowed, but Luke and Mack were already ahead of him. They activated their bounce jets and landed only a few yards in front of the team. Two of the enemy demolitionists fired rockets at them, which Mack intercepted with a shield before he formed the energy into a collected sphere and pitched it at one of their adversaries. It erupted and scattered the other heavies.

"Move your asses!" he called, albeit good-naturedly as the energy around his armor flared and he and Luke ran in to fight. The rest of the group readied themselves and sprinted to the now open entrance of the loading dock. All made it through before the shutters closed.

It was dark inside with only a few low-light lamps hung around the room. "Do you think there are many left inside?" Otto asked.

"Oh, I'd say about twenty at least," Raul replied.

"Why so specific?" Indre questioned.

"Because I activated my brights," the tracker admitted. "And that's how many I see on their way to us."

The rest of the group adjusted their HUDs and zeroed in on a group of mercs that approached from the opposite side of the dock.

"It's never easy." Cameron chuckled and closed the vent on his rifle. "But it wouldn't be fun that way, so who cares?"

CHAPTER FOUR

As Luke kicked off an enemy titan, a demolitionist lined a shot up and fired a missile. He activated his gauntlet shield to catch the blast but another missile powered into his back and he grimaced as he heard the cracks ripple across his armor.

"Dammit! Mack, are you busy?" he asked as he pressed the switch on his hammer and drove the head onto the ground. A wave of force knocked the demolitionists back to give him time to recover.

"Only a little." The vanguard grunted as a heavy with a flamethrower and another with a beam cannon both fired on him and forced him to keep his shields up. The necessity for continued defense depleted his energy rather quickly. "Wasn't Marlo supposed to—"

At an impact behind him, both looked back briefly and a third heavy in red-and-white armor nodded at them. "Sorry for taking so long. These are stubborn bastards, right?"

"No shit!" Mack grunted, exploded his shields, and

swept the weapons of the other heavies up as he backed away hastily.

Marlo activated a switch on his cannon and the inside of his barrel changed as he moved it to the side. "Get down!" he yelled and pressed the trigger to deliver a large beam. He swept it across the field and caught most of the enemy heavies whose shields depleted and armor melted after only a couple of seconds of contact. Only a few remained when his cannon overheated. "You got the rest, right?" the demolitionist asked as he unlatched the large vent on his cannon.

"Hell yeah," Mack confirmed. He activated the auxiliary generators on his suit to give him a quick boost of energy.

"I'm nice and angry now!" Luke concurred as he spun his hammer as if to make his point. "Let's get them!" he roared as he attacked the three remaining mercs.

As Marlo checked his weapon, a sound caught his attention. It was distant but loud and sounded like screech that seemed to be moving toward them. He immediately keyed his comms. "Hey, Flynn, do you hear that?" he asked. "What is it?"

The sniper took a moment to respond. "Hell no—get out of sight!"

"Is that the last of them? Cameron asked and looked belligerently at the fallen mercs.

"It seems like it." Izzy shouldered her SMG and looked at the tracker. "Hey, Raul, can you locate the control station or whatever we have to find to get the codes?"

"My drone is still outside," he admitted and checked the feed in his HUD. "I'll see if I can sneak it in."

"There's no need," Otto stated and opened a holoscreen.

"Can you hack in and find it?" Cameron asked and moved toward him.

"No. I have the map the commander gave us," he explained and flipped the screen to show the others.

"Oh," Raul muttered and folded his arms. "Well, that's handy."

"You need to remember these things when going on a military mission," Indre scolded.

"Come on. We never had maps during these last four years doing missions," Cameron countered, "Not unless we stole them. Easy mode wasn't an option."

The hacker spun the map again. "If we are here, we'll have to travel up to… All right, it's two floors up. Let's go out through this door." He led the others to an exit on the right side of the dock, knelt beside the terminal, and let his EI take control of it to open the barrier.

Immediately, they were greeted by a large cannon that unfolded from the ceiling and turned toward them.

The bounty hunter looked at Otto. "I thought you took care of internal defenses."

He looked at his holoscreen again. "It would appear some have reset and connected to a secondary power supply."

"Well, so much for easy mode." Raul grimaced.

"Would you all please move?" Izzy shouted as the cannon primed and red light filled the chamber. The group all flung themselves in separate directions. The weapon fired at the position where Cameron had formerly stood. The ordnance sailed past and into the wall to blow a giant hole in the side of the dock room and through into the adjacent area.

Cameron, Indre, and Izzy released a barrage that destroyed the cannon in a hail of laser fire. As they recovered, boots thudded in a rush down the stairs at the end of the hall. "Fantastic," Cameron muttered and prepared to take aim as Otto held a hand up.

"There is an alternative route," he said and reached back as a large disk unlatched from his pack, which he slung into the hallway. "Let's head that way. This should keep them distracted." The disk unfolded and three legs latched onto the concrete as the center arched back and a gun unfolded from inside.

"You have toys too, I see." Indre sounded admiring.

"All techies do, of course," he replied. The first two mercs to come down the stairs were fired on by the mobile turret that began to crawl across the floor while the targets retreated quickly up the stairs. They huddled together and took potshots at the droid as it approached.

"Let's go. Your lead," Cameron stated. Otto acknowledged him with a nod and led them to the back of the dock. He opened the main door and peered out to see if anyone was coming or if there were more cannons.

The group stepped out and the bounty hunter decided to take a moment to check in with the others. "Flynn, how are things outside?"

"They were dandy," the marksman muttered unhappily as

he dove behind the relative protection of the underside of a transport. When he peered out from beneath it, the feet of an enemy merc were lifted off the ground and the man thrashed and yelled as he was hoisted skyward. "We have devil birds out here, mate!"

The merc was dropped and made impact only several meters from him. He twitched for a moment before he lay still. Large talons landed on top of him and a massive beak descended and broke through the cracked armor to gorge on the man within.

Flynn rolled out from under the transport and looked around to see at least four of the mutant birds. The battleground, which had not exactly been relaxed to begin with, was now in a frenzy as both sides focused on the devil birds rather than each other.

Luke and the Omega titan he had battled with both swung their hammers at their mutual enemy. The giant bird screeched and swatted Luke away with a large wing as its head lurched forward and snapped closed around the other titan, who still tried to beat its head in as it shook him violently.

Mack and Marlo had broken off to face the two others. The vanguard blasted repeatedly at his target, together with a squad of both Resistance soldiers and Omega mercs, while his teammate tried to find the right point on his devil bird to fire at with his beam without killing anyone else—or, at least, any of their allies.

That left the one in front of Flynn. He wondered if he could kill the ravenous creature alone—how had Kaiden done it? As his hand slid to his waist, it touched his thermal container. He froze, looked at it, and focused on the mutant. Oh, right!

The sniper aimed at the devil bird's head and fired a shot through its eye. This stopped the beast's feast and it flapped its wings wildly and uttered a loud, pained screech. He vaulted on top of the carrier, retrieved the thermal container, and pressed the top switch that activated all the grenades within. With a smirk, he tossed it into the air above the bird and it arced into its gullet as it continued to cry out in protest. As it swallowed the container, it looked at its enemy with one remaining eye and rage filled it as it surged into an attack. The grenades exploded and its eye widened when its throat erupted. Flynn rolled to the side and almost tripped over its expansive wings as it fell and skidded a few feet to stop and lie still.

He smiled as he stood. "I guess I'm not so out of practice, eh?" he mused quietly before Luke careened into the transport behind him. He ran to the heavy and attempted to help him stand, but the weight of his armor made him more of a crutch than a real lifter. "Are you all right mate?"

"I'm gonna break that bastard's skull open," the titan threatened furiously. "Do you know how much this armor costs to fix? And he took my kill." He raced away to confront the mutant and Flynn joined him as he sent a message to Cameron. "We'll handle it, Cam, but if you could hurry, it would be most appreciated."

CHAPTER FIVE

The screams from outside were so loud, they could be heard by the team as they pressed deeper into the building. They glanced at one another each time something thudded on the roof and the sound of metal being ripped apart was interspersed with loud explosions and enraged screeches.

"You know, I thought I drew the short straw having to come in here," Otto commented. "I think I'm in a better position now."

"We need to wrap this up," Cameron ordered and glanced behind him. "Raul, how far?"

"It should be right around this corner," the tracker replied.

He nodded and prepared to move forward. "Right, let's get in and get out as quic—" As soon as he turned into the other hallway, laser fire streaked toward him. Raul and Izzy were able to yank him back before he was struck and Otto and Indre returned fire.

"Maybe not that quickly there, bud," Izzy told him as she retrieved her SMG and helped the other two in the fight.

"Where do they hire all these assholes?" Cameron muttered and pushed to a crouch.

"They've been around a while and I don't think they have high standards for grunts," Raul responded. He picked his teammate's rifle up and handed it to him while he readied his. "I think I saw about eight of them in the hall. There are probably less now unless our friends have terrible aim."

"Then let's get the rest." The bounty hunter took his gun and they dove around the corner. Sure enough, the number had depleted by two and each took half of the six remaining. Their shots struck home but only managed to drain the remaining shields of the Omega troops. Fortunately, the continued fire from Otto, Izzy, and Indre dropped them in quick succession.

Cameron swung his legs into the air and used the momentum to pop himself to his feet. "Right, back to what we were originally doing."

"Not getting shot or running?" Raul asked as the bounty hunter helped him up.

"Ha-ha, smartass." Cameron walked over the Omega's bodies and to the door they had been guarding. He tried to open it although it was obviously locked, fumbled in the container on his legs, and groaned when he realized it was empty. "Dammit, who has bombs?"

A couple of members of the team checked but Indre raised a hand. "You do know at least two of us can simply hack it, right?"

"I wanted a little catharsis." The bounty hunter grunted as he walked past.

"Killing those soldiers didn't provide that?" Otto grinned.

"That was work," he replied and waved them off. "Go ahead, do your thing."

She nodded, stepped closer to the terminal, and used a gadget to slide in and open the door in less than ten seconds. Izzy and Raul entered first and checked the room. Nothing fired at them so that was an improvement. The rest followed and Otto hurried to one of the consoles and began to work.

"Do you know what to look for?" Cameron asked as he took point at the door and made sure the hallway remained clear.

"I do, but if I didn't, would you know what to look for?" Otto countered.

His teammate flinched and shook his head. "Just get it done."

"I'm kind of surprised how take-charge you've been on this mission, Cam," Raul noted. "Don't you always go on about how you like to work alone?"

"That's only a bounty hunter thing in general," he replied. "But I haven't done normal bounty hunter gigs. I've done missions like these. While I don't like to be in charge if I can help it, I hate being told what to do more."

The tracker chuckled. "Fair enough."

"Oh...huh." Otto murmured and caught the attention of the others.

"Did you run into a problem?" Indre asked and stepped behind him.

"Kind of. I believe I found the codes we came for—along with many, many others," he stated and showed her the screen where hundreds of various lines of text were displayed.

"Wow. Uh, we'll need time to sort through all this," she said.

Izzy leaned against the wall and shrugged. "I'm sure the guys outside will be all right if we simply chill while you fiddle with knobs and buttons." Another loud bang on the roof was followed by repeated thumps, probably from a devil bird's beak.

"And we don't have the time to chill either," Cameron stated and ducked inside the room. "We have bots and a few more Horde grunts on the way."

Otto and Indre looked at one another. "I'll simply rip everything here and we'll sort through it at the base," he told her.

"I agree. That sounds good." She began to remove the pack on the back of her armor. "While you focus on that, I'll find us an alternative route out of here." She opened one of the side compartments and withdrew a couple of disks. "Hey, Raul, do you have any drones left?"

"I still have two spares," he said with a nod.

She returned the gesture and tossed him the disks. "Here, arm these and slap them on."

He caught them and studied them with a frown. "What for...oh." He sighed as he placed both disks in one hand and reached behind him to remove one of the two large cylinders on his back. "Requisitions is already pissed with how fast I go through these."

"Izzy, do you wanna join me?" Cameron asked. The scout smiled, took two thermals out of her grenade container, and threw him one. "I'd love to—on three."

She took a position next to him. On two, they each activated their thermals and on three, lobbed them down the hall. A panicked shout by one of the mercs cut off when the explosives detonated. The two teammates ducked around the corner and began to fire through the smoke, but their fire was returned immediately with two rapid-fire streams from the other side. "Shit, Havoc droids!"

The two scurried into cover. Cameron's shields had depleted rapidly in only a few seconds of getting hit. He checked his HUD after they had ducked into the room and his barriers had lowered to seven percent.

"It's about time they used something other than those shiny ones," Izzy commented.

"I wouldn't be excited about their replacements," he retorted.

"We're ready to go," Raul announced and two hawk-like drones hovered near his chest. "I can probably deal with the droids if I have a brief distraction."

Izzy looked at the bounty hunter, who shrugged. "My shields are almost depleted. You're up."

She rolled her eyes. "How nice of you."

"You were the one who was happy to see them. Get out there."

The battle medic grinned as she took her last two thermals out and switched places with him. She was about to dart out when a thermal from one of the Omegas landed outside the door. Without hesitation, she surged forward to scoop it up, threw it along with hers, and rolled across the ground as the Havoc droids fired on her.

Cameron poked his head out and fired to draw their attention, but the explosives did a far better job. The mercs scattered and the three Havoc droids hunkered down to bolster their shields in preparation for the blast. Izzy pushed hastily to her feet and ran into the room as the devices went off. Raul sent his drones out as the smoke billowed through the hall and easily located the droids through the feeds. Each drone streaked into one of the mechanicals and the explosives pinned to them exploded on impact. The result was even more powerful than the three thermals and it was clear that nothing would escape it.

"Got it!" Otto announced and backed away from the console. "Are we ready to go?"

"The hallway should be clear." Cameron checked the scope on his rifle, switched to thermal, and peered through it to look beyond the smoke. Four figures gathered at the end of the hall and others hurried to join them. "Scratch that. Who runs toward explosions?"

"Us, and on a regular basis," Izzy reminded him.

"Don't worry about it. I'm prepared," Indre stated as she backed away from the wall where her pack was now attached.

"Do you have something to cut through it in there?" Raul asked.

She turned to hold her arm up and show him the screen on her gauntlet with a message reading *Detonate.* The team looked at one another and then at the agent, who simply nodded. "You could say that."

Izzy looked at Cam. "Have you gotten your catharsis yet?"

The bounty hunter shrugged as he vaulted over one of the stations and crouched. "I could always use a little more, though. Everyone, get behind something!"

CHAPTER SIX

Luke swung his hammer against the beak of a devil bird. As it was forced back, Mack plunged from above, shoved an orb of energy into its face, and let it erupt. The explosion hurled the mutant into the dirt.

The vanguard landed next to the titan, but before they could so much as acknowledge their victory, another familiar screech made them both curse. The two heavies spun and located two more of the winged beasts that approached with single-minded determination.

"Good Lord!" Mack shouted and reached to his hip for a core replacement for his suit, only to discover none remaining. "How many of these are there?"

"There must be a nest nearby," Luke suggested and twirled his hammer. "I didn't think they traveled together —or not this many, at least. Then again, I can't say I know much about mutant migration."

A couple of Resistance soldiers were flung aside and landed in a tangle of limbs behind them. They turned and realized that an Omega vanguard, his heavy black-and-red armor coursing with white energy, barreled toward them.

Mack punched his fists together but his teammate stopped him from engaging. "Take a break and recharge. I got this one." He ran a few steps forward and activated his bounce pack to launch upward as he raised his hammer above him. With a shout, he descended on the Omega but the energy around his opponent's armor coalesced around his arm as he swung his weapon to meet the hammer in the air. The explosion was unbearably bright, and Mack shielded his eyes for a moment and heard Luke yell.

"Shiiiiiiit!" The titan careened past him on a direct path to the downed soldiers, who had barely recovered and managed to roll quickly to the side to avoid being injured by the falling heavy.

"Are you all right?" Mack asked. When his teammate pushed out of the dirt and shook his head, he pointed a thumb at the enemy. "Do you still want me to recharge or should I get in there?"

Luke waved him off. "Your turn. Take it."

He rolled his shoulders and raced toward the enemy vanguard while he pooled energy in his palm. The Omega clapped sharply and his energy flared as he braced himself for the attack. But instead of striking the merc, Mack jumped and launched the energy to the ground to flip the man without warning. As he landed, he spun and thrust an arm through the shield of the merc's power core and yanked it out. His opponent swung an arm to knock him back, but the effect was evident almost immediately. The shields vanished and he struggled to move.

Mack tossed the core up and caught it. "Thanks for this

buddy," he said, drew his arm back, and delivered a punch into the Omega's helmet that felled him. He tried to see if he could use the core as a replacement for his own but the earth seemed to tremble as something heavy landed behind him. He looked over his shoulder at a devil bird that opened its beak and pushed into an attack. Reflexively, he flung himself aside and the mutant's attack struck the downed Omega instead. The man was lifted in its giant maw and his armor began to buckle under the violent thrashing of the spiteful beast.

"He's having a hell of a bad day," Luke muttered as he stepped beside Mack and helped him up.

"How much longer do we have to deal with these damn things?" the vanguard asked as he removed his core and replaced it with the Omega's. "Did Cameron give you an ETA?"

"I haven't heard from him. Maybe Flynn knows some —" A large explosion interrupted the titan. The two turned and gaped at a massive hole that had appeared in the building Cameron and his team had entered. In the next moment, several figures leapt out of the aperture.

"Are those our guys?" Mack asked.

"Their armor is something other than black-and-red so I'll go with yes." Luke raised his hammer. "Let's get over there."

"Flynn, we're out!" Cameron shouted over the comms and yelled in his helmet to be heard over the sounds of metal and debris still raining from above. "Call the shuttles in."

"I already have, but you might notice something is stopping them from getting into the base," the marksman responded. He blasted the wing of a devil bird with several bullets that ruptured on impact. They coated the wings in a liquid that quickly hardened, ensnared the creature as it began to bend over, and forced it to land as the wings grew heavier and heavier.

"I guess we're gonna have to meet them halfway unless we can clear the air," Cameron muttered. He looked around, caught sight of an enemy sniper climbing one of the towers, and took aim and fired. The shot dislodged the enemy from the ladder and a smaller devil bird flew past and snatched his leg to haul him higher. The bounty hunter's attention was dragged from the mutant, though, when he noticed two large turrets on the still intact towers. They appeared to be in working order but offline.

"Indre, Otto, can either one of you get access to those?" he asked, marked the position on his HUD, and sent it to them.

"Well, we jumped out of the closest thing this base may have to a central command station," Indre pointed out. Her machine gun had overheated and forced her to open the vent as she switched to her pistol.

"I'm only looking for a yes or no, not sass," he retorted.

"I think I may have another way," Otto announced. "I'm sure at least a few of those codes are for this base. If I can get to the console that controls those guns—"

"Great—good idea, go!" Cameron shouted and Izzy and Indre ran to the hacker.

"You heard the man." The battle medic took the lead and her two teammates followed her across the field.

"Cam, we have bots," Raul warned and both men turned to focus on a group of assault and trooper bots that emerged from a partially wrecked warehouse. They began to fire on the devil birds and Resistance members alike and thus only added to the chaos.

Raul and Cameron found cover behind a large piece of metal that had buried itself into the ground, possibly from their recent escape, and prepared to fire along with several other soldiers. But as he was about to pull the trigger, a large flash erupted behind the droids and many mechanicals at the rear launched skyward or exploded. When they turned to attack their new assailants, many were crushed by the swing of a hammer.

Luke activated his gauntlet shield to block the incoming fire as he tossed his hammer up to catch it by the hilt in his left hand. He pressed the trigger and drove the head into the ground. The impact released a wave of energy that not only catapulted the bots in front of him away but also the metal Raul and Cameron were hiding behind. The bounty hunter flung himself back to avoid decapitation by the metal that had been made lethal by the force of the strike.

"All right, we're here," Izzy announced when they reached the first tower. "Get up there, Otto."

"Why? The console is right behind you," he said and pushed past her to locate and unfold the screen from its perch on the base of the tower.

"Oh...well, that works too," she muttered and kept watch while Indre joined him. "How long do you think it will take to sift through all those codes?" she asked the hacker.

"If I had to make it shuffle through all of them, up to ten minutes—assuming it doesn't lock me out," he replied. "However, I noticed a series of codes that all begin with the same combination—OB9. My guess is a designation for 'Omega Base Nine' or something similar. There's no reason to create complex passwords for a base they probably planned to burn, so if I am right and narrow it down to only those codes... Ah, wonderful."

A loud click above drew a small smirk to his face. The three looked up as the turret began to activate and Otto commanded it quickly to focus on the devil birds. It turned, targeted the injured one Flynn had previously shot at, and fired two large blasts.

They exploded on the back of the creature and savaged it. The beast shrieked briefly before it collapsed, and the turret turned to find a new target.

The trio was shocked at the destruction wrought by only two shots. "How many of these are there?" Izzy asked Otto.

He looked around. "There's one over there and another at the corner from what I see."

She smiled and held her weapon up. "Follow me. We'll be out of here in no time."

CHAPTER SEVEN

M arlo unleashed a blast from his cannon, but it was intercepted and blocked by the shield of an enemy heavy. He moved back and opened the vent of his cannon as he drew his heavy pistol. Two sniper shots streaked past his head and he grinned when they struck a couple of approaching droids. He gave himself a moment to watch them sputter from the impact before they fell.

"Nice shots, Flynn," he commended and looked toward the approximate area of the marksman's hiding place. "But close, don't you think?"

"For someone with my skills, there was more than enough room," his teammate boasted. "By the way, the heavy still has you in his sights."

"I know." He turned and tossed his cannon at the attacking heavy. The unexpected action surprised his enemy and he staggered as he tried to catch the hefty weapon. The demolisher used the opportunity to sprint forward and clothesline the Omega, which effectively dropped him and knocked the cannon out of his hands. He aimed his pistol quickly and fired three shots, careful not to hit his weapon nearby. "I kind of enjoyed it when we were all focused on the devil birds."

"Good things don't always last," Flynn muttered and scanned the area anxiously. "Amber, how are you and Julius holding up?"

"Very well, actually," she replied as she helped to soothe a massive burn on the leg of a military soldier. "We found shelter in one of the buildings near the gate and they haven't bothered us."

"Huh?" The marksman realized that his response might have sounded negative and quickly explained himself. "I mean good! But usually, you medics are the first they try to focus on."

"Trust me, I'm aware," she agreed. "A few did target us at the beginning of the battle, but Julius deployed some kind of mist around our position and it has wrecked anyone coming through it."

"None of our guys, right?" he asked quickly.

"Of course not," Julius replied and released a little more of the chemical from the barrel on his arm. "The mist is actually a virus I designed, and I made sure to inoculate everyone on the team before we began."

Flynn put his rifle down momentarily to think. "I don't remember having shots."

"It was in the water we used to toast with before we began the mission," his teammate explained.

Amber and the soldier she was treating looked at him. "I wondered about that," she told him. "It seemed out of character for you to suggest it."

"I assumed he was finally getting into the team spirit of

things." Flynn sounded distracted as he shifted his attention to focus through his scope and find new targets.

"I always have team spirit," Julius retorted and watched calmly as an enemy titan saw him and immediately surged into an assault with a large plasma ax. The large man encountered the rather muddled cloud in his quarry's vicinity and in one motion, dropped his ax and collapsed at the biologist's feet. "I am a medic. It is my job to keep the spirits of my team among the living."

"And that has what to do with creating a virus that seems to...I don't know, cover a person in smallpox and instantly kill them?" Amber snorted.

He looked over his shoulder and into the warehouse behind him. "It does nothing of the kind and simply causes massive simultaneous muscle spasms which leads to momentary heart complications. Most live."

Amber helped the soldier to his feet. "You explaining it so calmly is rather disturbing."

Julius turned to observe the fighting. "If it helps, I simply think of it as removing threats. I can heal and assist in fighting and both help. As I said, I made sure this wouldn't affect our troops, at least in small doses. If the truth be told, I didn't intend to create this virus. It happened by accident while working on a chemical to increase stamina and strength. There were a few failures there."

"I assume a fair amount of screaming was involved," she snarked as she folded her arms.

"Not by me," he responded. "As for the test subjects... Well, the sound of scientific progress is not always pretty but it is always sweet." Once he was sure they were safe for the moment, he walked into the warehouse. "We seem to be all right for now. Do you need any help treating the wounded?"

The battle medic looked at the group of soldiers waiting for treatment. A few shook their heads and one even sent a private message—*Please no*. She chuckled quietly. "I'll get these guys up in no time. You go do you."

He shrugged. "I suppose I have other trials I wish to run while we're here, but they are in early development so I'm not sure if I have the proper antidotes."

The soldiers shuddered and Amber merely slapped the side of her helmet in annoyance. "Keep manning the door, Julius."

"The second tower is online," Otto called rather unnecessarily as it quickly found its first target and launched deafening blasts at the massive mutant birds that still circled the base. One of the creatures saw its companion fall and tried to dive at the weapon, but the first turret locked on and fired before it could strike. The remaining mutants saw the force they were now up against and began to back off, while some flew away from the base.

"They are beginning to have second thoughts," Izzy shouted on her comms. "Let's get to the next one. Cam, the devil birds have started to leave."

"I noticed," the bounty hunter answered and tossed a cartridge of ballistic rounds to Raul while Mack strengthened the shield defending them. "I'm hailing the shuttles again, so keep it up. They should be here—" Shadows above them triggered an immediate fear that the birds had simply circled and doubled back but instead, three large shuttles cruised overhead. In the distance, he could see more on the way. "They didn't want to wait around, did they?" He chuckled and switched his comms to the team line. "Listen up! We have what we came for and the shuttles have arrived. Get to evac."

They didn't need a second invitation. The team, comprised of Nexus students and military, headed to the shuttles that descended to hover at various intervals. Spread out, they could pick up as many as possible as quickly as possible. Their bays opened and a few Azure Halo droids emerged to assist in the fight, which gave the soldiers room to breathe as they boarded. Others lingered around the sides of the ships to defend them while the wounded or soldiers with broken armor were the first to enter.

Flynn leapt off his perch and strode to Amber, taking quick shots with his rifle as he walked beside her. He was able to assist the soldier she supported to one of the shuttles. As Julius helped the other wounded out of the warehouse, a frantic Omega raced toward them with a long blade. The botanist snatched the pistol from one of the soldiers, shot the assailant in the chest, and felled him instantly.

"No weird purple goop for him?" the soldier asked rather cheekily.

"Occasionally, simplicity is the best option," he answered and guided the man to one of the shuttles.

More craft began to land. Marlo let one last beam rip from his cannon to obliterate a small line of droids and drive back a rather tenacious devil bird. He turned, made his way to a shuttle, and picked up a smaller soldier who struggled to board. Casually, he swung her in and sat on the edge to open the vent of his cannon.

"Third tower online," Otto shouted but continued to work on the holoscreen as the third cannon activated and joined the others in their assault on the devil birds.

"If we're good, then let's go," Indre ordered.

He held a finger up. "One moment... There!" With that, he shut the holoscreen, took his pistol out, and joined his teammates to jog toward the shuttles.

Raul and Cameron dove into a vessel as Luke knocked away the last of the close droids and Mack shoved with his barrier to scatter any enemy troops who came too close. As soon as the two heavies made it in, their shuttle took off, ascended, and almost skimmed the walls before it pushed to a good distance away from the mutants and turret shots that continued.

"Is everyone heading out?" Cameron asked.

"It looks like we're up and away," Flynn acknowledged. "Nice work everyone."

"Should we leave them with working turrets?" Amber asked.

"That's not a concern," Otto replied and eased back in his chair.

"Someone get a hold of those turrets," an Omega shouted. "Train them on those ships before they—" The weapons, as

Otto had programmed, turned to face the base. As no devil birds were remaining, they now acquired a new target.

"Oh, shit!" The massive guns began to fire and the mercs attempted to run out of the base or inside buildings for protection, despite the reality that it would do little good. A couple tried to gain command of one of the towers, only to find themselves locked out and a curious countdown on the bottom of the screen.

"They're rigged to blow! Get your asses out!"

As the shuttles settled into their homeward flight pattern, Otto and a few others watched on his holoscreen as the massive turrets erupted and large chunks of the weapons battered and crushed much of the remnants of the camp. The hacker merely whistled quietly in satisfaction as they returned to base.

CHAPTER EIGHT

"Teams one, three, four, and seven have finished their missions. Two and six are preparing, and team five is about to begin." Sasha placed the tablet on General Hartman's desk and leaned back in his chair. "So far, things have gone smoothly, although we'll have to wait for the debriefings to confirm that."

"No fatalities?" the other man inquired and took a sip of water.

"I would have considered that pertinent information," the commander replied, entwined his fingers, and rested his hands in his lap. "The Resistance has bolstered their ranks, freed the other Ark Academies during these last few months, and they have tasted blood in the water. They won't lose more than they already have, not to Omega hangers-on who don't know when to quit."

The general nodded but his grimace didn't leave his face. "For now, but you and I know these missions are basically practice to stay sharp for what is to come."

"That's rather a blunt way to put it." He sighed. "But I

do agree, as much as it unnerves me. Still, I have yet to talk to a soldier who isn't looking forward to the big push. Once we start, we will end this."

"It's better they keep the focus on that than what the final cost may be." Hartman placed the glass on the table, took his cap off, and ran his hand over his head. "The speculation and discussion by the other higher-ups... The only reason they agreed to attack this early without building our forces more was the agreement to spend the time in the meanwhile loosening the last remains of Merrick's grip on the planet. Remember that in case this doesn't go as well as you expect."

"I remember they had similar feelings when we went to take back the Academy," Sasha pointed out and shook his head. "Even with the patience age has granted me, the lack of faith the military shows has always been able to deplete it rapidly."

His companion fixed him with a calm look. "It's not a lack of faith, Sasha. It is practical and more importantly, strategy. We need to know what to expect and prepare for the worst-case scenarios."

"The worst-case scenario is always the same, General—complete annihilation," he countered. "I never saw the point of thinking that was an option."

Hartman's head lowered again, and although he exhaled a ragged breath in frustration, he followed that with a couple of honest chuckles. "I am always surprised by how thin the line between optimism and foolishness is. It seems to come down to how you frame it." He looked at Sasha, a small grin on his face. "Do you truly think this will be an easy task, Commander?"

"I do not," he stated firmly and leaned forward. "I think it will be immensely difficult. I believe that for decades, the soldiers and personnel who participate in the coming mission will remember it for potentially their entire existence as the hardest-fought victory of their lives."

"And yet you think there is no question that it will be a victory?" the man pressed.

The chancellor nodded. "I said it would be difficult, but everyone who has passed through Nexus—or any Ark Academy—has trained for difficult. They are there to be the soldiers who are called in for exactly this scenario. Merrick's forces may be numerous, but he works with thugs and droids, enemies my students cut their teeth on from day one." He took an empty glass and filled it with water from the pitcher on the desk. "And I'm sure the military would still like Merrick to answer for his crimes as well."

"There is no question of that," Hartman assured him. "It's simply that— Bah, there's no need to run through my qualms at this point. Heh, I should have you talk to the emergency council next time. You seem more gifted in changing hearts and minds than I am."

"I've had my fair share of debates over the years, dealing with the Academy board." Sasha took a sip of his water. "To be honest, I think that may have been a greater challenge than most of the missions in my youth."

The general uttered a brief but hearty laugh. "I'll send a message, then. I'm sure I'll have to deal with at least one more before we go."

"See that you do." He placed his glass down. "It's my

turn to inquire about how our preparations are going. When will the fleet be finished?"

The other man adjusted himself in his chair, rested his arms on the desk, and fixed his full attention on him. "The repairs are almost complete, new ships are being tested for any oversights, and we're bringing in more pilots for fighters and recruiting more volunteers for the assault. You were right to say the military wanted blood as much as your troops do. Many men and women lost someone the day Merrick destroyed the WC and have fought since that day to reclaim the sections of Earth he has taken. A chance to finish it all…well, many are more than happy to be a part of that."

"Indeed, and we should make sure that is what they know they are fighting for. It needs to always be on their mind." Sasha leaned back and his posture shifted. "I don't know what this will lead to. There will be considerable rebuilding and who knows how our alliances with the other races will change after this is all over. But we should get to that point first before we make plans. Defeating Merrick and ending this war is the primary goal."

"Agreed. Although to speculate a little about the future, can I hope you will join us in helping to repair those alliances when it reaches that point?" Hartman asked and raised an eyebrow. "From what I understand, you have a friendship with the Sauren War Chief at least?"

He shook his head. "That was Wolfson, but I will be there to at least tell the War Chief what happened. I doubt it will smooth things over much, though."

"Oh, I see." The general fell silent, collected his thoughts, and in a way, gave a brief moment of silence for the fallen and the chancellor's friend. "I understand. That will be difficult. I want to offer my—" He was cut off when the commander's tablet rang.

"It's Team One's leader." He looked up from the screen and his companion nodded so he answered quickly. "Kaiden, it's good to hear from you."

"Sasha, same here," the ace began. His tone was relieved but his face was grim. "Unfortunately, we have some bad news. We completed our mission, but Solos was killed before we could recover him."

He frowned. "I certainly won't shed any tears over the loss of one of the men who put us in this mess, but that was valuable information we lost."

"Not entirely," Kaiden replied. He looked down for a moment and seemed to fiddle with something. "Solos appeared to have lost a fair amount of love for his former boss and gave us access to his personal records. We found several cases of info and data he'd collected. We're preparing to transfer it to the command techs to have them go over it all."

"A silver lining. Well done, Kaiden," he stated. "I take it you've looked at some of it already?"

The ace nodded. "I have—a couple of videos and files on their droid program, but nothing that will give us any advantages. The vids merely confirmed Merrick's psychotic status to me, although that didn't take much."

Sasha nodded. "I see. Okay, we'll discuss it more once you return."

"How are the other members of my team doing?" the ace asked.

"Team Three has completed their mission as well. They

are on their way back and should beat you here by a couple of hours. There were some injuries during the mission but your friends seem to all be in the clear." He spoke quickly to reassure him and Kaiden's features lightened somewhat.

"And Chiyo?" he asked.

"Team Five had only begun their mission last I checked." The commander picked the tablet up, flipped to the relevant screen, and raised an eyebrow when he checked the feed. "And it would appear it is going quite well, although it seems they have forsaken stealth this time around."

The ace responded with a small grin. "Well, it's no surprise. Even Chi needs to let off steam now and then."

CHAPTER NINE

"Do you think we'll make it back in time for dinner?"
Fritz asked as he fired a couple of shots at the droid
fidgeting beneath him. "I'm starved."

"Didn't you eat before we started?" Kit asked, checked
the map, and made sure the different groups were all still
making good time.

"That was only a ration bar." He saw the top half of
another droid that crawled up behind his fellow Azure
Halo leader and fired a single shot through its dome. "I'm
not military. I'm not trained to simply bear with it."

"Your constant bitching makes that clear." She sighed
and turned the map off. "Come on, we need to go and—
behind you!" Both reacted as a group of six Arbiter droids
turned the corner. The three in front prepared to fire and
the two teammates ducked hastily. She opened another
menu to command their team of droids to return fire but
before they could, the three enemy droids in front of the
group were shot from behind by their fellow Arbiter bots.

The Azure Halo leaders looked at one another in confusion, unable to see who had hacked into the enemy mechanicals. A grate above was tossed down and Chiyo climbed out and dropped lightly to the ground.

"So, you're back with us?" Fritz grinned and glanced at the bots as she approached them. "Thanks for the save." The droids' heads began to shake and moments later, they erupted, the bodies fell to their knees, and one by one, they toppled. He looked at the infiltrator in confusion. "Couldn't you have saved them? We are in a factory that makes them so the more the merrier."

"The program I helped design to hack into the Arbiter bots only allows limited control and for brief amounts of time," Chiyo explained and looked at the group of over a dozen Halo droids behind them. "Besides, it appears we have more than enough backup."

"And this facility has run on emergency power for the last month and a half," Kit pointed out. "Production has stalled and most of the droids were used to defend the Ultra Ark Academy."

"Which we've already dealt with," the infiltrator reminded her and drew her SMG. "I tried to find central control but was locked out. From what I could gather, it wouldn't have been as much help as I hoped, though. It seems most of the AOs systems have some form of lockout when in emergencies."

"So it's not worth the effort?" Fritz asked.

Chiyo shook her head. "Not when we're simply here to destroy it. I did get a couple of heavy power readings, though. Honestly, at this point, the factory may well run out of power in another month or two without our help, but it's better to take care of it now."

"Since we're here and all, we can help." He chuckled, holstered his pistol, and drew his machine gun. "All right, where to?"

"I want to investigate the second large energy reading before we head to the core." She opened her map and sent it to the other two technicians' devices. "It is on the way and could simply be an auxiliary generator. As most modern power cores have that built-in, I want to see what the AO has devised in here."

"That works for me," Kit stated and gestured down the hall as the droids behind them set off. "I have the other teams searching the base to make sure nothing gets out to target us. They'll pick through anything useful and smoke the rest."

"I would make sure they don't try to get too deep into this facility," Chiyo suggested. "If we plan to blow it, they'll want to get out as fast as possible."

"I'm very sure our guys and gals are as interested in living as anyone else." Fritz chuckled. "They know the score and besides, there are only about fifteen of them, so it won't be a stampede to get to the exit or anything."

"Aren't you taking any of the bots?" she asked and looked from one to the other. "That will be quite an expense for the Halos, won't it?"

"It'll be pricey, but we've come into quite a few creds," he explained. "Working with the Riders and Kings has opened new opportunities and getting missions from the military has also been a nice boost."

"They tried to get our cooperation with the whole 'do it for your planet' schtick," Kit added. "It didn't work."

Chiyo frowned and wanted to argue but shrugged it off.

They were helpful and honestly, the freebies they had received from them were still because it was in their interest to help them—that and the fact that they owed Kaiden favors. She supposed she shouldn't give them too much grief for making this war work for them. They were a gang, after all, and allegiance was personal.

Metal clanged against metal, which told them more mechanicals were coming. The Halo droids took position and their arms transformed into cannons or chain guns as Fritz shook his head and readied his weapon. "They might not be popping these bastards out like they usually do, but they are still a nuisance."

"Madame, above!" Kaitō warned, and the infiltrator aimed upward at several droids that climbed on the roof. She fired and caught her teammates' attention. They joined her sustained volley as more Arbiter droids raced down the hall to fall before the Halos.

One of the mechanicals plunged toward Kit, who jumped back, tossed a spike at her attacker, and caught its shoulder. Electricity surged out of the end of the projectile to stun it and she fired her hand cannon twice into its chest and once into its head. Two more droids plummeted and Chiyo hacked into them, which caused them to freeze and land face-first on the floor. Fritz fired his machine gun into the back of one and she eliminated the other. Several smaller laser blasts rained from above and pummeled their armor's shields. When she glanced up, the Arbiter droids had their mouths open to reveal concealed barrels within from which they now fired.

"Those are new," Fritz shouted. He yanked a small force hammer from his belt and swung it a few times to build the energy before he pressed the switch and lobbed it at the roof. It connected and launched a wave of energy that swept the remaining droids off. They activated their cannons quickly, but the team and a couple of the Halo droids destroyed them before they had fallen very far.

Chiyo checked the hall cautiously. The group that had initially attacked had been reduced to four and they had lost three droids themselves, which meant they were down to twelve. Another group of Arbiter droids came around the corner and fired their cannons at Fritz. Two Halos intercepted the blasts. She set to work.

At most, she could take five and still make use of them, but she connected to all of them as she only needed to stop them for a moment. She was able to hack into all ten remaining Arbiter droids and forced them to stop firing for almost two seconds before she was overridden. Still, it was enough. The Halo droids reacted quickly. Each took a shot at a different mechanical and mowed them down despite the incredibly brief delay.

Fritz smiled and patted one of the droids on the shoulder as he moved past. "That's Halo ingenuity at its finest."

Chiyo relaxed and vented her SMG. "I wonder why you never used your talents to become a legitimate robotics corporation."

The man chuckled and gestured with a thumb at one of the mechanicals. "Do you think we could make something this good following regulations?"

She shrugged as she began to walk down the hall. "Do you think any robotics corporation follows regulations?"

He tilted his head in confusion and looked at Kit, who

merely laughed and followed the infiltrator. The droids ran ahead and formed an arrow shape in front as they led the way to the group's destination.

When they arrived, they paused in front of a massive doorway and Chiyo examined it carefully. "I'd say it's a kind of warehouse or building unit for larger machines."

"Do you think it could be mechs?" Kit asked.

The infiltrator looked at the terminal on the side of the door and accessed it in her HUD. "Perhaps, but we haven't run into any so far. Given that they've been on emergency power, it would be a wiser use of resources to simply build the small basic units instead." She unlocked the terminal and pressed the *open* command. The pressure released with a loud hiss and the doors slid open slowly. She was the first to walk in and the mechanicals followed at her heels. A long, dark hallway led to the left, where glowing blue and white lights flickered from large windows along the corridor.

The three teammates walked on as the droids checked the room. Chiyo approached the windows and her eyes widened. A large machine made of sterling silver contained an orb of energy. The sphere was surrounded by a few dozen circular objects that flew around it, caught discharges, and fed them into it again.

"What is this?" Fritz asked and stared at the contraption in awe.

"It's an engine of some kind," she stated as she scanned the readouts from her HUD. "Something like this… Honestly, this is powerful enough for a colossus."

"Do what? Another one?" He yelped and one of the droids on his left held its cannon up.

"Hostiles incoming!" it warned. The three became instantly alert as the other mechanicals ran past them. Several larger Arbiter droids with glowing chassis and wider frames than their basic counterparts appeared out of the shadows. The Halo defense fired and their lasers struck the enemy shields, which absorbed the shots and cannon blasts. The enhanced Arbiter droids' arms transformed into long-barreled guns and light formed along them.

"Get down!" Chiyo warned and fell prone with the others as the attackers fired. Several blasts caught the Halos and annihilated them.

When the energy dissipated, she looked up as the droids' guns vented, but for only a few seconds before they shut them and turned their attention to the humans. She tried to hack in but they pushed her out easily, even when she tried to access only one of them.

She grimaced and picked her gun up. It seemed they would have to deal with this using Kaiden's preferred method.

CHAPTER TEN

K it moved her hand to her weapon, but Fritz jumped in front of her. He held his gauntlet out and produced a shield that blocked three shots from the droids before it shattered. When he fell back, she stepped around him and tossed several small disks that attached themselves to the mechanicals and delivered pulses of energy along the enemy shields. They didn't seem to affect the droids themselves, but their shields dimmed rapidly. Chiyo saw her opportunity and fired with one hand and helped Fritz up with the other. Kit opened fire and yelled into her comms for any nearby team to come and assist.

"Thanks," he muttered as he stood and aimed his machine gun. "Do you still have that escape plan ready to go in case this gets worse?"

"I do." The infiltrator felt for one of her thermal grenades without removing her gaze from the enemy. "But I thought you said you didn't like the idea of having your body displaced by experimental tech."

"Duck!" Kit shouted, and the other two leapt to opposite sides as a charged blast rocketed past and into the wall at the end of the hall to blow clean through it.

"I'd rather not, but at least there's a chance I'll live compared to getting hit by one of those," he countered and readied his launcher as Chiyo tossed him the grenade. He slid it inside and held the trigger down to charge the weapon and explosive to increase the destructive power. Almost casually, he stepped over his mostly decorative barricade and fired. The grenade slammed into the center mechanical as its shield faltered again, blew the top half of its body off, and knocked the other droids aside.

"Heh, toss me more." Fritz stretched a hand toward Chiyo. "I might have been a little too antsy."

Red lights began to flash in the room followed by a chorus of loud hisses as several pods in the areas above began to open. More of the enhanced droids came online as the pod doors slid wide.

Fritz's arm wavered slightly when he saw them activate. "Or maybe I was right, as usual."

"Boss, we're here." Chiyo turned as three Azure Halo members raced in with additional Halo droids behind them. They stopped and glanced at the flashing lights and the enemy mechanicals. "What the hell are those?" one asked while another pointed through the window.

"To hell with the bots. What the hell is that?" the second asked.

"Focus on the bots for now," Kit ordered and continued to fire as Chiyo tossed Fritz her container of grenades. She looked at the engine and noticed several large cords on the ceiling and floor that were attached to it.

"Kaitō, look for the system that keeps the engine

powered," she instructed as she vented her SMG. "We may need to use excessive force."

"Understood. Shall I prepare the transport in the meantime?" the EI asked.

"I'll get to work on that. You focus on the engine." She shut her vent and fired at some of their adversaries above as they stepped out of their pods. One of those on the ground fired at the new arrivals to fell a Halo member and catch two of the droids in the explosion. Another two mechanicals made their way to the front, opened their chest plates as energy poured out, and created a large shield to cover everyone behind them. A third hurried behind them and held its hands out. Wires ejected and attached to their backs to allow its power to flow into them to strengthen the shields.

"Boss!" one of the remaining troops called as his teammate dragged the body of the deceased out of the line of fire. "The others are pinned down. It seems we have this place going now!"

"Dammit." Kit grimaced and looked at Chiyo and Fritz. "Should we retreat?"

Before either could answer, the shield the droids had made shattered with a large boom and a few of the mechanicals above jumped down. Their blades emerged from their arms as they attacked the group.

"It looks like we wouldn't get far," Fritz shouted, aimed his launcher at one of the mechanicals, and fired. He was able to hit one but those around it simply increased speed or maneuvered out of the way of the blast. The Halo droids in front popped their blades and engaged but were only able to put up a brief fight before they were cut down in quick succession.

"Get into the hall. There's more room to fight," Chiyo said and hastily took pictures of the engine using her helmet's visor. "I'm working on something. We'll retreat."

Fritz nodded but mumbled in a low tone about being scattered in pieces. The two women and a couple of droids maintained a sustained barrage at the Arbiter bots as they moved steadily out of the room. They had to dodge several blasts and Chiyo's shields failed after one that detonated behind her and caught her in its radius. She kicked off the wall and slid out as she took control of the terminal and shut the doors, activated emergency procedures, and let the blast doors descend.

"Madame, I am in," Kaitō informed her. *"Shall I begin a Genos special?"*

"Do it!" She opened a holoscreen, ran her hand across it, and made sure every dot that represented a friendly who was still breathing was marked. She set to work quickly and identified a location that was far enough away without pushing the system beyond anything they had already tried. This was experimental tech, after all. She had less of a problem with that than Fritz but she wasn't an idiot.

Blasts rumbled behind the door, followed by sizzling as plasma blades began to cut through slowly but steadily.

"Everyone, get ready," she shouted. Her teammates noticed a blue light that grew brighter through the holes in the door. Even the pounding seemed to decrease somewhat, an indication that the droids' attention had turned elsewhere.

"Chiyo, what's going on?" Kit asked, a growing concern evident in her voice.

The infiltrator closed the holoscreen. "We're finishing the mission. Kaitō how long do we have?"

"About a minute, madame. It seems the engine was not left in a very safe and shielded condition and didn't require that big a push," the EI informed her.

"That's fine. We're out." She pressed a switch on her gauntlet and exhaled a breath as she was pulled up and her vision went white.

───

Chiyo landed on her knees and reacted with a sputtering cough that was echoed by several behind her. She looked around at Kit, Fritz, and a handful of other Halo members. It looked like everyone still alive was there, at least.

"Where are we?" one of the Halo members asked as he removed his helmet and breathed deeply.

"I teleported us out but not too far. We're a little more than a couple of miles from the factory," she answered and stood.

"Will that be far enough?" Kit asked. "I assume you set that giant engine to blow?"

As if in answer to her question, a loud rumble drew the attention of the group to the horizon, where a massive plume of blue light surged skyward and dissipated. Even from their position, Chiyo felt like she would be picked up and hurled away by the force. A wave of energy ballooned from the initial blast and a few of the Halos began to retreat, prepared to make a run for it. Thankfully, it fragmented quickly and dispersed almost as soon as it had formed.

The team was quiet for a moment as they waited for another blast. Instead, pieces of metal rained from above and a particularly sharp one dug into the ground next to Fritz.

"That could have ended poorly," he stated and grimaced at a bang when an Arbiter droid arm struck the helmet of one of his troops. The man took a couple of steps back and held his hands to the side of his helmet before he collapsed. His teammate who had taken his protective headgear off replaced it quickly.

Kit stopped beside Chiyo. "Nice work. I'll have to remember that trick for the next run."

The infiltrator watched the darkened sky return to its original shade as the explosion began to fade. "I've learned over the years that it is…quite an effective strategy."

CHAPTER ELEVEN

"Soooo, it went well, then?" Professor Laurie asked as one of the technicians handed him a mug filled with dark coffee. "You pushed the teleporter to the max of its currently tested range, I see."

"Given the circumstances, I should have tried to put us down farther away," Chiyo replied and adjusted the feed on her end. "I think there is still some residual energy in the air. It's causing issues with our connection."

"It could be that." He took a sip of his coffee and his face tightened a little at the bitterness. "Or it could be the fact that we're processing so much information at one time that it's on our end. Communication has been an issue these last few days."

"Are they working you that hard, Professor?" she asked with a trace of laughter in her voice.

He rubbed a hand over his face. "You have no idea. I feel like I may drop before I have a chance to celebrate with the rest of you when this is all over." He refocused and took another sip. "We received a fair amount of new information via our dear friend Kaiden from one of the AO's former members. We're piecing it together and parsing it all. Hopefully, there is some information on weaknesses and perhaps still functioning codes if we're lucky. Fortunately, Team Three has finished its mission and obtained the codes for the stations."

"So we'll attack soon?" Chiyo asked, her mirth gone and replaced by a seriousness that was tense, even for her.

"I couldn't inform you of that, but once they know we have the codes to access the stations, I'm sure they will change them. Time is of the essence right now," Laurie stated and fixed her with a firm look. "So I suggest you get back as soon as possible if you would like to be a part of it. Ask your Halo friends if they would like to join us. I'm sure we could use all the hands we can get."

"We'll have to see. This might be above what they are willing to do but I'll certainly ask." She looked down and moved around the screen on her tablet. "I have something I wanted to pass on to you. Unfortunately, I wasn't able to get any info on it and had to destroy it on our way out, but we found this inside the factory." She sent the professor the pictures of the engine. He placed his mug down and studied it. "From the readouts I did take on it, this could have powered another colossus."

He frowned at the mention of the ship. "Send those readouts to me as well if you still have them. I agree with you simply by looking at it, but there is something different about this engine. It's more experimental and oddly designed for something that would merely be a big battery."

Chiyo nodded and tapped her screen. "Done. They're on their way and I'll be off now, Professor. See you soon."

"Come back safe, Chiyo," he responded and signed out. He examined the pictures again and scanned her readouts as well. If this was an engine design, he wondered, was it merely a prototype? Why would they risk building it on Earth? They had a hold on the planet, certainly, but it wasn't global by any means. Even at the height of their power a few months before, this would have been risky. He began to worry that this wasn't the only one Merrick had worked on. This was the beginning of mass production.

When the infiltrator had destroyed it and used it as a bomb, it was very likely that she might have unintentionally used it in the intended manner.

"Ah, it is good to be back!" Luke shouted, stretched his arms, and removed his helmet. He stepped aside hastily as medics arrived to recover the wounded.

"Get rest while you can, mate," Flynn replied as he walked past to the armory. "I'm sure we'll be sent out again in twenty-four hours or less."

"We wouldn't want to get too bored." Cameron chuckled and undid the straps around his gauntlets as the rest of the group made their way out of the dropships.

"Welcome back, Team Three," Sasha said quietly and spooked the team.

"H-hey, Chancellor!" Amber responded before she whispered to Izzy, "Man, I wish he would stop that."

"I don't think he means to do it. I think it is simply

normal for him at this point." She shrugged and they waited for the man to speak.

"Well done on the mission—very effective and with no fatalities." He paused when a couple of soldiers were carried off on stretchers to the medical building. "Some injuries, but it could have been much worse."

"Eh, it's become kinda easy now." Luke chuckled. "The Omegas are big and loud but it's like only some of them have any real training."

"You're gonna knock someone for being big and loud?" Indre asked.

The titan linked his hands behind his head. "At least I had training."

"So when is our next mission?" Cameron asked. Part of his chest armor was undone but he hesitated on the rest. "Am I getting undressed for no reason?"

"You deserve a break. There are other tasks but the most important ones are already being undertaken by other teams."

"Eh, I won't complain," the bounty hunter said and resumed the process of undoing his armor. "But don't feel you need to keep us locked up. This is the closest I have to therapy right now."

Alarms began to blare around the station. People stopped to retrieve tablets or open holoscreens to see what was happening.

"Sasha, we have incoming!" Hartman shouted into the chancellor's earpiece.

He activated the screen in his oculars. "What's going on General?"

"A fleet of Omega ships jumped into our space. They are engaging our blockade on the coast."

"That seems far enough away that you wouldn't need to activate a red alert," he commented.

"This is a large attack so it seems they are looking to strike at us in force now," the man explained. "I'm calling for any nearby units to help push them back and wondered if any of the teams you're looking after are in the area."

One sprang to mind. "I'll contact them."

"Team One?" Sasha's face appeared in the ace's HUD. "There is a large enemy fleet on the coast—"

"Yeah, the Omegas." Kaiden nodded. "We're already on the way. All of us felt the jumps and we weren't even close to their entry point."

"We're rallying all nearby vessels to assist but we cannot leave the base too unprotected in case it is only a diversion."

"It would be a hell of a diversion," Silas stated. "It looks like fifteen ships in all, from assault to corsair to destroyers. And that's not counting all the personal fighters."

"I am amazed that the Horde is able to muster such forces even after so long," Genos said thoughtfully.

"They have controlled their sector for decades," Jaxon replied. "I'm sure they've been building, stealing, and repurposing vessels the entire time. They are the largest mercenary force in the known galaxy."

"Not to mention all the terrorist groups that folded into them once this all kicked off," Haldt added. "There is a reason they've been so brazen, even after almost a year of fighting."

"We're heading there now, Sasha," Kaiden confirmed, signed off, and looked at the team. "Let's destroy this invasion attempt. The sooner we do it, the sooner we can take this fight to them."

CHAPTER TWELVE

"WCV Dionysus, we are a team of Resistance members currently designated Team One and coming in to join the fight," Haldt stated as he brought their dropship in and several others behind them broke off to land on smaller vessels.

"We're glad to have you join us," a technician responded. "As you can see, it's kind of a clusterfuck out there at the moment."

Kaiden studied the battle through the cockpit window. The approaching Omega ships fired blasts of red energy and rockets streaked toward their targets. Multiple dogfights were in progress and numerous smaller ships fought around the larger ones. At least a dozen of these were almost entirely obliterated in the frenzied chaos.

"No kidding," he muttered and turned to the pilot. "Drop me off before you head down."

"Do what?" the man asked with a frown. "Where?"

"Onto one of the enemy ships," he said curtly as he

pushed from the co-pilot's seat and began to walk to the bay. "One of the smaller ones, though. Aim for a corsair."

"Are you gonna take it yourself?" Haldt asked, his expression somewhere between amusement and disapproval.

"Maybe." The ace opened his weapons case, slid Debonair into its holster, and primed Sire. He looked at his team. "Does anyone care to join me?"

Silas nodded and stood quickly. "I might as well. Otherwise, I would probably be ferried onto another dropship or have to wait for them to come to me."

"I will as well," Jaxon offered and looked at Genos. "Will you, kin?"

"Given the current battle," the engineer began as he studied a screen with a feed outside, "I will probably be of more use as a pilot if they have ships available."

"Oh, they will," Haldt told him. "I served on a couple of destroyers and they are stocked to the gills."

"Then we will meet later." Jaxon stood and Kaiden tossed him his machine gun. The Tsuna activated it as they stood at the side door of the ship.

"Are we close yet?" the ace asked, his weapon at the ready as he crouched.

"I'm coming up to the side of one—they are opening the upper hatch!" The top half of the side door slid back and the three Resistance soldiers fired into it as the dropship circled above the corsair. They directed their attack through the aperture on the side of the smaller vessel as Haldt drew closer. A few shots were fired in retaliation, but a cannon blast from Genos ended the defense rather quickly.

"Heading out!" Kaiden shouted. The bottom half of the door slid away, and the three teammates leapt from the ship and landed in the top hall of the corsair as Genos stepped back. The door of their dropship closed and the ship backed away toward the military vessels.

"Where we headed?" Silas asked and checked their flank.

"Command deck. We're taking over," the ace responded and motioned for them to follow as he broke into a jog.

"And after that?" the Tsuna inquired.

"I haven't thought that far," he told them honestly. "I guess we can use it to attack other Omegas? I don't have mid-level pilot talents, though."

"Nor do I," Jaxon admitted and glanced at Silas, who shook his head. "Perhaps Chief can be of use?"

"Assuming they don't have some kind of junk OS, I can probably get something going," the EI responded and appeared in Kaiden's HUD. *"It was a nice-looking ship—until you damaged it, at least—and probably not repurposed so it should be all right."*

"Then I guess we'll—shit! Incoming." Kaiden fell to one knee and charged a blast as an Omega heavy rounded the corner. Silas spun and discharged his shotgun as a couple of mercs tried to flank them. Jaxon assisted and discharged his machine gun to keep the enemy at bay, although their adversary's shields nullified most of the damage. Kaiden fired in the same moment that the man raised his arms and launched a torrent of flames. The ace's charged shot blazed through the fire and connected with the heavy but only forced him to take a few steps back. Kaiden narrowed his eyes when he noticed the tank on his back and his now weakened shields.

"Help Silas," he instructed Jaxon as he withdrew a thermal, pressed the switch, and tossed it on the floor. It skipped for several yards and slid under the heavy, who steadied himself to fire again. The explosion preempted his planned attack when it shattered his tank and detonated a larger blast that shattered the windows. The force hurled the man out, and he spiraled inexorably to the earth below.

"Last one down!" Silas shouted as he eliminated the last of the mercs. "More are probably on the way."

"It's a safe bet," the ace replied. "Let's move but leave a surprise for them if you have some."

"Oh, definitely." The enforcer chuckled. The three sprinted up the hall but as they rounded the corner, a couple of shots from behind barely missed them. He withdrew two triangular devices and planted them on the wall as they pushed forward to the command deck.

"I'm picking up some energy signatures, partner," Chief stated. *"Droids."*

Kaiden held Sire's trigger down, spun as he turned the corner, and fired to hit a droid as it was about to fire. The explosion rattled two others behind it and these were immediately felled by Silas and Jaxon.

"I've noticed that there seem to be more Omega mercenaries than droids so far," the Tsuna remarked. He grimaced at a loud explosion behind them as their pursuers tripped the mines his teammate had left.

"There are less now," Silas retorted with a grin.

"We might have finally made some impact on their assembly lines," Kaiden reasoned and checked his weapon. "But we shouldn't get our hopes up and instead, let's focus on what we have to do now. We should be close to the

front of the vessel so the command would be right around
—" His words cut off when a turret descended from the
ceiling. He cursed and readied Debonair but a couple of
blasts from Jaxon destroyed the defensive unit.

"Yeah, we're probably very close," the enforcer reasoned
and nodded toward twin doors in front of them. "Let me
take point for a moment." He approached the entrance
slowly and held a few more mines up. "These have several
different functions."

"They were right outside, weren't they?" one of the Omega
mercs asked and trained his rifle on the door. "What the
hell is taking so long?"

"Just be ready to shoot," another instructed, and his
finger tapped the side of his shotgun. "These idiots won't
make it past the bots before we mow them down—unless
you get distracted."

"I'm not distracted. I'm only saying—what's that
beeping noise?"

The other man listened to a faint but increasingly loud
noise immediately behind the door. "Is that the lock?" he
asked with a frown before the beeping stopped and the
doors blew apart. The five droids that stood in front of it
were destroyed and a couple of the other mercs were flung
back. He fired reflexively but only managed a few shots
before machinegun fire depleted his shields rapidly and
drilled through his armor. His fellow merc caught the full
force of a charged bolt and was blown into the technicians'
terminals.

The last operational droid pushed its chest up and turned to fire but dropped after a shot from Silas struck home. The enforcer whipped the butt of his gun across the helmet of the closest merc before he fired two shots into his stomach. Jaxon's blade circled in a hissed arc and swung into the left side of the visor of another merc. A hail of laser fire felled the Omega man and the others scattered.

Even the non-combat members of the deck found weapons and joined the fray, but their eyes widened when several thermals streaked toward them. They panicked and tried to escape but were caught between explosives and machinegun fire. Some tried to surrender but it was a meaningless gesture as the thermals detonated and nothing could be done to stop them.

"It looks clear," Silas announced and waved his hand in the air to clear the smoke.

"To me as well," Jaxon concurred.

Kaiden walked in and scanned for any other hostiles, but it seemed they had been rather thorough.

"Well, you have the bridge," Chief told him and his gaze darted around as if to examine the room. *"It could use spiffing up now, though."*

"There's no point. It won't last more than a few minutes," the ace responded as he approached the commander's terminal and cast the EI inside.

"And why is that?" Jaxon asked and nodded as Silas posted himself at the door as a lookout.

"It's not worth staying on the ship. I'm sure there are more mercs who'll challenge us and I don't feel like wasting my time, no matter how much this feels like a turkey shoot," he explained and moved his fingers along a screen to check the map of the field.

"So what's the plan then—blow it?" the enforcer asked.

Kaiden nodded. "But not in the normal way. I feel like there's a more...efficient way to do things."

"Your definition of efficient is usually different than mine Kaiden," Jaxon remarked and made another slow scrutiny of the area. "Should we prepare by trying to find the escape pods?"

"You can but that would take you out of the fight." The ace found whatever he'd looked for on the map and pressed it, and the other two soldiers exchanged a glance when the ship began to increase speed. He turned to look at them. "We've been friends four years now. How much do you trust me?"

CHAPTER THIRTEEN

"You're both pilots?" the military crewman asked Haldt and Genos and studied the Tsuna especially.

"I have pilot talents and have trained for several hundred hours in their use," the mechanist offered with his hand on his chest. "Although technically, I am not with the pilot pro—"

"I have flown for almost two decades—since before my balls dropped." Haldt's firm but quiet tone interrupted the Tsuna. "This kid is almost as good as I am. Now, do you want us to fill out forms in triplicate or get out and fight?" Several explosions rocked the ship and he steadied himself on a pillar. "It sounds like bombers are making a run on the ship."

The crewman nodded. "Agreed, you're cleared. Get out there and deal with them."

"On it!" Haldt and Genos chose two available fighters, scrambled in quickly, and familiarized themselves with the systems as part of their hasty preparations.

"I'm heading out, friend Haldt!" the Tsuna announced

and the landing gear on his ship folded in as he spun his craft and accelerated out of the bay.

"Damn, he's quicker than me." The pilot pressed the switch to close the cockpit and brought up his landing gear. "I guess I now gotta prove I shouldn't have said 'I'm almost as good as he is.'" He touched the controls lightly to turn the ship and followed Genos into combat.

"Are you sure about this?" Silas demanded and directed a volley at a team of mercs who intercepted them in the hall. "I mean really sure?"

"About thirty-five seconds until impact, ya'll," Chief announced. *"You should probably have made your minds up by now."*

"No shit." Kaiden retorted as he shattered the last remains of the glass on the large window and holstered Sire. "Either take your chances with me or the ship. Now is the time to choose." With that, he ran across the hall and leapt out the window. Jaxon fired a few more rounds before he too ducked and jumped out while he stowed his machine gun on his back on the way.

"Well, screw me for liking sane plans," the enforcer muttered, took a deep breath, and followed his teammates. The Omegas who remained looked at each other in confusion as it was impossible for anyone to survive a fall like that. They were at least four miles above the Earth. One peered over the edge and recoiled as something rocketed past on an upward trajectory. He readied his gun before something else caught his attention and gaped at the side of an Omega assault ship that quickly became larger as their ship streaked toward it.

"Holy fu—" The corsair bulldozed into the side of the assault ship and effectively destroyed it when the impact blew a massive hole in the destroyer. The engines on the left side began to lose power as it fell slowly from the sky.

At a safe distance from the collision, the three Resistance teammates soared unperturbed, thanks to the jets on Kaiden's armor. "I need to thank Desmond for giving me this upgrade." The ace looked at the other two, who held tightly to his arms.

Silas tightened his grasp meaningfully. "Would you pay attention to where you are flying?"

"We should probably land on that military vessel," Jaxon suggested and nodded to a military lancer-class ship nearby.

"You probably know this, but you are well over the recommended weight capacity," Chief warned. *"So I would take the advice."*

"I will. It's not like I planned to carry them all in battle." The ace's jets increased in power and both soldiers held on tighter as he banked toward their destination.

"That's my third bomber down!" Haldt shouted. He, Genos, and several other military fighters had made quick work of the Omega bombers that tried to attack the Dionysus, so much so that they were now forced to stop their runs to avoid their pursuers. "It looks like I'll have number four here in a few seconds."

"Enemy fighters on the way to the left—or nine o'clock, rather," the Tsuna informed the group. His teammate focused on a group of ten Omega fighters on a course toward them.

Haldt frowned, fired at the enemy bomber in front of him, and destroyed its thrusters. As it descended rapidly toward the earth, he pulled away with a decisive nod. "I'll head to intercept."

"We're with you," one of the military pilots replied and he was joined by seven other pilots including Genos. "Preparing missiles."

The Omega ships fired on them and they retaliated. A couple of the vessels were able to release their missiles, but not from a good position and either missed or were shot down. Haldt banked his aircraft to pursue one of the fighters, locked on, and launched one of his missiles to obliterate his target.

He allowed himself a satisfied smirk but it faded quickly when he received a warning that he had been targeted. With a low oath, he checked the rear feed and identified two ships in pursuit. He prepared to bank sharply to return to the ship and catch them in his turrets during the maneuver, but one of the vessels fired a missile. Another muffled curse escaped as he pressed a switch to activate the rear turret and fired several shots before he was able to strike the projectile and spare himself a quick but nasty end. Unfortunately, he had no time to celebrate as the turret was blasted from above.

Haldt looked up and scowled at several more Omega fighters that descended into combat. "More incoming from above!" he warned and forced the yoke hastily to the left in an effort to gain distance from his pursuers before he faced more than he could handle. Moments later, a bright glow behind him made him check his rear feed again. His pursuers had been decimated and a large blue beam cut through four of the newly appeared fighters. "Who is that?"

"It is me—Genos," the Tsuna responded. "My apologies for not doing that sooner. The cannon takes time to charge."

"Cannon? You have a cannon?" he asked.

"Indeed. This is a dragon-class fighter. Yours is a challenger, I believe," the engineer explained as he drew alongside. The security officer finally noticed the differences between their aircraft.

"Lucky bastard," Haldt jested. "But we still have some of these bastards flying around. Let's get this done so we can go on the offensive."

"Certainly," Genos agreed. "It will take time for the cannon to charge again after two shots in succession, however."

"Take all the time you need." He pulled up and circled again. "It's time for me to have fun now."

Kaiden's group landed on the Lancer and a couple of guns barred their progress. They held their hands up immediately. "We're part of the Resistance and are here to help!" Jaxon announced.

"Call sign?" one of the soldiers demanded.

"Gamma-Beta 0202," the ace replied and the weapons lowered.

"Sorry. We're a little jumpy." The man nodded to the left where droid parts were scattered across the ship. "They keep dropping them in using fast transports so we haven't had time to get into position to do anything because we constantly have to fend them off."

"Did you guys see that Omega ship crash into the other one?" another soldier asked.

"That was us," Silas responded and folded his arms.

"Really? Damn, nice work!" the soldier said with a whistle.

"Oh, so now you think it was a good plan?" Kaiden snarked.

"I didn't say that, only that we did it," the enforcer countered.

At a loud bang on the top of the ship, all the soldiers snapped into action and turned toward a pod that had thunked into the hull. Two more followed before a transport of some kind swung sharply and accelerated out of range. "Sneaky bastards," a soldier muttered.

"Fire!" another roared. The three teammates drew their weapons as one and joined the soldiers as the pods burst open. As expected, droids surged out, but they were accompanied by a surprising number of mercs as well.

Kaiden retrieved his shield array and anchored it to the deck to create a defense for himself and those around him as kinetic rounds and lasers filled the air. He hunkered behind the barrier, charged shots, and fired them at the enemy before he ducked again while his adversary's shields were destroyed. Two soldiers were almost felled by an Omega with a launcher, who the ace dispatched with a charged round aimed at his gun to detonate the explosive contents inside.

"Kaiden, Jax!" Silas yelled and both glanced at him as he handed them each a mine. "This is the last of my stash so make them count. Use setting three."

The ace flipped the switch to three and lobbed it at one of the pods. The projectile connected and erupted to annihilate a couple of droids but also knocked the pod over. It began to tumble over the edge of the ship, upended a few mercs in its path, and shoved them off the side while they yelled in surprise. The sound grew more panicked as they fell.

"Damn, I wish I thought of that," Silas stated as his explosive dismembered a few droids with violent efficiency and shattered the shield of a merc, who was quickly gunned down by a marksman.

"Finish cleaning up," one of the soldiers—possibly the highest-ranking—ordered and activated his commlink. "Get us closer to the destroyers. We keep being attacked because we're an easy target."

Jaxon fired at a merc who seemed to try to retreat, although where he would go was anyone's guess. "I think we are clear for now."

"What? Are you joking?" the military leader demanded, and the three friends focused on him.

"What's wrong?" Kaiden asked.

"They said they are picking up energy spikes so more ships are jumping in. And they don't have familiar signatures," he explained.

"You're kidding me—the Omega are still coming?" Silas echoed the incredulousness they all felt.

"It's here." The man pointed above them and Kaiden gaped as the sky warped around itself for a moment before a massive ship appeared. It was much larger than a destroyer and closer to a dreadnaught. He studied it with narrowed eyes. It didn't have the Omega red-and-black or even the shiny white-and-silver of the AO droids. In fact, the design of the ship didn't look even remotely familiar.

It was alien, he realized, and when he saw familiar markings along the vessel, it clicked.

The new arrival was a Sauren ship.

CHAPTER FOURTEEN

"War Chief! We've finally arrived," Ken'ra announced as the doors to the front observatory of their ship opened to reveal a large red Sauren clad in white and golden armor.

He walked to the massive window and stared out. "Battle," he muttered.

"Indeed," his companion replied. "It looks like Earth military vessels are engaged in combat with an enemy whose colors and designs indicate—"

"It's the Omega Horde." Raza growled and turned to the other hunters behind him. "Prepare the gliders and chariots. We shall join the fight."

His warriors uttered bloodthirsty roars that echoed throughout the massive ship and wasted no time in complying with his order. "Come, Ken'ra," he stated and bared his fangs. "We'll aim for the head."

"Sauren?" one of the soldiers shouted in shock. "How did they get here? Are the gates open again?"

"I haven't heard anything," Kaiden replied, his attention focused as hatches on the side of the ship began to open. "I don't know how they got here, but they seem to be alive so that's a plus."

"Do you think Raza is on there?" Silas asked and kicked the severed head of a droid off the ship as he walked closer to him.

"That's the biggest vessel I've ever seen for a Sauren excursion," Jaxon noted. "And if they came to fight, I'm sure their War Chief would be there."

Kaiden nodded at the ship. "It looks like they came to do exactly that."

Dozens of small figures leapt out of the craft, all holding onto mechanical gliders that streaked through the airborne battle zone. Some dropped fighters individually, while others deposited groups onto Omega ships.

The ace held Sire close. "I'm going back in!" he shouted and launched himself off the ship and into the fray. Silas threw his hands up in frustration.

"Yeah, leave us here. That's cool," he muttered.

Jaxon turned to one of the soldiers. "You will continue to fight, yes?"

"Of course. That's what we're here to do."

"Good. We will join you." He grasped one of the railings.

The soldier nodded. "That's good to hear. We'll get the ship going again." He turned to enter the vessel and mumbled quietly, "It wasn't like you had much choice."

Kaiden zigzagged through a battle between fighters, charged a shot with Sire, and flipped to fire up as an enemy drone focused on him. He spun again and a hasty glance to his left made him move frantically up and to the left when the guns on a military assault ship swung to fire at an Omega ship nearby.

"Do you have any idea where you're going?" Chief demanded.

"Not really," he admitted and scanned the different vessels. "I wanna get in contact with some Sauren and find out what's going on."

"I think the debriefing can wait until we finish this."

"Well, I also wanna do some damage. I've seen what one Sauren can do alone so I wanna see what a group can do." Kaiden's gaze settled on another enemy corsair for a moment. One of the side hatches was ripped from its hinges and an Omega was hurled through it, followed by a couple of droids. He nodded and decided he'd found a place to set down.

Kaiden accelerated into his new course, flipped back, and eased the propulsion to slow himself as he sailed through the damaged doorway. He bounced off the wall, made another flip as his jets condensed, and turned, only to freeze in place. A Sauren in brown armor with thick scales of amber-yellow and darkened green eyes stared down at him.

"Whoa, hold up!" He held both hands up hastily, extended them in a claw-like manner, and pressed them together before he made a small bow, a motion that resembled a greeting in Sauren culture. "I'm Kaiden Jericho, working with the WCM as part of the Resistance."

"Kaiden Jericho?" the Sauren asked and leaned forward as he observed the soldier. "Our War Chief has spoken of you, I believe. You are from the Nexus Academy, yes?"

"Yeah, I am. Do you know Raza?" He almost slapped himself for his idiotic question. While he might have known Raza as a diplomat, he was the equivalent of a high-ranking leader on his homeworld. "Right, of course you would."

"Indeed, we have known one another almost from the time we spawned." The warrior turned and removed what appeared to be a shield off his back. "I am Lok. Talking can be done later, but for now…" He pressed a switch on the grip of the shield and numerous small spikes protruded from the edges. They began to spin as blue energy covered them. "We have prey."

Four Arbiter droids rounded the corner as he finished speaking. Lok threw the disc and while the grip remained in his hand, it sliced cleanly through one droid before it continued toward the wall. He pressed the switch again and the energy around the spikes flared for a moment before it made impact. It bounced off the wall and carved through two more mechanicals on its return to him. The Sauren caught the shield and set it again as the final droid fired. He blocked the attack with the barrier and waved it a few times to clear it as more droids rounded the corner.

The warrior glanced at Kaiden. "Keep my back protected," he stated before he turned, roared, and surged toward the bots. Although the ace instinctively aimed his rifle to help, Chief gave him warning of someone approaching from the hall alongside him. They obviously attempted to sneak up on him, so he dropped his rifle and used a quick burst from his jets to intercept the mercs.

A shoulder-charge shoved one back and Kaiden planted his feet, punched the second one, and cracked his visor. He grasped the man's chest plate and turned him as the other recovered and fired. The volley struck his teammate's back, and the ace flicked his wrist to release his blade. He kicked the man away and toppled him onto one of his teammates as they slid down the wall. With the blade held back, he paused for a moment, then cast it forward through the visor of the next man. His target raised his hand involuntarily as if to try to stop it, but the momentary reflex ended as soon as he fell.

With no further enemies, he hurried to snatch his rifle up as Lok crushed the head of the final droid and flung it aside. He lowered his rifle as the Sauren looked at him. "Finished?" he asked and the ace nodded. "Well done. The others have cleared a path to the bridge. We shall go there."

"On it." Kaiden ran forward as the warrior settled on all fours and raced away. Hastily, he stowed his rifle and activated the speed mods of his suit to keep up. Crazily, he almost had to move at a sprint simply to do so. When they arrived at the door, three Sauren, all different colors but equally as tall and heavily built as Lok, stood waiting.

"Military?" one of them asked.

The chief nodded. "One of the young ones Raza helped to train. From Nexus."

The three nodded in response and the one who had spoken turned to Kaiden. "We are preparing to breach. Will you join us?"

"Of course." The ace drew his rifle again. "We already took control of one some time ago so I have a plan if you need it."

Lok shrugged. "We planned to simply charge in and kill any who attempted to stop us. Does that sound good?"

Kaiden paused and thought about it for a moment. "Uh…yeah, it sounds solid."

The warrior nodded. "That's good." He turned to the others. "Kill."

The Sauren roared and slashed through the doors with their claws as laser fire erupted. Lok readied his shield and surged forward with Kaiden close behind. The ace managed a couple of shots and destroyed two droids, but the battle was essentially carnage. The helmsman and some of the crew fled, but all those who remained were savaged by the Sauren's claws and weaponry at an impressive pace. When it was over, he stood beside the chief as two of the warriors raced out the doors to pursue any remaining enemies.

"You know, I'm glad our people never had a war," he remarked and put his mostly unused weapon away.

"We are hunters, not conquerors," Lok stated. "War is a rarity for us, with the exception of amongst ourselves, unfortunately."

"Right. Uh, as you can see, we have a similar problem." Kaiden opened the map next to the commander's chair. "I had hoped to join up with Raza. Do you know where he went?"

The warrior approached and pointed at the largest ship. "He went to attack what appeared to be the Omega's main vessel."

"Right for the head, huh? It sounds about right." He sent Chief into the systems to begin piloting the ship.

"Shall we commandeer this vessel?" the remaining Sauren asked and Lok looked at Kaiden.

"We certainly can, but I used the last one I was on to ram into another ship," he explained.

The warrior bared his fangs but his lips twitched upward as he uttered clicking noises akin to laughter. "I like that plan more."

CHAPTER FIFTEEN

"Holy shit, do you see this?" a voice asked excitedly over the commlink.

"See what?" Haldt asked and immediately scanned the sky around him and checked his radar for hostiles.

"Look at the Omega command ship. Sauren are rushing at it on flying carts."

He turned and shook his head in disbelief at five floating machines that, while ornate and detailed, weren't much more complex than the pilot's flying cart description. The black ships nearby took notice too, judging by the way they turned quickly in that direction.

"Aw, hell. We need to get over there now," Haldt ordered and banked his craft into a hard turn. "Genos, are you with me?"

"I am already on the way, friend Haldt," the Tsuna replied.

"Good. Someone get on comms with the destroyers and assault craft. They need to pelt that vessel so the command ship's guns don't vaporize them."

"I think they are already on that, buddy," someone responded.

Bright flashes, a little too close for his liking, preceded massive energy blasts and kinetic cannon rounds that now fired in abundance at the large vessel. Its barriers and shields held but if it had previously had any attention on the approaching Sauren, it was now focused on different problems.

Haldt and several other fighters fell into formation and intercepted the approaching fighters as the Sauren chariots glided past the shields and into the ship. As he disabled an Omega fighter, a corsair flew overhead toward the command craft—but not to a hangar, he realized, and it wasn't slowing either.

"I should probably have mentioned that when I did this the first time, I bailed from the ship before it made impact," Kaiden warned as they drew closer to their target.

"That was a smart plan, then," Lok commented and primed his shield. "But we have our own protection."

The other Sauren quickly surrounded the soldier and each retrieved a shield. They were smaller than Lok's, but the same blue energy pulsed around the edges before it flowed to create a bubble around the group.

"*Impact coming in ten...*" Chief warned and counted down as Kaiden readied himself while the hull of the ship came closer.

"*Five...four...three...two... Hold on!*" The vessel powered into the ship, demolished the walls, and crushed the front of the Corsair. Their momentum was suddenly halted, and the group was flung through the newly created aperture. Their shield held and even bounced them a few times before Lok yelled for them to brake. The shield vanished and the Sauren all stopped themselves when they either dug their claws into the metal walls or floor or used their tails to grasp pipes or railings above.

Kaiden landed on his knees, slid across the bay, and drew Debonair quickly to fire at a grunt who raced to see what all the commotion was about. He recalled the thermals on his belt, pushed himself forward, and snatched them as he rolled and finally managed to stop. With the grenades hung on his belt, he stood and fired rapidly at approaching hostiles while the Sauren roared and lumbered past him to engage.

A rumbling sound made him look up to where the massive feet of a mech appeared around the corner. He holstered Debonair, readied Sire, and charged a shot. The jockey inside pressed a switch as he took the sticks and aimed at him. Lok's shield flew from overhead and thrust through the cockpit and into the jockey. His crumpled form forced the sticks together and made the mech's arms cross and point at the floor before they fired. A massive explosion shattered the decking and took the mech and several droids and any merc not caught in the blast down with it while the Sauren simply leapt to higher floors or grasped onto the walls.

The ace turned to Lok, who nodded at him. He aimed his rifle upward and fired at a turret that targeted at the hunter. When he saw the turret collapse, the warrior looked at Kaiden, who nodded in return. His lips twitched upward again as he pressed the switch on his grip and his shield returned to him from the hole in the floor before the two proceeded to a chamber on their left.

"You keep getting all the good kills," Kaiden stated.

"Machines aren't worth much. If this was a ritual hunt, I wouldn't have many points."

"There was a human piloting it," he reminded him.

The Sauren snorted. "Lacked ability, relied on big machine to compensate."

"So how many points do you think I'm worth?" he asked curiously.

Lok tilted his head from side to side. "You have ability, are sturdy, not easily frightened. Decent amount, but haven't seen much of you." He studied him briefly. "Show me more, maybe worth many points then."

Kaiden chuckled as they continued to run down the corridor. "That's some conflicting motivation right there."

"Sauren!" Raza shouted and held his duel-bladed staff high as they breached the command ship's hangars. "The hunt begins—for blood and glory!" His warriors roared as the shields around their chariots fell. They surged out and immediately pushed forward to engage the numerous enemy soldiers and droids that had opened fire.

The War Chief battered through the front of his chariot, too impatient to let it open on its own. He severed the head of a droid almost absentmindedly as he charged a bulkier one and pierced its chest with his staff. The mechanical fired its cannon while it still functioned, but he simply moved his head to the side and the blast streaked past him. He spun and cast the droid up to pound it viciously against the ceiling at least fifty feet above and watched it topple with a grin. A click alerted him that someone tried to sneak up on him. He whipped his tail, snagged a mercenary around the neck, and thrust him into a nearby column.

Drones joined the combat and added an airborne dimension. Raza slammed the bladed staff down as he drew his Taiko, one of the few gun-like weapons the Sauren made use of. He pressed the trigger once and three prongs popped up on the barrel. When he held the trigger, red energy collected in the prongs, which funneled into the barrel. He let go and the blast seared into one of the drones and erupted into a red orb to catch others around it or those that flew too fast to avoid it.

Three more Omega soldiers barreled toward the War Chief, who looked at them and bared his teeth but made no effort to attack. They aimed their weapons but before they could fire, two were pierced by lances. Claws wrapped the helmet of the man in the middle and as they sank in, his armor broke and visor shattered. He collapsed and Ken'ra grinned at the group of hunters behind them.

"What are your orders, War Chief?" he asked and Raza turned to him.

"If this ship has the ability to jump, disable it. We will destroy it and the enemy will see it happen," he stated and yanked his staff out of the floor. "I will head to the core."

"Alone?" the other warrior asked. "It would be faster with more hunters."

"I am sure it would but more will come. Should you run out of prey, join me." He twirled his staff as he walked away. "I have not been able to hunt in months. I desire a little personal pleasure."

CHAPTER SIXTEEN

"It would appear they are preparing to retreat," Genos notified the other pilots. Haldt took a moment to glance out his cockpit and confirmed that the Tsuna seemed to be right. Several of the smaller enemy ships either slowed their advance or turned away quickly and accelerated away from the fight. The destroyers and the last few remaining assault ships seemed to try to hold position or were engaged with the newly arrived Sauren. He could see a couple of them battling groups of mercs on top of one of the destroyers.

"Then get who you can," he announced, banked, and set a course toward one of the corsairs. "They might escape, but I wanna leave a reminder for them of how stupid it is to face us now."

"It's strange, but the command ship seems to make no attempt to retreat," the mechanist noted. "Viola doesn't even detect an energy spike to indicate an attempt to jump."

"Perhaps there's too much commotion or damage for

them to jump safely," he suggested, his focus on the corsair he'd targeted. "Or—and this is only a wild guess—they were boarded by dozens of Sauren. That might have something to do with it."

Kaiden lobbed one of the stolen thermals down the hall and the enemy soldiers either flung themselves aside or boosted their shields. He held Sire's trigger down and charged a shot. The explosive detonated and he moved quickly to the left to aim at a raider. The shot powered through the man's chest plate and the explosion shattered the pillar he tried to hide behind to spew debris and clouds of smoke around the hall. The ace tossed the second thermal into the smoke before he ducked through the door at the end of the hall and slammed the terminal to shut it as the second blast went off.

"Did you finish them?" Lok asked and continued to tear into the power lines of the jump engine to the command ship. The glowing sphere began to dim.

"Chief?" Kaiden asked and studied the door.

"There are no life signs, at least in the hall. You got them, buddy," the EI confirmed.

"We're good for now, but there are always more on big ships like these," he told the Sauren.

Lok thunked his shield into a console and yanked it out quickly, and a couple of terminals around the engine flickered before they shut down. "They are numerous but not strong." The hunter growled in what might have been disgust.

"*Change of status, partner. I have life signs coming this way but not human.*"

Kaiden walked closer to Lok and peered at the door on the opposite end and at the floors above. "It seems like some of your teammates are coming through."

"Yes, I can hear them," he said with a nod and straightened. "Stay close. They may be ravenous for battle."

"Naturally." He responded to his companion's hard look with a shrug. "Hey, I would think you would admit that the Sauren are known for being ferocious warriors."

Lok turned his attention to their surroundings. "True, but you cannot build a civilization through ferocity alone." A set of doors on the floor above were ripped apart and several Sauren ran through and vaulted over the edge. They landed with their weapons and claws bared but noticed both the now quiet engine and their compatriot, who held a hand up.

The final three landed and Kaiden noticed numerous markings and decorations on one's armor. The warrior straightened, checked the engine, and approached Lok, who placed his claw on the center of his chest plate. "Chief Ken'ra," he said with reverence.

The warrior placed a claw against his chest in a mirrored greeting. "You are a chief yourself, Lok. There is no need to be so formal with a brother."

"You know I felt it never suited me," the other Sauren replied and lowered his claw as his compatriot did the same. "We have dismantled their ability to flee."

"I can see that you have been thorough," Ken'ra noted and glanced at Kaiden. "Did this human help you?"

Lok nodded. "Indeed, this one has been most helpful.

Although he requires the aid of his technology to keep pace with me, his skills and strength are his own."

"I see. It's good to have useful allies." The new arrival strode closer and studied the ace. "We have wondered how it can be that after all this time, your species continues to show the tenacity that made us respect it. Who are you, hunter?"

"Kaiden Jericho." He glanced at Lok, who nodded. "Raza might have mentioned me."

"Indeed. Wolfson's apprentice," Ken'ra remarked and Kaiden twitched a little with impatience.

"Is Raza here?" he asked to change the subject. "If he is, I would like to fight with him."

The Sauren's mouth tweaked into a small smile, as did Lok's and a few of the others behind them. "We would all like to fight by our War Chief's side," he remarked. "He went to the ship's core and sent us here. The rest of our brothers and sisters are fighting around the ship."

"He's alone?"

"Has any of the force you've battled so far led you to believe our War Chief would be in danger?" Lok asked.

The ace shook his head. "Nah. I've fought Raza and even holding back, he kicked my ass. But my guess is it'll be a hell of a walk to the core by himself and he could use some company." He folded his arms, suddenly thoughtful. "How do you guys know where everything is anyway? Is it smell or hearing?"

"To some extent." Lok nodded.

"We have engaged this type of vessel before," Ken'ra explained and held a pad up—a rather old one by the looks of it—activated it, and displayed the layout of the ship. "The Horde has been an issue in our sector for many years. We downed one of these ships on one of our hunting planets and had a team of technicians examine it."

"Do you mind if I borrow that?" Kaiden asked. The war chief stretched to hand it to him. "Chief?"

"On it. Downloading." The EI downloaded a copy of the map in seconds and brought it up in the HUD. *"I assume you want a path to the core?"*

"I want to try to meet up with Raza, but heading that way is a start."

"All right. You need to go up."

"Up?" He looked at the catwalks and floors above. "Which floor?"

"No, just up. There's a space between floors on the ship near the top. You can use that to fly over to him without having to make too many detours."

"Right." Kaiden primed his jets and nodded at the Sauren. "I'll go to find Raza."

"And we will continue the hunt," Ken'ra responded.

Lok eyed his compatriot curiously. "Should we not make our way to our War Chief as well?"

"He said that if we run out of things to do, we should join him but he wanted…privacy," Ken'ra explained. "I'm sure he wouldn't mind an old friend joining him, especially one he hasn't seen in some time. And I doubt he will interfere much with the War Chief's hunt."

"Uh, sure thing." Kaiden crouched and vaulted up, activated his jets, and ascended rapidly while the Sauren watched him from below.

"Prepare to fire," Chief warned. *"Unless you wanna splatter*

on the ceiling and fall back in front of those warriors. That'll lose you some goodwill."

"Tell me when, smartass," he ordered, aimed Sire in front of him, and held the trigger.

The ceiling approached quickly and moments later, *Fire* flashed across his HUD. Kaiden did so and rode through the blast while Chief slowed the jets somewhat so he could get his bearings and scan the new area, which appeared to be a dark ravine-like conglomeration of pipes and wires.

"All right, now go straight," the EI instructed. *"For...a while."*

Raza swung an Omega soldier into another. The one who received the blow toppled over the railings and into the deep banks below, a fall of several stories. The War Chief crushed the head of the soldier in his hand. The final man, a titan, attacked with a large ax, pressed a switch to activate boosters on the back, and attempted to bisect him from head to toe. He simply turned, held his staff up, and blocked the strike, which also shocked his assailant.

The Omega leaned into it to increase the force of the boosters and gradually inched closer. He grew a little cocky when he saw the Sauren's arms shake slightly and added pressure to push his adversary back and swing the ax at him. The warrior bared his fangs, rolled to the side, and allowed the blade to drive through the floor inches from him. He roared and pierced the man's heavy armor with his bladed staff, yanked it free, and let the body fall and slide through the hole the ax had made. With a grin, he watched it fall and was about to turn away when he heard something mechanical approach.

A group of four thinner droids marched toward him. He had grown more annoyed than bored with them by this point and swung his staff in preparation to attack. A blast rang out from above as something blew through the ceiling and a figure in black sailed down. He paused as a wash of green energy swept the mechanicals and destroyed them in a single dramatic onslaught, and the figure landed amongst the sizzling energy and raining parts.

He turned to the War Chief, held his hands like claws and placed them together, and bowed slightly before he straightened and his visor slid away. The Sauren clicked his teeth together and let a smile form briefly. It had been some time, but he recognized the new arrival. "Kaiden."

"Hello, Raza," the ace responded and shouldered his rifle. "I heard you wanted to blow up a ship."

CHAPTER SEVENTEEN

Raza walked forward, his arm extended. "It has been some time, young hunter. I'm glad to see you still fight on."

"And on and on and on." Kaiden chuckled and took the Sauren's arm. "It's good to see you too, Raza. I don't think I ever got to thank you in person for helping with the Gin situation."

"There's no need. I was more than happy to end that wretch." The warrior grinned, released him, and stood tall. "How did you find me?"

"Lok and I destroyed the jump engine and met some of your other hunters who said you were heading to the core. Ken'ra gave me a map of the ship, which I followed to try to meet you until Chief picked up a life sign. Saurens kind of stand out."

"I see. Yes, I expected the trek would be long but I had hoped for more worthy fights than the ones I've had thus far." He growled his displeasure.

"I don't think you'll have much luck with that," Kaiden

told him. "We've fought for so long and we have the advantage now. They still have numbers but I think most of the guys left on Earth are basically the B-team." He pointed above. "If you want the good stuff, I assume most went back to guard the guy who caused all this."

"Hmm...I see." Raza clicked his teeth. "We will have to discuss the events before this battle, but we should finish this first."

"Agreed." The ace nodded, vented Sire, and closed his visor. "Lead on, War Chief."

The Sauren smiled again as he turned and began to jog, and Kaiden had to sprint to keep up. "I think this might be the first time I've heard you refer to me by my title."

"Well, this is a war so it seems appropriate," he reasoned.

Raza chuckled. "Tell me, where is Wolfson? Is he facing other foes outside the ship?"

He was glad his face could not be seen through his helmet. "He's...I'll fill you in later."

"Some other mission, then?" the warrior questioned with a huff of air. "Those are concerns for later, you are right. For now, we should...hold." He extended an arm, craned his neck, and listened. "Something is activating."

A rumble farther along the route confirmed his statement. Something significantly large was engaging its systems behind the big doors to the main core. Kaiden shut the vent on Sire, charged a shot, and aimed at the barrier as Raza leaned down and rolled his staff.

The doors opened and a massive machine emerged. A curved black body with red stripes lumbered forward on four pointed legs with four cannons, two on each side.

Kaiden saw no head, which meant no obvious weak points. It resembled a combination of a Goliath and Dragoon and as it marched out of the engine room, the glow of the power core illuminated its dark frame.

"That's...that's new," the ace muttered.

"Most machines are not worthy prey," the Sauren growled. "This one, I suspect, is an exception."

The cannons began to charge and both hunter and soldier darted forward rather than to the side, which would have meant off the ledge. Fortunately, the area close to the access point widened somewhat, but the cannons had more maneuverability than Kaiden had anticipated. Two moved immediately to target him and he fired instinctively down the barrel of one. It created an eruption that forced the barrel beneath it down.

When the second one fired, the large explosion flung him off his feet, but he rode the blast and rolled hastily to his feet. Smoke issued from the barrel he had damaged, but the light came on again as well. It was able to self-repair, obviously, or had at least enough power to force the weapon to function.

Raza sliced at the droid's legs and darted from one to the other as it tried to maneuver its cannons to enable a clean shot. A couple of loud clicks accompanied the mech's successful attempt to right itself and straighten its limbs, which began to pound the ground rapidly beneath it. The force was enough to stop the ace from getting close, and the Sauren was forced to leap back, running on all fours with his staff in his mouth. Their adversary turned all four cannons on the War Chief and Kaiden fired two more charged rounds to try to get its attention. He was successful and the droid rotated two of the weapons to retaliate. Thinking quickly, he retrieved his shielding array and began to run back while he activated it and he tossed it in front of a column that he dove behind.

"Chief, any ideas?" he asked and readied his rifle as the machine fired. The attack struck his shield, broke it, and impacted the column, and the force catapulted him away and cracked his shoulder pads and chest plate.

"Not dying is a good start," the EI recommended. *"I don't see anything we can break through, and we're gonna need a ton of power to defeat it. Which makes me think we can kill two birds."*

"What do you—" An arrow appeared in his HUD and pointed to the core. He immediately reached the obvious conclusion. "All right. So we only need to force it in there."

"Shooting the cannons made it step back," Chief reminded him.

"A little, yeah, but we need it to move more than only slightly. Probably, if I hit all four... All right, it's been a while since we've done this, but I have an idea."

"I think I follow. Let's do it, partner."

The ace nodded, swung Sire to focus on the target, and raced to the droid. Raza had pierced its chest with his staff and currently roared at it as he now tried to climb higher.

"Raza, jump!" Kaiden called, activated his last thermal, and lobbed it at the mech. The Sauren leapt off seconds before the explosive caught the rear of the enemy and damaged a piece of its armor. More importantly, it turned its attention to him.

He looked at the War Chief, made a shoving motion with his hand, and pointed at the core. His companion's eyes widened for a moment before he nodded, stowed his staff, and armed himself with what appeared to be a club. From the reverberating energy that issued from it, though, it was clearly a kinetic force hammer.

Kaiden turned and the mech loomed over him while all four cannons charged. "Chief, activate battle suite."

He raised his weapon as time began to slow and breathed out slowly. The energy coalesced in each barrel and he pulled the trigger—only a partial charge but enough for the blow-back. He switched to the left cannon, did the same, then repeated the process with the final two. Each shot struck home. While the combined blast forced his opponent back, he held himself steady against the pressure.

The mech staggered into the engine room and Raza seized the opportunity. With an aggressive bellow, he rushed at it and held the hammer high as it glowed a bright white. He drove it into the body of his enemy and a wave of kinetic force surged from it and hurled the machine back several more feet so it fell directly into the core.

The Sauren landed and Kaiden deactivated the battle suite. The engine began to disintegrate and poured out a wave of destructive energy. They dove to the sides as it funneled out of the room, consumed the path behind them, and melted the mech inside. The pressure gathered until the explosion rocketed skyward, blew through the ceiling, and caused the rest to collapse.

They had won but now, they were trapped on a ship that would soon be aflame.

CHAPTER EIGHTEEN

"D amn, something happened down there," one of the pilots exclaimed. Genos narrowed his eyes to focus as a large explosion ripped through a couple of floors of the command ship.

"It would appear that our Sauren allies have been quite effective on your left, C-2," he remarked and added a notification to another pilot of an incoming fighter.

"That vessel will go down hard. It's a good thing it didn't make it to shore so it won't drop over a city or anything," Haldt added.

"Indeed, a most fortuitous battle—if a battle can be fortuitous." The Tsuna scanned the sky. The few Omega ships that had gotten away jumped and finally retreated from the battle. "I wonder where Kaiden ended up."

"We might not have thought the plan through enough,"

Kaiden shouted as he scrambled to his feet and grimaced at the rapidly collapsing area and everything now on fire.

"*That's kind of normal for you, though, ain't it?*" Chief snarked. "*Still, it made one hell of a boom. I didn't expect that. It must have been a mixture of the power sources between the mech and the core.*"

He ran to check on Raza. "And you didn't factor that in?"

"*I didn't know what the power source to the mech was,*" the EI explained. "*I haven't seen one like it either. Also, it's not in my data and I have to work with what I have.*"

"Fine, fair enough." The ace knelt and checked the War Chief. "Are you doing all right, Raza?"

"I'm fine." He grunted and pushed himself up. His armguard was gone and his flesh had been gouged sufficiently that blood poured from the wound. "You know how difficult it is to kill a Sauren."

"Thankfully, but that looks like it could have done it," Kaiden replied and helped him up.

"War Chief!" A voice shouted from a communicator on Raza's belt. He took it off and activated it, and the screen displayed Ken'ra on the other end. "I'm glad to finally reach you. From this destruction, I feel secure in assuming you were successful?"

"We were indeed," Raza confirmed. "This ship will fly no longer."

"Unfortunately, we are on the ship," the ace reminded them.

His companion narrowed his eyes at him but exhaled a long breath. "There is that, yes. I shall send the order out to fall back, get going, and meet me on the ship."

"Of course, War Chief." Ken'ra saluted. "If you can give me a destination, I can have a chariot waiting."

Raza looked at the blazing trail that used to be the path to and from the core. "We are unsure of where that will be. Do not wait. We will find a way."

"Understood, War Chief." The Sauren placed a claw against his chest. "A successful hunt. We shall celebrate together."

"Indeed we shall." Raza shut his comm off and folded his arms. Already, a couple of scales had begun to grow back. "And not even a trophy to claim. What a waste."

"You do realize a trophy wouldn't mean much if we die, right?" Kaiden asked as he put Sire away. "Or can the Sauren survive a command ship crashing and exploding and I'm merely a frail human?"

"We could not survive such an impact," his companion stated. "You are a frail human, but that matters little right now."

"I'm beginning to wonder if this is tough love or simply tough." He sighed. "Chief, do you have anything?"

The EI appeared in front of them and displayed the map. *I don't see a way out of here with the bridge gone. Not conventional paths, at least.*

"But there are other routes?" Raza asked as he studied the map.

"Yeah, above and below," Chief explained and highlighted two markers. *"Head up and you can go through the pocket we came from, punch your way into the upper floor, and find a hatch or jump out the windows. As for down, this goes all the way to the bottom of the ship. Once there, you can punch your way through and you are golden."*

"Can we simply punch through? I don't have any explosives left," Kaiden asked.

"Buddy, this place is falling apart. The falling debris, compromised structure, and big explosions have done most of the work. A few charged shots and some Sauren muscle will get it done."

"All right, but I don't think I have the power in my jets to carry Raza. Or the strength, for that matter. Are my mods compromised?"

"Yeah, about that...your jets are partially compromised," the EI revealed. *"I can probably get you one good boost or slow your fall a couple of times at best."*

He felt behind him and grimaced at the heat that came off his jets and the melted parts. "Damn. Why bother talking about going up if that isn't a possibility?"

"Because it is. The War Chief would simply have to carry you."

The two looked at one another and the ace glanced again at the Sauren's wounded arm. It still healed far faster than a human's would but remained a problem. "So down?" he asked and pointed below.

Raza huffed in irritation and nodded as a large piece of metal landed behind them. Taking the hint, they both ran, leapt over the railing, and plunged down the deep cavern. "Chief, I'm gonna need you to pull double-duty right quick," he stated and twisted so his jet faced down. "Make sure I don't go splat and call Genos and Haldt."

"Hey, I'm getting a link from Kaiden," Haldt announced to Genos.

"As am I. Activating and going to group link." The Tsuna pressed a couple of buttons. "Are you there, friend Kaiden?"

"Yep, need a favor from both of you," he stated. "I'm with the Sauren War Chief and we have to take a rather indirect route out of here through the bottom of the ship. I assume the vessel is fairly high?"

Haldt studied the craft. "I'm having a look…it's over the ocean but there's a hell of a lot of rocks although it is high up. I'm sure if you wait a few more minutes you'll get closer to earth very rapidly."

"I'd rather not, thanks. I need you to come and catch us if you have the time," he requested.

"I'm on the way," Genos answered and altered course to the underside of the command ship.

"I'll swing through as well. Ping us before you bail." Haldt followed the Tsuna and they wove through the last remnants of the battle toward the command ship, which was now mostly broken and ablaze.

* * *

"Activating jets," Chief stated and caught Kaiden seconds before he landed. He stabilized himself and confirmed that Raza had made it to the wall after the jump and now slid down using his claws to slow himself before he vaulted off.

The ace nodded at his companion. "Nice. Now, where's a good place to break through, Chief?"

"Let's see…judging by current damage, the thickness of the

ship's plate, and power of weapons at your disposal, I'd say that big hole over there that's already been created."

He focused on the area highlighted and acknowledged that there was indeed an already broken section, probably the result of falling debris. "Well, that makes this easy. Ping them, Chief."

The two raced toward the gaping aperture and dodged a few pieces of metal and railing that plummeted from above. As they reached their exit and Kaiden flung himself through, he hoped his teammates wouldn't be late.

CHAPTER NINETEEN

"I have a ping!" Haldt shouted and his eyes widened when he saw the location. "Shit, other side—other side!" He and Genos banked sharply and accelerated toward Kaiden and Raza, who had now fallen through and plunged earthward. "I'll get the Sauren. You go to Kaiden."

"Understood. Going now." The Tsuna cut the comm and increased his speed while the security officer descended sharply to position himself under Raza. He slowed a little and hoped his timing was right. The answer came in the form of a heavy weight that pounded into the ship and almost made him lose control. Metal rent beneath the Sauren's massive claws and he focused on the large red head that stared at him through the left side of his cockpit and nodded to him in thanks. It had been a while since he had seen one and they were still as frightening up close as ever. All he could think of was that it was good to have a thankful one as his passenger.

Genos caught up to Kaiden quickly, positioned himself well below him, and noted his broken armor. "Kaiden, you need to decelerate. If I were to catch you now, it would still cause considerable injury to you."

"Yeah, Chief says the same. Get below and hover. I only have one last attempt at this." The ace tucked his legs and bent back. The ship had descended a fair distance, but his momentum made him come up fast. "Whatever is left, Chief, blast it!"

His jets flared to life, only for a brief spurt but enough to jerk him back a little and rapidly decrease his falling speed. He rocked forward, relaxed as much as he could, and landed on the wing of the fighter with a loud thud. His reflexive roll thunked his helmet against the cockpit window. God, he would feel that later, but he was alive. When he looked up, Genos waved at him. He returned the gesture wearily and a hasty glance confirmed that they were still fairly high with a beach in the distance below.

Genos opened his cockpit. "I should have assumed you had something to do with that destruction," he quipped.

"Yeah. Raza did his part too." Kaiden grunted and eased to a more secure position. "I'm glad to see you still flying. Did you enjoy yourself?"

The Tsuna nodded eagerly. "Oh, yes, indeed. I took part in some destruction myself."

"That's the spirit." He held onto the edge of the wing. "I need to check in with the others. Head to the beach, would you?"

"Certainly, it'll only be a moment." Genos leaned back in his seat and closed the cockpit hatch as Kaiden tried hurriedly to tell him that slow was okay.

"A bomb?" Hartman asked. "Do you think this is some kind of doomsday device?"

"It could be any number of things," Laurie stated and crossed his legs as he moved through the pictures on the holoscreen. "Chiyo thought it was an engine of some kind and that's certainly possible. But the containment situation with the couplings and the way it is handled makes me feel more like it wants to simply keep it in place rather than maintain it. If so, it means this was a prototype in the early stages, or it was being built as a weapon."

"Could it be for a cannon or mech of some kind?" the general inquired and studied the device more closely. He knew he didn't have the technical knowledge of the professor, which made it a pointless exercise. Maybe it was simply a hope that they didn't have a new problem now that they were so close to launching their offensive.

"That is certainly possible. As I've said, a number of things could explain it. But the reason I feel more assured in saying it is a bomb is the fact that they haven't worked on this for too long. If it were something more advanced and they still had plans to use it, they would be deeper into development by now," Laurie clarified, closed the holoscreen, and opened a hologram of the device. "This is a demonstration I constructed quickly to show how I believe it would work."

The silver arches around it began to spin and the plates keeping the energy in place compressed to force it into a tight ball before they fell away. The arches whirled faster and something within the light began to swirl. Hartman leaned forward and stared as the arches fell away in a few seconds and the sphere shrunk before it erupted in a massive white dome.

He dragged in a deep breath. "What would the destruction be like?"

"Massive. Anything caught would be eradicated," the professor stated grimly. "Something I noted was similar to the destruction of the colossus." He brought the holoscreen up to show a map of the area. "When the vessel erupted, everything was leveled and vaporized for miles. Even now sometime later, while there are signs life could possibly take root again, nothing has. Although we can't say for sure, of course, as this is the last real enemy stronghold here on Earth, and I don't think requesting a mission to plant flowers is top of the list for potential suicide missions."

The general frowned as he considered the information. "Merrick might have seen the destruction and decided building a few of these would be better and more practical than another colossus. Or they were for the colossus in case it needed to exchange one for another." He rubbed his brow. "Do we have any other confirmed sightings of these devices?"

"Not as yet, no, but I sent a request for teams that are currently on raid missions to look for more."

"I'll make it an urgent notice. Merrick's delusions have pushed him thus far. To have some kind of failsafe or trump card as a final way to beat us into submission wouldn't be beyond him."

"Agreed. I'll continue my work but keep you informed if I can deduce anything else for this device." The professor looked at the white dome and drew a sharp breath. "This is one of the few times in my life I hope my hypothesis is wrong."

Kaiden removed his helmet and approached Genos. "Jaxon and Silas are good. They're heading back on a shuttle."

"Should we join them so we can accompany them?" the Tsuna asked as he hopped off the wing of the ship and walked to meet his friend.

"Let me limber up a little and yeah, I'm not gonna head out on a shuttle. I'm sure they will want to escort the Sauren to the base and I should probably be around for that."

"I see. I should as well." Genos tensed a little and tilted his head to look at the ace. "I assume with all the fighting and chaos, you didn't have a chance to tell Raza about Wolfson?"

He closed his eyes and shook his head. "No, that will be the first thing I tell him when I see him again. He should hear it from me." A gust of wind above caught his attention and he frowned when something thumped into the sand. Raza stood behind him and Haldt's ship hovered above him before it moved to the left and landed.

"Raza?" Kaiden asked.

"The pilot wanted to bring me back to my vessel," the War Chief stated and regarded the two friends curiously. "I wished to make sure you survived."

"Oh, I see. Thank you." He looked at the Tsuna, who nodded to him. Haldt cut the engine of his ship, opened his cockpit, and looked like he was about to say something, but

Genos held his hand up to stop him. "Hey, Raza," the ace continued, "when we met earlier, you asked about Wolfson."

The Sauren snorted and nodded. "I did. I suppose the battle is over and we can speak. But I do not need to know what mission he is on. I can talk to him another time."

"No, you can't, Raza," he stated quietly, and a brief trace of confusion flickered in Raza's eyes before they widened in understanding. "We lost the Academy at the beginning of all this and initiated a large assault to take it back, during which—" His voice broke for a moment but he pressed on. "During which Wolfson sacrificed himself to save the rest of us from calamity. They planned to blow up a massive ship to try to destroy us when we were winning." He tried to offer a smile. "He jumped the ship with him inside, said that was what had to happen…and obliterated an entire enemy base with him."

The War Chief was silent, his eyes closed and his expression revealing nothing. Finally, he took a deep breath in through his nostrils and nodded. "I see. He went out a true warrior with honor, strength, and ferocity. It is fitting." He opened his eyes, walked closer to Kaiden, and placed an arm on his shoulder. "He saw you as a soldier, as I see you as a hunter. I'm sure he sacrificed himself because he is courageous and knew there was another who could match him in that regard."

The ace nodded and pulled his helmet on. "He always considered you a close friend and a great warrior. I think you might be one of the only leaders he truly respected."

Raza nodded and lowered his arm. "He will be missed." He looked at the Sauren ship. "I will have one of my warriors come for me. There is no need to cause more destruction to any of your ships."

He was about to say it was fine and they could help, but he saw something in the Sauren he hadn't seen before— mourning, he realized, which meant he was asking for something different than what they could offer. In silence, he simply nodded and walked to Genos' ship to climb on the wing as the pilot slid into his seat. Haldt turned his ship as well and they took flight.

Raza reached for his comm and requested a chariot. He barely let the Sauren on the other end finish saying, "Yes, War Chief," before he cut the connection. His expression focused on the sand, he took a few steps, looked at the wreckage of the command ship for a moment, and raised his head to utter a thunderous, pained roar into the sky.

CHAPTER TWENTY

Merrick looked down on Earth from the window of his office—the space he had hoped, to no avail, would be his headquarters by this point. He made a note of the lights and the cities they sprang from. Even in this dark hour, life continued. He ran his fingers along his face and pinched his nose in frustration.

One of the louts would be by soon to tell him what he already knew—the assault had failed. While he hadn't been optimistic enough to believe it would have been successful in destroying one of the military strongholds, he had hoped it would cause enough damage to the base to delay their eventual offensive. Perhaps it would have even subdued them a little and shaken off some of their ignorant hope that their attack could work.

He had to admit to himself that it could, especially now, and he should have had a failsafe ready long before. It wasn't much of a failsafe to have to destroy anywhere from a fifth to a fourth of the planet he attempted to save. Would they push him to do it? They should take hold of his vision and make him the progenitor of the warriors they now held in such high esteem, yet they cast their gift aside. He knew they were certainly capable of denial and fear and for once, he hoped they would give into them again.

The doors to his office finally opened. "Sir!" Merrick turned as one of the Omega leaders ran in. Skilz was one of a handful who had been promoted into his private organization after the passing of his predecessor—the most agreeable one, in his opinion, if a little stupid.

The AO leader wandered to his desk, spun the chair, and sat. "You here to tell me about the outcome of the attack, correct?" he asked and regarded him with an indifferent gaze.

The man slouched slightly. "Yeah, but my guess is you're already aware."

He nodded and leaned forward. "A good guess. I can see you have a rather deductive mind, Skilz. A pity you weren't down there yourself."

"Then you know the dragons showed up as well?" the man asked, approached the desk, and rested his hands on it.

Merrick nodded and his gaze traveled downward to settle on his hands as they began to tap on the surface of the desk. "I am, although to be fair, the Sauren are closer to how we picture dinosaurs. I have to give them some credit, however. They are a tenacious race to jump such a distance over months. I didn't think they had the technology to do such a thing without at least a partial warp gate run. It makes me wonder if the Tsuna and Mirus will join sometime soon. We could always do with more to take part in the fun at this point."

Skilz bared his teeth. "Are you mad? There are at least a few hundred of those scaled bastards now, not to mention the ship they rode in on. I doubt it's an unarmed peace-keeping vessel."

"It wouldn't be their type," he agreed and looked at the man. "I suggest you continue to prepare for war as you have been."

The Omega straightened and folded his arms. "We've brought up as many of our boys as we have left. Most of your facilities are now only guarded by droids and we even brought up all the terrorists and any grimy gangbanger who would be willing to shoot a gun for us for a few cred-its. But if they make a push now, we no longer have the advantages we used to. The WCM is reorganized, they have bots again, and our tech can't control them. When they attack, do you think we have the numbers to defeat them?"

"You are the Omega Horde, correct?" Merrick asked, his head tilted. "Final yet endless—I believe that was your motto at one point."

"Yeah, when we're out there." Skilz pointed behind him to indicate deep space. "We basically controlled everything beyond the fifteenth sector and no one could push us out. Who would bring a force so deep? But you brought us here"—he planted his index finger on the desk—"where everyone is. You promised a victory by now."

"I promised you my riches—or rather, your superiors my riches," the AO leader muttered, scowled at the offen-sive finger, and finally focused on his accuser's face. "Although I understand that those I originally spoke to have all died by this point. One during the invasion, two in a battle over London, and four of them during the reclamations of the Ark Academies."

"Another force we've lost," the man retorted. "And yeah, the big bosses are gone. How we work is the next in line gets the title, which means everyone you've chosen to take over as your 'council.'" The man leaned in so their eyes were only a couple of inches apart. "Without us, how many troops do you have? Do you think your shiny little metalheads will keep you safe? What if we all decide that now is the time to leave you to deal with the mess you've made, huh?"

Merrick stared at him as if in thought. When he stood, he walked around the desk and proffered his hand. The Omega leader looked at him in confusion, his anger still evident. He tried to knock the hand away, but the man blocked with his other hand and thrust the one he'd held out deep into the leader's armor. It crushed the plating and dug in, much to Skilz's shock.

The AO leader tightened his grasp and flung him into the window. He made impact with violent force but fortunately, the embassy windows were more than simple glass. Otherwise, both men would have been sucked into the void. When he tried to stand, Merrick drove his boot into the back of his armor and forced him to look out at the fleet of ships standing guard as he produced a switch. His captor knelt and showed the device to him before he pointed at the fleet. "I made sure all the repairs, upgrades, and retrofits came with a specific addition," he said coldly as he leaned forward and gestured expansively with the hand holding the device. "Choose."

"Choose? Choose what?" Skilz demanded. He tried to

force himself away from the window but Merrick didn't budge. It was bizarre how strong he was, especially since he wore no armor.

"Choose one of the ships," the man stated and studied the fleet almost clinically. "Or I'll choose far more than one."

Despite his fears, the Omega looked out and pointed at a small corsair in the distance. "That one. Is that what you want?"

"It'll do," Merrick muttered, and his eyes glimmered for a moment as he selected the ship with his oculars. He held the switch up, flipped the cover, and pressed the button. Skilz gaped as the ship disassembled and fell apart. Bodies spilled out and vessels around it quickly went to its aid to save who they could while the merc watched helplessly.

The AO leader finally pushed away from him, closed the top of the switch, and slid it into his coat. "I'll admit that not every ship has my personal additions at this point," he stated and took his seat again. "But would you like to guess how many do?"

"You bastard!" Skilz roared, drew his pistol, and aimed it at Merrick. "Why the hell did we ever—"

"Should I die without deactivating this trigger, all the ships with bombs will end up exactly like that one," the man revealed implacably as he folded his arms and leaned back in his seat. "Although I can tell you it will take much more than that to kill me, so either way, think hard."

Skilz's hold tightened and his hand trembled slightly where he sprawled beside the window, but he did not fire. Instead, he yelled his rage and barely resisted pounding the weapon on the ground. "Dammit!"

"It seems to me that our fates are rather intertwined," Merrick continued and looked coldly at the Omega leader. "Should my era end, so shall the Omega Horde's."

"Goddammit!" the merc cursed again and his gun wavered slightly, although he didn't lower it.

"There is no need to be blasphemous." The AO leader looked away. "Although I suppose if He were merciful, this wouldn't have come to pass to begin with."

"Fighting a madman's war—we should have mutinied." Skilz groaned, the sound low but emotionally charged.

Merrick spun, tired of dealing with the fool. "As I said when we began, prepare for war, Skilz. You certainly have the motivation now."

"Will you still honor your other agreement?" he asked and caught the man's attention once again. The merc looked fixedly at him, his eyes still full of hate. "You said you also wanted us as your army. If you win this, that's still ours, right?"

"Yes. Of course I need an army. That would be the reason I started this to begin with. Believe it or not, I want a united force and the Horde will be a part of that."

"Then why would you blow your own forces up?" he demanded. Merrick shrugged as he lost interest again.

"I suppose even I can succumb to hopelessness," he stated coldly and turned away. "You have your orders. I'm sure our enemy will come soon. Since you were not able to secure the other stations, make sure Icarus and Xuanzang are both well-defended. They will make their push and probably target Icarus first—or maybe both simultaneously. Whatever happens, I believe you can deal with it."

Skilz forced himself off the floor and holstered his weapon. "We have to deal with it."

"Whatever motivates you, I encourage it," the man said as he passed him. "Make sure to come up with a good excuse for what just happened. We don't want your people to get too spooked now, do we?"

The merc turned briefly to him with a scathing look but left without a word. As soon as he stepped out, he checked his tablet for reports about the ship. He ordered them to save who they could and recover any parts of the vessel they could as well. Perhaps, if he were lucky, they could salvage it and examine it to see how he'd rigged them to blow.

He realized it was pointless almost as soon as he finished the thought. Even if they did find out how his detonator worked, he doubted they could deactivate them without him knowing and that would merely be another thing to set him off. Planting bombs to destroy his army was one way to keep them under his thumb. Merrick might be insane but he wasn't an idiot. Although that might be debatable, of course.

The AO leader watched the doors close, drew in a deep breath, and checked his hands. He'd sustained tiny cuts from where his fingers had dug in but they were repairing quickly and were almost normal once more. He spun to look out the window again at the planet below. This time, he saw no lights, no cities, and no ships, only darkness that obscured the world below.

One that used to be so full of life.

Kaiden hopped off the fighter and rolled his shoulders as Genos killed the engine and climbed out of the cockpit.

"It's not my favorite way to fly," the ace admitted as he removed his helmet, "but there are worse options. Thanks, Genos."

"My pleasure, friend Kaiden," the Tsuna stated and took his helmet off as well. "I suppose we should find a shuttle?"

"We can take Haldt's," he suggested and looked at his companion as a thought occurred to him. "Did he wreck it after I left?"

"It's fine," Haldt shouted and they turned as he approached quickly. "Thanks for the vote of confidence."

"Hey, man, it's a battle. Things get hectic."

"Hardly a real battle," the security officer replied and shrugged. "I'm not saying it was a cakewalk but given some of the fights we've had thus far, this didn't seem like some grand play on the Omega's part."

"I merely assumed we had become much better at dealing with them," Genos interjected.

"That's a part of it, sure," Haldt agreed. "But they attacked one of our main bases with a force designed for a quick strike. Even if they don't have good intel, they had to know there wasn't a chance in hell they would break through with something so paltry."

"They also didn't expect the Sauren to join the party," Kaiden pointed out.

"That too, but even if they didn't, this wouldn't have ended well for them," the man insisted.

"So you think this was simply to divert our attention or something?" the ace asked.

Haldt shrugged and placed his hands on his hips. "I

think it was meant to cause damage, but it wouldn't ever destroy the base or take it over."

"Do they have the forces to try to screw with us?" he questioned and Genos tapped his infuser in thought.

"They could be trying to stall us—or they could be trying to distract us like you said," the security officer stated. "Either way, they know we're coming."

"I think they've known that for a while now." Kaiden frowned. "Probably from when we refused to get on our knees and kiss their feet and all. I don't know any terrorist who is optimistic enough to wait it out."

Haldt chuckled. "Sure, but there could be something more. I guess we'll have to talk it over with Sasha and Laurie. They might have found something by now."

"Agreed. Should we depart?" Genos asked.

The security officer nodded and began to walk across the hangar to the shuttle. "Yeah, let's go before they ask why I have claw marks on my fighter."

CHAPTER TWENTY-ONE

"The Sauren have arrived?" Sasha asked and glanced at Hartman. "Well, that explains the massive warp reading we saw. How did they get here?"

"Raza can fill you in," Kaiden replied. "They're heading back to base with us—or I guess I should officially say we are escorting them to base. Their ship doesn't exactly need protection, though."

The general moved his hand to the screen on his desk and brought up the feed from outside the base. His eyes widened as he focused on the approaching vessel.

"I can see that," the chancellor stated dryly. "When they land, I would appreciate it if you could bring the Sauren War Chief to me."

Kaiden nodded. "No problem. I'll bring him to you soon."

When he moved his hand to turn the screen off, Sasha stopped him. "One moment, Kaiden."

"What's wrong?" the ace asked and the chancellor drew a deep breath.

"Does he know?" he asked. The ace closed his eyes and nodded briefly. "I see. All right. I'll be waiting."

"Understood. Signing out." The feed disconnected and Sasha turned to Hartman. "I'll get Laurie and bring the War Chief. If you could let the other generals know about the new developments, I would appreciate it."

"I'm already on it," the general said and opened messages on his screen. "It would appear we will have to move our plans up. The men and women are ready and I doubt the Sauren will want much of a break."

"Do you think this will finally get the other leaders on board?" he asked.

Hartman chuckled. "If they still have objections, I'll tell them they'll have to tell the Sauren themselves."

Raza had retired to his den since his return. He knew he didn't have much time to himself as they would arrive at the human base soon, where they and he would have questions. Now, however, he took the time to think of Wolfson and their meeting. Their fight had continued for days and he recalled the exchanges, the insults traded, and the blood shed—blood that would create a bond. He had developed a fondness for the soldier and when the Sauren were made allies, Wolfson was there to greet him and had even learned his name.

It was then that he acknowledged the name Raza—one he had disliked at first but grew to accept, mostly because it was used by one he respected. The man had never been one to acknowledge tradition or even complications like his full name. Now, when he heard others call him by that, he recognized how it had spread thanks to Wolfson. He knew he could never banish it and oddly enough, it was something of a gift now, bestowed by his friend.

A knock on his door disturbed his reverie. "Open."

Ken'ra walked in dressed in full gear and bowed. "War Chief, we are approaching the base and crowds are gathering."

His gaze drifted to look out the window. While he'd known that the trip wouldn't be long, it felt so much faster than expected. "How long until arrival?"

"We are inside the perimeter and will land shortly," his aide stated. "Should I have the other hunters wait onboard?"

He shook his head firmly. "No need."

Ken'ra studied him curiously. "War Chief?"

Raza returned his gaze with a gleam of anticipation. "We will fight alongside those we meet on the ground. If there is any issue between us, we should deal with it now instead of later."

His companion saluted and nodded. "It'll be done, War Chief." As he turned to leave, he paused and looked at him again. "We were contacted by the soldier. He says he will escort us to the leaders."

"Is that so?" the Sauren leader mused and chuckled. "I see. It's quite fitting. I suppose he is taking Wolfson's mantle up after all."

———

"Damn, who ordered the flying fortress?" Luke asked. He

and the others gaped at the massive vessel of the Sauren as it entered the base.

"Cameron is gonna be pissed he missed this," Izzy noted.

"It's his fault for staying asleep." Flynn laughed.

"I wasn't asleep for two months." Cameron groaned and the group turned to where he stood and ran his hand through his short hair. He was dressed only in lounge pants and shoes. "You kept blowing my messages up and my EI woke me, and what's so damn excit—Jesus!" The bounty hunter went slack-jawed when he saw the ship.

"We have new friends." Luke laughed and slapped him on the back. "You might have the right idea. We should rest while we have the chance."

"Do you think Raza is on there?" Marlo asked.

"I would say it is a safe bet." Chiyo looked through her messages. "Kaiden says he will escort him to Sasha."

"Then let's help him," Flynn suggested and jogged ahead. "He was nice enough to fight a battle for us."

"This seems unnecessary," Raza muttered as Kaiden met him once he'd disembarked. Many of the other Sauren exited from different points of the ship and met the soldiers, technicians, medics, and other crew of the base. For many, this was their first time to see a Sauren in person, especially in such numbers.

The ace shrugged and looked at the visitor's guards. "Hey, Lok," he called and drew the Sauren chief's attention. "If we came to your world in a massive military vessel and wanted to meet Raza, what would the protocol be?"

"We'd keep our eye on you," he responded.

"We would take you to our leader as allies," Ken'ra corrected.

Kaiden nodded. "Same here. This isn't for safety or anything. Sasha simply wants to get to you quickly."

"You would think he would meet me personally, then," Raza countered, and Kaiden had to agree.

"I see we think alike, Ran'ama." They all turned as Sasha stepped out of the crowd. Despite his calm demeanor, he seemed to be breathing a little heavier than normal.

"You must have run to be here so quickly," the ace noted with a grin. "I don't think I've seen you move faster than a brisk walk outside of combat."

The chancellor straightened his shades. "Given the circumstances, I believe I should make sure this is my top priority."

"I would say that is correct."

Raza walked forward and studied the man before he placed his claws together and bowed. "It is good to see you are still with us, Commander."

Sasha bowed in return. "And it is good to see that you could join us, War Chief." He looked at their ship. "I'm amazed you were able to construct a ship that could remain intact through so many jumps in space."

The Sauren nodded and glanced at the vessel behind him. "This is a prototype we have created in conjunction with the Tsuna. When the gates went down, most returned to Abisalo before it was finished. We completed it ourselves and made our trip here its first mission."

"It was untested?" the commander asked. "I thank you for taking the risk."

"We received no answers on what had happened," Raza explained and focused on him again. "So, we decided we had to find them ourselves. I believe I have a general understanding of what has been going on, but I am willing to hear the rest."

"Of course. You deserve that much," Sasha said with a nod. "And you can hear our plans going forward. I'm sure you would like to join us in righting this."

"It is the best use of our skills." Raza agreed. He, Lok, and Ken'ra began to follow when voices called to the War Chief. They paused as Kaiden's friends forced a path through the crowd.

"Ah, Wolfson's other trainees," the Sauren leader stated and followed it with a low growl, but not of anger. The ace walked out and held his arms up in front of his friends to stop them in their tracks.

"Hey, guys," he began and lowered his arms. "Raza and Sasha gotta talk. You can catch up later."

Some of them looked like they planned to protest, but a massive claw on his shoulder made him glance at Raza, who nodded to him. "Hello again, young hunters," he said calmly. "It is good to see you are all well. That is a relief. But as Kaiden has stated, I have other priorities right now that I must attend to. We can exchange greetings later, I vow to you."

Any words of disagreement died in their throats and they simply nodded and waved him off. He withdrew his claw and joined Sasha to walk briskly into the main building.

Kaiden looked at Cameron and narrowed his eyes as he studied his friend. "I see you got comfortable while I was defending the base."

The bounty hunter threw his hands up. "You beat them?"

"Yeah, of course," he responded.

The other man folded his arms. "Then I guess I was smart to trust my life to you."

The ace smirked and shook his head. "Finally, it gets through." He grimaced and unlatched a lock around his left shoulder pad. "I gotta get to the armory to make sure my armor is ready for the big push."

"Is it finally time?" Flynn asked. "We've been waiting for more than a month. Are you sure?"

"Sasha may not show it but he's as anxious as we are to move against Merrick," he stated, undid the final lock, and removed the pad. "And he's moving with more purpose than someone who only wants to talk about maybes. Which means I need to get to the armory and make some calls."

"The Arbiter Organization?" Raza asked as he studied the files on the screen. He glanced at General Hartman. "I do not recall ever being told about such a threat."

"That would be because up until the invasion, they were considered a myth," the general explained. "To be honest, they technically still are. From what we have found out, this organization has only been in existence for a couple of decades, not the few hundred years they have supposedly existed."

"So it would be akin to us warning you of the Ava'don tribe," Lok ventured.

"I believe there are differences," Ken'ra interjected. "But that could be comparable."

"Well, we're all ears," Hartman replied. "After all, if we had maybe taken the commander's warnings more seriously, we could have prevented this mess."

"The Ava'don are a disgraced tribe that has continued to hunt, even after death," Raza stated and looked at Lok. "It's a story for children to make sure they take their hunts seriously. As you have shown, this myth of yours is a threat in reality."

"True enough," Sasha agreed. "But one we hope to deal with quite soon."

"Indeed." Hartman nodded, cleared the screen, and brought up a display of a hologram of the embassy, two stations, and a fleet of ships. "We're preparing an attack. Although other leaders want more time to build forces and make sure the planet is left defended, we've noticed that the longer we take, the more the primary target is secured as they bring reinforcements from their non-important bases to help with the defense of the embassy."

"So they have taken the embassy," Raza muttered.

"I do not think we had any delegates out at the time of the gates shutting down, War Chief," Ken'ra told him.

"Perhaps if we had, this problem would have been dealt with by this point." Lok growled with open displeasure.

Sasha zoomed in on the embassy. "From what we know,

there are at least three thousand hostiles on board and they have control of the defenses."

Lok snorted. "Humph. Well, there would be less."

"Quiet, Chief Lok," Raza ordered and silenced the hunter. "When do you plan to attack?"

"Within days," Hartman confirmed. "We are prepared to go at a moment's notice in case of a premature strike. But there has been a new development here on Earth that we wish to confirm before sending the majority of our forces out to attack."

The Sauren widened his eyes. "And what is this development? Can we deal with it quickly so we can begin the assault?"

The general was somewhat taken aback by the question. "Well...uh, I am thankful for the offer of assistance, but the issue is that we still have to confirm that it exists and how much of a threat it is."

"Then I have good news and bad news," Laurie stated as the door shut behind him. "Hello, Raza."

"Professor. I take it you can tell me of this development the general was informing us about?"

"Always with the vague words, you military types," the professor quipped as he approached the desk. He stopped and shook his head. "I can indeed, Raza. It is a bomb." He focused on Hartman. "That is mostly confirmed at this point. We know where it is and yes, there is only one more, which is the good news."

"And what is the bad, Laurie?" Sasha asked.

The professor changed the holographic display to reveal the device he had previously shown Hartman. "This was the original device Chiyo found—particularly nasty on its own." He placed his fingers at the edges of the image and stretched it. "We were able to discover another when we focused on locking down the energy signature, which is rather unique as you would expect. Like I said, we only found the one and it's located in their stronghold in Russia."

"The Arbiter's?" Hartman asked. "That would be their Ark Academy."

"That would be correct. I see how you got a command," Laurie joked before he caught himself. "Sorry, I become a little sarcastic when I try to mask my concern with humor."

The general and Sasha looked at one another and the latter placed a hand on the professor's shoulder. "Concern? What's wrong, Laurie?"

The man collected himself and looked around the room with a slightly haunted expression. "We found the device—I might as well call it a bomb because using it as a power source would be difficult and overkill at this point if that was their intention. This one appears to be more than five times larger than the one Chiyo found, which meant the first was a prototype or merely a smaller model for a different plan. This one could eradicate the entirety of Russia as well as parts of China for good measure. Assuming they don't move it somewhere else, of course. And I would guess that since they have no plans to blow themselves up, that's the plan, which is the bad news."

The room fell silent and he stared fixedly at the image before him. "The even worse news is that it is almost complete."

CHAPTER TWENTY-TWO

"How long do you think they are gonna be in there?" Indre asked, her expression impatient as she looked at the group.

"Eh, you know how long those official meetings take," Luke muttered and waved his hand dismissively. "They gotta go over charts and readouts and all that junk. Plus, I'm sure the debriefing between Raza and the military is gonna take a while."

"Where the hell are Silas and Jaxon?" Kaiden demanded, his arms folded. "I had to go to the armory and fill out all those forms and they still aren't back."

"Kin Jaxon has started something of a ritual when returning from combat," Genos explained. "He replaces his infuser, cleanses his body, and applies cooling gel as it helps with our injury recovery."

"It sounds kinda standard for guys who went through… you know, getting shot at," Cameron replied.

"Where's your infuser, then?" Izzy teased and he frowned at her.

"All personnel, please report to hangar one," Sasha bellowed over the intercom. "This is urgent. Unless you are working on a priority job, drop everything and make your way to hangar one."

"I guess that didn't go on as long as you expected," Indre remarked and patted Luke on the shoulder as she walked past. The rest shared curious glances as they all left the barracks and hurried to the hangar.

"Go ahead with the briefing, Commander," Hartman stated as he sat at his desk. "I'll handle the other leaders, although I doubt they will have many complaints once they understand the severity of the situation."

"And yet the severity of the situation until now hasn't stopped them from finding complaints." Laurie sighed. "On the off chance that they do, tell them the one upside is that with a quarter of the Earth gone, they will have fewer things to worry about."

The general glared at him but sighed and nodded. "Like I said, I doubt it will be an issue. We've had to move plans up many times before, although usually not on this scale. Even if they won't cooperate or aren't ready, we will go."

"Of course we will. We have to." Sasha saluted the general and turned as he beckoned the professor. "Come on, Laurie."

"Do you need emotional support?" his companion asked as the two left the office and proceeded to the hangar.

"You will have to explain the situation with the bomb,"

he stated. "I think it will have more impact coming from you."

The professor chuckled darkly. "Oh, really? Do you think I'm that good a public speaker?"

"On some occasions," he responded as they proceeded down the stairs. "But I think our technicians will immediately offer to try to trace and hack the device to stop it remotely. In dire situations, even the best-trained individuals can be prone to the obvious pitfalls. With you speaking, I think they will understand the severity of the situation."

"Because they will know I already tried," the man finished glumly.

"You have, haven't you?" Sasha asked with a quick look over his shoulder.

Laurie frowned. "Of course, Sasha. Isn't that…oh." He hesitated and gave himself time to think it over. "It is rather dire, isn't it?"

"It puts things in perspective," the commander reasoned. "I had begun to think we were getting too comfortable in all of this."

The two reached the bottom, where Raza stood waiting. "Raza?" The professor looked at him in surprise. "I thought you went to address your people."

"Lok and Ken'ra can handle that," he stated and stepped beside them. "I should be there to represent the Sauren as we will go into battle together."

Laurie scratched the back of his head. "I appreciate the thought but I don't think it is—"

"Understood. Come with us," Sasha interrupted and gestured with his hand as he continued toward the hangar.

Laurie trotted beside him. "Is this necessary, Sasha?" he asked. "I'm sure the Sauren need to prepare as much as we do."

"I agree," the other man replied but didn't slow his gait. "And Raza has taken measures to begin that. This may only be a formality but we don't have time to debate. The fact is, we have little time to prepare as it is."

"Man, seeing everyone together like this…" Cameron muttered and stared at the thousands who filed into the massive hangar from their position on the catwalks above. "I guess the base has always been busy but I never realized how big the force was."

"This is one of the bigger bases we have," Chiyo told him. "It's in the top five, at least. That's why we are usually called on to handle assaults and are sent out on so many missions. We have people to spare."

"Do you think this is finally the go order?" Flynn asked and looked at Kaiden, who scanned the room intently. "Kaiden?"

"Hmm? Sorry, I'm looking for Silas and Jaxon. I thought I saw them but it was another guy with dreads next to a Tsuna."

"You can't be worried about them making it back. Their shuttle checked in with everyone aboard," Izzy reminded him. "They are fine and as Genos explained, he has his rituals or whatever. Now, back to Flynn's question."

"About what?" he asked.

"He's asking if you think this is the announcement of our attack, dumbass," Chief snarked.

"Oh. Okay, the odds are good," he reasoned. "Those codes you guys were sent to get are only good for a little while so we gotta make use of them before they are reset."

"That would be good news." Marlo turned to the ace. "The problem is they have had codes in the past and let them go to waste. Usually, the excuse is they are still building the force up and can't risk it."

"We do only have one chance at this," Chiyo reminded them. "If we lose here, it will take a long time to build up another fleet for a second attempt. That means enough time for Merrick to devise something new to worry about." She looked down and muttered under her breath, "If he hasn't already."

"What was that, friend Chiyo?" Genos asked, but before she could reply, Kaiden gestured ahead.

"There he is." He leaned forward and noticed two other figures. "With friends too. I don't see the general."

"He must be taking care of business." Raul narrowed his eyes as several large holoscreens opened throughout the room and displayed Sasha's face.

"A good evening to you all," he began and took a moment to scan the crowd. "I have come to announce our current situation. I know many of you are ready to take the fight to our enemies in full force, rather than in the small skirmishes that have been our main priority up until now."

Although no one called out or hollered, the movement of the bodies below showed a general agreement and unease amongst the people gathered. "I know the feeling, and despite knowing you are willing to go into battle, it is always with a heavy heart that one such as myself must announce that it is time. That is why I am here."

"Called it," Flynn whispered.

"We will be attacking in two days, starting at 0600 hours," he announced calmly. The statement caught some off-guard. Although they wanted to strike, mobilizing a large force in such a small amount of time was rather unusual.

"Something has happened," Chiyo stated and straightened as she focused on the commander.

"We discussed the assault plan before," he continued. "The majority of our forces would attack the embassy and take the nearby stations to gain a foothold and access the security systems that would allow us a way into the embassy station itself. We would leave a smaller force to defend against any flanking attack from the enemy still stationed here on Earth. That, however, has changed"—he glanced at the man a few paces away from him—"as a result of critical information from Professor Laurie."

The professor nodded and stepped forward beside the commander. "Due to a discovery by one of our technicians during a mission, we were able to trace an energy signal to the Ark Academy in Russia, the largest stronghold of AO forces here on Earth." He opened a holoscreen and his massive hologram of the device appeared above the heads of those gathered. "We hoped this was merely a power unit or jump drive the enemy was creating in an attempt to rebuild the colossus. Given that this was the better outcome, it should prepare you for what is to come."

"Oh no," Chiyo whispered and covered her mouth with her hand.

"This is, in fact, a bomb—a very, very powerful one. The explosion this would create could destroy anywhere from a fifth to a fourth of the planet. While the aftermath effects aren't completely known, the initial destruction would be...total, for lack of a better term." He stepped back and Sasha took center stage once again.

"The force we intended to leave behind will now launch an attack on the Ark Academy and deactivate this bomb. We will go almost all in now, so there will be very few ships and soldiers available in a security capacity." He nodded at Raza. "The Sauren have offered their aid and they will make up for the ships that were assigned to be a part of the main assault force that will now assist on the Earth mission. Due to the new objectives, we will reassign personnel to other positions according to who will be a part of which force. Fortunately, we've been building that list for several weeks and now only need to make a few changes. You should have your orders by the time the night is upon us."

The commander paused to collect his thoughts and stood tall. "For those who have followed me until now, I know it seems that every time we go into a battle, I make a point of saying how important it is. Please know that it is not simply my way to speechify. We have found ourselves in the largest war in a couple of hundred years and every battle is important. And we have been winning most encounters to this point. With this battle, we could have a chance to end it once and for all. Although I have not given you long to prepare, be ready, give it all you have, and your rest will come with victory."

The gathered forces nodded. Some clapped and others

cheered, but Sasha raised a hand to quiet them. "Save it for the declaration of victory. For now, ready your armor and weapons. Once you receive your assignments, report in and memorize your objectives. Remember what we lost and what we fight for now." He saluted and the gesture was returned by all present. "Dismissed."

The group of friends looked at one another. Kaiden nodded to them and walked away without a word. "Where are you going, mate?" Flynn called.

"To the armory to make sure my armor is on rush order," he stated. "Before everyone else gets there."

CHAPTER TWENTY-THREE

Skilz looked out from one of the embassy lobby windows at the forces below. He had decided to tell Farah and Niles, a couple of the other Omega leaders, about the bombs, but kept it a secret from the rest. To be honest, he might have kept it from them as well, but he needed to lighten the burden and they seemed the most likely to keep their mouths shut.

He rested his head against the glass and peered past the ships to the Earth below. For such a large force, only a couple of hundred Omegas were Earthlings and he was one of the few born on the planet. Most had been born on stations, outer colonies, and the like. He hadn't been back since he'd left as a kid, and now that he had returned, he would help someone who had lived there for most of his life try to rule it.

Admittedly, he might not have held much attachment for his former home, but he had distance. Was this merely a desire for power on Merrick's part? Or was it a warped version of care? He had asked himself this question ever since he received the first orders but still hadn't settled it in his mind.

"Hey, Skilz, we have a problem." He recognized the voice as his lieutenant, Darren. Skilz leaned back, rolled his shoulders, and resisted the urge to make a crack about how the man had no idea how right he was. Instead, he nodded to signal for him to continue. "We have considerable movement from the military bases down there."

"Which ones?" he questioned.

"All of them," the man stated and passed him a tablet. "They aren't trying to be sneaky anymore. Everyone is running around like the world is on fire and we haven't even reached that stage yet."

"We knew this moment was coming," he muttered as he studied the info and pictures on the tablet. "I had hoped we could get a few more mercs and gangs under our colors. The military wasn't as weakened as we would have liked, and I'm sure they've been building night and day since the invasion. This is gonna hurt."

"The other leaders are getting together. I have the girls and boys in the ships and stations all at the ready, but they've been that way for at least a month now," his lieutenant told him. "I'd estimate that we have five days at most. They aren't being subtle about this anymore and will come through like a junker with an overheated engine."

"I doubt we have even that long." Skilz tossed the tablet to him and hurried past. "Have the others gathered in the usual place?"

"Yeah. They didn't mention needing to change it," Darren confirmed and put the tablet away. "I'll send the engineers and technicians to have a look at the ships. We don't want another accident like we had earlier."

The Omega leader halted for a moment as an unexpected thought crept in. "No, an accident would be problematic," he muttered. "But with a little planning, we could make it work for us."

"We found juice!" Marlo hollered as he and Luke lugged in two barrels each. "Mack found something too. It could be kinetic bullets or nuts. We haven't cracked it open."

"It's gotta be nuts. There would be more clanging if it was metal," the vanguard declared as he dropped a mid-sized crate on the floor. "Did you guys scrounge up anything?"

"Yeah. Funnily enough, the cafeteria had a wide selection." Silas grinned as he speared a piece of meat on his plate.

"You took from the cafeteria?" Luke asked and dropped his barrels onto the ground.

"It's still open, genius," Cameron replied, his mouth full. "Did you think they would shut down simply because the big day is tomorrow? Sending troops to fight on empty stomachs wouldn't end well."

"I knew that," the titan countered. "But we were looking for something a little extra. There's no big gathering this year but we should still celebrate, don't you think?"

"It's not a bad idea," Indre said with a shrug and examined the containers the teammates had brought. "But if those aren't from the cafeteria, where did you get them?"

"In one of the supply tents near the workshops," Marlo told her and lowered his barrels carefully.

"Near the workshops?" Janis clarified.

"Okay, his crate might be peanuts," Izzy said and gestured with her fork. "But are you sure that is juice? You could find yourself drinking fluid or chemicals."

"It's labeled juice," the titan said and turned one of the barrels to show her where *Juice* had been written on a white label. "It seems like a good sign."

"It depends on whether an engineer wrote it or not," Genos pointed out. "We have become quite fond of our personal keywords. Juice could very well mean oil, burner fluid for boosting, or any number of things depending on the person."

The two heavies looked at one another and Luke shrugged. "Find me something to crack this open with and we'll find out."

Kaiden chuckled, finished his meal, and shook his head as he put his plate down. He wasn't as anxious as he thought he'd be but being around his friends was probably the reason for that. Honestly, he had thought he'd spend the night before the big assault checking his armor and weapons. While he still planned to do that before he turned in for what sleep he could manage, at least he wasn't alone in a darkened room doing it over and over while his mind dwelled on all the possible outcomes of what lay ahead. That probably wasn't healthy.

Chiyo tapped him on the shoulder and he turned quickly as she beckoned for him to follow her. He nodded and wondered if he should tell the others he would be back soon but saw most of them were focused on finding things for Luke. The titan tried to pry the lid off the barrel with his hands before he thumped it fruitlessly a few times. With a small smile, he let them be and stood to follow her down the hall and into another room. "What's up, Chi?"

"I only wanted a few moments to talk." She took a seat on a nearby chair while he leaned against the wall. She waved her hand and a small holoscreen appeared to display her messages. "I received my orders about half an hour ago. I'll be a part of the group going after the bomb."

"I assumed as much," Kaiden admitted and folded his arms. "You were the one who discovered the first one. I imagine that deactivating it will be tricky since we don't know much about it. You're one of the best we have so they gotta send you where you would be the most beneficial."

She smiled, closed the screen, and crossed her legs. "So by that logic, I assume you will be part of the main assault force?"

"If this were a bet, you wouldn't get that many creds for stating the obvious," he joked.

She uttered a soft laugh and ran a hand through her hair. "I had kind of hoped I could accompany you on the mission or have you with me."

"Because I'm so good at getting the enemy to shoot at me and not you?" He kept his tone light and teasing.

Her laugh was a little louder this time. "That is a perk, yes, but...I've thought about what Sasha said—how this will probably be the biggest battle we ever take part in. Thinking about that has also made me realize it will probably also be the deadliest."

Kaiden held a hand up. "Hey now, it doesn't have to be." He walked closer and dragged a chair with him so he could sit across from her. "Look, these assholes may have gotten the drop on us during the invasion but we pushed them back, recovered the Academy, and we've run missions against them for months now. Those fancy droids they have might as well be junkers to us by now, right? Except maybe those bulky glowing bastards."

He frowned for a moment and shook his head. "I ain't going to suddenly be an eternal optimist now. I know there'll be blood spilled on both sides. The thing is, though, that ain't gonna change—at least for me—even after this is done. I fight so I can see the next day and see all my friends and you." His tone sounded wistful for a moment and his head lowered but his gaze remained fixed on her. "There are a hell of a lot of them, sure, but they ain't got nothing on me, you, or any of us. They've already taken so much from us all, so I know everyone who will fight tomorrow won't let them take anything else if they can help it."

Chiyo smiled and met his gaze. "I…I know, I shouldn't dwell on things. We may not set out together, but once the bomb is taken care of, I will be on one of the ships that join the main assault. Be sure to have one of the stations captured by then and meet me on it."

The ace nodded and returned the smile. "Of course. I'll fight hard to make sure you can hold me to that."

They gazed at each other for a moment before she leaned closer. He met her advance and their lips brushed hesitantly before they pressed together and their eyes closed. Kaiden raised a hand to run it over her hair as the kiss deepened. He gave in to the need and allowed himself to experience a peace he hadn't felt since this all began.

"Oh, this is quite lovely." A familiar voice intruded and

they drew apart slowly. His head spun and his gaze settled on Genos holding a cup at the door. "Luke finally opened the barrel and it turned out to be juice—and remarkably good too. I came to inform you and saw your display of passion. I have hoped this would be the outcome between you two friends. I am glad you have become so affectionate."

"Hey, Genos, do you want to know what's customary to do in these moments?" the ace asked in almost a snarl.

"Celebration?" the Tsuna responded and took a sip of juice from the cup.

Kaiden pointed a thumb down the hall and jerked his hand to the side. "Get the hell out, buddy."

"I see. How odd." The engineer nodded and took another sip. "Well, enjoy each other, then come and enjoy some of Luke's juice."

"We will, Genos." Chiyo waved him off and the Tsuna stepped into the hall.

Kaiden sighed and glanced at her. "That was a nice moment—and literally a moment."

She giggled and placed her hand on the side of his face. "We'll continue when we meet again."

He raised an eyebrow. "We're technically meeting right now."

"Technically, yes," she agreed, removed her hand, and stood. "But it wouldn't provide an incentive for you to survive to see me again if we continued."

The ace folded his arms as she moved past and out the door. Alone, he shook his head and muttered, "Clever, sneaky girl," before he stood and followed her out.

CHAPTER TWENTY-FOUR

"So you want us to be cops?" Zena asked sharply and Desmond chuckled beside her.

"We want you to help with patrols," Sasha corrected. "Very few of the military forces will remain here on the planet, so we're calling in favors with every organization that could be of assistance to help maintain the peace we've fought for until now. This includes both of you."

"Okay, I can understand that," she said with a nod and folded her arms. "It's simply...ironic, I guess. No matter how technical you want to make it sound, you are asking us to watch over the area and make sure no one is doing anything stupid. That's very cop-like."

"You can view it however you choose," he replied. "Can we count on you to do this?"

"This battle you're heading out for," Desmond began and focused on the commander's hologram. "This is it, right? The big one?"

"We are hoping this is the final battle of this war." He

removed his oculars for a moment. "If we fail here...well, things won't be hopeless, but it will be devastating."

"Devastating doesn't sound much better than hopeless," she muttered and glanced at Desmond, who nodded in response. "Fine. You've paid a retainer to us for a reason. The Fire Riders will help look out for things down here."

"Same with the Kings," Desmond vowed and thumped his chest. "Don't sweat it, we'll keep the skies clear."

"Much appreciated, both of you," the commander stated and prepared to sign out. "I'll make sure to get you a list of other organizations who are helping with patrols, and that law enforcement green-lights you, although I should mention that it is only a temporary measure."

"Eh, we wouldn't get too hopeful." Desmond laughed and gave a half-hearted salute. "Best of luck to you all, Commander."

"Appreciated." He looked up and nodded to the holograms. "And the best of luck to you as well."

He sighed and collapsed into his chair as he reminded himself he still had other calls to make and wanted to check in with Janis to see how many droids they had ready. With a sigh, he replaced his oculars. It was 02:13 AM. There were less than five hours before departure.

Sasha studied his hands for a moment. Did he honestly intend to sit there while he sent others out to battle? He was not a general and he knew there were things that needed to be done. Despite this, he didn't want to get simple tasks done while others—including his students— were sent out.

His mind made up, he stood abruptly and retrieved his tablet. "Isaac, send messages to the remaining benefactors, ask for their final answers, and notify me once they respond."

"Of course, sir," the EI replied. *"Where are you heading?"*

"To get suited up," he said. "The rest will be waking up in an hour or less and there will be quite a commotion before we set off."

The shoulder pads on Kaiden's armor buckled into place and gears in the chest plate spun and tightened against his torso. He slipped his boots on and they fastened themselves as a low hum initiated in his helmet. His HUD came online and his shields charged slowly. He picked up a case containing his weapons and gear and nodded at Jaxon and Silas, two who would join him as their teams headed into space.

"It's nice that those of us who are going were grouped together, don't you think?" the enforcer asked as he flipped his helmet in his hands and put it on.

"I'm sure that was done by the chancellor," Jaxon responded and checked his infuser. "It makes sense to place those familiar with one another in the same group and should yield better results."

"Assuming we have a chance to fight," Kaiden reminded him. "Until we get to the station, all the fighting will be done by the ships and pilots unless we are boarded."

"Is this your first space battle?" the Tsuna asked.

He nodded. "My first real one. How about you two?"

"I've had ship battles," Silas replied.

"They are different from space battles," Jaxon stated.

"You have more autonomy and options for retreat in a normal ship battle. As Kaiden said, unless we are boarded, we can do nothing but perhaps run to an escape pod." Jaxon drew his pistol and examined it. "As for me, I've practiced for space battles on Abisalo and run them a couple of times in the Animus, but I cannot say I've been in one."

"Something tells me that'll be most of us." Kaiden took a seat on the bench behind him. "I went into space a few times in the Animus—usually only travel, although I managed a couple of battles in there that I could participate in."

"Are you feeling rattled, Kai?" Silas questioned.

He chuckled and shook his head. "Nah. Hopeful, to be honest."

"Hopeful? For what?" Jaxon asked.

"That they will attack and board us on the way," he admitted. "It'll give me something to do during the ride."

The Tsuna shook his head while Silas chuckled. The conversation ended, however, when they received a message to tell them the group assigned to ship *Fenrir* should make their way quickly to the hangar and onto the ship.

The ace stood and lifted his case. "Well, gents," he began as he headed to the door, "let us cry havoc and all that."

"Hello, friend Chiyo." Genos greeted her cheerfully as the two friends met on the way to their ship. "Are you prepared?"

"As much as can be," she admitted and smiled at the Tsuna. "How about you, Genos?"

"This is merely another mission," he stated and returned her gaze calmly. "I shouldn't be too concerned. After all, we will have many more like it in the future."

She smiled as they reached the line at the entrance of their ship. "Yeah, there's no need to be shaken by this. It would make you a mess in the future."

"Especially if you plan to see the future," he agreed. "Do you?"

Chiyo nodded, her gaze on the waiting vessel. "I promised him I would."

"We will make this Arbiter Organization pay for harming our allies," Raza roared from the holoscreen as Hartman and Sasha looked on. "We will finally rid the universe of the Omega Horde. By the end of this battle, we shall have trophies for every tribe on our homeworld. The Sauren will show that the legends of our ferocity and skill should never be challenged!"

"He certainly speaks well to his people," Hartman noted as bellows of agreement and bloodlust issued from the other Sauren in attendance. He could hear them from the screen but he could almost swear he heard them from inside the ship as well, almost a mile and a half away.

"He's the equivalent of a chieftain to their entire race," Sasha noted and picked a case up. "He has to lead by both words and example."

"Like yourself?" the general called after him as he

headed to the door. "You didn't mention joining the fight yourself. I had hoped you would choose to be a more strategic leader this time around."

"Perhaps I will be one day, but not this battle," Sasha stated but didn't turn back. "I will be a chancellor once the Academy is up and running after this is all over. For some of my students, this is their last year. I should join them. After all, this is truly my last battle as a commander." He left and Hartman watched him go, having no reason to stop him. Instead, he checked his watch, an old antique passed down through his family. The hour hand near seven and the minute hand close to six almost looked like an arrow pointing to the sky.

Their forces would follow that direction soon.

"Hey, Chief," Kaiden said as he slid his case onto a bench in the room he and the others had been assigned and popped it open. "Send Chiyo a message for me, would you?"

The EI appeared in the HUD. *"Sure, what'll it say?"*

"Tell her I look forward to seeing her on the station— just a reminder." He placed a few of his tools and gadgets on his belt and in his armor's compartments.

"Only that? Don't you want me to spruce it up a little?" Chief asked with a trace of humor.

"Keep it simple. I'm not trying to write sonnets here," he instructed as a few more of his friends entered the room. He waved to them and proceeded to check his rifle yet again. Hopefully, this battle would be kept simple as well.

Merrick looked down at the planet once again, having just heard that the WCM forces had been mobilizing for the last few hours. His gaze shifted to his forces—hundreds of ships all prepared to engage the coming army.

He felt both sadness and a thrill at this sight. Sadness from the inevitable loss of life he'd attempted to prevent in the first place but the thrill of the victory in his grasp. After their loss at his hands, he could finally bring humanity together to stop the approaching darkness.

CHAPTER TWENTY-FIVE

"We are officially into the stratosphere, ladies and gents," one of the helmsmen announced over the speakers. Kaiden checked his weapons reflexively, even though he'd lost count of how many times he'd already done so. It was purely instinctive when he knew things would become rather intense in thirty minutes or less.

"Do you think the others have already infiltrated the Ark Academy?" Raul asked and looked from Kaiden to Silas.

"We're not tracking them. They are trying to stay dark and all, so I can't say," the enforcer responded, folded his arms, and leaned back. "If they are fighting already, it means the stealth portion of the mission already went to hell."

"They'll be fine," Otto stated firmly. "It's why they launched the strike at the same time we left. The defenders won't be able to get reinforcements."

"At least ones worth a damn," Mack added. "And that

means we have many more to deal with. But if you think about it, within a week or so—if this works out—we'll have finally ended this mess."

"We shouldn't consider ourselves in the clear yet," Jaxon reminded them as he pulled his chest plate on again. "These upcoming fights will test us."

"Do you think the chancellor will consider this our graduation test?" Julius asked. "Or are we considered on furlough right now?"

Kaiden shrugged. "I guess that's something we'll have to ask when it's over. It's another reason to make it out of this alive."

"We don't need many more," Mack said acidly. "This bastard has already taken more than he should ever have. Like hell will I give him the satisfaction of taking me out."

"I'm sure you're on a list somewhere," Silas joked. "He'd be really happy to mount your helmet on a wall."

This earned a few chuckles, although it did trigger a new thought process. "So who gets his?" Izzy asked.

"His helmet?" Raul asked.

"Or his head," Julius remarked.

"I would guess a Sauren," Jaxon commented. "They like their trophies. Although I'd imagine that the WCM will require it for examination given his link to the original super-soldier program."

"So it's not up for grabs, then?" Mack spoke with deliberate sarcasm because they knew none of them would get it, even if they wanted it. Hell, if it came down to it, the military would probably want him alive if they had the chance to capture him.

Kaiden rested Sire across his lap and made sure it was

balanced before he drew Debonair and inspected it. "Wolfson asked me to put a couple of holes in Merrick for him." When he looked up and saw the others staring at him, he twirled the pistol a couple of times. "I plan to make that happen and damn the consequences."

His teammates exchanged understanding glances, nodded, and stood. "Well, we won't snitch," Mack promised. "And when you get to him, if I'm not there, add another for me."

The ace laughed as he holstered Debonair. "Of course. You don't even need to ask."

"We have incoming, people!" the captain warned over the comms. Anyone who wasn't already armed stood quickly, retrieved their weapons, and ran out of the rooms, although Kaiden and his team remained as they were.

"That didn't take as long as I thought," the ace commented and shouldered Sire.

"Let me see what's going on," Otto offered, opened a holoscreen, and connected to the video feeds outside the ship. "It looks like we have...not a fleet incoming?"

"What?" Julius asked and most of the group crowded around the screen. "They intend to take on more than sixty percent of the military and not send all their forces?"

"Not to mention that it's only a group of smaller ships," Otto added and flipped the screen.

"This is madness," Jaxon muttered, his eyes narrowed to focus on several dozen ships on a course toward them. "Even if this is a diversion to slow us, what can they hope to accomplish with it? If it does derail us it would only be momentarily."

"Maybe they are priming a big weapon?" Mack

suggested. "They could have been making upgrades. It's been almost ten months."

"They are coming in rather fast," Kaiden pointed out and frowned as the enemy vessels were systematically annihilated by the various military vessels. "Do they simply want this over with?"

"Kaiden, I don't detect lifeforms onboard," Chief informed him. *"They are guided by EI—simple EI, not ones used to man ships. And aside from a handful, most of these seem to be retrofits or junkers, not the normal Omega craft."*

"Wait, what?" he responded but it didn't take long for the implications to fit together. "Shit! They are going to ram us!" He tried to contact the bridge but couldn't get through. Frustrated, he turned to Otto's screen and scowled when he saw that other ships had already been impacted by the enemy kamikaze attacks. The vessels exploded with more power than they should have. "They have explosives on board."

"What should we do?" Izzy asked.

"I doubt they will waste these attacks on our ship," Jaxon reasoned. "It looks like they are aiming for our destroyers and dreadnaughts in an attempt to take the stronger ships out of the fight."

"Or simply trying to get the most bang for their buck." Kaiden grasped a railing above him. "For once, there is nothing we can do—unless you wanna find an escape pod and eject."

The group looked at one another. Some were nervous but didn't move to leave, and Julius and Jaxon donned their helmets.

The ace nodded. "All right, then, we weather this," he

stated and shifted Sire against his shoulder. "Soon enough, they'll board us or we'll board the station. Either way, we'll have our turn."

———

"Zetta, sir! We have incoming!" The former vice-chancellor of the Ark Academy made his way to the desk and checked the screens. "It looks like a military force is trying to assault the base."

Zetta, however, was unimpressed. "With this paltry force?" he asked disdainfully as he counted only a few dozen ships approaching. "This is hardly bigger than the force we sent to their base in Washington. Our stronghold is many times greater than that. Is this some kind of mockery?" He pushed himself away and gestured with a hand. "Prepare the cannons and send out the airforce. We should have this finished within the hour."

Suddenly, alarms blared all around the base. "What is this? Who set the alarms off? I told you that—"

"Sir! More ships are inbound."

He ran to the screens again and his eyes widened as many more ships began to jump into view. "They must have sent this force to act as connections for the jumps. They weren't the primary forces."

"Look, something has launched an assault toward the gate!" another shouted. Zetta and a number of technicians leaned closer to gape at tanks, mechs, and hovercraft that bulldozed through the forest and leveled it as they approached the entrance.

"How did they get through the outpost towers without

setting off a warning?" he demanded, but no one had an answer. "Prepare all defenses. Get every soldier armed and every droid primed," he ordered and pounded his hand on the console. "Move!" The technicians immediately rushed into motion. Ark soldiers and Omega mercs were already at the gates and prepared to fight. He had known this would come eventually, but with how close they were to completing the device Merrick had created, he had hoped they'd have a little more time.

It didn't matter. They might have been allies under normal circumstances but they were enemies now, and he had to crush them or risk his future standing. Still, perhaps it would be best to call for help to end this quicker so they could go back into production.

"Call for assistance," he stated. "Tell those above about the attack."

"I've tried, sir," one of the technicians responded. "But I don't receive anything. I can't establish contact with anyone."

"What?" Zetta demanded and leaned closer to the technician's face. "Are we being blocked?"

"We might be, sir, but I also received this message when the ships first appeared." He pointed to his screen and as Zetta turned to look, his face paled.

They have begun their assault.

"Knock, knock!" Luke roared as he and several other titans drove their hammers into the western side of one of the walls. It crumbled and fell as raiders, scouts, demolition-ists, and other soldiers raced through the gap they created and into the stronghold.

The enemy troops who were positioned behind the front gate quickly took notice. Many broke off to engage while the front gates endured a relentless battering from the opposite side. The cannons and sentry towers wouldn't activate, and all their aerial forces scrambled quickly to intercept the vast military forces on a headlong trajectory toward them from the horizon.

The gates finally fell to reveal mechs and tanks that surged through. Ark mechs went to meet them as chargers and lancers roared outside the stronghold to attack the military intruders. Ark soldiers quickly manned stationary turrets and cannons around the base. They fired on the invaders as hovercraft and a few shuttles made their way in to drop off more soldiers, who quickly returned fire.

Marlo charged a shot and launched it at an enemy lancer that drove past. A charged ball of energy pounded into the side of the vehicle and flipped it, and the driver was flung out when the entire side ripped open. Flynn eliminated one of the turret gunners above with a headshot before he shot a line to the edge of the building and pulled himself up. He knelt and fired at any enemy soldier or droid that entered his sights. "The western wall has been breached along with the front gates," he shouted into his comms. "Sabotage teams, are you in yet?"

"Team one on the way!" said one voice.

"Team two at the southern wall," another announced. "We're about to enter."

"Chi?" Flynn asked and scowled as a merc shoved a corpse off a cannon and tried to take control of it. The marksman snapped a hasty shot and the man stumbled and fell off the roof to join his former teammate.

"Landing now," Chiyo stated as she, Indre, Cameron, and Genos leapt out of the shuttle as it flew past the stronghold roof. They landed on one of the edges and surprised a couple of guards who were quickly felled by decisive stabs from Indre and Cameron. The infiltrator accessed the automated lock on the door and opened it deftly. "We're heading inside."

"All right, we'll keep them busy. Get those codes and take care of that bomb." Flynn noticed several droids file out of the door on his left. He tossed a thermal behind them as he dove off the roof and fired his line behind them to swing to the ground as the explosive detonated.

"Stay safe," she responded as her group descended. Heavy bangs and the sound of machinery grew louder as they moved closer to the door at the bottom of the stairs.

"Where are we?" Cameron asked. "Is this a hangar?"

"Of a sort," Indre said with a nod as she scanned with her visor. "It is either a hangar, factory section, or repairs. I see a mech being repaired in there and there are numerous grunts walking about or running out."

"Perhaps they will leave of their own accord?" Genos suggested.

"They will more likely be sent to defend the bomb," Chiyo countered. "This is fairly close to the lab where it is held, not to mention the server room nearby. That could probably hold some of the codes we need to get into the lab or take control of the systems controlling the bomb."

"Are you sure about that?" Cameron sounded cautious.

She shook her head. "I need to get in there to see and will have to check several."

He nodded. "Okay, you take care of that and we'll create a distraction."

"Do you have something in mind?" Indre asked.

The bounty hunter nodded again and turned to Genos. "Hey, you can pilot all kinds of things, right, buddy?"

"I can handle most smaller craft and some more mid-sized vehicles as well," the Tsuna responded, his expression thoughtful. "What do you have in mind?"

His teammate snickered and glanced at Indre. "Do you think while Chi is hacking into those servers, you can get Genos a ride in that mech?"

She considered it for a moment and looked at the engineer. "Does that sound like fun to you, Genos?"

The Tsuna nodded. "I must say, it does indeed."

The ship shuddered and several loud bangs followed. "Shit, have we been hit?" Mack asked.

"That didn't sound like an explosion," Jaxon stated and primed his machine gun. "More like an impact or rupture."

"We've been boarded," the captain shouted. "To battle!"

"It looks like our turn finally arrived." Kaiden raced out of the room as Mack energized his armor. Jaxon, Raul, and Izzy held their weapons up, Julius checked his concoctions, and Otto closed his holoscreen. Mack, Otto, and Julius separated from the group. "We'll circle, clear anything we find, and meet up with you again," they called and the ace waved at them to go. The rest followed him quickly as he sprinted down the halls, looking for the nearest group of hostiles. "Chief, do you have anything for me?"

"I have several breaches deeper into the ship. But if we're in the thick of it and they are attacking us for real, there should be some more coming up in—droids!"

Several Arbiter droids ran around the corner. Kaiden fired a blast at their feet to force them back and provide enough time for him and his team behind him to get around the corner. Now that the mechanicals had reached them, they moved back from where they had been in order to weave through the grid-like pattern of the structures for cover and distance. Silas stopped and charged his cannon. Kaiden followed suit and readied a shot as Jaxon, Izzy, and Raul readied their weapons. When the bots arrived, they all fired as one and felled their pursuers before they could respond.

They continued to press forward and found a fallen soldier, who had a droid's leg crushing his chest. As Kaiden raised his weapon, it aimed to fire into the man's helmet. Raul pressed the trigger first and knocked the mechanical off the fallen jockey, but he hadn't vented his gun and it overheated. The droid looked at him and fired. Kaiden grabbed him and dragged him down as the lasers flew overhead. The ace retaliated and his shot obliterated his target's legs. Once the top half fell, it pushed up and aimed at them again. The ace dropped Sire, drew Debonair, and fired three rapid shots into its head to end its attacks.

Before they had a real chance to catch their breath, something pounded into the wall next to Kaiden. The force was enough to hurl him into the opposite wall. He hopped up hastily and scowled at a large pod, the front shot off, that had gutted the wall and would have flattened him had he not been thrown clear. An Omega merc pointed a heavy pistol at him and a red light charged in the barrel.

CHAPTER TWENTY-SIX

Chiyo moved quickly and quietly through the ducts, her mind conflicted as she tried to focus on her priority of getting to the server and trying to keep herself calm as the battle raged around her.

"Chiyo, are you there yet?" Cameron whispered over the comms. She hurried to a vent along the route and looked down into a room with several servers and three guards loitering nearby.

"I'm here," she responded and continued to scrutinize the room. "Three guards are blocking my path."

"They won't be there for long, I imagine," he assured her and she could hear him rustling around over the mic. "Cameron, your mic is live."

"Oh, my bad. I'm only getting into position. The jock ran off so Genos has a clear path to the mech."

She sighed and switched her comms to Genos. "Are you sure about this?"

"It is a good opportunity," the engineer said calmly.

"Plus it would be a waste to not use an opportunity presented to us, no?"

"Okay, but…please be careful." She sighed quietly and continued her slow crawl forward.

"Oh, I have every intention to continue living. Jaxon would be mad otherwise," Genos promised.

Although trepidation nagged uncomfortably within her, Chiyo couldn't help but smile. "So would all of us, so do your best."

"Of course, friend Chiyo."

She nodded and hunkered down. "Tell me when you're about to begin."

"In a while. I'm only waiting for someone to get the damn hatch open." Cameron growled his frustration and snuck a look over the crate he currently hid behind to check the mech.

"Don't bitch to me. The systems in it are all messed up. It must have been cracked by a dimwit who forgot to pay attention during the class on operator resets," Indre all but hissed and focused on her holoscreen. "I'm cleaning it up and getting it prepped for ya."

"It merely needs to work. We don't need it to have video streaming and automatic cup holders. Air conditioning might be a plus, though," Cameron conceded and nodded at Genos.

"I'm talking about making it move and fire right. If Genos wants it to walk forward instead of dancing to the left when he pushes the movement joystick forward or firing the cannons instead of activating the self-destruct function, you need to give me time to fix it," she retorted.

"Good Lord, how badly did they mess it up?" he demanded.

"They're a collection of intergalactic thieves and murderers with no pride in their mechanical and technological work." The agent scoffed. "I assume that applies to the students here too."

"I apologize for the trouble. Perhaps there is a more suitable option nearby," the Tsuna interjected.

"Don't worry about it, Genos," Indre said and gestured to the mech. Genos and Cameron peered over their hiding place to see lights flash in the pilot's chair. "It was annoying but nothing I couldn't handle."

"Your timing could have been a little better. The jock is coming back," the bounty hunter said and aimed at the pilot as he walked to the mech.

"You can't rush a proper recalibration," she stated and pressed a few more buttons on her screen before she closed it. "I'll warm it up for you."

He nodded and activated the comms. "All right, let's get this going. Chiyo, get ready. It'll get hot damn quick."

"Understood. Good luck," she acknowledged.

Genos looked at Indre. "Please open the mech's hatch."

She complied and the entrance to it opened. The jock paused in confusion and the two mercs beside him gaped at it, which gave Cameron a perfect sight of all their visors.

He fired at the men and lined up three straight shots through the weak point in their helmets, and they all fell in rapid succession. Quickly, he pointed to Genos and then to the mech, and the Tsuna nodded, leapt over the crate, and sprinted forward. He vaulted onto the leg and pushed himself into the pilot's chair.

"Shutting the hatch and activating the mech," he announced. The opening closed and he grasped the two joysticks on the dash. The console lit up with various toggles and switches and a screen in the middle illuminated to display the fuel level, cannon and boost charge, and integrity.

Genos looked out at a few guards who stared at him in surprise. One pointed at the bodies nearby and seemingly shouted to get the others' attention.

"They are coming," he exclaimed, took a firm hold of the controls, and brought the cannons up. "It is time to begin. Let us make the most of this distraction."

"We'll be right behind you!" Cameron promised as his teammate fired his first shot from the cannon. It dislodged a chunk of the roof that fell on top of a group of Ark soldiers and he turned the other arm to the right to fire at some canisters on the wall. A large explosion resulted and began to spread flames along the floor. "Or maybe a little farther behind you."

At two loud blasts from outside the room, the guards scattered quickly and ran out the door to leave the area empty and allow her to abandon her hiding place in the vents. She dropped down and quickly located the correct server. When she retrieved a drive and slid it into an open port, Kaitō appeared in her display.

"What do you require of me, madame?"

"I need you to locate the files we need from this server and the first part of the code for the main server above. I'll see if I can access the turrets and any other safety features on this floor from the console over there," she explained as she left the server to walk to where she needed to be.

"Should I make sure to block any alerts being sent out?"

Another round of blasts rocked the room and dust and debris fell from the walls and ceiling. "I don't think that's much of a concern for the enemy right now," she stated and hoped in the back of her mind that Genos didn't accidentally level the room. "We're prioritizing efficiency over caution right now."

"Then it should only take me a couple of minutes to locate and download the files. I'll be back shortly." With that, Kaitō disappeared and she began to look through the various commands on the console. She found the main security functions and the turret commands.

"Cameron, are you there?" she asked.

"I'm a little busy! I have a couple of those little zappy bastards running around me an—oh, Genos stepped on one," he replied, a note of demented mirth in his tone.

"I need the mech's registration number and the team's IDs. That way, I can command the turrets to fire at everything but you and your mech."

"What was that? Sorry. I'm too busy sniping," the bounty hunter responded.

"Sorry, Chiyo, he's having too much fun at the moment," Indre replied. "I'll send you the IDs and the mech's registration is…AN1-SC78."

"Understood. Thank you, Indre. Inputting now."

"Wouldn't putting our IDs in be a faux pas in this situation? Like they would know who to look for after we got out of here?" the other girl asked.

"Normally, it would be," Chiyo agreed. "But the mission is to level this place, so there isn't too much to worry about."

"Fingers crossed." The agent chuckled.

"Miss Chiyo, I have finished my objective and am ready to disengage from the server," Kaitō announced.

"Good work, Kaitō. I have just finished changing the security protocols." She shut the cameras and alarms off, more out of habit than a real need given the circumstances, along with changing the turrets' attack parameters. "We won't have to worry about those, at least. I'm activating the maintenance ladder." She pressed a button on the console. A hatch opened in the back of the room and a ladder descended.

She walked to the server and took the drive out, placed it in her pouch, and made her way to the ladder. "Genos, I have retrieved the first batch of data files. I'm heading to the next floor now. How are you faring?"

Genos launched another blast from the cannon and a group of five mercs was blown to smithereens or hurled away and into the walls around them. "Chiyo, I am doing well and enjoying myself, I must say."

"As am I," Cameron shouted, as he eliminated an enemy sniper off one of the walkways above. "It's a pity there isn't another mech around, though. I wouldn't mind taking one for a spin."

"That is a good point," the Tsuna replied and took a moment to survey the area. "I know many are fighting outside the base, but there should be at least a few more mechs in here in case forces such as ourselves gain entry. It is curious that—oh dear." A flash of light cut his words off seconds before he was catapulted back. Red lights flashed in the cockpit and he noted on the information screen that the mech had taken damage on the left shoulder. "It seems they have finally arrived."

"Aw, hell," Cameron muttered and lowered his rifle as two mechs entered the bay. "They look seriously pissed too."

The engineer manipulated the machine onto its feet and looked through the screen at the two new arrivals that lumbered down the hall side by side. One was equipped with cannons like his and the other was outfitted with a large laser ray on the left arm and a claw on the right.

"These bastards will ruin all the fun," the bounty hunter protested and sprinted to the left to dodge an incoming blast from one of them. "Do you think you can handle them, Genos?"

"They are not more advanced models, nor do I detect any unique mods or functions," his teammate noted and prepped his cannons. "It all comes down to who is the better jockey, and I have yet to see an Omega I respect." He pulled the mech rapidly to the side as a laser blast streaked toward him and nicked the left leg of the mech.

"I can understand why you wouldn't, but it looks like they don't respect you either," Cameron declared and attempted to take shots at the jockey's canopy. His efforts were hampered by having to constantly shift his focus between them and the other mercs still present and who were focused on him. "Indre, can I get a little help if you're not too busy?" he yelled before he turned as a merc was thrust off a platform a couple of stories up by one of her drones. "That works. Keep doing that. I have an idea!"

He spun at a loud crash behind him. One of the enemy mechs had taken a blow that destroyed a cannon and had been knocked down, but it regained its feet quickly.

"They keep getting up," Genos muttered. "It is rather irritating." A laser struck one of his cannons and was barely affected by the remnants of his shield. He would have to improvise.

With new resolve, he turned his focus to the screen, powered down non-essentials, and funneled the excess power to the shields. He also dropped some of the armor and uncoupled it from the mech in favor of maneuverability. None of the mercs fired explosives or heavy weaponry at him so he needed to focus on the other mechs for now, which meant he needed to dodge rather than take a beating.

"Keep them busy, Genos," Cameron told him. "I have a plan."

"I shall do what I can." The engineer seized another joystick, pushed it up, and activated the rockets on the back to go airborne. These were meant for short hops rather than sustained flight, but it gave him a chance to fire down at the enemy mechs from above. They tried hastily to adjust their aim, but his power had already begun to run low. He cut it as he hovered over a catwalk, landed on it, and crushed it on the way down to take a few other mercs with him in the fall.

"Hey, make sure you aim around the one with the lasers," the bounty hunter requested. "Go crazy on the other one."

"Might I ask why—oh." Genos landed and lunged to the left to avoid another assault. "I think I know why, but please be quick."

"Stay alive for a couple more minutes and focus on the one with the cannons. I'll be right back." With that, his teammate disappeared.

"Understood. Go ahead, friend Cameron," the Tsuna confirmed as he jerked the sticks to the left to dodge the beam and his mech toppled heavily. He tried to aim the cannons at the approaching enemy, but one of the weapons was caught under the mech's weight, which meant he could rely on only one.

Calmly, he aimed for the opponent the bounty hunter had asked him to focus on. He hoped the plan would work and more importantly, that it would work quickly. His shot struck the left leg of his target and the machine toppled noisily. It was down but not out, however.

"That should buy me some time," Genos stated briskly but immediately noticed the other enemy begin to fire. "Oh, dear."

With no other options, he activated what remained of the boost and skidded across the floor, trailed by the laser ray from the hostile. He drove into a wall, which forced the mech upright but thunked his head into the side of the cockpit. His vision blurred and his head pounded but he grasped the controls and tried to aim at the last adversary. It seemed Cameron's plan wouldn't work as planned.

The viewscreen illuminated as his barrier was impacted

by a blast powerful enough to hurl him into the wall. He recovered and glowered at the adversary that now faced him squarely. "You bastards are real killjoys, you know that?" He growled as he tried to move the mech upright.

The enemy marched forward as its laser charged. Genos began to wonder if he should eject. Given the circumstances, though, he had little confidence in the odds of being effective without the machine.

As his determined assailant aimed at his cockpit, the bright light almost blinded him through the screen and he narrowed his eyes to remain focused. Air issued from the sides of the door, it flung open, and the jockey inside was confused when Cameron ran to the top of the machine. He vaulted down, caught hold of the merc, and flung him out as he slid into his place. Without the slightest indication of hesitation, he grasped the sticks, turned the weapon to the other mech that had now found its feet, and fired.

The stunned Tsuna gaped as the hatch closed and his teammate gave him a thumbs-up. The mech lurched into motion and crushed the previous pilot as it walked forward. It extended its claw to help the engineer back to his feet.

"That was a little close, wasn't it?" the bounty hunter declared when he appeared in the viewing monitor.

"I was not aware you had talents in mech jockey," Genos responded, still a little shaken.

"I don't—only one, which is enough to pilot basic models," his friend explained. "The rest is what I picked up from my dad and uncle. They've had to learn how to be tricky and didn't have Animus training before they became bounty hunters."

The engineer nodded. "You take after them well, friend Cameron."

His teammate chuckled. "I've learned some neat things, I guess, but honestly, that's kind of a mixed compliment."

"So we have two mechs now, huh?" Indre asked and peered at them from above, her drones hovering close. "In that case, I'll meet up with Chiyo and help her."

"It sounds good," Cameron acknowledged. "Kaiden would probably be pissed if anything happened to her."

"Certainly more so than if something happened to you," the infiltrator quipped.

Cameron rolled his eyes. "You know what I mean."

"How are you doing so far, friend Chiyo?" Genos asked as he checked his weapons and ran a diagnostic test on the mech to see if anything was badly damaged.

"I'm almost finished with the second server. I'll head to the third one right away. You should begin to make your way to the lab. My guess is that most of the heavy guard will be posted in that direction, and we'll still need a distraction."

"We're on our way," the bounty hunter acknowledged and began to walk the mech to a service elevator at the end of the bay.

"I've hacked into their cameras and there is a large group of mercenaries converging on you from all points in the building. Given the damage you've dealt them and how many are still in combat with our teams outside and in front of the stronghold, I would say these are whatever is left of their forces."

"A hundred and seventy-seven units remaining by my count,"

Kaitō confirmed. *"Primarily droids and ark soldiers as most of the Omegas are engaged in the other battles."*

"You didn't happen to see any other mechs did you?" Cameron asked.

"At least you learn eventually." Indre laughed.

"I did not, although we are only working with a partial map and IDs. There may be some guarding the bomb," the fox EI responded.

"Then I guess we should get a move on." The bounty hunter resumed his walk to the elevator.

"I have your location, Chi. I'll meet you in the vents," Indre stated as one of her drones cut through a grating. When it fell, the mechanical folded and landed in her pack as she fired a line to the shaft and hoisted herself up.

Genos followed Cameron past the destroyed mechs and bodies of Ark soldiers. He thought it a pity that they ended up like this, merely puppets for another's personal vendetta. At the same time, he knew there would be someone out there who would want to remind him he was a Tsuna fighting for a race that was not his own. While that was true, he was on this planet with no way home until the war was over. The main difference was that he was fighting for his friends.

While it might be something the Ark soldiers were doing as well, they unfortunately had the wrong friends.

CHAPTER TWENTY-SEVEN

The merc was about to release the trigger on his pistol when both he and Kaiden were knocked away by something that made impact with the ship. The ace recovered quickly, rolled along the floor, and managed to stop himself when he knelt and planted his foot for stability. He looked up as he charged Sire. Two more mercs rushed out of the pod and turned to fire but took a short volley in their backs from Silas and Raul. He fired the charged shot from Sire at the first merc. The blast caught him squarely in his chest and he careened down the hall while pieces of his armor fell from his body.

More mercs and Ark soldiers raced up the hall. He fired quick shots from Sire at them and delivered two into the shoulder of one of the approaching enemies. One of the Omegas scrambled out of the way and shoved an injured soldier into Kaiden's path. The ace grimaced and fired a few more shots into the oncoming group as Silas and Jaxon joined him before he twisted to target the escaping grunt.

The shot barely missed and drilled into the wall as the man turned the corner. While the discharge knocked the fugitive into the wall opposite him, he simply bounced off and continued his retreat.

"Dammit." Kaiden grunted and wondered briefly if he should pursue him before another eruption rocked the dreadnaught. He stumbled and leaned against the wall to balance himself. "Chief, do you have any idea what is going on?"

"It might not be obvious to you, but the ship is under attack," the EI responded,

"I can see that." Kaiden growled. "I mean what is the situation? Are we still on course for the station?"

"I can't tell unless you can get me into an observation system or console to boost my scanner. Everything is muddled between the various energy outputs of the ship and whatever the hell is outside. The only thing I can say is that I'm picking up multiple readings but nothing too big. My guess is there might be a team of fighters and bombers or something similar out there."

"Trying to take on an assault ship with a handful of fighters? That's goddamn stupid." Kaiden thumped his hand against the wall in frustration and looked at his teammates. "I guess I'll have to find a window to see what's going on but first, let's make sure no one will blow this bastard up while we're still on it."

"Why haven't the defenses activated?" Jaxon asked and studied the ceiling. "No turrets or blast doors are working and the alarm didn't even sound. Only the captain let us know what had happened."

"The enemy has used jamming devices all this time," Chief

explained. *"They probably still have some but they aren't the strongest—at least, they aren't affecting me."*

"Small miracles." Kaiden sighed as he considered the possibilities. "Do you think you can get them going if we can get you into the systems?"

"I'll try but whatever they are doing is targeting specific systems so it'll probably be more of a pain than it's worth. I still say they can't be that powerful, though, given that they haven't tried to shut down the ship's oxygen systems, artificial gravity, or core."

"Not yet, at least," Silas interjected as he double-checked his helmet to make sure it was secure.

The ace winced at a bright flash from the corner of his visor and immediately noticed a fire forming on the other side of the hall. Whatever was attacking them gave the ship hell, and quickly too. He tried to think what was best to do because they were well and truly in the thick of it now. They needed to deal with the enemies on the ship, for one thing. If they made it to the station, why bring more hostiles with them?

Were their orders simply to destroy the vessel? They would probably try to blow the core up, something that worked well judging by all the times he had done it. He looked at the pod. They wouldn't escape in those, so would they try using their escape pods? He looked at his team, most of them ready to go or waiting for another pod to break through. He turned to them. "All right, we have to—"

The next blast didn't come from the ship itself but from behind him. He whirled with Sire drawn but lowered it and breathed a sigh of relief. Mack stood in the doorway with the doors in a heap ahead of him.

"It's good to see you're all right, Kai—damn, what happened here?" the vanguard asked. Julius and Otto pushed through from behind, the latter with an SMG and Julius holding a pistol with some kind of dark liquid in the chamber.

"The same thing that's happening everywhere on the ship right now." Kaiden pointed Sire at the pods. "Is everything all right on the other side?"

"We had only a few Omegas on our end. Most of the WC soldiers were already dealing with them and we simply helped to clean up," Julius explained and checked the group for injuries.

"I've picked up some interference," Otto said and opened a holoscreen that was completely blank. "I assume you've noticed it as well."

"Yeah, no internal defenses or alarms was the tip-off," Silas replied. "Chief thinks it's another jammer but weaker than the big-ass one Kaiden encountered before."

"Or not close enough." the hacker pointed out.

"It's blocking some of the doors as well." Julius pointed to the now battered doors on the floor. "Mack didn't do that because he felt like it. They wouldn't budge even though we all have access."

"I have over a dozen uses, but battering ram is one of the most fun ones." The vanguard chuckled. "But now we have a few moments to breathe, I guess we can look around and come up with a plan?"

"I can't get any readings on the other ships without a connection. We need to get to the bridge and see what is going on," Otto suggested.

"That would be helpful, but I'm sure the enemy is here to destroy this ship, not commandeer it," Jaxon stated.

"It wouldn't be smart to demolish your ship unless that is the plan," Raul agreed.

Kaiden looked at each of his team members. "We have enough people to check both. My feeling is that if they are trying to destroy the ship from the inside, it means they won't fire on us that heavily. It's a bonus in some ways, but they are probably targeting the core."

"It's a safe bet." Silas nodded and paused with a frown. "Technically, I guess not—would they honestly blow themselves up along with us?"

"They don't exactly strike me as zealots—or not the Omegas, at least. Who knows about those Ark guys?" Kaiden held his hand to his helmet. "Chief, are you there? I need a map of the ship."

"Yeah, yeah...give me...." The reply hissed with static.

"Dammit, is it the jammer?" Kaiden asked, awaiting the evitable headache, but nothing came.

"It's definitely similar but weaker, like I said. I think the technician is right. It and a few others are probably stored on different ships. As we move through the battle, the waves will most likely come and go. I should be fine and was only disrupted because I felt three different waves. But it gives me an idea of how to block them."

"All right, let's hear it."

"Send me with Otto. He wanted to go to the bridge," Chief suggested. *"I'll get your map first."*

It appeared on Kaiden's HUD and he minimized it quickly and looked at the hacker. "Do you have a spare tablet or EI pad?"

Otto nodded and tapped a circular device on his waist. The ace cast Chief into it and focused on his teammate. "Take him to the bridge. He says he might have a way to deal with the jammers. Julius should accompany you. The rest of us will head to the core in case my hunch is correct."

"Incoming," Silas shouted and Kaiden spun as a group of Ark soldiers marched toward them. One held what appeared to be a cannon, already charged and aimed directly at the group, and he fired almost immediately.

Mack formed a shield hastily and blocked the attack. The soldiers continued to fire as the ace pointed behind him to order Otto and Julius to leave. The technician and biologist headed quickly toward the bridge while Mack reinforced the shield to form a wall. He poured more energy into the barrier and it sparked and solidified like it had at the terminal. When he was satisfied, he shoved it forward and drove it into the squad as it connected to the wall in the distance and shattered.

Kaiden took point and raced closer to fire on the guards who were able to dodge the wall. He felled one with a few quick shots but the other activated a portable barrier. Quickly, he flipped the knife in his gauntlet out, took the blade end in his fingers, and threw it at the guard as the man began to fire his rifle. The knife went through the barrier and found its mark in the enemy's shoulder between his neck and his shoulder pad. He swore in pain as the ace used the opportunity to run closer and kick him in the face.

The Ark soldier fell and Kaiden fired a few shots from his rifle to make sure he stayed down. He heard loud shots behind him and turned as Mack fired his hand cannon at the clustered group that had been driven back by his energy wall. Silas, Raul, Izzy, and Jaxon had made their way past and directed a concerted volley at additional mercs, droids, and soldiers who approached steadily.

The ace opened the map and scanned it quickly. The core was relatively close but one level down. Still, if it was close for them, it was close for the enemy too. They didn't have time to deal with combat situations if they would simply encounter constant waves. Fortunately, it appeared Mack had a similar notion.

Although he didn't take the time to look back, he felt a pulse of energy behind him and a light flared to indicate that the vanguard had begun to charge his energy. As the enemy closed in and his team worked together to keep them at bay, Kaiden stepped to the side so Mack could pass him. The man's entire body was aglow with blue light that both coated him and trailed around him.

The vanguard began to run down the hall, focused on a group of mercs and droids, and barreled into them before he let the energy erupt. Kaiden and the team shot the airborne bodies as methodically as they could and rapidly eliminated all the enemies they could see. A few tried to retreat, but Kaiden and Jaxon focused on them while the rest faced those who still tried to retaliate. He snapped to each target, pulled the trigger once, and held it only briefly before he switched to the next. Their adversaries fell far too slowly, though, and they walked backward and returned fire when they should have been in a full sprint to race out of sight.

Their determination, he decided, was also their mistake.

He continued his measured assault and Mack joined him with a few rounds from his hand cannon. Now, the enemy were in full retreat, but their numbers were down to only three remaining Omegas. Kaiden shot two, one in the back of the head and one in the stomach. The vanguard claimed the last and severed the man's leg in a single shot as the fugitive reached a room down the hall. His cries of pain muted as the doors closed.

"We need to go now while we have a reprieve," Jaxon advised, his machine gun still aimed at where the man had vanished.

Kaiden agreed. "The core is down a level and about three hundred yards out." He pointed down the hall. "The stairs are that way, though—up there on the right."

"We could simply use the elevator," Raul said and pointed in the general direction. "It is next to us."

"Do you think that's smart with enemies all around us and jamming everything they can?" Izzy questioned.

The tracker pressed the button to call the elevator. "What's the worst that could happen? Do you think they are stupid enough to pile into elevators to be mowed down when it opens?"

"Do you think we are?" Kaiden challenged.

Raul shook his head. "Good point. Okay, to the stairs." They were about to turn as a group when the elevator doors opened and revealed a small group of Omegas and droids within. The ace, almost incredulous, froze for a moment in disbelief. Fortunately, his teammates reacted faster and delivered a solid fusillade before the enemy had the time to react.

"Holy hell, they were that stupid." Raul laughed and gestured with his rifle.

"That wasn't the worst thing that could happen," Izzy pointed out. "But it could have ended badly."

"I already agreed to take the stairs," Raul reminded her. "You can throw your snarky comments later. Let's get moving."

"We're almost there," Otto stated as he and Julius continued their run to the bridge.

"It's awfully quiet around here," his teammate commented. "There were bodies along the way, both military and enemy. It's odd that they wouldn't at least attempt to take the bridge, though. I would have thought it would make their attack smoother even if the plan is only destruction."

"I guess we should be ready for whatever is awaiting us," Otto suggested. "I still can't get any readings."

"I'm picking some up, though. Hold on," Chief ordered and the teammates came to a halt at the wall a few steps before they rounded it to the door of the bridge. *"The turrets are armed in front of the door."*

"That's a good thing, isn't it?" Julius asked.

Otto shook his head. "If they had control of the defenses, shouldn't they have brought them down all over the ship?"

"I'm glad one of you is quick to catch on," Chief responded. *"Does either of you have something to throw?"*

Julius thought for a moment before he withdrew his knife. He leaned against the wall and threw it underhanded across the hall. It was shot out of the air before it could fall.

"Well, they have either been trapped in there, are all dead, or someone has taken the systems over."

"I can deal with the turrets," Otto offered and ran his hand along the wall. "Is there a way to know who is inside?"

"I can still read life signs but I'll have to get in close," his teammate told him.

"Okay, give me a moment." The technician pushed into the wall and a section popped out and opened to reveal a console inside. He pressed a few buttons but after a negative reading, he sighed, took a cable out of his gauntlet, and plugged it into one of the slots on the console. The screen began to scramble before it shut down. He drew his blade and tossed it across the hall. Thankfully, it simply fell at the end of its trajectory and spun for a moment before it stopped.

Julius waved a hand and when nothing happened, ran up the hall, and stopped to lean against the door. "I have life signs inside. This bridge crew is comprised of twenty-nine members. I read twenty-three."

Otto approached from behind. "Some either escaped, weren't here when the attacks began, or—"

"They are dead," Julius finished. "There could be Omegas in there and robots, of course."

"They are all Stealth-model droids," Chief told them. *"Their engines have unique energy signatures. We've fought enough*

Omegas to know what their suits run on and I don't pick anything up."

"All droids?" Julius asked as he retrieved an orb with yellow markings. "Well, that's convenient. I have something I've been meaning to try." He looked at Otto, then at a panel above. "You wouldn't happen to have any small drones on you, would you?"

CHAPTER TWENTY-EIGHT

Indre caught hold of the lever and grunted as she forced it up until a hiss of air released and the hatch opened. She ushered Chiyo into the crawl space and followed, then quickly grasped a handle on the inside of the hatch and closed it behind them.

"The ladder is directly ahead," the infiltrator said, as they scurried rapidly and as quietly as they could through the vent. "So far, no one seems suspicious—or at least they aren't looking for us given the chaos outside."

"We'll be fine," her companion assured her. "The other teams should be inside by now. I don't think the defenders will look for a few people poking around when they have a fleet of ships and tanks on the outside and two mechs wreaking havoc on the inside."

"You certainly seem to be positive about that." Chiyo hauled herself out of the shaft and into a small circular area with a ladder that led up four floors.

"This kind of thing usually goes well for you, right?"

Indre asked and gestured casually around the small area. "You've survived this long, after all."

"I usually have more control of the situation," she countered and pressed herself against the wall to give her companion enough space to climb out of the vent.

"And here I thought your most lauded skill was vent-crawling," the agent joked as she pulled herself up and held onto the ladder.

Chiyo brought the map up on her tablet and turned her visor off momentarily. "We need to go to the top of the ladder. That'll take us to the tenth floor and seventy yards from the security room. You go first and scout for guards."

"I'm on it." Indre nodded and ascended without hesitation with her teammate close behind. "How should we get into the security room?"

"That won't be an issue." She held her gauntlet up and pointed at the screen. "Even if they lock it down, Kaitō will have no issue getting in."

"*It should be well within my abilities, madame,*" the EI confirmed.

"There will probably be guards inside—or at least technicians," the other woman pointed out.

"If it is only technicians, that shouldn't be a problem," Chiyo stated. "If there are still guards there, I can eliminate them while you secure the room."

"By yourself? I would guess there are at least a few guards in there. Do you want me to head in first? Or maybe one of my drones?" Indre reached the top, which revealed a small ledge and another shaft to crawl through. She leaned forward and began to traverse it without looking back.

"I'll be fine against a small number of guards. While I usually leave firefights to Kaiden, I have enough experience," the infiltrator assured her.

"You mean to the soldiers in general, right?" her companion asked. Chiyo reached the top of the ladder and followed her inside.

"Yes, I suppose so, but we have run many missions together. I guess I'm simply used to it being him," she stated, her voice low.

Indre chuckled. "It's nice how that works out, huh?"

"Wait, what was that?" she asked curiously and held a hand up to silence her teammate. Both listened intently and a few moments later, rapid thumps sounded outside their hidden passage.

Indre turned to her. "We're almost at the end. Let's go silent for a moment." They crept to the vent opening, this one a simple grate instead of an emergency hatch. She reached back and Chiyo handed her a small curved prong. Cautiously, she peered through to make sure no one was coming, slid the prong through the openings of the grate, and unlatched the locks. She checked the hall again and looked left and right before she opened it slowly and climbed out. As she landed, she drew her pistol and held it ready. She knelt and helped pull Chiyo out of the vent, closed the grate, and clicked the latches in place.

"This is what I have so far." The infiltrator handed her teammate her tablet. "I was able to get access to the doors around the lab, but not the lab itself or the controls to the bomb."

"I guess we were a little hopeful, huh?" Indre asked.

"It's why I decided to target the security room next. It'll

make our lives easier if we can shut down any advantages they might still have, but it would also be the place where they would store most of the access codes. Either that or the main command center."

"Let's hope it doesn't come to that." The agent handed the tablet to her. "How do you think the guys are holding up?"

Cameron swung the arm of the mech into a group of four mercs and upended all of them. As one of his adversaries moved to retrieve his gun, he fired a blast from the laser and not only disintegrated the heavy but also created a hole in the floor that two of the other mercs fell into.

Genos disabled a turret above them and an enemy heavy attacked his teammate with a hammer. The bounty hunter raised a massive mechanical leg and crushed his would-be assailant with ease. A couple of mercs tried to dive behind a metal panel for cover and their panic amused him somewhat. He merely aimed one of his cannons at them and fired to destroy both them and their rather ineffective defenses.

"Man, I should have been a jockey," he hollered in glee as he searched for more targets.

"This has proven most efficient, hasn't it?" Genos asked with mirth in his tone. "Although we are on the inside, most of the heavy units are battling outside. The stakes are very different."

"We'll see if we can help out when we are finished here," Cameron responded.

"For now, it is best we—enhance shields!"

Cameron looked down hastily and thumped his shield button as several rockets careened into both mechs. He spun and fired a beam in the direction from which they had come to destroy two turrets that fell into a messy heap. "Are you all right, Genos?"

"I am fine," the Tsuna stated and manipulated his mech into the upright position. "That did more damage than is desirable, however. What a pity I could not replace the armor."

"I still have mine so I'll make sure to lead." The bounty hunter lurched his mech forward. "Sorry. I'm having a little too much fun but there are still things in here that can make this a pain for us."

"We are getting closer to the lab," Genos noted and eased his mech into motion again. "I believe it is safe to say the forces will be concentrated around that area."

"The other sabotage teams should be on their way too. Hopefully, they can find a way in if the girls can't," Cameron reasoned. "Chiyo must have not had much luck so far, huh?"

"She would not tell us needless information and prefers efficiency," the engineer said and aimed his cannon at a closed door that blocked their route. "But she will get us what we need, and she has Indre's help. We will be victorious."

"So we simply believe, then?" his teammate asked. Genos looked at him through his cockpit as if confused by the question. "I'm not given to much sentimentality, but I do believe we're gonna keep kicking ass."

"Hmm," the Tsuna responded and settled his thumb

above the firing switch. "That is a good start, I suppose." He pressed the switch and fired to obliterate the doors, and the two marched forward.

"We have a straggler coming," Indre whispered and held her fist up as prongs extended from the knuckles. "Hold on a moment."

She raced forward and as the guard turned casually into the lobby, she thrust her fist into the front of his helmet. He tumbled but she caught him before he fell. It sounded like he tried to yell but his words were mumbled from the shock and his helmet's mic no longer functioned. She punched him twice and he went limp.

"Cyra made a good recommendation," she said and admired the gauntlet for a moment as electricity sparked between the pins. "I gotta remember to use this more often." She clenched her fist three times and the gauntlet deactivated.

Indre slid the guard down. Without warning, Chiyo drew her pistol, placed the barrel against his head, and fired, startling her teammate.

"Uh…nice double-tap?" she asked.

The infiltrator held the pistol up. "A strike like that would only keep him cold for a few minutes and it's best to make sure he stays down," she explained calmly. "The handgun is a Yokai so it's silent. There's no need to worry about alerting anyone if there are more around."

"Interesting, but I have an idea." Indre held her hand out. "Do you mind if I see?"

Chiyo spun the weapon and handed it to her. She removed the magazine, looked at the spiked bullets, and chuckled. "Do you have any to spare?"

"Come on, who's next?" An Ark heavy with a chainsaw blade growled a challenge as he stormed around the three bodies at his feet.

Luke blocked his path and planted the head of his hammer into the ground. "Go ahead. Start that and show me what you can do."

The man paused for a moment and studied the titan with a hint of trepidation. He grunted before he lifted the blade, grasped the handle at the base, and tugged it in one swift motion. A loud whine erupted from the weapon and the chains jerked in place a couple of times but did not spin.

He cursed and glanced from the blade to his opponent for a second before he yanked the handle again. Another loud whine issued, and the chains began to inch around before cracking sounds could be heard. He stared at the weapon as the noise continued but it ended a few moments later with a sudden metallic snap. The chains ripped free of the blade and whipped down his helmet and the front of his chest plate.

The Ark heavy cried out as he clutched his face and blood dripped from it through the damaged helmet and down his armor.

Luke laughed. "What the hell do they teach you here?

You should have realized good weapon maintenance is far more deadly than threats and pointy weapons alone."

He bared his teeth and spun to confront him, holding the blade high. "I'll still slice your—" His words died in his throat and the last thing he saw was the barrel of the titan's hand cannon firing.

"Whatever you were about to say, I doubt that too," Luke quipped. He hung the weapon on his belt and took his hammer up. The Ark soldiers had been better behaved and trained when they had tried to reclaim the academy. This one had been…almost feral seemed appropriate.

He shuddered to think what they had gotten into after all this time, or was that simply how the man was? Maybe they were desperate for bodies now. He studied the field carefully and noted that whatever fight they had faced in the beginning had already begun to peter out. Hell, the force he had seen amassing to defend against the ships was nothing compared to that which the Resistance had come with.

His gaze drifted to the stronghold. Hopefully, the teams inside were close to success because if he had come to that realization, surely the enemy had as well. It left them with two options.

Surrender or detonate the bomb early. If they could take everyone there out with them, they could claim a victory, even if they didn't live to see it.

The two teammates reached the security room and Indre removed her pack. Chiyo pointed at the opposite wall and motioned for her to move there. She complied and the infiltrator took her previous position.

"When I open the door, you eliminate the guards within," she ordered.

"Not a problem. I'll show you what my babies can do," the agent said as she pressed a button on her pack and three drones rocketed out, unfolded, and hovered above her. "Especially with the new toy you provided."

"It is a good idea but using lasers or electricity could damage the systems in such a tight area," Chiyo warned. "Are you sure they won't jam?"

"I'm sure. They were a perfect fit." She looked at the wall, activated her visor, and scanned the room. "We have six in there. I'm making my marks."

"I'll get the door." Chiyo accessed the lock deftly. "It's automated, so tell me when."

Indre nodded and directed her drones to the front of the door. "Ready. Let's do it."

The infiltrator swiped with her hand to open the doors and the drones swooped in. Each focused on two targets and fired several spiked bullets provided by Chiyo through the visors of the technicians within. They barely made a sound other than a muted thump on the tiles. The two women followed quickly, their weapons at the ready in case, but nothing fell from the ceiling and none of their adversaries stood.

"We're clear." Chiyo hurried to the main console. "Let's hope we don't have to climb any higher."

Indre set the drones to guard the hall and joined her to study the configuration. "Is there anything we should look for besides the codes?"

"Information, access...the normal things," her teammate responded. "I think I might have something—records on the project, by the looks of it. They call it Project Beta, probably as in plan B."

"Did they store that on the security console?" her companion asked.

"No. I'm using the access from the security console to get into one of the central systems," the other woman explained. "It's better to do that than have to access it directly."

"Man, you're quick," Indre said admiringly and looked at her screen. "I think I might have found access to internal defenses, or some at least. I'll see if I can get them all. I'll probably only be able to shut them down, though. It would take too long to mark friendlies."

Chiyo was silent as she read the files she had found. Her teammate could tell something unnerved her. "What's wrong?"

"There was another part of the project—one they weren't working on at the other facility," she stated. "I wondered how they intended to move this."

"Couldn't they simply put it onboard a ship?" Indre asked and leaned closer to look at the screen.

"It would potentially create too many risks. They could have had the bomb go off in transit or simply shut down without a proper power source," she explained. "Especially one of this size with a core that is so unstable. I had thought they would simply disassemble it and move it to another location—maybe another secret facility—set it up again, and detonate it there, but that would require time.

It's clear they realized a while ago they didn't have the time for that."

Indre continued to read the file and her eyes widened. "They planned to teleport it?"

Chiyo nodded. "Using a warp gate. It is so obvious. We have been without them for so long it never occurred to me. But they have access to all of them. They could send this bomb anywhere they need it to be."

The agent looked at her, surprise evident in her demeanor. The infiltrator returned to work. "I'll get the codes for the lab and console," she stated as her fingers almost seemed to blur over the keyboard. "And, if we're lucky, there is a possibility we can use the warp gate to turn this to our advantage."

CHAPTER TWENTY-NINE

The *Fenrir's* captain watched as three bots tinkered with the main control console of the ship. He looked around grimly. The odds were heavily stacked against them, of course. He and the crew had either been killed or captured and he counted at least twenty of the bots. Dammit, he had to do something. While he wasn't sure if the enemy wanted to gain control of it to use it against the other military vessels or simply set it to self-destruct, nothing they did would be good for the ship.

His concerted mental effort was diverted when a small device—no, he realized, a drone—seemed to drift out of a narrow vent above, carrying several small orbs. The mechanical sailed around the room and dropped the spheres, which burst and emitted a yellow gas. The droids did not react to much other than to the sound of the escaping contents. After all, what could gas do to them?

The captain held his breath, as did many of the crewmen. Some were forced to inhale when it didn't disperse, but nothing happened to them other than a few teary eyes and loud coughing. The crew was confused as to the point of this. It did not seem to affect the droids or the humans on the bridge. The doors didn't unlock so this was not a smokescreen, and why weren't the enemy venting the gas? It might not harm them but it could still obscure visibility. The captain shifted impatiently and noticed that the droid that had kept watch on him didn't move to follow. In fact, it seemed stuck and dark-brown spots had appeared on its chassis. He narrowed his eyes and realized that the marks consumed more and more of it.

He stood abruptly and his crew watched, openly curious. When he placed a hand on the droid's chest and pushed, it toppled and parts of its body cracked and shattered on impact. The team rushed to follow suit and surged forward to accost the mechanicals, while some hastened to take the controls and another turned to the vents. The doors to the bridge opened and the ship's crew all scrabbled for the weapons their captors had conveniently left on a nearby table. Two figures in armor marked with Resistance emblems on the shoulder entered.

"We are with the military," one shouted. "Signal Alpha Gamma Foxtrot 027."

"U-understood!" The captain coughed as the crewman finally began venting the gas. "I take it the two of you are responsible for our rescue?"

"Yes, sir. We're glad to be of assistance," Julius said and retrieved a small container that contained tiny octagonal pills. "Also, you might want to take one of these. The gas is designed to erode synthetics, but it's not completely harmless to organics." He opened the top of the vial and gave one to the captain, who swallowed it quickly, and walked past him to the rest of the crew, shaking the vial. "Right then, who else wants to live?"

"I'm sure he's exaggerating," Otto said dismissively as the captain's eyes widened. "The droids tried to take over the ship. Can you get it under your control again?"

"Already done, Cap!" one of the men shouted and took a pill from Julius.

"Well, that's good at least." The technician sounded relieved.

"What's it like in the rest of the ship?" the captain asked and attempted to bring up a hologram of the vessel to check the damage.

"About what you expect from a boarding assault," he said with a shrug. "My teammates are heading to the core. We think they might try to destroy the ship from the inside."

"They are ramming their ships into ours and have some kind of explosives onboard that create even more destruction," the captain stated. "Thank you for the rescue. Now, I need to focus on getting us to the station to begin repairs. Your team can handle the saboteurs, correct?"

Otto nodded. "Oh, I have little doubt about that."

"Get the hell out of the way!" Mack yelled as he shoulder-charged a group of droids, released a blast of energy from his arms, and fried them as he and the rest of the team continued their sprint toward the core.

"I pick up more droid readings around the corner," Raul

informed them. "And some life signs too. Given that they are in front of the droids and haven't been shot in the back, I have to say it is probably Omegas."

"Do you have thermals?" Kaiden asked and looked at Silas.

"Do you honestly think it's best to blow up our own ship?" the enforcer asked as he held a shock grenade up.

The ace shook his head. "Fine. I have some of those as well." He took a shock grenade out and as they approached the corner, they activated the devices and bounced them off the wall. They arced around the corner to the surprised shouts of the enemies waiting there.

They detonated as Kaiden charged a shot and both teammates slid along the floor, turned into the hall, and fired. Silas fired his shotgun into the Omegas while his partner launched his charged shot at the droids behind them. The combined attack destroyed the mechanicals and flung the Omegas overhead and into the wall, where they collapsed.

"Showoffs," Raul muttered as he, Jaxon, and Mack ran past the two, who stood and fell in behind them. "It's getting hotter the closer we get to the core."

"That's normal," Jaxon stated. "The heat spike isn't too bad so hopefully, they haven't started overheating it yet."

"They could also be trying to shut it down," Silas suggested. "It would leave us dead in space."

The door to the core was mere seconds away and Kaiden began to charge a shot as they approached. "Whatever they could be doing doesn't matter," he said as he yanked the bolt and burst through the door. "Because they won't get to do it."

"Incoming!" Jaxon shouted, caught the back of his teammate's armor, and hauled him back as a rocket sailed toward him. They flung themselves prone and the missile sailed overhead, passed them, and pounded into the wall and the unfortunate Omegas who still sprawled there unconscious.

The ace looked at an enemy in heavy armor with a rocket launcher attached to each arm. He peered beyond him into the core room and identified several other Omegas at the console before he turned to his team. "Hey, Mack, do think you can take this guy?"

The vanguard snorted. "Are you kidding me? Of course!" He slammed his hands together and his armor flashed with white energy.

"The rest of us need to get past. More Omegas are inside, working on the core," Kaiden informed them.

"Will you take lead?" Raul asked.

He vented his rifle. "Now that's a dumb question. Of course."

"Uh, guys," Izzy shouted and pointed down the hall. "You might want to pay attention to the guy with the explosives."

Her teammates followed the gesture and their gazes settled on a heavy with open compartments on his shoulders revealing several smaller rockets. He aimed both launchers at them.

"You see, Sy? Using thermals wouldn't have been that big a deal," Kaiden snarked, but the enforcer simply shook his head in annoyance.

"Everyone get down!" Mack bellowed and placed his hands together as an orb appeared. The ace activated his shielding device as a precaution when the heavy fired his salvo and Mack spread his arms wide. The vanguard covered the group in a massive dome and the missiles made impact in an eruption of fire and smoke.

CHAPTER THIRTY

Flynn fired three more shots before he vented his rifle. This had begun to feel more like a horde attack in the Animus than a large-scale battle with trained troops. The droids were relentless and their numbers vast, but he felled them with headshots so rapidly that he wondered if there would be a pile by evening. The Ark soldiers and Omegas fought hard too, but there did not seem to be much leadership or strategy. He reasoned that it was because they were focused on the air battle—where they were currently significantly outnumbered—in hopes to avoid reinforcements.

But when he saw more and more enemies pour out of the building, another thought occurred to him. Maybe they had more specific orders than simply to stop them. Despite the significant casualties on the defenders' side, they held the line at the main entrance of the building with a ferocity that could almost rival the Sauren. Perhaps their orders were to stop them from entering, but why? Surely that bomb couldn't be—

"Everyone, this is Chiyo," the infiltrator announced over comms. "We need backup. The bomb is farther along than we realized."

"Do what?" Cameron asked and Genos stopped his mech beside him. "Will they blow it here?"

"That's the next thing. They have an active warp gate in the building. It's deconstructed and it appears they plan to use it as a one-way jumper to send the bomb to anywhere they wish."

"Well, shit," Luke muttered. "Things just got a hell of a lot more tense."

"Indre and I are working on slowing it remotely, but we need to physically disconnect the bomb from the teleporter. Even if we could manage to sneak closer, the lab is crawling with soldiers and droids. We have to do this loud."

"It works for me," Marlo replied and snapped the vent on his cannon shut. "I can't exactly do stealth anyway."

"We should hurry, friend Cameron," Genos prompted and slid into his seat. "We should clear the way."

"How will the others even get in?" the bounty hunter asked.

"We'll find a way. Get moving!" Luke ordered and ran to Marlo. "You're with me, big guy. Let's see if we can find a point to break through."

"Falling in. I'll see if I can find some eager volunteers for this little diversion," Flynn announced and launched his line to one of the towers before he leapt off the side of the main building.

"Come on!" Mack roared as he charged the rocket heavy. The enemy returned the gesture by firing at him, but he simply folded his arms in front of him as his shields brightened. He took the impact but ran through it and drove into his adversary as he launched another blast and hurled him back into the room, where he collided with one of the soldiers inside for bonus points.

"Nice job, Mack!" Raul cheered as he and the others rushed past to engage the saboteurs.

"Shut it down or blow it, but hurry!" an Omega shouted and pointed at two technicians at the console as he brought his rifle out.

"Izzy, lock them out," Kaiden ordered, dropped to one knee, and fired on the hostile party.

The scout nodded and looked at the console. "Got it, and for an added bonus…" Pained yells made him look at where the two technicians clutched the sides of their helmets and tried to rip them off. "They were remotely connected and I sent a burst of feedback. It's not the most pleasant sensation."

"I like the improvisation." The ace turned his sights onto the techies. "I can help ease the pain. Give me a—"

"The big guy is up," she warned and he glanced over his shoulder as the man pushed to his feet.

"Dammit—Mack!" he shouted and loud bootsteps thudded past him.

"I've got him!" the vanguard declared, formed an orb of energy in his gauntlet, and lobbed it at the enemy as the man prepared to fire. The sphere collided with the rocket to generate a large explosion in the room that catapulted the heavy into the wall and broke pieces of his armor.

Mack leapt over a console, his right arm burning with energy as he drove his fist into the chest plate of his adversary. With a brilliant explosion of light, the blow shattered the man's armor and bulldozed him through the wall.

Seeing this, a couple of the enemy mercs tried to surrender and dropped their weapons. Silas and Jaxon stepped forward and knocked them unconscious with the butts of their guns while Kaiden, Izzy, and Raul dealt with the remainder.

"Well, that's one disaster averted for now." The scout sighed and vented her SMG.

"We won't be blown to bits," the tracker agreed. "But dying is still an option. Does anyone know how close we are to the station?"

"I'll try to make contact with Otto and Julius," Kaiden offered and put Sire away. "Chief, have you had any luck with that jamming signal?"

"I had an issue as uninvited guests were on the bridge when we arrived," the EI explained. *"It's all taken care of and I'm now working on the signal. How are things going for you?"*

"Fine now. We were right. They had targeted the core." He kicked one of the unconscious grunts. "We dealt with them and should probably head up."

"A couple of us should stay behind," Jaxon reasoned. "In case they make another attempt."

He nodded at the Tsuna. "It's not a bad idea. Hey, Chief, how long until we reach the station?"

"The captain says he'll make this ship fly as fast as she can once everything is back in place. He's working on getting the internal defenses online and activating the lockdown shields in

certain areas. We're almost done, though, so you might want to find a place to brace yourself."

"Chief says we're about to speed to the station and to take hold of something," he warned his teammates.

"There's probably still a horde of these bastards running around our ship," Mack stated as he moved to join the others. "Do you think it's all right to try to make a break for it? They will probably realize both their plans have failed soon and come looking to fix that."

"If they are wise they would retreat for now," Jaxon suggested and looked to the side in thought. "Although they appear to be caught in bloodlust or utter desperation given their tactics thus far. There are other areas they can compromise like the engines and thrusters."

Kaiden grimaced and nodded as he pointed to his fellow ace. "That's a good point. Hey, Chief, should we leave these Omegas unleashed? It's no use blasting toward the station if they cut the thrusters."

"There's no need to worry about that, partner," the EI assured him. *"There might have been some hiccups, but the ship is under the crew's control now. The captain tells me there are effective ways to deal with them."*

Red lights began to flash around the room, handles appeared on the sides of consoles and came up from under the floor, and the team looked at one another and the unexpected handholds. *"Tell all the ladies and gents to hang onto something,"* Chief instructed. *"Otherwise, you may end up dancing amongst the stars like the Omegas will be in a minute."*

CHAPTER THIRTY-ONE

"Are the techies done yet?" one of the Omega jocks asked in the comms.

"They're still getting everything together," an Ark soldier responded. "This is delicate work and is being done under rather stressful conditions. Keep watch and we'll keep you posted."

The jockey gritted his teeth and turned his mech to continue his patrol. "Shit, you think it's stressful in there? Try being out here hearing the sounds of combat and knowing there's a bomb directly behind the wall you're guarding."

"Do you see anyone?" He looked out of his cockpit but saw only three Omegas.

He shook his head and drew on his vape stick. "Nothing, and it's fine by me if we never do. Rather let them finish that bomb and get it the hell out of here before anyone shows—" The large doors beside him blew open, pounded into the mech, and hurled it over as the Omegas scattered.

"We're close," Genos announced and noticed the scrambling defenders. "Do we have a plan?"

"I thought we agreed to clear a path," Cameron countered and aimed at the mech as it tried to find its feet. "There's only one way to do that at the moment."

"Agreed. Let us do that." The engineer pushed into motion to pursue the Omega troops who attempted to flee. He hoped they would lead him to more. With a couple of rockets available, he would like to have more use out of them if the opportunity presented itself.

"And hit it," Luke ordered. He and two other titans swung their weapons into a wall compromised by Marlo and a few other demolitionists. The construction crumbled to leave a large hole and provide access to the western side of the stronghold. "Hell yeah! Nice work. Let's get in there!"

Flynn landed beside them and retracted his wire as he contacted Chiyo. "Hey, Chi, we're in. Do you have a map or coordinates for us?"

"Of course, my apologies. I should have sent them sooner."

"It's all good. How are things on your end?" he asked as the map appeared in his HUD.

"We have been able to slow them by making small changes to their data and orders. Unfortunately, they will notice soon enough," she explained. "After that, I'm sure we'll be locked out. Hopefully, by that time, we'll be close enough to disabling the bomb that it will be a nonissue."

"We'll make it happen. You sit tight," Flynn promised

and joined the group of soldiers as they made their way into the base. A hasty scan of the battlefield confirmed that a few more troops ran toward the main entrance, and he allowed himself a satisfied smirk while the group headed to the lab.

Combat continued to rage on the *Fenrir* as military forces battled Omegas and droids. Suddenly, heavy blast doors began to separate various combatants, tethered grips descended from the ceiling, and the WCM soldiers nodded to one another as they took hold. The Omegas were immediately confused. It appeared that the ship's defenses had been reactivated, but no turrets or troop droids were deployed, so maybe they only had it partially restored?

The ship began to increase speed incredibly quickly. Realization dawned for some, who tried hastily to grasp the edges of corners or doorframes, while others began to fall back as the vessel ascended and its speed continued to build. The pods that had crashed into the ship began to buckle and twist. A couple fell out, followed by a few more, and left large holes in the side of the craft. As the artificial gravity was cut off in those sections, the Omegas were dragged through and into space in the midst of the massive battle that still raged.

In the rear of the ship, airlocks were opened and Omega soldiers and droids were ripped from their positions and out into the great dark. WCM and Resistance soldiers either activated their mag boots, held onto the provided tethers, or locked themselves down in seats with security bars as the ship vacuumed out the intruders. After some time, the captain called for the shields to be raised, activated the outer shields of the ship, and closed the airlocks once again. Some of the blast doors opened as the soldiers released their handles and unlatched themselves.

"We are close to the station, soldiers," the captain announced. "Thank you for defending the ship while we took control and got everything restored. It appears we are one of the first to arrive, so we must maintain our current position and defend the area to make sure nothing sneaks in from behind. Please head to the shuttle bay or lock yourselves into the specially marked escape pods. They have been modified to pierce through shielding and metal. We can give the Omegas a taste of their own medicine."

"Which is closer?" Kaiden asked as he pushed off the floor. "Personally, I wanna grab a ride in one of the pods."

"You're in luck, then," Chief announced as he reappeared in his HUD. "Head upstairs. There will be one of the special ones on your left. Also, I'm back now."

"I'm glad to have ya," he responded. "Where are Otto and Julius?"

"They will hang back for a while. Otto will make sure the ship's systems are back to normal after the droids' tinkering and Julius will help to heal the injured. They said they will join us when they are finished, assuming we haven't taken the station by then."

"Okay, it sounds good." Kaiden looked at his team. "Are you guys ready to do what we came here for?"

"Is that right?" Silas retorted. "What exactly have we done until this point?"

Jaxon answered before the ace had the chance. "Warming up."

The group nodded to one another before they vented and holstered their weapons and followed Kaiden down the hall and up the stairs. They filed into the waiting pod and the six of them sat with two seats remaining. These were quickly filled by two WCM soldiers, who greeted them with a nod. Once the men had locked themselves in, the pod went dark and white glow strips illuminated the interior after a brief delay.

The ace looked above the door, where a countdown from ten was displayed. He rested his hands on the safety bars and released a breath as it went down from three to two and finally, one. Reflexively, he braced himself as the pod launched toward their target location. Something activated on the front and it began to spin. It jostled as it thunked into the side of the station and he looked around to check on everyone. No one was hurt, but they were certainly eager.

The harness loosened and a hiss sounded from outside the pod. He pushed the harness up quickly, drew Sire again, and shut the vent. Mack was in the front and traded his moderately depleted power core for a fresh one. The vanguard slammed his fists together and his armor was covered in blue and white light. Something jettisoned from the front of the craft and was followed moments later by surprised yelps and angry growls. It seemed they had a reception committee. Kaiden placed his hand on Mack's shoulder and his teammate looked back and nodded before he wove his energy into a large ball.

The doors to the pod opened and the vanguard leapt

out and flung the ball forward. It unfurled into a shield wall to give the team protection as they all ran out. A team of droids and a handful of Omegas stood ready, their ranks supplemented by what seemed to be various small-time gang members. Kaiden snickered quietly. He was fairly sure he saw the emblem of the Freak Magnets on at least a couple of them. Merrick must have been desperate for bodies.

He charged a shot as Jaxon and Silas sprinted forward and pushed in close to deliver a concerted volley at the Omegas. Mack shoved the wall forward and upended many of the droids. The ace fired his shot and it annihilated three droids before it exploded in a small group of them. Shaking from the walls and beneath their feet indicated more pods striking the location, which meant more reinforcements. From the debrief, there were thousands of hostiles on these stations and they had control of the defenses. This might be hard work but at least it wouldn't be boring.

As he prepared to fire another shot, a loud and aggressive roar from above caught his attention. He narrowed his eyes as several large figures landed on Arbiter bots and crushed them easily before they vaulted off and drew spears, kinetic clubs, heat-blade claws, and other unfamiliar weaponry. The warriors snarled and roared at the enemy and Omegas who had rushed to join the combat faltered quickly or began to attack from a distance when the hunters began their assault.

It appeared the Sauren had also made their way onto the station, so maybe this wouldn't be such a challenge after all.

CHAPTER THIRTY-TWO

"We gotta get in there," Cameron shouted and surged forward in his mech, almost into the oncoming path of a missile. If it weren't for Genos' quick maneuvering and grasp with his mech to haul him back, his charge would have been suicidal instead of merely reckless. "Damn, that was a close one. Thanks, Genos."

"My pleasure." The Tsuna looked at his screen and studied the oncoming foes. "I agree that we need to get into the lab as soon as we can but we need to be cautious, at least until the others get here. There are two more mechs and it seems the Omegas have brought their demolitionists into the fray."

"Terrific." Cameron grunted and readied his cannons. "Flynn, where the hell are you?"

"Communication is out," his teammate replied. "I've tried to stay in touch with Chiyo during all this and she has not responded either." He fired a blast at the floor beside the corner of the hall in an effort to keep the approaching horde at bay. "There are a number of reasons for the loss in signal. I honestly hope for any but one in particular."

"Why? What's wrong?" the bounty hunter asked and fired at one of the mechs that tried to peer around the corner. His volley forced it back and he walked his mech alongside his partner.

"When a gate is being activated, signal disruptions are quite normal," Genos said and Cameron caught his meaning quickly. The engineer tightened his hold on the mech's controls and pushed forward. "I must agree with you in this case that we need to push forward. Be sure to remain on guard, but let's bring the fight to them."

"I'm right with you," his teammate shouted and the two hurried around the corner to face the forces that tried to prevent them from completing the mission.

"Dammit!" Indre cursed as she thumped the screen on the console. "I think either I've been detected or they have begun to smoke the system as a precaution."

"It appears they have put more EI power behind fixing our small disruptions," Chiyo stated. "I have to agree. I think they suspect something."

"How much time do we have?" the other girl asked.

The infiltrator shook her head and stood. "We need to move, I think. Flynn's group has almost reached the hall and Genos and Cameron are nearly at the doors. We can shut it down easier from the lab itself rather than trying to do it remotely."

Her teammate nodded and summoned her drones to her. "Are they doing all right?"

"I cannot tell," Chiyo admitted and studied the map. "I haven't been able to make contact in a while but I still have their signals, so that's something."

"Cameron and Genos have done good work with only two mechs," Indre commented and drew her pistol. "But that can't last forever during an onslaught."

"Agreed." The infiltrator nodded and checked her SMG. "Hopefully, Flynn and his group get there before we do. They would be far more helpful than a couple of technicians right now."

"Keep following the destruction!" Marlo hollered as the group raced headlong through the base. "Man, what did they get into here? I saw multiple destroyed mechs."

"That's because they have mechs too," Flynn replied. "Chiyo showed me on the map. Genos and Cameron are on their way to the lab in a couple of borrowed ones."

"I like their improvisation." Luke laughed. "Are we close? They've had all the fun so far."

The marksman pointed to the right. "We can make a shortcut through this room ahead." The team turned toward it but some hesitated when they noticed there was no way out to the other side.

"Are you sure you have that right?" Marlo asked with a glance at his teammate.

Flynn nodded at the demolitionist. "Yeah. I said we can *make* a shortcut." He pointed to the wall. "The hallway they are in is directly through there. The alternative is to run along at least another mile of halls and who knows what else to reach the same location, so if you don't mind?"

The heavy nodded and a couple more demolitionists stepped beside him. "We're on it," he acknowledged as the group came to a stop. One of the three ran to the barrier, took a large pack off his back, and placed it on the wall. He pulled on a switch in the middle of the pack and it latched itself in place. Satisfied that it would hold, he nodded at his fellow demolitionists, who nodded in return and began to charge their cannons while he found cover. The rest of the group hunkered down for a moment and waited for the explosion. It came swiftly as the cannons finished charging mere minutes later and they fired in tandem at the charge.

When something detonated violently behind them, Cameron spun in his mech, ready to fire, but he quickly aimed the cannon away and grinned. "It looks like our luck is finally turning—ah!" His yelp resulted when something pounded into the back of him. He held himself in place as the machine began to topple and checked the screen. It had sustained major damage and the power unit was compromised, and he cursed under his breath. He should have paid more attention. "Genos, I need to bail. My mech is about to erupt."

"Understood. I'm rather surprised I was the one who lasted longer," Genos commented as he continued to fire.

"Yeah, yeah, rub it in." The bounty hunter pulled on a lever and the cockpit hatch on the front opened. He grasped his rifle and scrambled out. "You should get away before it—what are you doing?"

Genos had taken hold of the damaged unit with both his mech's arms and began to spin. "You said it was about to blow, correct?" Two rockets soared toward him as he released it. He held the mechanical arms up to defend himself and routed as much power to his shields as he could. The attack powered through with significant damage to the machine—so much so that he could barely make it walk. Still, that was fine, he decided when his teammate's mech bulldozed into the two remaining enemies. Flames poured out of the back as it caught fire before an explosion tore through it and the enemy and scattered the forces on the ground.

The invaders rushed in and Luke and Flynn caught up to Cameron and Genos. "Damn, I can't tell if this was good timing or terrible timing," the titan muttered.

"I got careless," the bounty hunter admitted. "It's good to see you, but I'm not sure how much time we have to chat."

"Is something wrong?" Flynn asked.

"I fear they may already be activating the gateway," Genos replied. "I am unsure if they have finished the bomb or not, though. The best scenario is that it is unfinished and they are merely trying to move it to another location. It would be an issue, but it would buy us more time and… well, it means it wouldn't go off."

"So that's the good possibility?" Luke asked as he rolled his hammer. "Like hell we'll let them get it away from here."

"I never suggested we would," the Tsuna reminded him.

"It's merely a possibility. I am not completely sure they have begun the transfer. It is only speculation at this point. My thought was that since I was unable to communicate with anyone and there was—"

Light flashed through the massive doors of the lab and energy began to hum. While most of those involved in the battle were too focused to notice it, the group certainly did. "Although now, I think it is more than merely speculation." Another flash of light followed the sound of something crackling inside with loud snaps like thunder. A few soldiers on both sides finally jerked out of their fervor and looked at one another in confusion or shock.

"You know, you sometimes gotta hope you're wrong." Luke patted the engineer on the shoulder. "But this ain't one of those times, buddy." He lifted his hammer and crouched. "Now, let's get in there before they blow the planet up, aye?" Without waiting for a response, he roared a challenge and charged the doors. Some Omegas and Arbiter droids prepared to fire on him but the military forces began to fight again. Genos and the others followed and prepared themselves for what looked like it would be the deciding moment of this mission.

CHAPTER THIRTY-THREE

"We have droids!" Silas shouted as he and the military troops delivered a fusillade at the oncoming group of mechanicals. The portable shields they had used for defense finally began to give way.

"We've had droids for a while." Kaiden retrieved a thermal and lobbed it into the group. He aimed with Sire and fired a charged blast at the explosive to trigger it and strengthen the effect of both so the result destroyed much of the hostile group. As the smoke settled, he prepared to fire again, but two Sauren leapt into the smoke. Sparks and mechanical parts scattered like shrapnel before the two raced through to the other side of the lobby to join their brethren and leapt to a floor above.

"It buys us some breathing room," one of the WCM soldiers muttered as a small team began to move forward with glances at the Sauren. "We'll head up and try to reinforce the halls and keep the battles tight."

The ace nodded to them. "Then we'll focus on getting

to the center and—" A thought occurred to him. "Hold on…doesn't Otto have the codes to this station?"

"Every techie has them," Izzy replied. "Like we would risk this mission by having one guy carry the only set of codes."

"Oh, all right." Kaiden sighed and shook his head. "I wondered why—"

"I have them too, ya know," Chief interjected.

His eye twitched. "I did not know, and you could have mentioned it before we got here."

The EI rolled his eye in the HUD. *"I didn't think you would freak out. You've done so well all this time but that tunnel vision of yours can still creep up."*

"Save the ribbing for later," he retorted as more pods impacted the station. "We still have more reinforcements on the way. Not to mention any coming by shuttle, but we should get started anyway. Even if we're not the first ones there, it means we can clean the station up on the way."

"Agreed," Jaxon said and scanned their surroundings. "Although I've noticed that all we've seen are hostile forces. Where are the inhabitants?"

"That's a good point," Izzy replied thoughtfully. "You don't think they—"

"Killed them all?" Kaiden asked and both she and Mack flinched.

"Nah, they wouldn't have gone that far," the vanguard stated firmly.

"I know it's been a while, but you do remember this started with them blowing up Terra and the Council, right?" Silas pointed out and his teammate folded his arms.

"Yeah, but I agree with Mack." Kaiden immediately

drew the others' attention. "Merrick, in his own demented way, has proven that he is doing this for what he believes to be the benefit of humanity. I wouldn't put it past him to have killed some to make examples of them, but the rest are probably locked away somewhere."

"Thousands live on this station," Jaxon protested. "Where could they put them all and keep them corralled?"

"They may not care if they are corralled or not," Silas replied. "They could simply want them out of the way."

The ace recalled his Animus missions aboard stations and the pirate takeover scenario sprang to mind. "The underside of the station," he said, thinking out loud rather than making a definite statement. "Each one has a vast network of tunnels used for transport and storage, foundation work, and all that. They could simply herd them down there and lock the exit."

"It's certainly possible," Jaxon agreed. "If that is the case, we should still make getting the station under our control the priority. As long as they are not in immediate danger, we cannot shift focus right now."

"I agree, but it doesn't mean we can't multi-task." Kaiden pointed to Jaxon and then forward as he placed a hand on the side of his helmet. "Jax, take point. I'll follow but I'm gonna make a quick call."

The Tsuna nodded and gestured for the rest to follow him through the lobby area and up a flight of stairs. Kaiden activated his comms and hoped he could still reach the man this far out.

"Hey, Sasha, are you there?"

"Kaiden, it's good to hear from you." The commander's tone sounded approving but also stern as if he focused intently or was busy, which made sense as he was one of the people coordinating all this. "What do you need?"

He was quite impressed that he could hear the man so clearly given the distance between them. "We're on Icarus, heading to the main control deck," he explained and took care to keep his eyes open and remain aware as he followed his team. "But we were talking and noticed that we haven't seen any civilians. We didn't want to assume the worst and I thought the area where they could be secured is in the bottom of the stations."

"It's a good deduction and also a fairly typical maneuver when stations are seized," Sasha replied. He now seemed to breathe a little more heavily, which was disconcerting.

"So you already came to that conclusion?" he asked and paused in front of a ladder Jaxon had led them to while each of the team climbed one by one.

"We've planned this assault for some time, Kaiden, and already have plans in place. Certain leaders have orders to search for the civilians and keep them safe." When the man answered, the distinctive sound of laser fire in the background was unmistakable. What the hell?

"Sasha, is the HQ under attack?" he asked.

"Not that I've heard so far," Sasha replied, the statement punctuated by another round of shots. "I am, however, although it's nothing to be too alarmed about."

The ace's hold on the ladder slackened slightly. "Wait, what? How does that make any sense—where are you?"

"I'm on the other station," the commander told him. "I suppose I forgot to tell any of you that, didn't I?"

"Yeah, you did!" Kaiden snapped and pulled himself up quickly and through the hatch. Mack closed it behind him and he looked at the group. "Sasha is a part of the assault, apparently."

"He's here?" Izzy asked.

The ace shook his head and pointed to the east. "The other station."

"Do you mind if we pick this up at another time, Kaiden?" the commander inquired and heavy steps could be heard. "Something has come up that requires my immediate focus." A loud blast was immediately followed by equally loud yelling in the background. "Very immediate."

"Right, I'll see you soon." He canceled the link and looked at Jaxon. "Yeah, they already thought about the civilians. They are on it. Our job is still a go."

"As we thought." The Tsuna nodded. "It was a good idea to check in, though."

"So where did you bring us exactly?" Kaiden asked and scanned the area. Their ascent had taken them to some kind of cramped hallway with a few pipes and locked boxes on the wall. It was possible these were tunnels for maintenance or crewmen.

"According to the map, I've brought us to the ninth floor," Jaxon explained. "Using the ladder—which is meant for emergencies only—I found a way to get here without having to fight through every floor."

"Oh, well, nice work," he responded approvingly. "And this certainly would qualify as an emergency."

"We won't have a clear route, though," Izzy stated and adjusted her visor. "I'm getting hits in the scanner and there are more than a few grunts and other assorted Omega standing out there."

"What? Are they simply loitering around?" Mack questioned.

"No, they are setting up sentry guns and placing bombs on the main door," she explained. "And we have a couple of our teams approaching. It's an ambush."

"Then we need to take care of it before they take our forces by surprise." Silas tried to cross to the exit but she stopped him quickly.

"I don't think you understand how many of them are out there right now," she said firmly, her tone serious enough to give him pause.

Jaxon crept to the door at the end of the hall and examined it. "We can't all go out as one, either. The exit is too small," he told them. "If we aren't careful, we would simply line ourselves up to be gunned down."

"Let me out first," Mack volunteered and his shields brightened. "That's what I do best, I'll keep the lasers at bay, you come out after me with guns blazing, and together, we tear them all a new one."

They looked at one another and Izzy shrugged. "There's a number of heavy hitters out there. They might bum rush through your shields if you're their only focus."

Kaiden put Sire down for a moment and dug in a container on his belt. "It's still a good idea but needs a little change in strategy."

Mack thumped his fists together. "What are ya thinking, Kai?"

"I'm thinking offense instead of defense," he responded and focused on the vanguard. "Do you remember that mission we did with the women from logistics?"

His teammate nodded. "Yeah, the first day of our second year."

He returned the nod and opened his hand to reveal a handful of shocks. "Remember that trick you showed everyone in the hangar?"

Mack looked at the grenades and chuckled as he nodded enthusiastically. "I'm glad I made such an impression back in the day. You're on."

CHAPTER THIRTY-FOUR

"The other teams are close," Izzy warned and turned to her two teammates. "Are you guys ready?"

"That's up to the big guy," Kaiden said and rolled the shocks in his hands. "I only have to lob them when he says pull."

"Yeah, I'm almost there. I had to recalibrate the output real quick," Mack explained and clapped briskly. "I'm ready to go."

Jaxon nodded at each of them and took hold of the handle to the door. The ace stood next to him and gestured for the Tsuna to pull it open. Mack barreled out as Kaiden lobbed the grenades out of the doorway ahead of him. As Izzy had suggested, the Omegas in the hall uttered a few surprised yells but immediately began to fire upon the vanguard.

He pounded the floor and released a wave of energy that covered the entire room as the shocks detonated. The electricity caught the energy from his suit and burgeoned into a nova of electrical surges that fried the droids, sentries, and bombs they had been placing. It also began to drain any of the Omegas' shields before it sent them into convulsions when the electricity coursed over their armor and deep inside.

Silas and Raul forced themselves closer to the walls as licks of static crept into the small tunnel. "You're cutting it close, don't you think?" the tracker asked and stared at the display outside.

"I didn't hear you offer to calibrate his output," Kaiden chided. "We're good. He's got this!"

Mack stood, his shields momentarily drained, and moved to draw his heavy pistol. Any Omegas left standing were only that way temporarily as they were still in the throes of the shock. They finally buckled and fell with no attempt to stop themselves. The vanguard waited for the last of the waves to subside before he called to the team as he went to open the large doors. "We're clear!"

Everyone filed out and waved at the approaching teams as the doors opened. "What happened here?" one of them asked as the soldiers lowered their weapons.

"They were setting up a little surprise party," Kaiden replied. "We thought now wasn't a good time and asked them to kindly stop."

A few of the other soldiers noted the sentries. "We could have taken a few losses here," one mentioned and inclined his head to the Nexus team. "Much appreciated."

"It's all good." The ace gestured behind him with his thumb. "The main control room is on this floor. We should get moving."

"Right!" The military officer nodded and his group formed up and pressed on as Kaiden, Silas, and Raul followed. Jaxon and Izzy walked with Mack as he removed his power core.

"Do you have enough juice?" she asked.

"I have one more full core," the vanguard stated, took it out of the container on his belt, and slid it into the generator on the back of his armor. "I also still have that partial, though. If I gotta nova again or I get tapped, it'll be faster to replace it with the partial and charge from there so hopefully, I can make it last."

"Well, remember what comes after this," Jaxon reminded him. "The embassy is our next destination, assuming nothing goes wrong in capturing the other station."

"This will seem like a cakewalk by comparison," Izzy warned.

This only amped the vanguard up and he pounded his fists together and activated his shields. "Good. We don't want this to be too boring now, do we?" With that, he began to run to catch up with the others, and his teammates increased their pace to keep up.

"This way," the military officer whispered as the group crept slowly toward the main hall. "The area is circular with the main station in the middle. Keep your guard up. They can come from anywhere."

"That seems to be the general vibe," Raul muttered and touched his gauntlet. "Hold for a moment. I'll send my tracker out."

The man held a hand up for everyone to stop. Raul

knelt, took an oblong device from his belt, and tossed it above him, where it unfolded into a winged device. He sent it down the hall and opened a holoscreen so others could see its feed. Not that it mattered because as soon as the tracker entered the space, it displayed a large cylinder that stretched a few stories in the middle of the room surrounded by rows of curved consoles and a few droids. Unfortunately, they could also both see and hear a blast impact it and cut the feed.

"Well, they are quick on the trigger," Kaiden commented. Raul shook his head, took his rifle out, and adjusted the barrel to a shorter length.

"It looks like they are waiting for us." Silas held his shotgun ready. "Shall we keep them waiting?"

"Think about everything they were preparing at the door," Izzy reasoned. "Do you think they haven't prepared the room for a ton of soldiers to come barreling in?"

"We're hardly a ton," Mack protested and tapped his chest. "Although I might be on my own."

Orders were issued inside the room and the team members looked at each other. "They aren't waiting anymore," the officer announced.

Kaiden poked his head around the corner and whipped it back when laser fire singed the wall. "Quick on the trigger indeed."

Jaxon opened the map of the station. "There is the other entrance on the other side. If we rush, we can make it there in two minutes or less from here."

"Assuming there are no Omegas along the way," Raul reminded him. "Do you think we'll be that lucky?"

"Plus we would simply have them tailing us as we tried to circle," Izzy countered.

"We would need some to remain here and keep them distracted," the Tsuna answered and closed the map.

"We'll stay and fight," the military officer stated, and his team nodded in agreement. "We'll keep them busy. They will probably send the droids to keep us at bay. If you can flank them, we can use the distraction to push in ourselves."

"I'll stay too," Mack offered, "and keep them secure. It's not like I can run all that fast anyway."

The others nodded and the ace took another hasty glance around the corner. "Godspe— Shit! It's those glowing bastards!"

A group of advanced Arbiter droids approached the group from the hall. Kaiden, Jaxon, Silas, and a couple of the WCM troops immediately launched a fusillade of concerted fire that met their shields. The enemy retaliated with blasts from their cannons to force the soldiers back as Mack stepped forward.

He formed a shield quickly as he jumped to the entrance of the hall. The ace darted closer to him as several large orbs streaked into the shield and pushed him back.

"Get moving!" the officer ordered as the troops formed up to support the vanguard, who created several small holes for them to fire through. Kaiden and the others left the area quickly, raced out of the doors the military team had come in through, and circled along the walkways to the other side of the floor. A few turrets dropped along the way but were eliminated by the soldiers who did not break stride.

Several rappel lines were attached to the railings and it seemed most enemy mercs along this route had gone to join the fighting below. It made their route easier to travel, although he hoped the thought had not jinxed it.

Jaxon blasted the console in front of the door and it instantly unlocked. He and Raul forced it apart and when Izzy and Kaiden entered the hall, it was clean. "We're good," she announced, although she hastily readied her weapon when a heavy thud was heard.

A large droid came around the corner from the hall that led into the central chamber. It was red with a curved head and white trim. When it turned to look at the group, it revealed a single shining eye. They opened fire on it but its shields simply absorbed the various blasts while it scanned the small team. When they were forced to vent their weapons, the mechanical continued to approach them. Its eye switched to red before it aimed its three-barreled cannon at them and the massive weapon began to prime.

"It looks like this might take more than a couple of minutes," Kaiden muttered and retrieved his shielding device. "Get clear!"

The droid's barrel began to spin and fired rapid bursts of charged energy bolts at the team. The ace threw the protective device out and dived behind it as he held Sire's trigger down. The shield broke and the enemy focused on him, its eye fully red as it locked the cannon on its new primary target.

CHAPTER THIRTY-FIVE

"Someone get those doors!" Luke roared as he pounded his hammer on one of the enhanced droids, crushed its chest, and kicked it away seconds before it exploded.

"Isn't that your job, titan?" Raul retorted and fired a shot over his teammate's shoulder at an approaching assassin droid. "Just break them down."

"Look at those doors." He swung his hammer into the side of an Omega soldier before he spun it as he slid across the floor and drove into the large doors to the lab. They didn't give an inch. "I can't break through with force or explosives."

"Hey now, don't make assumptions," Marlo countered and gestured to two other demolitionists beside him with launchers. He charged his cannon as his companions loaded their weapons. Luke and any soldiers near the door moved away hastily as the three took aim and fired as one. Their projectiles struck home and generated a massive explosion, but when the flash and smoke dissipated, they only had light damage and scuffing to show for their attempt. Marlo opened the vent on his cannon as the other two reloaded. "All right. Luke might have a point."

"We gotta hack them, then," Flynn reasoned and opened the directory containing the names and specialties of team members around them. "We gotta have at least a couple of techies here, right?"

"Where are the other stealth teams?" Cameron asked and smacked an Ark soldier off him with the butt of his rifle before he aimed it and pulled the trigger to finish him off. "Are they still caught on the other side of the building?"

"I don't know, but what about Indre and Chiyo?" Genos suggested. He held the head of a droid with the claw of his gauntlet and twisted it off. "Perhaps they can access it from their position."

"That's a good idea," the marksman agreed. "Can you give them a call while we keep the rest of this trash off—" From above, spikes streaked into Omega grunts and droids and Flynn and Genos caught a glimpse of several drones. "Whose are those?"

"Who do you think?" Indre responded over the comms. The marksman looked up as she and Chiyo landed on a rail above. "Are you guys still stuck at the doors?" she asked before she noticed the damaged mechs. "And you lost the mechs."

"Give us a hand now and mock us later," Cameron retorted and he fired at an Ark marksman who aimed at the new arrivals.

"I'll get the doors," the infiltrator stated and vaulted over the railing. "You clean up the rest. They still have forces waiting in the lab, and we need to be quick."

"Mopping up," Luke hollered, thunked his hammer into

the floor, and hurled soldiers and drones away. The other soldiers used the opportunity to decimate their ranks and force the survivors back. Chiyo caught a hanging banner and used it to slide down before she jumped off onto the wall and bounced to the floor. She ran to the doors, cast Kaitō into the terminal as she drew her SMG, and quickly demolished two Arbiter droids on her approach.

"Madame, I've almost opened the door," the EI informed her.

"Did you have any interference?" she asked, still alert and watchful. By this point, however, most of the hostiles were at the end of the hall, being pushed out or eliminated by the Resistance forces.

"No, and it's rather curious. In fact, I would say they have no interest in stopping me. I think they are too focused on fixing whatever remains of your disruptions and getting the bomb activated."

Chiyo frowned and vented her weapon, while Indre descended by using one of her drones to allow her to glide down. Flynn, Cameron, Marlo, and the remaining soldiers who weren't driving the enemies out of the hall joined her. "The door is almost open. Get ready. We don't have much time."

"That's been well-established," Cameron stated and closed the vent on his rifle.

"Do you believe we can still shut it down?" Genos asked.

"That would be the best outcome," the infiltrator confirmed and shrugged. "But even if we can't, we will not fail here."

Kaiden cursed in a low tone, aimed hastily, and charged a shot. The barrels of the red droid—aimed directly at him—began to spin ominously again.

"Hold on for a sec." Chief vanished without explanation.

"What the hell are you talking about?" he demanded and frowned as light began to glow from the barrels while they charged. He aimed his rifle away and shifted so he could roll to the side and push to his feet. The droid did not follow, thankfully, and the cannon began to slow.

"Did it break?" Silas asked warily as he approached with his shotgun still at the ready.

The enemy's red eye changed to white again and it straightened, aimed its cannon up, and nodded to the team. Kaiden tilted his head thoughtfully as he examined it. "Chief? Are you in there?"

"You got it, buddy," the EI chirped. *"Taking over one of the scrawny bastards almost doesn't seem worth the effort. This one —an Arbiter Prime model from what I see—is worth it."*

"You could have let me know a little sooner," he muttered and strode past the droid.

The mechanical shrugged as it followed him. *"I was working on it and am not good at multi-tasking."*

"Bullshit," the ace retorted. "Whatever. Let's get down the hall and take the station."

"We'll still need to clear it," Jaxon reminded him. "The mission will not be a success until we have complete control of it."

"Having control of the defenses and security bots will help with that," Izzy replied.

Kaiden held a hand up. "We're here." He pointed to the droid, then down the hall. "Chief, get in there."

"You want me to lead the charge?" he questioned. *"I have the feeling you think I'm expendable."*

He shook his head. "Of course I don't," he said and tapped the mechanical's chest. "But that body you are in is, now show us what it can do."

Although he couldn't see Chief's avatar, he was fairly sure he was rolling his eye. *"This seems like petty revenge, but whatever."* The droid's shields activated as the cannon barrels began to spin. *"I hope you meat bags can keep up."*

The droid lurched into a run on long legs and barreled into the central room. The team followed with a few paces between them and the mechanical, and as soon as the EI had enemies in his sights, he began to fire. The attack surprised the Omegas, whose focus was still on the other hall. Kaiden and Jaxon were the first of the team inside and fired at soldiers above. Silas and Izzy demolished two droids that dropped from higher up and watched the hall behind them.

"They made it," the military officer shouted. "The enemy is breaking—push forward!"

"Let me," Mack offered, formed the shield wall into a ball, and cast it ahead. It plowed through a few soldiers before it struck the cylinder in the middle of the area, erupted, and hurled the enemy soldiers and droids across the room.

"Kaiden!" Jaxon called and dodged the large blade of an Omega heavy while he planted a thermal grenade on the man's back. He vaulted over a set of consoles as the explosive detonated. "Get inside the central station. Upload the codes."

"Chief has them," the ace replied and yanked his blade from a merc's neck. "Chief, leave the body."

The EI annihilated three Arbiter droids. *"Are you sure? I still have—"* A loud crash cut his words short as another Prime droid dropped in. *"Aw, hell."*

"Quick—take it out!" Kaiden ordered and charged a shot before a droid dropped behind him and a blade unsheathed from its arm. He side-stepped the attack and fired into its chest while Chief exchanged fire with the first mechanical. Rapid energy blasts were exchanged but the ace ducked hastily, and the droids quickly destroyed each other's shields before each annihilated the other.

"Well, shit. Never mind." Chief groaned as he reappeared in the HUD. *"Let's get in there."*

Kaiden knelt and vented his gun for a moment before he shut it and charged another shot as he approached the central chamber. He found the entrance and fired at the door to demolish it in a flash of green energy. In response, a small orb of blue energy sailed out, caught him in the chest, and forced him back.

"Shields are down to thirty percent," Chief warned. *"It looks like they saw that coming."*

"I noticed." The ace growled his annoyance as he retrieved a thermal. "Let's see them respond to this." He lobbed it into the room but one of the droids snatched it from the air and prepared to throw it back. "Nope." He sighted his rifle and fired at the explosive, detonated it, and obliterated the enemy.

"Lucky that wasn't near anything important," Chief pointed out. *"Let's try to not destroy what we came here for."*

Kaiden was silent for a moment as he had to admit Chief was right. "Noted." He sighed, stood hastily, and ran inside. "I'll try to keep the destruction a little more moderate."

This time, he did see Chief roll his eye.

CHAPTER THIRTY-SIX

Luke removed his hammer from the chest of the assault droid on the floor and rested it on his shoulder. "Is that the last of them?"

"It seems to be," a raider stated and looked around. "Do you think we should push deeper into the complex or head out?"

"That bomb is our priority right now," he replied.

"He's right," a military officer agreed. "We need to get back there and assist the team. Who knows what else is coming through to try to stop us?"

Alarms blared and the entire group turned to the red lights that flashed at the end of the hall. A door opened and a large black mech pushed through before the entrance had even opened fully. Large cannons were affixed to both arms and two turrets were mounted on its shoulders.

The titan hefted his hammer in both hands as the group began to back away. "Is it too late to place a bet on a Goliath droid?" he quipped.

"Yeah, betting on that is off," the officer grunted and

checked his team quickly. "But I have a new bet if you are interested."

The mechanical aimed its cannons at them. "Yeah, what's that?" Luke asked.

"How long do you think it'll take us to destroy this?" the other man replied.

Luke smiled and twisted his hammer. "Whatever you are thinking, I'll take the under." He pressed the trigger on his hammer and surged toward the enemy with two other heavies and two raiders alongside. Undeterred by their aggressive approach, the Goliath fired on them.

"The doors are open, madame," Kaitō stated as the large doors began to move with a hiss of escaping air. *"I suggest you defend you—"*

Before he could finish his warning, they faced a fusillade of laser blasts. A couple of heavies popped external shields quickly while the others ducked or leapt out of the way and spun hastily to return fire.

"Indre, Chiyo!" Genos called. "Focus on the bomb. We will make sure you are not interrupted."

"Much appreciated," Chiyo acknowledged and ran in with Indre on her heels as she dispatched her drones to assist. The lab was massive and extremely high-tech, but it seemed cleanliness had not been a main concern, at least recently. Various machines and components were strewn everywhere. Droids and pieces of armor seemingly took up an entire corner of the facility, but the large box in the middle that glowed white with a large ring hovering over-head drew their immediate attention.

The infiltrator aimed at an Ark soldier in their path, but two of Indre's drones swooped to launch spikes and small kinetic rounds through his helmet. He fell and both technicians vaulted over him to a large terminal and console set up outside the box. Several technicians in gray coats turned to them as they approached.

"We are unarmed," one stated breathlessly and held his hands up.

"Technically, no, you aren't," Indre countered and gestured at the box. "We're here to shut that down."

"It's too late," another technician shouted, although her tone was more concerned than malicious. "We were ordered to start it early because of your attack. The levels fluctuate constantly, though, and we can't keep them in check."

"Are you saying it'll explode here?" Chiyo demanded and prodded the man with her gun.

"It does not have to," he stated. "We intended to send it somewhere else."

"Do you care to explain where?" she pressed. He turned away and remained silent. "I assume somewhere that would have caused millions if not billions of deaths. But now that I give it a little thought..." Chiyo put her SMG away, shoved the technician aside, and took the controls. "Indre, keep them secured."

"Not a problem," the agent responded and trained her gun on them as she summoned a couple of her drones to guard them. "What's the matter, Chi? You sound tense."

"Which is not abnormal given the situation," her teammate responded and continued to work while she sent Kaitō into another part of the system.

"You've done very well keeping your cool until now, at least," the agent added. "Something must really be wrong, huh?"

Chiyo nodded. "It's only now occurred to me that there is no place on the planet to which we can send this that won't end in a massive loss of life," she explained. "Even if I do find a location in the middle of the ocean that would be sufficient to make sure no one dies from the blast, the bomb seems to eradicate anything within the explosion radius, along with creating great force. That would cause havoc with the ecosystem and potentially lead to natural disasters such as earthquakes and tsunamis, which would lead to devastation either way."

"Then send it into space," Indre reasoned and motioned with her pistol to a technician who seemed to be trying to back away.

"That's what I realized, but there are space stations and the army to consider," she replied. "I need to send it deep into space and without another gate open, I can't make it travel that far."

Her teammate pressed her gun against the chest of the lead tech. "Activate more gates," she ordered.

"We couldn't help you there even if we wanted to," he snapped. "The gates are controlled by the stations and embassy."

"Shit," she muttered and turned to Chiyo. "Is that true? Is there no other way?"

"It is, but that doesn't mean it's hopeless." The infiltrator opened her contacts. "Although it means we have to hope he's made better progress than we have."

———

"Son of a bitch, go away!" Kaiden yelled and fired Debonair through a droid's head and shoved it off him. "Chief, can't you do something about all these bots?"

"Do you wanna whine or do you want me to get this station under our control?" Chief retorted. *"It's not like I have it easy either. Even with the codes, they've already started switching certain systems to a different set. Not many but enough to be a pain, and I think they have hackers trying to stop me."*

"Ugh, fine!" Kaiden whacked his blade into the chest of another droid. They seemed as concerned as he was to not destroy the room and attacked with smaller arms and melee weapons. "I'll keep busy."

"Quit squawking and I can— Hey, we have a message from Chiyo."

"Really?" Kaiden kicked the droid off his blade and it smacked into another behind it to impale itself on its comrade's weapon. Kaiden fired a shot through the second droid's head before he reacted to the unmistakable sound of an electric charge and ducked as electricity arced overhead. He straightened and threw his blade through the attacking mechanical's skull and finally eliminated it with two shots to the chest. "What's up? How is she doing?"

"Not the best, it seems," Chief revealed. *"They have reached the bomb, but the enemy techs have already activated it. She has a way to teleport it, but she needs a gate opened to send it far enough away for it to be of no harm."*

"All the gates are down," he said and scanned the area. No more droids were visible, so he finally gave himself a moment to breathe. "What can we do?"

"The fact that we're on this station means we can fix the problem," the EI confirmed. *"Stations Icarus and Xuanzang also control several gates. That's part of the reason we have to take them back."*

"Can you activate them in time?" he asked, his gaze focused on the entrance to the room.

"Yeah, but I need a boost. I gotta activate the battle suite."

"How's that gonna help you?" the ace asked and exchanged Debonair for Sire. "It's to increase my fighting ability."

"We have a special relationship," Chief explained. *"We're not like other soldiers and EIs. I can get a boost to all my systems."*

Kaiden looked at the options the EI scanned quickly. "Really? Why haven't you brought this up before?"

"Because we've never needed it. I do easy hacking stuff and never had to dip my nonexistent toes into the job of a techie," he replied. *"And there is a catch—to you. In the same way the suite basically intertwines us but to your favor, this is the opposite. I'll be able to work beyond peak efficiency, but that's gonna be unloaded onto you."*

Kaiden raised an eyebrow. "Meaning what exactly?"

"The best-case scenario is you'll probably get a bit loopy. At worst...remember how you felt when Gin shut the Animus down and kept you in it?"

"I do, yeah. My brain could have been fried if I recall correctly," the ace muttered with a grimace. "Whatever. Just do it."

"Make sure the others know and I'll try to make this quick," Chief told him somberly.

He activated his comms. "Whatever you guys are doing out there, keep it up, but I need you to make sure no one gets inside. I will be out for a moment."

"Out? Where are you going?" Silas asked.

"I'm gonna get loopy according to Chief," he responded. "Or hopefully, that's the worst that can come from it." He silenced the comms and nodded. "Do it, Chief."

"Initializing suite." Kaiden's vision grew brighter and he became lightheaded almost immediately. The EI's computing ability improved dramatically and he immediately shut out the other hackers and technicians and got to work. *"All right, you pathetic excuses for techies. See if you can stop me now."*

CHAPTER THIRTY-SEVEN

"Is everything well?" the captain of the *Fenrir* asked.

"As well as it can be given that our job is to be a shield," one of the crewmen responded.

"Shield and sword," he corrected. "I have no desire to fall on this day either, so if you could focus on the sword part, I would be most appreciative."

"I'm on it, sir," the man acknowledged with a small chuckle.

The captain approached Julius, who watched over four other crewmen, all asleep on the floor. "Will they be all right?"

"Hmm?" Julius looked up from his medical case. "Ah, them? Yes, they will be. There are some moderate to severe wounds but nothing critical. The elixir I gave them puts them into a temporary sleep to aid in accelerated recovery." Julius picked up the arm of one of the crewmen to show the other man a scar about four inches long. "This used to be wider and much deeper, and this is the progress after a little more than a half-hour."

"Remarkable!" the officer responded with genuine approval. "Is it your own product?"

"I can't take all the credit," the younger man said as he stood. "I came up with it during my advanced year in a group of four. I'm still ironing out the kinks so I had to give them a much smaller dose since I couldn't dilute it properly. It is still not good for soldiers on the battlefield as they are physically weakened and have some mental disconnect to their EI for a short time. These crewmen should be back at their posts within an hour, though."

"I'm glad to have your help," the captain said graciously. "I've spoken to the medics in the bay. They have treated who they could and are taking care of others. Those who weren't KIA are also on the path to recovery. Most are rather stubborn and are determined to return to combat."

"Well, that's what they came for," Julius reminded him. "I think myself and my compatriots were worried about not getting to the fight at all, so I'm glad it didn't come to that."

"Due in part to you and your comrades' assistance."

"Which reminds me, has Otto reported back yet?" the medic asked. "I can swing by the medbay to offer a few healing gels and serums I have, but I should save the rest to help my team and we should be off soon, now that the worst is over."

"Right, of course." The man checked his pad. "I haven't received any messages since he left. I could call him if you would like me to."

"Are you looking for me?" Otto asked and dropped from the ceiling, startling the captain. "Sorry. I had to get into the guts of the shield system and simply crawled here.

The other techs and I made sure everything is back in working order and keyed the jamming signal in so the enemy's tech can't mess with the ship anymore. They are sending the instructions to other ships, but it appears most have been able to find their own workarounds."

"That's a relief." The officer's frown eased a little. "I was thanking your partner for his help, which applies to you also. Will you be off now?"

"We probably should be." The technician glanced at his teammate. "We're happy to help but we are here to assist with taking the station."

"I wonder if we are even needed anymore," Julius said thoughtfully. "We've seen Kaiden and the others in action, and backed up by the WCM's best, it should make this a rather brief assault for this station, no?"

"Captain!" a helmsman called. "We have enemy destroyers and a dreadnaught approaching."

The officer frowned again and returned to the front of the bridge with Julius and Otto in his wake. "Keep the front bulkheads closed and activate the holomap."

"Aye," the helmsman acknowledged, and a large map appeared in front of the captain's chair. It displayed several destroyers en route toward the line around Icarus. "We can hold against the destroyers together, but that dreadnaught will be an issue," the man muttered. "Are any of our dreadnaughts available to assist?"

"All are currently engaged. We have other destroyers, corsairs, and assaults coming up from behind, though. Still, I'm not sure we have enough firepower to destroy or disable it before it inflicts significant damage to the line and perhaps even the station." The helmsman shrugged unhappily.

"If we are winning, they would probably rather destroy the station outright than relinquish it to us." The captain stroked his beard as he considered the likely scenarios.

"We'd better hope they haven't activated the self-destruct on the station," Julius muttered.

"The stations don't have a self-destruct function," Otto explained. "They have a way to cut the power off in dire circumstances, but if we needed to scuttle the station, we would simply destroy it remotely. It's a good thing it didn't come to that since Icarus is one of two stations designed for battle."

"You're right," the officer shouted and drove a fist into his upturned hand. "Icarus' main cannons could make all the difference." He strode decisively to the middle of the bridge. "Everyone make contact with the officers on the station. See if they have control yet and tell them we need those weapons asap."

Julius looked at Otto, who had activated his comms. "I'll contact our team to see how they are faring." He shrugged as if the rest of his thought was obvious. "Maybe they are in a position to help."

"Chief, I ain't feeling so good." Kaiden moaned, now on all fours and buried by a wave of nausea as if he were about to vomit.

"Hold tight, partner. I'm almost there. I have control of most interior defenses, not that there are many left. Also, I have

control of life support and main systems and I'm working on auxiliary and weapons."

"I might need life support after this," the ace mumbled and eased himself back so he could lean on one of the consoles.

"Kaiden, I think I saw an Omega soldier heading inside to where you are," Izzy warned.

He shook his head, picked Sire up, and held the trigger. "You had one job," he muttered as the barrel began to glow.

"Uh…you are still on comms," she replied.

"I'm well aware." He fired as soon as he saw a hazy figure round the corner. A green haze appeared as the shot erupted but he heard the crack of the Omega's armor and him making impact with the wall down the hall. "Hopefully, that solved the problem." He pressed his hands against his helmet and dragged in a deep breath.

"Kaiden? Are you there?" a voice inquired.

"Who is it now?" Kaiden growled annoyance.

"It's Otto. Are things all right?" the technician responded, concern in his tone. "You sound ill."

"That about sums it up, yeah," the ace replied. "As for if things are all right…technically, sure, we almost have control of the station."

"That's great and it's what I'm calling about, actually," his teammate stated. "Listen, we're about to come under heavy attack. There are enough ships to hold off most of the assault, but the Omegas are bringing a dreadnaught in. We need it taken care of and could use the station's weaponry about now."

"Did you get that, Chief?" Kaiden asked and turned his head slightly.

"*I did. It's good timing,*" Chief confirmed. "*I've gained control of the station's weapons, so I'll focus on that while you get that gate working for Chiyo.*"

"Easier said than done, bright light," he grumbled and struggled to his feet.

"*Hmm? Oh, yeah. I can deactivate the suite now. We're good.*" He felt immediate relief but also something akin to vertigo. Quickly, he stripped his helmet off and drew a deep breath.

"Thank God—all of them." He pressed his fingers against his temple. "Okay, what do I need to do to get the gate working?"

"*Go to the blinking console,*" Chief instructed and the ace located a flashing panel. "*Initiate the boot-up sequence. I've taken care of all the particulars. Then contact Chiyo so she can give you the coordinates and you can connect it to whatever she is using to move the bomb.*"

A little of his strength returned and the ace hurried to the console, activated the screen, and initiated the program for the warp gate. He took another deep breath and replaced his helmet. "Chi, are you there?"

"Momentarily," she responded. "Is the gate available?"

"I'm getting it ready. Chief says I need to link up to you and get the coordinates."

"Good, I'll open the link. I'll put it under my name. If you grant me access to the systems, I can send it myself," she instructed.

He opened a menu that contained dozens of channels but identified hers without difficulty. "Got it. I pressed the go button and it's linking."

"The go button?" she asked and he could hear a sigh. "I am grateful for your help but why isn't Chief doing this?"

"He's busy with something else," he replied.

"I have the cannons ready," Chief advised him. *"You might want to make sure your feet are planted securely. These are big guns!"*

"They are closing in and are almost within range, sir," the helmsman announced.

The captain took his seat. "Then prepare to fire. Focus on the destroyers but don't break the line," he instructed, leaned forward, and clasped his hands tightly. "And hope they can get those cannons online before—"

"Cannons!" a crewman bellowed. "Icarus' cannons are taking aim at the dreadnaught."

He smiled. "Well then, belay the order not to move. You'd better make sure we aren't in their way."

CHAPTER THIRTY-EIGHT

Luke—elevated by about fifteen feet—rocketed into a wall. He shook his head and opened his eyes, and as he peered through his cracked visor, he realized that one of the Goliath's turrets aimed at him. A hasty scan of his HUD wasn't encouraging. His armor's shields were at twenty percent and certainly couldn't deflect a shot at this point. While his gauntlet shield was at thirty-three percent and slowly charging so might be able to protect him, there was a strong chance that doing so could overload and break it. Possibly, he acknowledged morosely, it might even fry the gauntlet.

A red light flashed in the turret, which immediately prompted him to activate his bounce jets as he began to slide down. They launched him across the room and over the laser blast. He took hold of his hammer and pressed the button on the handle that activated the booster on the rear of the weapon seconds before he was about to collide with the giant mech. He roared as he pounded it into the side of the Goliath's head to create a large crater and a crack that spread from the top part of the head to below the neck.

"We have an opening!" the military officer shouted and indicated the damage the titan had caused. "Demolitionists, focus on the weak point and fire!" he roared. Two ran up, one with a cannon and the other with a launcher. They aimed as Luke landed and fired as the enemy attempted to right itself and eliminate him with one of its cannons. The heavies fired together and the missile struck the target first, followed seconds later by the charged blast from the cannon. While they weren't able to destroy the head, they caused additional damage that extended the crack down the mechanical and into its chest plate. The weapon aimed at Luke failed.

"It's busted," he shouted and twirled his hammer. "Bust it more."

"Everyone fire as one," the officer ordered and the group released a combined barrage that attempted to obliterate it. The Goliath tried to push them back with its turrets as it struggled to stabilize itself, but they were destroyed quickly by another missile from one of the demolitionists and a grenade thrown by a raider. Luke was joined by two other military titans. One held a hammer similar to his while the other held a large mace.

He studied the latter weapon with real curiosity. "How does that compare to a hammer?"

"Have you never given one a whirl?" the man asked and he shook his head. The military heavy pressed a switch and prongs emerged all around the spherical head and began to glow. "Have a look." He charged the Goliath and activated his jets when he was a few yards away. They enabled him to leap onto the mech's torso and he drove his mace into the giant robot. The chest burst open when a wave of energy was dispersed from the weapon on contact and surged from the weapon in a blue flash.

"Heh, pretty lights." Luke chuckled, grasped his hammer, and nodded at the other titan. "But let us show him what the classics can do." The man held his hammer aloft as they both raced forward once the mace-wielding titan had retreated. Both followed his movements and jumped at the Goliath while it was besieged by volleys from the rest of the group. They each pressed the triggers on their hammer, condensed the kinetic force stored inside their weapons, and struck the enemy together. The force of their attack shattered its midsection and it broke apart. The top half of the machine fell in pieces while the bottom toppled to the side. Luke and his attack partner landed and the military titan clapped him on the shoulder as the rest of the team roared in victory.

The military officer approached them. "Moments like these are why it's always good to have a couple of titans at your side," he remarked and gestured down the hall. "But we have to get back there. We've lost enough time and they will need our help to keep the Omegas—" He was cut off by a rumble that made the floor shudder. Luke stared in disbelief and concern as arcs of white energy destroyed the doors to the lab. Ark soldiers and Omegas retreated in fear.

"I know it's only a few hundred yards down," the titan muttered. "But are we gonna get there in time to help at all?"

"Don't think," the officer shouted and began to sprint toward the lab. "Just move—double-time!"

"I have the dreadnaught in my sights," Chief yelled and Kaiden heard a loud whirring that seemed to echo around the station as the EI positioned the cannons. *"You might wanna plug your ears. It'll be loud!"*

"I can't right now. I'm still working with Chiyo," he replied. "How are things on your end, Chi?"

"Energy is spiking in the bomb," she explained. Sizzles, snaps, and pulses were audible over the comms. "It's sending out errant waves of powerful energy. The droids nearby have all ceased to function and it's melted the armor of a few Omegas who were hit."

"Shit, be careful," he responded.

"I'd rather be rid of it entirely," she retorted and he snickered quietly. "Right. We're linked up. I've already had Kaitō find a remote destination, but you'll have to make sure the gate is not shut during transfer and to guide it through the—"

"Hold up. I thought I was done?" he protested. "What happens if I fuck the next part up?"

"There is a good chance the bomb doesn't travel the full distance and will more than likely explode on-planet or even in the middle of the battle in space," she explained.

"Fuck that!" Kaiden balked. "Chief, take over."

"Do what?" the EI demanded. *"But I'm about to fire the big guns."*

"I'll do that, but this is more important and you're better at it," he pointed out with no leniency in his tone.

"Well, yeah, but—dammit! Get off the controls," he welched and appeared in the screen as Kaiden stepped back and

moved to the cannon controls. For a brief moment, the EI turned an annoyed red. *"Talk about blue-balling a guy."*

"This should have been how it was to begin with," the ace pointed out as he studied the screen where it showed a reticule aimed toward the dreadnaught closing in on the blockade of military ships. "Damn, that's a big bastard," he commented and turned his attention to the side of the screen that showed various outputs for the cannon. "Hey, the power output is only a little over half," he noted and adjusted it to full. "Did leaving the suite dumb you down that much?"

"All right, Chi. I have it locked. We're ready to—wait. What was that, Kaiden?" Chief asked but by this point, Kaiden already hovered his hand over the large red button to fire the cannon.

"Firing!" the ace shouted and pounded the button. He lurched back as both barrels of the cannons fired at the dreadnaught and the station was jostled enough that lights began to go on and off. Shocked, he caught hold of the edge of the console and hauled himself toward it to stare as two massive blasts of blue energy rocketed through the dreadnaught and combined in a massive eruption.

The crew inside the *Fenrir*, all the blockade ships, and those who could see the blast from the windows at the edge of the station, all stopped momentarily. They gaped at the destruction wrought by the attack. Fighting soon continued, but damn if it wasn't impressive.

"Good God. It's a damn good thing they never had the weapons ready," Kaiden exclaimed.

"Dammit, Kaiden!" Chief remonstrated furiously. *"You're lucky I still had access to the station. A blast at full power could*

have caused a temporary shutdown. I had to divert power to make sure the link between us and Chiyo didn't crash."

The ace looked bemused. "What? Shit, sorry," he stated with honest regret. "Have you been able to get the bomb away yet?"

"I'm waiting for Chiyo to press the go button," he replied.

"I have the gate working on my end," Chiyo responded. The box containing the bomb began to brighten increasingly with both the energy of the device and the beginnings of the warp field. "The coordinates are set...only a little longer."

"Hey, stop!" Indre shouted as two of the Omega scientists made a break for it.

"Don't bother, Indre," the infiltrator told her. "If this goes wrong, they have nowhere they can run to fast enough to avoid it."

"She is quite right," the lead technician confirmed. "If you manage to pull this off, I must say I will be impressed."

"You should be thankful," the agent snapped. "We're the ones fixing your mistake and saving your ass."

"It wasn't a mistake," he corrected. "It was an order."

She scowled and held her gun trained on him. "See how well that defends you once we're done with this."

"I'd imagine poorly," he replied.

"I'm warping the bomb, Chief," the infiltrator stated and backed away from the console as the box glowed to its brightest hue. "It's on you now."

Energy continued to spread and Indre, Chiyo and the

scientist retreated a little farther as it moved closer to them. Chiyo worried for a moment that she was too late or the teleporter did not work properly. Soon, however, the energy condensed into itself before it vanished altogether. She raced to the console to check, but it was down. "Kaitō, what's wrong?"

"It is a momentary surge, madame, and should correct itself," the EI reassured her. He had no sooner finished his statement when the monitors turned on again. She opened a separate screen quickly and searched for energy signatures of the bomb on Earth. Thankfully, she found nothing.

"Chief, are you there?" she asked, "Is it gone?" She received no response. "Chief?"

"Sorry, darlin'. I had to concentrate and make sure I didn't slingshot it into a star or something," he finally responded with a mirthful chuckle. *"I'm happy to report the bomb is gone and has done a grand total of zero damage to anyone or anything. Great work."*

She released a sigh of relief, looked at Indre, and nodded. Her teammate reciprocated and even the Omega technician seemed somewhat pleased. "We still have to deal with the rest of the enemy forces here, but our main objective is complete," she reported. "I take it you are on schedule?"

"For the most part. We still gotta deal with all the hostiles and free the civvies, but we have control of the station so it's only a matter of keeping it," Chief confirmed. *"I'd tell the others to wrap it up quickly if you want to join the main attack on the embassy and the push to defeat Merrick. Once we have our foothold, I doubt we will have the luxury of waiting around—not that many will want to."*

"Understood," Chiyo said. "Assuming we have the advantage and now that the bomb is dealt with, they'll probably send small teams to join the main force."

"Still, there's a fair number of scraps and enemies along the way here. You'd better make sure you're in fast and agile ships unless you want to be drawn into it," the EI warned. *"I gotta go. Your boyfriend found out how to manually control the cannons so I have to make sure he doesn't go hog-wild and drain the station's power or cause any damage to friendly forces."*

"Boyfriend?" she whispered and chuckled softly. "I suppose so. Tell him I hope we'll see each other soon."

"I'm on it. Be safe until then." He dropped out of the link.

As she took a moment to breathe, a ruckus at the doors of the lab heralded a group of soldiers who raced in with Luke in the front. "We're here. Point us at them," he roared before reality clicked in and he noticed the only remaining soldiers were friendlies. He sighed, planted his hammer, and rubbed his helmet. "Shit, I take it we missed it?"

"You did." Indre twirled her gun as two military soldiers took the lead technician away. "But all things considered, that wasn't a bad thing."

"The bomb has been taken care of, but there are still more enemies to deal with," Chiyo pointed out as she crossed to her teammates, followed by Genos, Cameron, Marlo, and Indre. "And we can begin prepping ships to take us to the main assault force. Do you care to join me?"

The titan looked at the military officer, who nodded. "I'll get on the link with the other officers and captains. We'll get ships ready," he replied. "Head to extraction, but you might wanna run some quick repairs first."

Luke holstered his hammer onto his back and saluted.

"Yes, sir. I'll try to find someone to take a look." He turned and followed Chiyo out of the lab. "But I ain't missing my flight."

"I wonder what happened to the other infiltration teams," Genos said thoughtfully. "I have not heard from them."

"I checked in," Indre responded and took her tablet out. "They were a little sidetracked, but they've put considerable work in." She tossed the device to Genos, who looked at the screen with Cameron and Marlo peering over his shoulder to see the feed from outside the stronghold. Animus droids attacked Omega and Ark soldiers and automated turrets fired on enemy vehicles.

"I see." Genos passed it to the agent again. "It has been quite a productive day hasn't it?"

CHAPTER THIRTY-NINE

"Targets marked," one of the Resistance marksmen reported. "Ready for takedown."

"Do it," Sasha ordered. He and several other soldiers turned the corner and fired no more than two shots apiece to annihilate an approaching group of Omegas and droids. "Well done. Move in."

"Commander, this is Blue Leader," a voice announced over the commlink. "We're in position at the rear of the central station and are heading in."

"Roger. We're approaching the front entry," he responded. "We will breach momentarily."

"Yellow Leader here," another officer interjected. "We've reached our destination and are ready to come down on your mark."

"We may want to get this wrapped up fast," Blue Leader told them. "We've received reports that Icarus is already under our control so we're lagging now."

"I've kept an eye on the situation," Sasha replied and motioned for the two demolitionists in his team to prepare the explosives for the door. "Icarus is currently under our control, but they still have more hostiles to contend with than we do." His men placed the breaching charges on the door with quiet efficiency. "The race is still on. We are prepared to breach. Yellow, the explosion will be your signal. Blue, flank and help us eliminate any remaining targets in the room. We'll have Xuanzang under our control momentarily."

"Roger," Blue Leader acknowledged.

"We're waiting for the boom," Yellow confirmed.

Sasha gestured for his team to back away and let Isaac scan the room, mark targets, and send them to his soldiers' HUDs. Once that was done, he nodded to the demolition-ists who each pressed buttons on their gauntlets to activate the charges and blow the doors. The team proceeded rapidly into the central chamber.

Quick, precise shots felled enemy troops and droids before most could aim sufficiently to fire on them. A team of twelve military soldiers dropped from above and most landed on Omegas as they joined the fray. The doors to the back entrance opened and a small unit of Arbiter droids attempted to assist their masters but were mown down when Blue Team approached from behind.

"Sandra, Collen, with me," Sasha ordered as they hurried to the control room "Techies, follow us. Let us take this station from the enemy."

Merrick scowled at the battle that raged for miles in front of the embassy. He still had a large line of defense, but he had already lost control of Icarus. It was prudent to believe that Xuanzang was not far behind. He looked at the shimmer on the outside of the window of his office. With control of both those stations, they could force the shields down, an emergency contingency they had in place in case the embassy was taken. He had to admit, despite how little he thought of their leadership, the former world council were annoyingly practical in other areas—or simply cleverly paranoid.

The bomb was gone now as well, and they had access to the gates, or at least one of them. Fortunately, it didn't seem they could use it to bring anything through yet, only send things away. This meant they could not gather any reinforcements still caught in deep space for now. All his plans, conceived and prepared over many years, had been countered by strategies concocted in a matter of months or even days. This whole preposterous war should anger him, but a piece of him was relieved and even proud. What was it? Perhaps, even if he lost this day, humanity could be prepared to face the oncoming destruction he foresaw?

It would still be his doing. This was humanity improved by having to live a life based on its own decisions, not ruled from on high by a council of uncompassionate and meek leaders who would rather hide their faults than admit to them and improve. He had revealed their faults, and those who remained saw them and took control of the world for themselves. It was merely a pity they saw the same faults in him because it showed that they were, in part, still blind.

He walked to a large capsule and turned the dial on the front to open it. A set of armor rested inside, one he had commissioned over a year before. He was prepared as well, although he had not thought he would have to don it for defensive reasons. It was silver with glowing white lines through the chest and arms and included a helmet with a darkened visor and protruding rivets at the top, akin to a crown. He had hoped to wear this as his battle armor for when he led his armies to show the people he would not simply hide behind the lives of others. His purpose was to lead them and fight alongside them.

He would prove that now but under less heroic actions. But as he went through his remaining options, a dark thought took hold. If they wanted him to be a villain, he might have to play to that to be victorious.

―――――――

"Skilz," one of the Omega lieutenants said tentatively and turned in his chair to look the Omega leader in the eye. "Harken's dreadnaught—it's gone."

"What? Were there complications with the jammers?" he demanded.

The lieutenant shook his head "No, gone—as in it blew up." The leader's face fell and his eyes widened. "The military took control of Icarus, powered the cannons, and obliterated the ship while he attempted to rush the blockade. That makes three dreadnaughts lost so far."

"Dammit to hell!" he cursed and thumped his fist on the holomap table. "We won't sit here anymore. Gather all surrounding assault ships and destroyers. We'll head in."

"But we're the front guard," one of the other lieutenants countered. "We can't simply leave. Besides, we haven't finished checking the ship to see if it has the same problem as the one that blew up the other—"

"Don't worry about it," he snapped. "He wouldn't do anything to us right now because he's still crazy enough to think he'll win this."

His muttering earned him confused looks from most of the crew around him. "What are you talking about?"

He looked up and waved them off. "Like I said, don't worry about it." He walked to the captain's chair, sat, and folded his arms. "Now, get moving. I'm not gonna sit here and be that bastard's shield. We'll handle this like Omegas, got it?"

The crew nodded and some shouted and hollered in approval as orders were sent out. He looked at one of the screens that displayed the embassy and a part of him realized it might be one of the last things he ever saw. Hopefully, seeing him disobey his orders would be one of the last things Merrick ever saw.

***

"A dropship is waiting for us," Flynn reminded his team. "Let's get a move on."

"We're already running," Cameron retorted as they raced up the stairs. The marksman was the first to reach the balcony and the side door to the dropship opened as soon as he appeared. The others filed in one at a time and a few military soldiers joined them.

"Come on, now," the pilot remonstrated sharply. "We might be winning this but there's still danger around so no loitering."

"We're in," Luke shouted and slammed the door. "Let's head out."

The man nodded, engaged the thrusters, and flew out of the stronghold's perimeter. "Nice work in there," he complimented. "Disabling those automated turrets made this an easy pick-up."

"That was the other team," Chiyo replied. "But I'll send your compliments."

"How long will it take to reach the station in this dingy?" Marlo asked as he set his cannon on the seat beside him.

"Are you kidding? This is a Thunderbird dropship, made for quick extractions and drop-offs, not long-range travel," the pilot protested and pointed to the horizon. "I'll take you to a destroyer. You'll be able to run repairs and rearm yourselves before you head out from there."

"A destroyer?" Indre asked. "Can we afford to take one out of the fight?"

"If we can afford to take six of them out along with assaults and corsairs, I think one is fine." The pilot chuckled.

The soldiers looked at one another in real interest. "Is the sky battle going that good?"

"It was hardly a battle," the man explained. "The initial barrage when we arrived dealt with most of their bigger ships. I think most of their space superiority came from the embassy or other bases. They weren't prepared for an assault of this caliber from us, especially so suddenly."

"There still appears to be some skirmishing," Genos noted and peered out the window at dogfights between fighter ships in the distance and a group of Ark ships engaged in battle with military destroyers and assault ships.

"I didn't say these guys were smart," the pilot quipped.

Chiyo turned her attention to the combat outside the ship. "It could be they are more afraid of what will happen if they surrender."

"Given what happened to the scientists after the raid on their facility last year," the Tsuna added, "I can say... Well, it is unsettling, although I would imagine all their options lead to death."

"I'd rather die fighting," Cameron muttered and folded his arms. "I may hate these guys' guts, but I can understand that at least."

"They could be under mind control," Flynn pointed out with a grimace. "I guess it's no use thinking about it. We have a mission to finish."

"A war to finish," Amber corrected.

"That's right." Luke nodded. "So the sooner we get there, the sooner we can help bring this to an end." He knocked on the top of the dropship a few times. "So let's get to the destroyer already. My hammer is getting cold."

"Does that matter much?" Marlo asked.

The titan shrugged. "You know what I mean."

"You're certainly a feisty team." The pilot laughed. "Hold on, we're heading in."

Raza and Ken'ra looked up as Lok entered the war room and bowed. "War Chief, the hunters we sent ahead have reported success in their battles. One of the stations is under Resistance control and the other should be taken shortly."

"What are the losses?" Raza asked and stood to his full height.

"They are minimal. A few warriors lost their lives in the fighting, but we had a larger force perish in the destruction of an enemy ship. They were caught on board when it was destroyed from within."

He nodded solemnly. "They will be honored when we return. Make sure their names are remembered."

"Of course, War Chief." Lok straightened. "However, the hunters and warriors aboard are growing restless. We have yet to unleash our full might upon the enemy."

"I know," he muttered and paced slowly. "The fighting is too spread out for a coordinated assault right now. I had hoped we would be assaulting the embassy by now and could unleash the full might of our forces."

"What about the power of the vessel?" Ken'ra suggested. "This ship holds more than any ship we have seen amongst the enemy forces."

"I agree once again. However, we were not able to calibrate the weapons systems properly before departure," Raza pointed out. "It would be a large drain on our resources if we used the main cannon for more than two shots. As a result, we should focus on gaining the maximum impact and get the best use out of our weapons rather than simply fire them out of boredom."

"War Chief!" a pilot called from the bridge. "We have enemies approaching, sir."

"How many?" he asked as his two chiefs moved to stand at his side.

"A group of eleven vessels, sir. They seem to have broken off from the defensive line in front of the embassy. From their visual course, they seem to be heading toward one of the stations and will no doubt attempt to strike where the military blockade is weakest."

"I see," he muttered and looked at Lok and Ken'ra. "Engage them. We now have an opportunity to properly honor our new ship with the blood of our prey." Raza stretched to retrieve his ceremonial helmet from the table and donned it calmly. "And give our hunters another chance for glory and trophies."

CHAPTER FORTY

Sasha pounded his boot on the head of a fallen droid. "Technicians, get in there and take control," he ordered and the four of them in his team hurried into the central control room of Xuanzang. "I want this station under military command in ten minutes or less."

"Yes, sir!" they called in unison, cast their EIs into the station, and set to work. He stepped out of the room and studied the situation. The other soldiers in his team as well as teams Blue and Yellow swept the area to eliminate any remaining threats and make sure no new ones got through.

Those who had accompanied him walked beside him. "Take positions here," he ordered and pointed at the doorway. "I'll go to check in."

"Sir." Both nodded and stood guard as he walked away.

"Isaac, open channels to Red, Green, and Purple teams," he instructed as he left the central chamber.

"At once, sir. Channels are open and ready."

"This is Commander Sasha. How has the recovery of the civilians progressed?" he asked briskly.

"This is Red Leader. We've reached one of the entrances to the underside of the station," a man reported. "It's been a hell of a time breaking in and I have a couple of techies giving it their best, but it may be under a lockdown code. If so, there's not much we can do from here."

"This is Purple Leader," another officer announced. "We're closing in and are about five hundred yards off. There are guards on standby but we're dealing with them no problem."

"Green here and our sitrep is much the same as Purple, but we have more internal defenses," a woman stated. "Nothing we can't handle—turrets and reprogrammed security droids—but they are dotted all along the halls and hinder our progress. Still, we should be at the doors within ten minutes."

"Understood. We've taken control of the central station and should have access to security measures within ten minutes. We'll get those doors unlocked once we do," Sasha assured them. He peered around a corner to where a military titan pierced an advanced Arbiter droid with a large blade.

"Commander, we have approaching enemy ships," one of the captains of the blockade declared.

"How many and where?" he demanded.

"It looks like eleven—a mixture of assault ships and destroyers. The indications are they broke off from the main force in front of the embassy and are coming from the rear. We're less defended here and the front of the blockade has to remain steadfast as they are still dealing with strikes."

"Other vessels should be nearby. Send a call for help," he suggested.

"Most are currently engaged in combat. A few responded but were intercepted on the way. Xuanzang is not as heavily fitted with weaponry as Icarus, but once you have control, please prepare them for— Hold on, something is coming...it's the Sauren ship!"

"Raza?" the commander queried. "Open a connection to your feed."

"Certainly," the captain replied. Sasha opened a small screen in his HUD and while he made sure to keep track of his surroundings, he watched the large Sauren ship fly in front of the blockade. The front of the vessel glowed.

"They are powering their main cannon," he noted and immediately wondered what kind of firepower they had on board. Sauren weren't known for that. Their hunting ability and ground troops made most fear them as adversaries. They were hunters and warriors but weren't space combatants unless it came to raiding ships. Surprisingly, it fired its main cannon and a stream of white energy sliced through several of the enemy craft in a single streak. Several smaller ships left the main vessel and turned toward the remaining Omegas as they quickly changed course.

He had forgotten that this vessel was a combined Sauren and Tsuna design, and the Tsuna were certainly much more well-known for their firepower.

"What the hell was that?" Skilz bellowed. "Report. What's going on?"

"Some big-ass ship eliminated five of ours in one shot," a crewman told him. "We lost three assault ships and two destroyers, and we have incoming."

"Bring it onscreen," he ordered and scowled at a holoimage of the massive ship that had obliterated almost half his fleet. "What is that?" he demanded. "It's not a military ship."

"That's the Sauren vessel," one of the lieutenants responded. "I thought Sauren didn't have ships with guns that could deliver that kind of damage."

"Sir, those other ships are still approaching. I think they plan to try to board us," the crewman shouted.

"Like hell they will. Don't let them get near us," Skilz commanded seconds before his ship was rocked by impacts.

"Pods have breached the hull," the man informed him.

"It looks like we don't have a say on whether they board or not," one of the lieutenants muttered.

The Omega leader merely growled and snatched his helmet and machine gun from next to his chair. "Then we'll have to kick them off!" he roared and dragged his helmet on. "Everyone to arms."

"How are things going, Chief?" Kaiden asked and checked the screens that displayed the blockade.

"*Fairly good. The Omegas are giving us a wide berth now that we have the cannons online. We have some of the damaged ships from the fighting coming in for shelter as the hangars are mostly clear. I sent a message to send technicians to get in here and take over."*

"Hey, Kaiden." He turned as Silas entered the control room, followed by Izzy, Jaxon, and Mack. "Everything is finally clear out there. The military team went to help clear the rest of the station."

"Cool. Chief has everything on lock," he explained. "We'll be relieved soon."

"Is there anything to report on the civilians?" Jaxon asked.

"They've been found. I had to unlock the doors to the under-belly of the station," Chief replied and appeared in the air in his avatar form. *"No surprise, but they weren't exactly treated well while under the AO's thumb. Most of the medics on the station are being sent there to help. They apparently all had to share what remained of their meager rations. Needless to say, they are quite relieved now."*

"Baby steps," Silas noted. "I'm glad to give them some hope, but we still gotta deal with the big bad before we can say this is all over."

"Most of the preliminary fighting is wrapping up," Kaiden stated. "Chiyo said the force on Earth will send teams up now that they have completed their main objective."

"That fast?" Izzy was impressed. "Do they already have control of the stronghold?"

"Not quite," Chief answered. *"But the big threat was the bomb, which they dealt with thanks to a little help from yours truly."*

"Are you not gonna mention the fact that you almost

blew it because you wanted to fire a big gun?" Kaiden snickered.

The EI spun to fix him with an affronted look. *"Technically, I almost blew it by relying on your technological skills,"* he retorted sharply. *"I will admit that was a mistake on my part. I've been too lax in trusting your brain. I'll make sure to factor it in from here on."*

The ace rolled his eyes. "Yeah, yeah, smartass."

"Is there any news from the other station?" Mack asked and leaned against a wall. "Are they close to taking control too?"

"I haven't heard anything from Sasha, but he was heading to the control center around the same time we were."

"Is the chancellor also in the fight?" Jaxon asked in surprise. "I thought he would direct everything from Earth."

"Yeah, me too, but I guess that's not his style." Kaiden shrugged. "If they are about to plant the flag, we should get ready to head out again."

"Do you think they'll send us to the embassy this quickly?" Silas asked. "The whole point to taking these stations was to give us a foothold near the embassy to prepare for the final assault."

"Technically, it was also so we could take the shields down," Chief explained. *"And I've tried a couple of times but without confirmation from Xuanzang it's a no-go, so I don't think they have control of it quite yet."*

"I doubt they will make us wait long," Jaxon interjected. "While these stations are intended as our foothold for the time being, having the embassy so close with a bulk of their forces ready means we are not safe to rest for long."

"And personally, I don't want to wait when we're so close to victory." Kaiden pushed aside his next words when he received a call on the comm from Otto.

"Kaiden, head to the hangar," the technician instructed. "I have a shuttle waiting to bring you and the others onboard the *Fenrir*."

"I'm still waiting for the—oh." A group of technicians entered the control room and Chief appeared in his HUD again as they took over. "Okay, never mind, but why do you need us on the ship?"

"*Fenrir* is one of the vessels that has been cleared to assault the embassy," his teammate told him. "We've already been given the go-ahead for an initial assault and it will happen within the next few hours."

"Damn, we really are moving in for the kill now, huh?" Mack muttered.

"You need to get aboard, get patched up, and check your weapons and all that. If you think the first leg was fun, this final stretch will be a hell of a lot more exciting."

"I'm looking forward to it." The ace ended the call and gestured for the others to join him as he left the room. When they stepped into the main area, they had to take hasty steps back as two Omega soldiers plummeted to splatter almost at their feet. As one, the team looked up. A Sauren stood several floors above and peered at the bodies to make sure they didn't move again before he left. "Huh, I almost forgot they were running around," he quipped. "I wonder what Raza is up to."

"We've had more impacts throughout the ship," an Omega lieutenant reported. "I am attempting to compensate with shields. Who knows how many of those scaly bastards are running loose in our ship now?"

"It doesn't matter if it's ten or a hundred," Skilz snapped and brandished his gun. "We'll kill them all and mount their heads like they'd do to us."

"And that doesn't worry you at all, Skilz?" the lieutenant asked. "Sauren are feared for a reason. We've tangled with them before."

"And we killed them, didn't we?" he replied. "It's proof that they aren't immortal."

"We lost eight to ten men per kill," the other man pointed out. "Maybe we should be in a bigger group."

"We have more than enough men here." He turned and his eyebrows bunched in confusion. "Wait, where the hell did the others go?"

The three men who were with him spun and realized only one was following them. "Weren't there a few more guys with us?" the lieutenant asked in bemusement.

"Maybe they broke away," one of the others suggested.

"I didn't tell them to," Skilz muttered. "Where the hell did they go?"

"Hey, did you hear that?" the third man asked. The small group quieted and caught the distinctive sound of something dripping on metal. One of the mercs crept forward and something dropped again from above. He looked up instinctively at a rather large hole—like a powerful force had savaged the ceiling—before a long tail snaked out of the aperture, wound around his throat, and hauled him up.

"Holy shit!" the lieutenant shouted as the remaining three aimed their weapons at the ceiling and prepared to fire. The wall beside them erupted and a large amber-colored Sauren battered through. Without pause, he thrust his claws into the two mercs and the lieutenant and pinned them to the wall.

Skilz backed away and aimed at the warrior, but before he could fire, a claw encircled his weapon and crushed it. He turned and was skewered in the stomach by a spear that pierced easily through his armor and lifted him off the floor. He looked into Raza's eyes, and the War Chief bared his fangs at him and growled. "Humph, he is hardly a worthy trophy." He opened his jaws and Skilz's last image was of the inside of the massive maw.

CHAPTER FORTY-ONE

S asha stood on the edge of the Xuanzang station. His vantage point provided a sweeping vista as the Omega ships that were previously a threat were now besieged by Raza's warriors. Some still tried to retreat and a couple had ceased to function, all while the Sauren's primary vessel stood off to the side, prepared to fire at them once again. It was almost hilariously macabre.

A soldier walked up behind him. "It's a good thing they are on our side, right, sir?"

"Indeed." He nodded. "I never had to fight a Sauren as an enemy. An old friend of mine did—not much intimidated him—but even he admitted it would have been a while before he voluntarily went toe to toe with one again."

"Sergeant Wolfson, yeah?" The soldier realized his mistake quickly when the commander turned slowly to look at him. "I'm sorry, sir. I know it must still be painful to think about—"

"It's all right," he stated quietly and returned his focus to the ships. "It's better that people still think of him and remember him—better than fading away."

"I…understand, sir." The young man cleared his throat. "I came to report. The station is now fully under our control, as is Icarus. We are moving the civilians out and ships are docking in the hangars. We'll launch an offensive strike at the main target soon."

"I see." Sasha put his rifle away. "Are there any remaining hostiles on board?"

"We're sweeping to make sure," the soldier clarified, "but it appears most have bailed, given the number of escape pods that have been launched recently. The techies in the control room are uploading our IDs and now use the security system to scan for any remaining soldiers. We're confident that there are no more hostile droids."

"That is good to hear." He began to walk away. "I'll head to the hangars to join the assault."

His companion took a few steps after him. "Uh, wouldn't it be better to wait to join one of the later waves, sir? We could use your help to monitor the station until everything—"

"There are many other officers and commanders on board," Sasha said without breaking his stride. "And as I said, we should always remember those close to us whom we have lost. The best way I could do that is to help to bring this to an end as quickly as possible."

"Damn, there's been some brutal fighting up here," Luke muttered and stared at one of the screens that displayed a view of space outside. Broken and battered ships and bodies floated through the abyss. "The Omegas did this with one assault?"

"They have a rather substantial force," Genos explained and studied one of the screens as well. "But this ship here, and this one—both seem to be Omega ships. Repair and patchwork suggest they were junkers, but the recent damage looks like the explosion came from the inside, along with impact damage. They could have been sent as large missiles to attack our forces."

"They kamikazed our ships?" Flynn asked, almost incredulous. "If they are so desperate, why not give up? There's no point in wasting your forces."

"I'm sure the ships were not populated," the Tsuna said.

"And as we've discussed, they may not have the option to," Chiyo added. "I don't have sympathy for the Omegas and Ark soldiers. They have committed crimes even without the help of Merrick and the AO, but that doesn't mean there isn't a gun to their heads right now given the circumstances."

"And it's not like we would give them leeway after we win," Amber agreed.

Indre pushed a tool into one of her drones and deftly extracted a piece of shrapnel. "I think Chiyo means that Merrick might be forcing them to fight. You have to admit, even for a mercenary company—and no matter how many creds he is paying them—there comes a time where no amount is worth the hassle."

"Or blood," Flynn interjected.

The door to their compartment slid open to admit a military officer. "Hey. I was passing through and wanted to tell you the stations have been taken. We are preparing for the final assault and this destroyer will be a part of the force that initiates the first strike."

This drew the focus of the entire group. "When is it happening?" Chiyo asked.

"Soon. The current guess is within an hour. We're trying to assess the damage to our forces and to designate who will go with each wave. Since we're reasonably fresh, we'll be a part of the first force. If you need to get patched up or need a breather, I would say something now so you can take a shuttle to one of the stations."

The team members looked at one another and no one raised a hand. "I'd say it looks like we're ready to continue kicking ass," Flynn said for all of them.

The officer nodded. "That's good to hear. Still, double-check your equipment before we commence the attack." He saluted them. "Fight well."

They responded in kind and he lowered his arm and pressed the switch to close the door again.

"Well, it looks like this is it, boys and girls." Flynn grinned and checked his rifle. "Are we all ready to end a war?"

"Welcome aboard, guys," Otto said, and Julius waved as Kaiden and his team stepped off the shuttle.

"For however long it lasts." The ace chuckled and folded his arms. "Wait, how are we gonna board the embassy? We used most of the pods to get onto the station."

"That's why we're meeting you here," Julius explained.

"While we have a few pods left, the fighting outside the station will be constant. It is doubtful the *Fenrir* will be able to get close enough for the pods to be effective. Instead, we'll use the shuttles, escorted by fighters and interceptors."

"So we should simply stay put, then?" Silas asked and prepared to sit in the shuttle next to Izzy, who hadn't moved.

"Well, if you want to go into battle with only moderately durable armor," the technician said and pointed to Silas' and Kaiden's broken armor before he gestured to the back of the hangar. "They have repair stations set up and also all the remaining gadgets, grenades, and knick-knacks you could want...assuming they still have it as they aren't as stocked up now after the initial assault."

"It would probably be best for us to at least go through basic armor repairs," Jaxon suggested. "We should also recharge our shields."

"And probably see if they have any spare cores," Mack agreed.

The ace shrugged. "It can only help. We'll be ready." A light flashed in his HUD and a message appeared. *Omega forces are mobilizing. Prepare for battle. Final assault to begin in twenty.*

"Well...shit," he muttered and the team hurried to the repair station as the *Fenrir* began to break from the blockade.

Raza tossed the body of the Omega soldier aside and

looked around the bridge. "Without the power of the vessel, they seem to be pitiful prey." He studied the forces he and the two chiefs had decimated with such ease.

"War Chief!" Ken'ra called and the War Chief looked up as the Sauren checked one of the military tablets and handed it to him. "It appears it is time."

He took the device and looked at the brief message, nodded, and handed it back. "So we shall finally bring this farce to a close and avenge the lost with the head of this Merrick." He growled and pressed a switch on his spear to shorten it. Raza moved to place it on his belt but instead, looked at it before he shifted his gaze to Ken'ra and offered it to him. "Take control of the forces here. Lok and I will return to the ship and assist in making a path to the embassy. Once you have destroyed the remaining forces here, join us quickly."

The chief nodded and took the spear. "It will be done, War Chief."

Raza returned the nod and strode out of the bridge. "Come, Lok!" he ordered. The Sauren dropped from the levels above, his teeth and claws a bloody red. "We should not keep the prize beast waiting."

CHAPTER FORTY-TWO

"Sir? The military is preparing to assault our base," a concerned voice stated over the comm on the desk. "As in right now, sir. They are amassing ships in front of both stations and will launch an attack from two sides."

"Three," Merrick corrected as he drew the helmet of his armor on. "You forget the forces they are bringing in from Earth along with those breaking from the initial battle."

"Um...right, sir," the underling agreed. "I recommend that you leave. They will have targeted you and I'm not sure how long we can hold them off before they—"

"I will not run like a coward," he stated, his voice monotone. He approached the window and surveyed his forces with a calm others might have found unnerving. If he zoomed in with his visor, he could make out the forces assembling against him far in the distance. "If I cannot win this day, my last act will be to show them what I was willing to risk to achieve the preservation of humanity." He activated a switch on his gauntlet and powered up the rest of his armor. "Maybe then, they will see their folly."

"Understood, sir," the man said and signed off. The AO leader sat in his chair and shook his head. If this was to be the day he fell, it wouldn't merely be his last day. It would be the end of the Arbiter Organization and the Omega Horde as well.

"Well, things got damn real damn fast." Luke dragged his helmet on again. "Did we even get to a station?"

"It appears we will be a part of the force striking from the center," Genos explained and studied a holoscreen that provided the formation of the ships. "They said we are to be a part of the first strike, correct? It appears this will be rather large for an initial assault."

"We have a host of enemies to push through, mate," Flynn replied and rested his rifle against his chest and shoulder. "I assume the second wave will be backup for the ships fighting outside the embassy, and whatever is left will be backup for the forces heading inside."

"That sounds correct," Chiyo agreed. "Which means we'll have to make do with what we start with."

"Heh, it'll be enough," Luke affirmed and thumped a fist into his hand. "I can't wait to introduce that bastard Merrick to the business side of my hammer."

Genos looked at him. "Isn't that technically both ends?"

"It's a figure of speech, buddy," the titan replied and patted him on the shoulder.

"It's a pity we couldn't meet up with the others." Amber sighed. "It would have been nice to go in as a group."

"I'm sure we'll meet up," Indre said reassuringly as she

placed the repaired drone into her pack. "We gotta focus on surviving to see them, though."

"Do you think Kaiden will wait?" Flynn challenged them. "He's been very anxious to face Merrick. I doubt he's the only one, so that will only make him want to be the first to reach him."

Chiyo looked away and gazed in the direction of the embassy. "He may, but I'm not worried."

"Really? You think he can defeat the guy alone?" Amber asked.

The infiltrator raised an eyebrow. "You've seen what he is like when he wants nothing more than to win," she replied. "And he promised we would meet again."

"Can you still not connect?" Kaiden asked as he picked his repaired chest plate up and put it on.

"*Nah. They might be too far back or there's simply too much interference right now. There are many channels going at once,*" Chief explained.

"Then we'll have to make sure to connect once we've landed." He retrieved Sire and placed it on his back as he headed toward the shuttle. The opening to the hangar was only sealed by a shield so allowed him to look into space at a dozen other ships waiting alongside. "It looks like it's almost time."

"*Drink it in, partner. This'll be the last time you see a force on a scale like this,*" Chief said. His eye shrank, then enlarged. "*Hopefully.*"

The ace narrowed his eyes and peered beyond the ships

and into the distance. Although he couldn't see it, he stared directly at the embassy. "This would've been around the time we would take our final, right?"

"Almost." Chief nodded. *"I think this'll count toward your graduation."*

He chuckled and stepped aboard the shuttle. "I'm in good with the chancellor. I think he'd agree."

"Do you want me to contact him? He's close enough," Chief offered.

Kaiden sat and nodded. "Yeah, him and Raza if you can."

"Bringing them up."

Chief opened a commlink with both the War Chief and chancellor. Raza seemed to accept the call, but the ace could hear nothing. Sasha joined a few moments later. "Hello again, Kaiden."

"Hey, Sasha. I had hoped Raza could join us but—"

"This is Raza, can you hear me?" the War Chief asked and finally joined the call.

"Ah, good, you were able to join us," Sasha said warmly. "I wanted to thank you for your assistance in taking Xuanzang."

"My pleasure. It was hardly a good hunt, though." The Sauren huffed with real disappointment. "My apologies for the delay. We're getting into position and the vessel is a hive of activity."

"It's all good, War Chief," Kaiden assured him. "I only wanted to tell both of you good luck and that—" He was interrupted when an alarm activated and a message popped up in his HUD. *We are go. Prepare for assault.* "Sasha, we're heading out."

"As am I," the commander replied. "I will meet you on board. I assume we shall see you there as well, Raza?"

"Of course. I will not sit idly by when Wolfson needs to be avenged." The War Chief growled for emphasis.

The ace looked down and nodded. "That was the other thing. I intend to find Merrick right away."

He could hear Sasha draw in a sharp breath. "Don't do anything too reckless, Kaiden. The initial attack will be large. Trying to push through it quickly could cost us."

"Do you have his position?" Raza asked.

"No, but I'll find him or Chief will," he reasoned.

A rough, gurgling sound issued from the Sauren. "I will help in your hunt. Merrick will be my trophy."

"He'll be my penance for Wolfson," Kaiden stated.

Sasha sighed. "I understand your feelings, both of you, but he could have retreated by now."

"Where would he go?" the War Chief asked.

"No warp gates are active. Chief made sure to turn the one we had off." The ace waved as Mack, Silas, and the others boarded the shuttle. "He wouldn't risk heading through us to reach Earth."

"You are…most likely correct," the commander agreed. "But have a little patience. I will join you as well."

"Shouldn't you lead?" Kaiden asked.

"Do you intend to stop me avenging my friend as well?" the man demanded.

A small smile formed on his lips. "It's nice to know you don't always have to play the resolute commander."

"I am very resolute," Sasha replied but was distracted by shouting on his side. The thrusters of his ship began to power up. "They are preparing to bring down the embassy's shields. We are heading out now."

The *Fenrir's* thrusters activated moments later, and the vessel shifted slightly. "We are as well. I'll stay in touch. Again, good luck to you both."

"Good fortune in the hunt." Raza silenced his connection.

"I will see you there," Sasha promised.

Kaiden deactivated the link and glanced at his team. "Are you ready?"

"About as much as we can be without a pilot," Izzy commented as a man in a blue jumpsuit entered.

"Sorry for the wait," he told them and slid into the pilot's seat. Kaiden noticed the Resistance emblem on his shoulder.

"Are you from Nexus?" he asked.

The man chuckled as he prepared the shuttle. "I was but I'm military now—five years in."

"It's nice to meet a graduate," Julius said.

"I noticed the Resistance emblem," Kaiden said with a small gesture at it. "Not all Resistance members wear it, so it isn't like it's official."

"Hey, technically, we're all Resistance now," the man replied. "Exactly like all of you are soldiers now."

He nodded and gave his team a thumbs-up. "Well, you have a point there."

CHAPTER FORTY-THREE

General Hartman and a party of other leaders and crew who had been left on Earth watched the giant holomap. Numerous icons represented their forces and moved slowly to a large collection of red icons that represented the enemy. "This is it, ladies and gentlemen," he began and focused on the group. "Today will be the day we liberate Earth."

"Excuse me, sir?" A crewman held a hand up.

"What is it, Ensign?" he asked.

"I know we have to deal with this Merrick guy for the good of everyone," the younger man stated. "But he's doing this because he believes there is a dark force coming—like maybe an alien one we don't know about. What if he turns out to be right?"

"Are you saying we should let him take over?" another soldier demanded.

The ensign held his hands up. "No, hell no! But what if there is a chance he could be right?"

"That's simple, Ensign," the general said as he turned to

look at the map. "We show here and now what humanity is willing to do to be victorious. We set an example."

The *Fenrir's* captain focused on the enemy as they approached steadily. "Don't stop for anything," he ordered. "Weapons ready. Hold nothing back."

"How many do you think we can eliminate, sir?" one of the helmsmen asked. He turned to him and wanted to say something about focusing on survival and making sure the soldiers could make it onboard. When he saw the wry grin on his face, one mirrored by other members of the crew, he realized that now, they needed to hold onto hope.

He returned the smile and stroked his beard in a show of thought. "I'm unsure, why? Did you want to place bets?"

The helmsman and crew laughed. "Sir, that doesn't sound like military professionalism."

The captain shrugged. "Perhaps not, but it doesn't answer my question, son."

The man looked around at a few members of the crew who either held hands out or called numbers. "I'll say about seven."

"Really? I intended to say three," he replied.

The helmsman frowned. "That low, sir?"

"Three destroyers," the captain corrected and held three fingers up. "The small ships don't count."

The other man laughed again. "Three destroyers eliminated by an assault ship on its own?"

"I'm sure we'll have some help," he clarified. "But I don't

want you boys and girls slacking. We need to keep things interesting."

"Fair enough." The helmsman took a tablet out. "Since we have the rules established, I'll take everyone's guesses."

"Make it quick," the captain ordered. "We're about to engage the enemy."

"War Chief, we are closing in on our prey," Lok shouted to Raza, who was seated on a throne at the top of the bridge. "The cannon has cooled enough for another shot, but we won't be able to fire it again until some time has passed if we use it now."

"Then make sure we decimate as many as we can," he ordered, stood from his seat, and pointed into the void. "Close in, prepare the cannon, and keep the shields up. We will not fire until we can cut completely through their ranks."

"Yes, War Chief." Lok thumped his chest and leapt to join the crew below. Raza looked at one of the screens around his throne and noticed that several destroyers had joined them on either side. He walked to the front of the balcony. "Remember this day, my pack!" he roared. "We shall be the force that rids this galaxy of the Omega Horde. We shall show that no one can strike at the Sauren or their allies and be safe. For honor and glory!" His proclamation drew the approving roars from throughout the ship.

Merrick maintained an almost icy calm as the military closed in and his forces prepared to intercept. However this would end, it would not be with a whimper.

"The Omega are approaching!" the helmsman shouted and the *Fenrir's* commander nodded but held firm.

"Let them come. Lock onto corsairs and junkers and get rid of the gnats first," he commanded, and his subordinate nodded and repeated the orders.

Silence descended over the bridge as the Omega ships began to move on a direct trajectory toward the line, of which the *Fenrir* was one of those in the front. "They will be in firing range in ten seconds, sir."

"Then fire in ten." He stared at the approaching forces. In his oculars, the clock counted down from ten. The cannons of the enemy vessels had begun to charge.

"Fire!" Raza bellowed and was almost hurled into his throne as the main cannon unleashed its payload into the Omega ships. It destroyed at least a dozen large vessels before it powered into the side of a dreadnaught and created a large hole.

"We have a path!" Lok shouted.

"Then cut through," Raza demanded. "Leave none alive! They have no worth as trophies."

Both sides launched volleys at each other. Fighters and all other personnel ships quickly engaged in a massive swarm as the large craft passed one another. Military assault ships and corsairs maneuvered quickly through the space the Sauren had created to move closer to the embassy. They were either intercepted by Omega forces or caught in combat.

The embassy's shields fell, but their defenses remained active. Bombers and interceptors closed in quickly and destroyed the outside turrets and cannons. A few flew past Merrick's window. The embassy would sustain damage but they wouldn't risk destroying it. They still needed access to the warp gates and to save the ambassadors and politicians aboard, not that there were many to save at this point. He observed the group of ships that now pushed toward the embassy. In one strike, they had made significant progress—more than he'd thought they would.

He walked to his cabinet and armed himself with a long blade, a shotgun, and two pistols. One option remained. It wasn't one he had wanted to resort to, but it could provide a bargaining position as one last hope. They had forced him to this, he reminded himself.

"Can we go now?" Kaiden demanded as the *Fenrir* rocked violently in response to impacts from the fighting.

"We're still not close enough," the pilot answered. "I can do amazing things in space, but there's considerable crossfire and the embassy still has their defensive cannons. We need to wait for the order to—"

"This is Captain Oliphant. All shuttles and dropships

need to leave now," he ordered. "The fighting will only get worse from here and this is your best opportunity."

"Well, my ass is covered," the pilot stated, shut the doors to the shuttle, and pulled up on his throttle. The ace sat and secured the safety harness along with the rest of his team.

"Hey, Mack, if the shuttle blows, how long do you think your shields can keep us alive?" Otto asked.

The vanguard looked at him. "Oh, we'd live through the explosion."

"Really? That's incredi—"

"We would simply suffocate once our oxygen ran out," his teammate finished as the shuttle began to head out of the hangar.

Otto's demeanor wilted and as Kaiden and Silas chuckled, the pilot looked back. "Don't worry, we'll get there," he promised and eased the craft out into space where flashes of massive laser fire and fighter ships streaked around them. "But if any of you happen to be religious, praying might help." With that, he activated the thrusters and accelerated with a suddenness that prevented a response.

CHAPTER FORTY-FOUR

"The shuttles are away, sir," a lieutenant stated and observed the holomap with Hartman.

"The first wave," he replied and gazed as the dozens of smaller dots began to swarm the map. "Even if they all make it to the embassy, it'll take a hell of a lot more than that to bring this to an end."

"Even if they are able to find and eliminate the leader?"

The general glanced at him. "I would be impressed if they could achieve that so quickly, given the circumstances," he stated. "Hundreds—potentially thousands—of enemy soldiers and droids are waiting for them there. To find their way in and be able to break through will take considerable mettle."

"Sir, it appears the Sauren vessel is moving rapidly to the embassy." The lieutenant pointed at the holomap where the large image of the ship moved inexorably toward the target with surprising speed. "It appears they are launching those chariot-like craft as well."

"So they will join the first assault?" Hartman said thoughtfully. "That may make the difference."

***

"Jesus, that was close!" Otto shouted as several large laser shots passed their shuttle.

"Would you not fall on me?" Silas demanded and shoved the techie off him. "I've barely finished making repairs."

"Rushed repairs," his teammate added and studied some of the remaining scuff marks and small cracks on the enforcer's armor.

Silas shrugged. "It's not surprising. We started when it was time to go."

"Still nothing, Chief?" Kaiden asked.

I can detect them but can't establish a link. They are probably bringing up the rear if they are on the shuttles. But they could be coming in pods. That would probably make them part of the second wave, technically, the EI clarified.

"Okay, but be sure to get me in contact when you can," he stood quickly and walked to the pilot as the shuttle jostled. "Hey, man, are we there yet?"

"What the—get the hell back in your seat," the man demanded as he swerved to the left to dodge an attack. The abrupt movement toppled Kaiden on his ass.

Some explosions outside the shuttle were rather close. "Those are probably some of the other shuttles," Izzy said mournfully.

The ace slid into his seat again. "Can you confirm that, Chief?"

"Yeah, I've kept a count of the shuttles after departure. So far, twenty-one have been destroyed, which means about fifty are left but more are coming."

"How many per shuttle?"

"Anywhere between four and eight," the EI replied. "We're looking at a few hundred soldiers on landing assuming the rest make it...damn. We lost another two."

Kaiden held Sire tightly and breathed deeply. "We'll make it and ensure they are avenged in the process."

"We're going in!" the pilot shouted and the group focused on him. "Get ready to bail. Opening the doors in twenty."

They stood and Mack activated his shields. "Get behind me, you guys."

"Do you think you can face every gun they have waiting for us in that station?" Izzy asked.

He chuckled. "Do you think I can't?"

"Please, try to keep yourself alive too," she responded and drew her SMG.

"We're coming in hot so you have to boogie. Opening the doors," the pilot announced, and he'd barely finished speaking when the doors on the left side of the shuttle opened. Mack popped a shield wall that was immediately targeted by laser fire. The shuttle landed on one of the side balconies of the embassy, given artificial gravity by a projected barrier. Kaiden's team joined several other shuttles on the landing. The vanguard leapt out, followed by the team, and they immediately engaged a group of Ark soldiers.

"I can't say I've ever been impressed by their abilities," Julius muttered. He fired a bullet from his gauntlet into the neck of one of the soldiers and his adversary stiffened and collapsed.

Kaiden delivered a charged shot into one of the approaching heavies and hurled him back. A Resistance titan killed him by skewering him with a massive blade. Izzy, Silas, Jaxon, and Otto fired as a group to force the enemy back as more shuttles swooped in to unload troops onto the balcony while other craft swirled around the embassy to locate other drop-off points.

"We need to get inside quickly," Jaxon stated as he eliminated a shotgun-wielding Ark soldier. "If they decide to drop this biosphere, that will make things complicated."

"I didn't want to sit this battle out and take the view in anyway," Kaiden responded. He drove the butt of his rifle into an Ark soldier's helmet before he drew his blade and ran it across the man's throat. "Push forward!"

By this point, their force was over sixty strong and together, they surged inside. Omega soldiers and droids soon joined the combat as the invaders pressed on toward the embassy itself. When he saw the mechanicals, Otto walked back to join a small group of other techies. They synced up hastily, opened holoscreens, or worked on the screens on their gauntlets to take control of the automated threats.

The Omega soldiers were temporarily caught off guard by the sudden attack by their own units, but once they realized what had happened, a marksman positioned himself to fire on the military techies. One took a shot in the head and another in the chest. Their combined shields broke and disrupted their hold on the droids. Several shock grenades were lobbed by military soldiers at the hostiles and massive arcs of electricity powered through them, shocked the Omegas and Ark soldiers, and shorted the mechanicals.

"Press on!" one of the officers shouted. At this point, explosions, laser fire, and kinetic shots both above and below them seemed to indicate that they had a foothold. A few more Omegas joined the fray, but when they caught sight of the fallen, they retreated hastily. The military pushed into a run behind them to pursue them through the halls.

Turrets dropped from the ceilings above, accompanied by both Arbiter and Security droids. The techies took control of some of the mechanicals, but most were mowed down along with the turrets as the team spilled out of the halls and into the foyer that overlooked the vast central lobby of the embassy.

It was surprisingly well-kept. The large fountain redesigned several years before was still standing, the banners of each race still hung proudly on the ceiling, and the large window provided a view of space. The original warp gate floated in the distance and was framed in the center, still intact. Aside from the plethora of Omega and Ark soldiers who flooded the room, it was a peaceful sight.

Kaiden leapt over the foyer railing, followed by a number of other soldiers, while teams stayed behind to fire at the Omegas from above. He landed and was immediately beset by an Omega Assassin that attacked with twin plasma blades. Before he could fire, the Assassin met an energy-charged punch to the face from Mack. It launched the would-be killer into a small group of its compatriots and the vanguard took point to generate another barrier as laser fire erupted from all sides.

"We're surrounded," Jaxon shouted, his weapon kept busy by a group of Omegas who surged from the entrance hall behind him.

"Good. It means we can't miss," Kaiden responded, retrieved a thermal, and lobbed it down the hall to where the Omegas were too bunched to scatter.

"More soldiers are joining the fun," Izzy told them. "But we're gonna need more firepower if we hope to push through at this point."

"We need demolitionists," Silas agreed as he fired his shotgun to drive an approaching Assassin droid back. "Or a team of titans."

The battle was interrupted by a chorus of roars from above—a familiar sound to Kaiden, and a frightening one to the Omegas. "How about a team of Sauren?" he asked with a grin.

Silas and Jaxon looked to where the roof was torn asunder and several Sauren bulldozed through. They plummeted onto the battalion below and the Omegas immediately began to shoot wildly as the reptiloid hunters pounded into them. Bodies were thrown carelessly and cries of pain and shock accompanied the Sauren's bloody assault.

"Yeah, that'll do it." The enforcer chuckled and hefted his weapon as their group fought toward the center of the fray.

CHAPTER FORTY-FIVE

S asha pursed his lips as the shuttle was rocked by a blast. "How is the battle going?"

"There aren't enough forces for this to be a real battle, sir. The Omegas have the upper hand when it comes to their numbers on the embassy," the pilot told him. "Any battleships here are simply to clear a path and make time for the teams to retrieve hostages and objects of importance. I'm not sure when they'll pull back."

"We should have thirty minutes at least," a marksman suggested.

"We can rule out that they will have reinforcements," the commander noted and, out of habit, checked his gun again. "We have the remaining forces on Earth, but I haven't heard about the next wave's departure."

"Don't worry about it, Commander. We've got this," a raider promised.

"Are everyone's weapons at the ready?" he asked and all his soldiers confirmed. "When we get inside the embassy and we have oxygen and gravity, unlock the doors and we'll lay down covering fire until we can find a position to slow enough for us to jump."

"The oxygen is no issue but the gravity is, sir," the pilot stated. "It looks like all our landing positions are occupied. We are being diverted toward the central area of the embassy. I see a destination I can fly through but the artificial gravity field in that chamber is out."

Sasha popped the chamber of his sniper rifle open, removed the kinetic core, and replaced it with an energy core. "Only in that section or the whole station?"

The pilot opened a holoscreen and displayed a map of the station. "Right now, only in sections C and D according to reports. Most of the battle is taking place in the central lobby and on the far side of the embassy. You'd be about five floors up and hundreds of yards away from that." He eased the shuttle through a small chamber in the guts of the embassy and entered a dark tunnel.

"That will be fine," Sasha told him. "When we're near a bridge or landing zone, bank to the left and open the door. We'll use the mag boots." He looked at his team to check they had the equipment and received nods from all of them. "Some of us will eliminate any immediate targets when we're still airborne while the others get below. All of you, be careful. Mag boots will help to keep you in place, but you won't be capable of quick movement while you have them on."

"I didn't plan to run anywhere except toward the target, sir," a soldier stated.

"Which is what, exactly?" the marksman asked. "Are we going after Merrick, sir?"

"While most of the enemy forces are concentrated in the lobby and hangar areas, we should see if we can find any hostages," Sasha told them and sent a copy of the embassy map to each of the soldiers. "We have no confirmed sightings or positions, but these are the best possibilities. If Merrick is seen, notify me immediately but do not move to engage. He is still considered a dangerous target, even for a squad."

"I can't believe he used to be the chancellor who ran Nexus," the raider muttered. "I think he was still running it the year before I went there."

"Then I would take this opportunity to show how far you've come," the commander responded as the shuttle emerged from the tunnel. It glided through a large interior section of the station with many bridges and pieces of floating metal and debris. Small firefights took place throughout the area. "And that you've surpassed him."

"Aren't you the chancellor now, sir?" one of the soldiers asked.

Sasha held his rifle tightly. "I am, and I recommend the same advice."

The craft shifted as if to begin to nosedive. "We're heading into the port now, Commander. I'm gonna try to drop you off at a safer point," the pilot advised.

Sasha stood, held onto the railing in front of the door with his sniper rifle at the ready, and took a final look at his team. They had all lined up behind him and seemed resolute and calm. "You have your orders and jobs," he said, turned away, and held his weapon in both hands. "Let's get this done and bring this war to an end."

"I'll open the door in five...four...three..." The

commander braced himself as the light on the lock changed from red to white. The door opened and when he dove out, the lack of gravity almost made him spiral but that was the plan. It allowed him to quickly scan around him. His trained eye located almost a dozen targets, although they seemed more distracted by the remaining Security bots than the new group in their midst. It would not remain that way for long.

Two of the marksmen followed him. Both held their rifles and the trio began to find their targets and eliminate them methodically. The energy blasts had much less kick-back than kinetic rounds, but they were still tossed around and back somewhat. Rather than pose a problem, it simply made finding new targets easier and each man focused on a different direction than the others. The main group was able to pull themselves to the ground with hooks. They landed and all soldiers immediately delivered lethal volleys at anything that was not military or Resistance. They largely ignored the Security bots as they were hacked anyway.

"Sir, I've found a route that will take us toward one of the meeting areas," one of the scouts informed him over the comms. "That's one of the sections where they believe the hostages could be held."

"Understood. Good work." He delivered one more shot at a desperate pirate who tried to fly toward him while his back was turned. Sasha took the hook shot from his belt and fired it at the bridge. "When we have gravity again, I recommend switching to kinetic rounds. They will get through their shields easier."

He reeled himself in and activated his mag boots once he landed. The others followed suit, used hooks themselves, and jumped between pillars and debris—or, in the raider's case, using a quick burst from his jet.

Once he'd checked for any immediate threats, the commander turned to the door, where one of the soldiers was already placing a breaching charge. "Once we get through this, we should have gravity again, sir," she informed him. "But we'll also have more Omegas and Ark soldiers to deal with, along with the droids."

"We knew that coming in," he reminded her and glanced at the raider, who peered at the screen on his gauntlet. "What are you looking at, soldier?"

"A buddy of mine was one of the first guys to land. He's fighting in the lobby." He extended his arm so Sasha could see. "It's wild, sir, and looks more like a riot than a real battle."

"When you have two sides fighting desperately, most battles devolve to that in this situation," he explained. "Is the charge ready?"

"Yes, sir!" the woman shouted and backed away. "Counting down!"

"Get behind a wall and turn your mag boots to full capacity," the commander ordered and found a position behind a wall. "You don't want to potentially be blown into space."

"Three...two...one," the soldier counted and pressed the activation switch on her gauntlet. The door was ruptured to leave a small opening. Sasha turned the mag boots' connection down and approached with the team. Four of them took hold of either side of the doors and pulled to open the entry a little more. Two Omegas had run into the hall to see what happened but were felled by two shots from Sasha delivered in quick succession.

"Proceed," he stated crisply and the team pushed into the station.

"Kaiden," Chief said but the ace was busy. He drove an elbow into the visor of an Ark soldier before he spun and fired a charged shot at an Omega Heavy who tried to attack Silas from behind *"Kaiden!"*

"What?" the ace demanded, vented his rifle as he drew Debonair, and fired at two droids that had focused on him. "Are the others here yet?"

"Yeah, I just picked them up, but there's something fishy going on."

He noticed an Omega taking aim at him through a screen in his HUD that checked his rear. Reflexively, he ducked, dodged the shot, and whirled to fire several shots from Debonair into the man's chest. His adversary collapsed as he closed Sire's vent and holstered the pistol. "Do you care to be more specific?"

"I feel slight fluctuations in the embassy's core," the EI explained. *"It could be simple flare-ups because the fighting is pushing the power higher than normal after a very long time."*

"Could it mean that it'll blow?" he asked quietly.

"I wouldn't push it that far. It could also mean they are activating warp gates, which is another big problem—among a few others."

"And we can't afford any of those right now." Kaiden fired a few shots from Sire as he pushed through the crowd. "Send a message to the others that we will investigate."

"Fine, but you are heading the wrong way," Chief warned.

"I'm gonna see if I can get a tagalong," he retorted.

Raza hurled an Omega heavy into the fountain's statue and uttered a fierce roar as he drove his massive ornate blade through three Arbiter droids at once. Something raced toward him and he spun to face an Ark soldier who aimed a launcher at him. He growled and bared his teeth as he whipped his curved blade to the side and slid the droids off it toward his attacker. None hit as a blast from the side upended the Ark soldier and made him miss his shot. The explosive fired and struck the ceiling as a couple more Sauren dove from the floor above.

He looked at Kaiden, who approached him like a man with a purpose. "War Chief."

"It is good to see you in battle again, young hunter," he said to return the greeting. "Do you have Merrick's location?"

"Not yet, but something is going on at the core," the ace told him. "It's probably not caused by us this time. I'm going to investigate. Do you wanna come along?"

Raza scrutinized the battle. It was large and ferocious but he was not satisfied with it. He nodded and slid his blade onto his back. "We will fix this issue and then hunt for Merrick."

"Agreed." Kaiden nodded and they hurried toward the core. Neither imagined that it might be where their true prey awaited them.

CHAPTER FORTY-SIX

"Coming in hot!" the shuttle pilot shouted and banked sharply as a blast from a fighter behind them sailed past and struck the embassy. The enemy craft was quickly intercepted by two military fighters as the shuttle pilot changed course and soared higher.

"We may need the shields turned on if this fight lasts a long time," Chiyo commented. She looked from Indre to Luke, who waited eagerly at the exit.

"Come on!" He exhaled a frustrated breath. "There aren't gonna be enemies left if we take any longer."

"I am sure there will be, friend Luke," Genos reassured him as he drew his cannon. "At least statistically, but perhaps not enough for your liking."

"Do you think there is a chance they will simply blow the station?" Indre asked and folded her arms. "At some point, they will realize the best they can do is spite us."

"If they haven't already," Cameron added.

The infiltrator shrugged. "It is a possibility. But with

Xuanzang and Icarus under our control, they should be able to control remote detonation."

"I did take a moment to look at the schematics of the embassy." Genos tapped his infuser as he thought. "It is possible to begin an overload manually, but to do so is almost a suicide mission. It would require one to deactivate the shield containing the core and drop the balancing grid. Of course, it would take a fair amount of time for a small group to do this, and you have to deactivate the shield before taking the grid down, which is done in three parts."

"I can see that taking a while," Flynn agreed. "But what makes it dangerous?"

"While you deactivate the grid, you also drop secondary safeguards. As the core destabilizes, it releases loose spikes of energy and with nothing to contain it, almost anyone in the immediate vicinity would be fried. From my understanding, even with specialized suits, it is not guaranteed that you will succeed."

"Still, even if they were able to get through two of the checkpoints, that would be enough to cause issues with the core and power sustaining the station," Chiyo pointed out.

"Oh, certainly." The Tsuna nodded. "It is not recommended."

"I've found a place to land," the pilot informed them. "Get ready as I have to bug out immediately."

"Finally!" Luke shouted eagerly. "Let's get in there."

"Commander!" one of the soldiers called but was immediately struck by an energy blast from above. Sasha and another marksman aimed quickly and fired two shots apiece at four droids that targeted the group from a walkway above. All four found their marks and the kinetic rounds drilled through the robots' heads.

The commander raced to where two others were helping the wounded soldier to sit. "Are you all right?"

"Yes, sir. It only depleted my shields," she confirmed and shook her head. "The impact thumped my head fairly hard but never mind that. I'm picking up vital signs in that room." She pointed to the doors she had inspected. "It might be hostiles but I didn't pick up any energy readings that indicated weapons or armor."

"Let's take a look." He helped her up as his team hurried forward to surround the door. The terminal was in lockdown so he cast Isaac into it. "Can you get it open, Isaac?"

"It will take a few moments longer than normal, sir. My apologies for the wait."

Sasha shrugged as he aimed his weapon at the door. "It's fine. Can you make guesses as to what is inside?"

"I can only confirm the CPO's words. There are people inside and no indication of weaponry or armor." As the EI spoke, the terminal glowed green. *"Doors unlocked and opening."*

They slid open and the team entered. Ten occupants were present, eight humans and two Tsuna, all backed against the far corner of the room.

"Are you here to finish it?" one of them asked, a woman with tanned skin and long black hair with a few silver streaks. She looked drawn and unkempt from her time in captivity. Sasha recognized her as one of the delegates representing the UK.

"Amoli Harris?" he asked. She studied him cautiously but nodded slowly.

"They aren't dressed in Omega colors," one of the Tsuna representatives told the others. "Are you the military?"

Sasha nodded, lowered his rifle, and motioned for the others to do the same. "We are. Do you know if there are others?"

"There might be," Amoli stated. "They separated us about a month ago, but they've…made examples of us since the takeover. I do not know who remains."

"Then we need to press on." He activated his comms. "I'll see if we can get a shuttle to rescue you for now." He pointed to two of the soldiers in his unit. "Stay with them. We need to see if we can find the others if there are any."

"On it, sir!" They saluted and he sent a message to all shuttle pilots and ship commanders in range about a possible pickup as they returned to the meeting hall. Hope remained that there would still be more to save.

A squad of four Omega soldiers jogged down the hall, flanked by six Arbiter droids. They had been commanded to break away from the fighting and report to the core room, but the purpose of the order was still unknown. A large blast rumbled behind them. One caught a green flash as he spun to see the droids had been blown apart. He uttered a yell as he pointed up before he and the soldier next to him were crushed underfoot by Raza who plunged through the ceiling above. The other two raised their weapons quickly to fire, but the Sauren snatched the barrels of the guns to draw them closer, released them, and sank his claws into their throats. As if to punctuate the attack, he pounded their heads together before he tossed them aside.

Kaiden leapt down behind him and patted the War Chief on the back as he walked past. "Nice work."

Raza snorted and nodded as he walked over the bodies. "Are we close?"

"It should be down this hall—right, Chief?" he asked.

The EI popped up in front of them and bobbed up and down. *"Yeah, I'm still picking up a growing energy reading but it's not being funneled anywhere that I can tell. It's more like quick spikes."*

"Is that odd?" the Sauren asked and the two teammates increased their pace as they ran down the hall.

"From the core, yeah. The shield should equalize any power fluxes and I shouldn't detect anything to begin with. That's why I thought we should take a look."

"So maybe that run on the dreadnaught was a warm-up, huh?" Kaiden asked.

Raza bared his teeth. "I only hope there is another worthy adversary. I do not wish to have abandoned the battle for nothing more than suspicion."

"Like I promised, we can hunt Merrick when we're finished here," the ace reminded him and focused on the way ahead. "Do you smell anything?"

"I smell nothing, which is odd," Raza told him.

"Why's that? Doesn't that simply mean there's nothing around?"

"But there is. I smell the machines down the hall and the scent of the embassy itself I have yet to acclimate to.

But there is this...blankness amongst it all." The War Chief sounded perplexed. "I believe something is awaiting us."

Kaiden hefted Sire and patted Debonaire with his free hand. "I'm not sure what a 'blankness' is, but let's be ready." They proceeded a little more cautiously to the end of the hall, where two large doors barred their way. He pointed to the access terminal. "Get on it, Chief."

The EI's avatar vanished and reappeared in the terminal. *"Uh...it ain't locked, partner."*

"Well, that's a nice change of pace. Open it, then."

"There is an emergency warning," Chief stated as escaped air hissed from the doors followed by a loud mechanical chugging and they began to separate. *"Something is going on."*

"Yeah, a battle in the embassy," Kaiden snarked and stepped closer to the entrance.

"Not only that, idiot, inside the—look out!" A flash of white blazed inside the chamber and his eyes widened when an arc of white energy rocketed toward him. Raza grasped his shoulder and hauled him clear before both stepped to the side. The arc seared into the metal floor of the hall, burnt into it for several yards, and left a hot orange and red mark.

"The core's shield is down!" Chief yelped as he appeared in the HUD. *"That's not good!"*

"Can you fix it?" the ace asked as he and Raza peered into the room when the doors opened fully. The large white core flowed brightly and several more beams and shocks struck the large walls and ceiling of the circular chamber.

"If you get me into the main console, I should be able to get

*the shields up again. That won't stop it entirely but it will
contain it while I—"* Chief was interrupted by a jarring crash
that seemed to fill the room. One of three large pillars—
that had previously glowed—went dark and the upper half
slid and collided with the bottom half.

"What was that?" he demanded.

"That's part of the balancing grid," the EI explained. *"It's
what keeps the core from going nova. Someone is deactivating it."*

"Dammit, where are they? The security station? Maintenance?" Even without answers, he began to stride away
from the chamber.

*"The only way that can be done is manually. Whoever is
doing it is in there, Kaiden!"* Chief insisted.

"Then we need to find him, Raza." He turned to the War
Chief, but the Sauren did not look at him and instead,
stared at the stairs that lead to a curved walkway that
circled the core. His focus made the ace look more closely.
It appeared they wouldn't have to search for the perpetra-
tor. A figure walked from behind the pillar to the top of the
stairs, dressed in elaborate armor—and certainly not
anything he had seen among the Omega—and stared at the
two of them. The sloped visor on the helmet didn't slide
back or open. It appeared to simply disperse to reveal a
man with tanned skin and silver eyes who regarded them
with a knowing look that included annoyance.

It was that knowing look, as he shifted his gaze from
Raza to Kaiden, which made the ace realize who this was.
"Chief, send out a message," he said and aimed his weapon.
"We've found Merrick."

CHAPTER FORTY-SEVEN

"Of course it would be you." Merrick growled an inaudible curse and his gaze turned to a glare at the sight of Kaiden. "The curiosity that became more than it was worth."

"Have you seen this cur before, Kaiden?" Raza asked as he drew his blade.

"I haven't, but for a while, he and his buddies were watching me," he explained and charged a shot. "They wanted Chief."

"We wanted one of Laurie's specialized EIs. Yours would have sufficed," the AO leader stated coldly and descended a few steps. "You could have been a part of the solution, boy, if however small—"

"Yeah, I've heard enough of your 'solution,'" he snapped and fired a charged shot directly at his target. The man raised a hand with the palm facing outward. It connected but without the expected result and caught both Kaiden and Raza off guard.

Merrick raised his arm and some kind of shield or

energy surrounded the blast. "You are so temperamental. How you've survived this long baffles me."

"I'm not gonna let this asshole run his mouth," the ace muttered and aimed again. "Let's see how many of these he can take." He fired several smaller shots and although his adversary hardly moved, he was still able to dodge most of them. The two that did strike simply sparked against his armor's shields. The man moved his arm back and cast it forward, and the charged shot hurtled toward him as both he and Raza leapt out of the way of the explosion.

Kaiden rolled along the ground and vented his rifle as Raza roared. He looked up when the War Chief attacked the AO leader, who had now descended the stairs. The Sauren lunged at his prey with his blade held aloft. Merrick's visor reassembled itself and he raised a leg and folded it in. Was he insane? Did he think he could kick a Sauren away who weighed close to a thousand pounds?

The man lashed out with the limb and caught Raza in the chest. The Sauren's leap was halted and, in fact, he was knocked back. He landed heavily and slid until he was stopped by a wall. The ace's eyes widened at the display. "No way," he muttered. "He must have some kind of mod or mechanical appendages that let him—"

"I do have mods," his adversary stated as he approached slowly and with infuriating calm. "But my strength? That is my power alone." He held his right arm up and a long blade released from his gauntlet. "It is a power gifted to me by the so-called leaders of my species." His pace quickened as he drew his arm back and prepared to run Kaiden through. "And all this has merely been my way to return what they gave me."

The ace slammed Sire's vent shut, aimed at his attacker, and pulled the trigger to fire a point-blank shot as the man descended upon him.

———

"We found another group, sir," the raider reported. "It's smaller than the last, though."

"It's something," Sasha reassured him. "I've had reports from other teams and they have found small groups of other delegates and employees. It appears any military and security forces on board were among the first to be disposed of."

The other man simply nodded solemnly. "Have we had any luck with an evac?"

"They are putting a team together. We should round up who we have and move to a pick-up area. There's one nearby in the next section and there shouldn't be many hostiles along the way. Most have joined the main fight."

"On it, sir." The raider nodded and returned to the office where he and the team had found more hostages.

Sasha began to continue his search when a message popped into his HUD from Kaiden.

Found Merrick.

All of his training and ability to keep calm under pressure could not stop his heart from racing. "Isaac, send a message to the team that they must take the hostages to extraction. Connect them with the shuttle team," he ordered and fixed a lock on Kaiden's position. "I am needed elsewhere."

"Good Lord, are there enough of these guys?" Luke asked rhetorically as he swung his hammer into two droids and drove them into a wall.

"I thought you were looking forward to this," Marlo replied and fired his massive cannon at an Arbiter Prime to shatter its chest.

Two droids fell, deactivated by Chiyo, who immediately took her SMG out and fired at an Ark sniper who attempted to poke his head around the corner. He was smoked out by two of Indre's drones and a set of spikes launched by one drilled into his visor.

"We need to—" Chiyo was interrupted by Kaiden's message and her eyes widened. "It's Kaiden. I need to go."

"What? Where?" Luke asked and a noticeable pause indicated that they had all received the message. "Go, we'll hold them off."

Genos ran to her. "I am going with you," he said firmly. She merely nodded and they sprinted away while the rest of the team beat back the combined assault of Omega and AO forces.

Kaiden groaned as he forced himself up. His blast had created a sufficiently large explosion, but did it do any damage? He narrowed his eyes and peered into the smoke where a red glow indicated that his opponent's blade remained on course. While he couldn't be sure that the answer was no damage at all, even if he had managed to inflict some, it wasn't enough. He aimed what he believed to be Merrick's chest before he wondered if the man would try to catch his attack again. Something streaked toward him from inside the smoke and thankfully, he saw it in time to step to the side. A spike pierced the floor and would have gone through his knee if he hadn't reacted.

"Kaiden, explosive—move!" Chief warned as the top of the spike began to emit a red light. He dove to the side seconds before the explosion detonated and Merrick attempted another leap at him with his blade at the ready. The ace activated his armor's jets in an attempt to fly back and gain some distance, but the man caught his leg and held him in place, even when he increased the power to his jets. How strong was he?

The AO leader prepared to slice through his captive's leg. Kaiden deactivated the jets quickly and let himself fall as he drew Debonair. He fired several shots at the man's helmet. One was able to burn the visor, which forced Merrick to position the blade close to his head to block the blasts. The ace rocked himself forward as he drew his blade and stabbed his opponent's hand. This finally forced him to release him, and Kaiden rolled away and holstered Debonair as he charged a shot in Sire.

His adversary removed the blade from his hand and when he saw the Resistance soldier was ready, he aimed his left gauntlet at the weapon and launched another explosive spike that pierced the barrel of the rifle. Kaiden immediately realized what was about to happen and hurled the weapon at the man, who raised a hand and created a shield seconds before the explosive spike and collected energy in the weapon generated a large explosion.

The ace checked his arsenal. He had Debonair, a few thermals and shocks, and a spare blade on his belt—not the best position to be in. "Chief, get inside Debonair and reconfigure it for heavy fire."

"You'll overheat the weapon in a few shots," Chief warned him.

"I think we've at least seen that normal shots don't do that much to him. I'll worry about that on my own time." He drew the pistol again and readied himself for another encounter. Merrick never came, however, and when the smoke cleared, he was gone. Both confused and disturbed, he held the pistol up and scanned the room carefully. Where the hell could he have gone? They were in an open section of the chamber and there weren't many places he could hide. A memory flashed in his head of Gin and his stealth generator. *Shit.* "Chief, scan for—"

"Behind us!" the EI yelled and Kaiden whirled as the man reappeared and his blade moved closer. A lance soared past the ace's head, buried itself into his assailant's shoulder, and drew a pained growl from him. He fired two shots from Debonair. The beams were larger but more compact, and his adversary's shields shuddered from the impact. The AO leader backed away and generated a shield with his left hand to protect himself as he hacked through the lance with his blade. He yanked the remainder from his shoulder, withdrew his blade, and activated his stealth generator once more.

"That won't protect you!" Raza bellowed and raced past Kaiden with his weapon poised to strike. "Whatever you use to mask your smell, it only aids me. You have no scent and you are a hole in the room, but I can find you!" The

Sauren raised his blade and when he swung it down, a clash of sparks resulted.

Merrick reappeared and used his blade to defend against the larger one. The War Chief removed a hand from his weapon and lunged at his opponent's throat with his claw. The man grasped it with his free hand and launched a vicious kick, but Raza closed his claws around his hand, opened his jaws, and snapped them viciously. The AO leader was forced to dodge the attacks without being able to move away as he struggled against his captor, who simply planted his feet, twisted his body, and pounded him into the back of a large machine near the circular walkway. With another violent shake, he drove him into the floor, spun his blade around, and pointed it in preparation to finish the fight.

The man recovered faster than anyone should be able to from such a beating. He rolled and pierced Raza's right leg with his blade, and the Sauren uttered a pained roar. Kaiden stepped forward, ready to fire, but their opponent seized the opportunity, managed to scramble to his feet, and sliced cleanly through the large hand around his wrist to release himself from the iron grasp. Raza responded with a furious roar and held the stump as blood leaked from it. Kaiden called to the War Chief and fired two shots from Debonair at Merrick, who created a small shield that deflected the blasts into Raza's chest that knocked him down.

"Dammit!" The ace growled in frustration and grimaced when Debonair burned in his gloved hand. He slid the vent back, took his spare blade out of his belt, and prepared to close on Merrick. The man had managed to pry the still locked claws of Raza's severed hand free and tossed it carelessly aside.

The AO leader did glance at the ace, but he turned to the War Chief. Kaiden's eyes widened as their adversary raced toward the Sauren and he immediately did the same in an attempt to stop him. Unfortunately, Merrick was too fast. He watched in horror as the man descended on his wounded friend and raised his blade in preparation to behead him when a shot rang out from behind them. The man's helmet cracked and his assault was stopped.

Kaiden slid in front of Raza, shut the vent on Debonair, and fired two shots at the other man's head. Both struck the shields around the helmet and shattered. Merrick glared at the ace, who returned it with equal hatred and readied to fire a third time. His target launched another explosive spike and this one landed next to Raza. The ace lay sprawled on the floor, and if he moved out of the way, the Sauren would take the blast. His enemy vanished again as he turned away from the threat and tried to think of a way to protect his friend. Another shot, entirely unexpected, destroyed the top of the spike where the explosive was held.

The ace looked up when he realized that help had arrived. Sasha stood at the entrance to the chamber, reloaded his rifle, and nodded at him. "You couldn't wait, could you?"

CHAPTER FORTY-EIGHT

As Sasha entered and scanned the room for Merrick, Kaiden helped Raza to sit. He checked his wounds and his gaze lingered on the severed hand. "How are you holding up, War Chief?"

The Sauren growled, folded his legs in preparation to stand, and hissed from the pain of the injury on his leg. "It will take more than this for me to give in."

He helped to steady the warrior. "Yeah, I guess it's death or nothing." He placed Raza against the back of the circular walkway and vented Debonair as he turned to Sasha. "Thanks for the save."

"You could have prevented this if you had called in before engaging," the commander chided and his gaze scanned the area.

"I didn't realize we would find him here. We came because the core was fluctuating," he explained and closed Debonair's vent. That brought his focus to what had led them there to begin with. He looked at the core, from which errant arcs continued to jettison. Most were directed toward the ceiling. "We have to get it back under control. Otherwise, it'll blow the embassy."

"And destroy much of the force nearby," Sasha added. "Can Chief do anything about it?"

"I'm locked out and it'll take time to get the system open," the EI explained hurriedly. *"The problem is that he's already begun to take down the balancing grid. I might be able to get the shields up but putting the grid back to normal is delicate work."*

"Then shouldn't you get started?" The ace checked on Raza, pleased to see that the wound on his leg had already begun to heal.

"I can if you wanna risk it," Chief replied. *"We don't know if he's left traps in the system. If something happens to me, it will also affect you."*

Kaiden took a few steps forward when he realized Sasha had moved a fair distance ahead of him. "Dammit…I would risk it if we at least had an idea of where—"

Raza lunged and almost toppled forward. "Commander! He's behind you!"

Kaiden aimed hastily at where he thought their enemy might be. Sasha turned and leapt back, and a hole appeared when something pierced the chest of his armor. The ace fired three shots, but they were stopped in midair when Merrick appeared again and kicked the other man away. The ace retrieved a shock grenade as his adversary formed the three blasts he'd fired into a single orb. He readied himself to dodge but the man looked away and toward the core. Conscious only of the need to stop him, he pressed the trigger on the shock and lobbed it as Merrick tossed the orb at the pillar he had already deactivated. The sphere stuck to it and seconds later, a large red blast preceded an avalanche of pieces of the pillar. A loud crashing issued from below the floor.

"What the hell did he do?" the ace demanded and gaped as the shock grenade detonated next to the AO leader. The electricity coiled around him before it was all absorbed by a generator on his back. "Great. I juiced him up, didn't I?"

"The bastard compromised one of the grid stations!" Chief yelled. *"To hell with it. Get me in there. I need to see if I can save it."*

"Then go, Chief!" Kaiden ordered and cast him into the core's terminal as Raza joined him. Merrick held both arms up and his blade retracted as two pistols ejected into his hands from the underside of his gauntlets. The Sauren drew his Taiko and he and his partner aimed at their aggressor. The man aimed one of his guns in their direction and the other toward Sasha, who had recovered and shortened the barrel of his rifle as he approached his target from behind.

The four stood motionless and waited to see who would make the first shot, while the core continued to flare behind them.

"Down the hall, Genos!" Chiyo instructed as they sprinted toward the open doors at the end, where they could see a brightly glowing orb and heard explosive and static sounds.

"That core is not in a good state," the Tsuna muttered. "It appears our concerns were accurate."

"Can we do anything about it?" she asked and darted him a concerned glance.

"It all depends on how far gone it is," he replied. "Between us, we can possibly get the shields back on. If the grid has been tampered with, however, that will require much more work. At best, we may have to simply shut it off. There should be a temporary power backup that will allow us to at least evacuate the station."

"I don't see Kaiden," she told him and checked the map. "It says he's still in there."

"And alive, so that is fortuitous," he added.

"Commander Sasha is in there as well, but if neither of them is working on controlling the core, they must be in battle...perhaps fighting Merrick," Chiyo reasoned and her voice shook.

"Then we may have other concerns before we can work on the core," the Tsuna pointed out as they approached the doorway. The core flashed and several streaks of energy launched free. One seared into the ceiling of the hall. The two teammates pushed on and entered. Her gaze was immediately drawn down the room to where Raza and Kaiden stood motionless and aimed at something.

"Kaiden!" she shouted. The ace reacted to hearing his name and turned slightly toward her. A loud bang accompanied a shot from Raza and a large orb of yellow energy rocketed forward as Kaiden dove to the side. Genos hauled her down as a kinetic round flew overhead, struck the wall behind them, and blew pieces of metal apart.

"Help Chief!" Kaiden shouted at them and pointed at the core and the station in front of it as he pushed himself up and fired at someone in armor. She stood and stared at the figure and knew, when a pair of piercing silver eyes settled on her, it was Merrick.

"Chiyo, we must go!" the engineer insisted and all but dragged her to the stairs.

The ace fired two shots from Debonair, but his adversary ducked under them. The AO leader prepared to return fire, but blasts came from behind and one struck his shoulder. He fired at both Kaiden and Sasha. The younger man caught a shot in the leg and even with his shields, the armor around his femur cracked. Sasha took two hits, one in his left shoulder while the other skimmed the side of his helmet. He fell back, retrieved a thermal, and threw it toward Merrick.

His teeth gritted, the ace rolled forward, took a thermal out as well, and hurled it. The AO leader had begun to holster his guns so he could use his shields to block the blast. As the explosives hurtled closer, Kaiden took aim at his and fired a shot. It struck the grenade and caused it to blow prematurely. The blast triggered Sasha's and the explosion consumed the man. Their adversary leapt out of the blast, however, with two disks in his hand. He flung one at each of them.

Raza stalked forward and charged another powerful shot in his Taika. The two soldiers were able to shoot the projectiles, which unleashed a wave of force on impact and hurled them both away. The War Chief bellowed a challenge as he fired, and Merrick held his hands up and created a shield as the large yellow orb careened toward him. Even with the shields, the power of the blast slid him back. He made impact with the wall as he tried to contain the ball of energy and struggled to hold it aloft and return it. The Sauren moved his hand to his belt, took his force hammer out, and activated the switch before he hurled it at Merrick.

Even from his somewhat distant position, Kaiden could see a twinge of shock in the AO leader's eyes. The hammer connected as he tried to throw the orb. It fell out of his hands, landed a few yards away, and exploded. Raza held his arms up to shield himself as the man was consumed by the blast.

"I'm surprised this system is still holding together," Chiyo muttered and studied the options presented to her.

"You're telling me!" Chief yelled, his avatar distorted on the screen. *"I'm glad you guys came along as I'm not sure if even I could hold all this together myself."*

Genos returned quickly after having examined the grid. "The node is damaged internally. I'm not sure if it would be stable enough to contain the core even if we can set it in place again."

"What options does that leave us?" she asked and looked from him to Chief.

"There is one more failsafe," the EI mentioned. *"It's below deck, a station that activates a generator that will siphon the excess energy being poured out of the core."*

"That sounds like the most preferable option." The Tsuna nodded at her.

"We still need to get the shield going," the EI reminded them. *"The generators are in the same area, and with how much power this thing is pouring out, anyone who goes down there...*

Well, they may be able to tough it out and activate it, but they would be fried before they could get out."

"The shield will need to charge even if we turn it on," she pointed out.

"Then we might have a use for the node after all," Genos said quickly and turned to look at it. "There is still power inside it. I can arrange for it to transfer into the shielding generator when you get it working again."

"Boosting the charge rate...it's a good idea," Chief agreed. *"Get on it."*

CHAPTER FORTY-NINE

Raza put his Taiko away and the remains of the energy from Merrick's fumbling attempt to use the collected energy began to disperse. He grasped the hilt of his blade again, but before he could draw his weapon, two shots from within the yellow cloud caught him in his chest and erupted in ballistic explosions. As he was thrown back, Kaiden cursed and fired into the cloud at almost the same time as Sasha.

Light flared, the sign of impact against shields that were close to giving way. He took a few steps forward before a warning in his HUD let him know that energy was building around the man. When he confirmed that the commander had withdrawn, he ran to Raza and flung himself down as a large wave of energy was dispersed to clear the air and reveal Merrick. Pieces of his armor—his left shoulder pad, right gauntlet, and the upper half of his chest plate—were broken. Blood dripped down his forehead and more was evident on his armor, most likely from wounds beneath it.

The AO leader aimed both pistols at Kaiden, who leveled his single weapon, ready to fire. "Prepare the jets," he ordered and heard them start as he pushed to his feet. "Raza, can you still move?"

The Sauren uttered a growl and shifted slightly. "I guess that's an affirmative," the ace continued. "I'll give you a shot in a sec, so be ready." He tilted his head and studied the Arbiter leader. "So, was this how you expected the new age of humanity to be?" he challenged.

The man didn't respond at first and when he noticed Sasha taking aim, he moved to aim one of his guns at the commander in a mirror of how the fight had begun.

"You know, you said back when this all started, you expected something to attack us," Kaiden recalled and moved forward a step. "What is it? Some new alien force? A big-ass meteor? Demons summoned by an intergalactic death cult? I prefer the last one honestly. That's at least new."

"Would you believe me? You've proven you would rather fight against salvation than fight for it," Merrick responded and focused on him again. The ace felt this was something he never got enough credit for—his quick wit, or big mouth as some of his friends might say.

"And you never gave us the choice," he snapped and took another step forward, his jets almost ready. "You attacked the planet and allied yourself with terrorists and the number one outlaw merc company in the galaxy. Some of your lackeys went on about how you were such a god and a strategic genius, but your PR is shit."

He expected his adversary to fly into a rage or perhaps scoff but either way, to take the bait. Instead, the man lowered his head slightly, although he did grit his teeth but more out of the frustration of trying to hold something back. "I have spent decades of my life in the service of our people. I was to be the representation of what the future of the human species would be but the council's gift to me only brought me madness."

"No shit." Kaiden snorted. "So you faked your death and decided to take care of things for yourself. Is that about right?"

"Do you believe there was an alternative? I tried them all!" Merrick growled and looked at him again. "I was forced into this—not by personal pleasure but by necessity. I regret the sacrifices but they had to be made."

"You would save the Earth even if you had to break a few eggs to do it, right? Why does that always mean genocide to psychos like you?" He scoffed. "You know, I think I worked out what this big bad thing that will wipe humanity out is."

"Enough!" the man yelled and fired a shot at his two opponents. The ace activated his jets and elevated sharply. Sasha dove back and fired two shots from his rifle. Both struck their adversary's chest and shattered the remains of his armor and Kaiden shut his jets off as he descended. The AO leader swung toward him to fire, but Sasha's shots toppled him and made him miss. The ace found his mark and delivered a strike directly into the tyrant's head.

Merrick cried out in pain, the first Kaiden had heard, before he dropped one of his pistols and clutched his face. He brandished the other at him before a tell-tale roar gave scant warning and Raza leapt on top of the man. While he tried to kick his attacker off, he was only able to push him over. The Sauren War Chief was finally able to sink his blade into the Arbiter leader.

The ace landed and spun to level Debonair at Merrick, who now coughed as traces of blood trickled from his mouth and down his chest. He walked closer and Sasha jogged to help Raza to his feet. Kaiden kicked Merrick's pistols away and fixed him with a hard look. His face was now blackened, scarred, and burnt, and Raza's massive blade was buried in his chest and down into his stomach. He knelt beside him and removed his helmet to stare into the Arbiter leader's eyes. "You know, seeing you like this now…" he began and placed Debonair against his temple. "In a weird way, I almost wish this wasn't how it ended. It makes everything feel so damn pointless."

The man caught his arm and he began to press the trigger of his pistol as Merrick stared directly into his eyes. "So what did you see?" he asked. "You said you had an idea of what was coming. Does that mean you are prepared? Do you think you could do any better in my position?"

"I already am," he stated and broke the man's hold with his free hand. "You said this thing comes for humanity and tries to destroy it? That only you can save us? I think maybe you could have if you'd made a different choice."

Merrick looked at him in bewilderment, but they were interrupted by a loud bang. Kaiden and the others looked up as another node in the grid collapsed. "What the hell?"

"His shots must have destabilized it," Sasha stated. Unlike the first node, this one didn't merely sink in place. It fell off its railings and plunged floorward at the rear of the room.

"Chiyo, Genos!" Kaiden shouted and stood quickly to

run to his teammates. A hand caught his ankle and he looked coldly at the wounded man. "I intend to kill you anyway. Do you merely want to make it happen quicker?" he demanded and brandished Debonair.

"What choice?" Merrick demanded and his features betrayed desperation and even a touch of the madness he suspected had hidden in him this entire time. "What was the choice that could have changed this?"

He ripped his foot away from the man. "It was you, Merrick," he responded. "You didn't have a vision. You lost your mind and made a fake vision real. Whatever the hell you saw that would destroy humanity, that darkness was you." Merrick's face scrunched, first in anger, then in confusion, and back to anger, before his eyes widened and he let his head sag against the floor. The ace turned away and strode to the core's terminal to help his friends, while the AO leader uttered a loud, drawn-out laugh behind him.

"Of course! It is such an obvious solution." The man continued to laugh as he stared at the ceiling and arcs of energy began to tear into the walls and floor around him. "As humanity has always done, it creates something to destroy itself."

CHAPTER FIFTY

"Chief, what can we do?" Kaiden demanded as he ascended the stairs.

"Well, we had a plan," the EI stated. Intermittent waves of energy pushed against him and slowly drained the rest of his shields as he waited for the full explanation. *"But that ain't gonna work now."*

"We can still get the shield on," Chiyo assured him.

"Will that do anything?" he asked,

"It'll buy us more time to evacuate." She looked at him and her visor slid open to show eyes filled with concern.

"Can we even get out of the blast radius?" he asked.

"Maybe. It would be close, but it all depends on if we can leave right this second. Even then, most wouldn't be able to make it out. It's not like the Omegas will simply lay down their arms at this point," Chief elaborated.

"There is the failsafe, remember," Genos called and ran from the other side of the walkway.

"What failsafe?" Kaiden asked and turned to the Tsuna.

"The siphon—below the room." The engineer pointed down. "It can stabilize the core by absorbing the excess energy."

He threw up his hands. "Why wasn't that the first option?"

"Because it's dangerous, Kaiden!" Chiyo replied. "It was dangerous even before we lost the second node. All the excess energy will be siphoned to the generators and at the current rate the power is being expelled, it could tear the person activating the failsafe apart."

"And is it any less dangerous to let it explode?" He made his mind up and put his helmet on. "Where is it?"

She shook her head. "No, Kaiden! We can find another way to—"

"I'll get the hatch open and lead you to it, partner," Chief offered and appeared in the HUD. An image of a hatch opening followed a moment later.

"So you're good with this then, Chief?" Kaiden asked. "You know they can't simply pop you into another soldier."

"I wouldn't want another one anyway," he said. *"You've been enough of a pain in the ass that you've grown on me."*

"Kaiden, don't!" Chiyo demanded. "Please, give me time to—"

"I'd give you all the time in the galaxy, Chi," he said as a streak of energy struck the roof and sparks immediately followed. "But it ain't mine to give right now. I can save you, though. Chief can take care of any of the tech stuff while I flip the switch and hold it down."

Genos folded his arms across his chest. "I could perform those same functions, Kaiden."

"I have no doubt, Genos," he assured him. "But I don't

wanna answer to Jaxon, and you have to get back to your people when this is all over. I expect you to make songs about me."

"That isn't our strong suit," the Tsuna said with a small chuckle. "I will do it, nonetheless."

"I appreciate ya." He turned to the infiltrator. "I know we had that talk before heading out, but don't use that as an excuse to…" His words faltered when he saw the tears forming in her eyes. "At least let this mean something, yeah?"

She hesitated and sadness overwhelmed him. When shots rang out, they turned quickly to where Sasha sprawled on the floor, his armor broken. Merrick was gone.

"No!" Kaiden cried as the three ran down the stairs. He raced toward the door to the chamber but didn't see the AO leader making an escape.

"Kaiden, the hatch!" He turned and scanned the place where Merrick had been impaled. Blood surrounded it and Raza's blade lay on the floor. Movement caught his eye and he realized their adversary had somehow managed to ease into the hatch and now began to shut it. He fired three shots but only struck the metal when it snapped closed. Furious, he ran closer and yanked on the cover, but it would not budge. "Chief, open it!"

"It's sealed manually," the EI told him. *"I can't do anything about that."*

"Shit! Genos, check on Sasha and Raza. Chiyo, we need to see if there's anything we can do. That bastard won't win here!"

Merrick had given up on winning, possibly even before they invaded the embassy. He let go of the ladder after he'd climbed down only part of the way and landed a couple of stories down. Weak, he wavered and stumbled forward and he checked his wound. It had begun to seal but even with his regenerative abilities, it would never completely heal. All he needed was to last for a while longer. He looked up, located four large generators in a square, and hobbled down the illuminated path. Red lights flashed and monitors warned of the imminent eruption of the core.

When he reached the end of the pathway, a few stairs led to a small cylindrical chamber with two levers, one each on opposite ends. He ascended slowly and a small console asked for a fingerprint to access the chamber. Irritated, he looked at the glass-like material surrounding the tube, drew his arm back, and hammered it through. It offered very little protection anyway.

Something ripped into his back and his skin tingled. The energy was already working through to the chamber. He felt the generator on his back and realized that it was sparking and had been damaged. Well, this would hurt a little more then, a slight penance that made his choice easier.

He walked into the middle of the tube, stretched his hands to the levers, and released a deep breath as he closed his eyes. This was his moment. He would still stop the darkness he saw—the one Kaiden had helped him to see—even if it was only at the last moment. Calmly, he took hold of both levers and began to push down. An alarm blared when the generators roared to life. He could hear the strikes of energy on the floor around him. A shield formed around the cylinder but he knew it would not hold long. He continued the pressure and when he opened his eyes, large beams of energy were being funneled into the generators. They reached a limit and dispersed it around the chamber into buffers. Some of it surged against the shields and depleted them in a single wave.

Merrick held firm and pushed the levers lower to increase the speed of the siphon. More arcs of energy erupted throughout the room. He looked at one of the generators and noticed a circular tracker was close to full. Another pulse was released and he braced as it tore into him. He clenched his teeth and continued to push down while the remnants of his armor disintegrated. When the levers were almost to the bottom, he looked at the generator again and the circle that filled relentlessly. He looked into the bright light of the core and yelled as he forced the levers all the way down and a large wave of energy swept free. The room went white seconds before he closed his eyes.

The monitors Chiyo and Kaiden were watching went black and they looked at each other with wide eyes.

"He...he went to stop it?" he asked, baffled by the fact that he had seen the enemy of humanity sacrifice himself.

"I don't understand," she muttered and worked on the console. "Why try to destroy the station only to stop it at the cost of his life?" She looked at him. "What happened during the fight?"

He glanced at the place where they had fought and the pool of blood where Merrick had laid. "I only…ran my mouth and talked back to him," he answered and placed his helmet aside. "I guess I was the first one to do it in a long time."

CHAPTER FIFTY-ONE

"Can someone give me a situation report?" Hartman demanded and pounded his fists on the holomap table. "What's going on in the embassy?"

"We have reports of hostages being evac'd." one of the officers told him. "We are preparing wave three, the ship battle is progressing well—"

"I can see that on the map," he stated and pointed to the holomap that still displayed the current space battle outside. "But are we any closer to taking the embassy itself? What about Merrick? We haven't had any reports from anyone since landing and I need to know—"

"Hartman, this is Commander Sasha," a voice said in his comms. "Are you there?"

"I am. Finally, someone responds." He sighed. "What happened, Commander? We received reports about a power flux in the embassy."

"It's been taken care of, General, along with Merrick," Sasha responded and the general's eyes widened.

"Merrick? You have him in custody?" he asked and the

question stirred chatter amongst the soldiers and crew behind him. He activated a switch on the table to put the other man on the speakers.

"No, he's dead, sir," the commander said. "I'll fill you in later. For now, we are gaining access to the embassy and will transfer it to you in a few minutes."

Hartman allowed himself to smile. "Excellent work, Commander, and we know exactly what to do."

"The *Fenrir* is on her last legs, sir," a crewman shouted as the ship was rocked by another blast from a barrage of enemy fighters.

"Damn, they were good legs." An officer chuckled and pushed off the floor.

"We almost made those destroyer numbers." A lieutenant sighed. "You would have won yourself a big pot, sir."

The captain nodded and adjusted his hat. "I could have paid for a nice vacation after this was all over." He turned to his crew. "Evac the ship. I'll take control while you—"

"I'm not going, sir," the lieutenant stated. "Discipline me if you want to, but I don't think it'll matter soon anyway."

His superior's eyes narrowed. "You shouldn't be so thick-headed. Can't you see that—"

"I think he speaks for all of us, sir," a crewman responded. "He simply didn't want to be presumptuous."

"That's about right." The lieutenant nodded, folded his arms, and regarded the captain with the same fixed look as the crew. "We're staying here, win or lose, sir."

The captain could feel a tear in his eye and he nodded

and prepared to address them when a number of lights shone through the front window of the bridge. He turned and saw that they came from the many warp gates in the distance. Surprised, he laughed as the crew cheered. "I'm glad you all decided to stay, ladies and gentlemen!" he declared. "Because it looks like this is the grand finale!"

Dozens of ships raced through the gates—human, Sauren, Tsuna, and even a few Mirus, followed by a massive Mirus mothership. The Omegas were all caught slack-jawed by the sight. "Numerous new targets coming, ma'am," a pilot in an Omega destroyer shouted. "Do we engage?" The leader looked at the new force—almost a hundred strong with more pouring through—and had to laugh. For a second, she and the other leaders thought they could probably still do major damage before they retreated to see another day.

She collapsed in her chair and shook her head. "I don't feel like dying today, not like a rat among lions." She sighed. "If the others wanna perish, let them. Stand down."

Little did she know she spoke for most of the Omega forces.

"The gates are active," a military soldier cried as she thwacked an Ark soldier across the head with a kinetic hammer. "We have reinforcements pouring in."

An Omega took aim but was shot in the back by Silas.

"Does that mean the fun is over?" he asked and scanned the battlefield. Even without the fresh troops, most of the fighting was done in the lobby. Either the Omegas and Ark soldiers had retreated or laid on the floor, their fight finished.

"There's a better question!" Silas and the others looked at a group of soldiers above them, Flynn and his team among them. "Does that mean we win?"

The soldiers looked around and the few remaining hostiles exchanged confused glances. "If the gates are open, does that mean we lost control of the embassy?" one asked.

"Does it mean the boss is dead?" an Ark soldier asked. The others either looked at each other or averted their eyes in fear or sorrow, and some dropped their weapons. A few Omegas initially tried to knock sense into them, but they soon came to the same realization. One by one, they abandoned their weapons and held their arms up.

The military and Resistance members held their arms aloft as well but for them, it was in victory.

Lok and a group of Sauren pushed into the power core chamber in search of their War Chief. When they found him being held by Kaiden and Sasha, battered, cut, and missing a hand, fury welled inside them. "War Chief! Where is the cur who did this?" Lok roared and pointed to the stump.

"Dead, Lok," Raza replied. He pushed away from the humans and stood tall. "Merrick is dead, but no trophy can be claimed."

"That is a pity." The Sauren sighed but clasped his hands together along with the others and bowed. "Did you have a good hunt?"

"I feel it could have been better," their leader said thoughtfully and ran his tongue over a cut along his jaw. "But we are victorious. That will suffice."

"The gates are open and more of our kin join the ranks," Lok told him as he straightened. "Although they will be disappointed in the pickings."

"So the station is secure?" Sasha asked.

"The enemy has surrendered. We will not claim cowards."

"So it is over, then?" Genos asked. "Were there Tsuna among them?"

The Sauren nodded. "All the species of the alliance have arrived in swarms. Even the Omegas engaged in space combat have surrendered."

"Hartman works quickly," Sasha commented. "I need to check to see if there are any remaining hostages who can be—" His legs failed him and he almost fell before Raza and Kaiden caught him.

"You need rest," the ace chided. "You just got this chancellor gig and need to live to make it official when Nexus is up and running again."

"There could still be—" the man began and was interrupted by Raza.

"You have made your people proud, Commander," the War Chief complimented him. "But you are no use to them if you are broken. Rest now."

Sasha sighed but nodded, and the ace took him under

his arm. "Let's head to Earth and enjoy however long this peace will last now that we've earned it."

"You know it won't be for long," the man muttered as they left the chamber. "Even after everything, there will be those who will take advantage of the disarray and see Merrick as a martyr."

"Then they will also know how we dealt with them," he countered. "That should buy us a few hours to relax at least, right?"

Sasha chuckled and studied his students. "Although I have my doubts, I'll let hope have its moment for once."

CHAPTER FIFTY-TWO

"And did we let them take our planet?" Luke hollered to a growing group of military crew and soldiers in the yard of the Seattle HQ. Some threw their hands up and others raised their weapons in celebration.

"Hell no!" they shouted in unison.

"Did we let them get away with trying to take our home?" he continued and Kaiden watched from the sidelines with an amused grin.

"Hell no!" the crowd responded again.

The titan pounded his hammer on the crate he stood on. "But did we kick their ass to space and back?"

Cries of "Hell yeah!" and "Ooh-rah!" followed this question, and the ace wondered if his friend had any aspirations to lead a unit. The man certainly seemed to have the charisma for it.

He pushed away from the wall and strolled to the hangars with a case in hand. Along the way, he noticed Silas and Flynn and nodded to them. They returned the greeting and watched him leave. It had been a few days since the end of the war, congratulations and stories had been exchanged, and this was the time for reconstruction and catching up with the world. Small talk could wait for a while.

When he reached the entrance of his hangar bay, Jaxon and Genos were talking in the foyer. Kaiden attempted a polite nod to them as he continued, but the engineer noticed him and ran up quickly. "Hello, friend Kaiden."

The ace chuckled. "Hey, Genos. What's up?"

"Kin Jaxon and I were discussing the immediate future," he told him. "Due to the circumstances of the war and having not been in contact with our people in quite some time, all Tsuna who were stationed on Earth have to report and declare their intention to stay or return to Abisalo."

"Really?" He swung his case over his shoulder. "Will you head out?"

"We will report in," Jaxon confirmed. "But we will stay on Earth for graduation. Chancellor Sasha offered to simply send any Tsuna's diploma and paperwork to an ambassador for record-keeping, but we felt we should be here with the others we've trained beside."

"And fought alongside," Kaiden reminded them and pointed a finger at the Tsuna ace. "Don't forget that."

"Of course." Jaxon nodded.

"I understand from friend Chiyo you are going some-where?" Genos inquired.

"Not far. I'm heading to Nexus," he revealed and gestured deeper into the hangar with his thumb. "Haldt is giving me a lift."

"Back to Nexus?" Jaxon asked. "Is it already up and

running? I thought it would be another month or so before they start housing again."

He shook his head. "Nah, they are still doing repairs. I'm going to see if anything of mine was found in the wreckage and to take a walk around. It's not like any of us who are graduating will stay there before the big day."

"I see." Genos tapped his infuser before he pointed upward in a moment of realization. "Ah, yes! Speaking of friend Chiyo, I saw her here a few minutes ago. Perhaps you should see her before you go."

"I plan to." Kaiden smiled. "She's coming with me. Do you care to join us?"

The engineer tilted his head and thought about it. "It's tempting…"

Jaxon placed his hand on his kin's shoulder. "We are waiting for a shuttle to report to the Tsuna main fleet around the embassy. They would not appreciate us failing to arrive after we scheduled a meeting."

"Ah, you are right." Genos nodded but looked disappointed. "Sorry, friend Kaiden, but we will meet again soon."

"We'd better," he replied and continued his walk. "We need to celebrate properly, and drinks are on me."

The two Tsuna watched him go and Genos frowned. "Do you remember which drink made me ill in our third year?"

"I do not," Jaxon said and shook his head. "Just don't drink anything with artificial coloring."

He nodded, but a moment later, his frown deepened. "Hmm, that limits my options."

Kaiden reached the second floor of the hangar and

located the dropship. Chiyo and the security officer chatted easily as he approached and the man noticed him first. "There he is!" he called. "Did it take you that long to pack?"

"I had to say a few goodbyes and watched a friend run for parliament," he responded and shook Haldt's hand. "Are you doing all right?"

"Decent, but I'm still getting over not being able to join the battle." He sighed and scratched the back of his head. "People needed dropping and things needed running, I guess."

"Speaking of which…" He looked from one to the other. "Are you ready to go?"

Haldt nodded and moved to the dropship's entrance. "I have the ship prepping. Let me finish—it'll only take a few minutes if you wanna climb in."

"Sure thing. We'll be in there in a second." Kaiden looked at Chiyo. "How are you doing?"

She regarded him warily. "Fine, why do you ask?"

"I guess my curiosity is getting the better of me," he explained with a shrug. "You've been kind of distant since we got back and I haven't heard what your plans are now."

"Really? I thought it would be obvious." She took a few steps away and nodded as if to reassure herself. "As for being distant…well, I suppose I'm still getting over having to prepare myself for my lover to throw himself into the abyss."

"Are you still on that?" He rubbed the back of his head with his free hand. "I mean…it worked out. Besides, it would have been heroic."

"Humph." She sighed and turned to face him. "So because it would have looked good it is all right?"

"Well...it helps, right?" Kaiden suggested but she did not seem to accept that. "Fair enough. I'm sorry I put you through some kind of trauma, I guess?"

She chuckled and shook her head. "I'm not sure I wanted an apology, but that was a terrible one nonetheless."

"God, you're picky," he retorted. The dropship began to activate and he motioned her inside. "By the way, now that you've had a few days, did you think of anything that could have been done besides using the failsafe?"

Chiyo was quiet as they boarded and Kaiden laughed. "I tell you what. If you can give me a good idea before we land, I'll try to come up with a better apology."

"Hmm, what do you want in exchange?" she asked.

"That the next time I do something idiotic you simply smile and nod."

She sat on one of the benches and folded her arms. "How long do we have?"

He sat opposite her and placed his case beside him. "About twenty minutes."

With a small frown, she leaned her head back. "Let me think."

"We're heading out!" Haldt called and the dropship elevated a few feet before it accelerated out of the doors of the hangar and returned to Nexus.

"No, that doesn't count," Kaiden insisted as he and Chiyo stepped out of the ship.

"Why not?" she demanded.

"Because your ideas have to be reasonable," he explained and turned to her with a frown.

"Using a droid would have been reasonable. There were enough of them available," she said defensively.

"Most of them were in pieces," he pointed out. "Besides, how would you have made it work even if there was one available? Hack it and send it down to activate the siphon? Even if it got there in time, one of the discharges would have simply destroyed it."

"Yeah? Well, it's only a matter of…" Her words faltered and she folded her arms and looked up.

"Yes?" he asked teasingly. "I'll give you one last attempt."

"Fine, you win," she conceded. "But please try to make the next idiotic stunt less…idiotic."

The ace smiled, leaned forward, and kissed her, catching her by surprise. The kiss lingered for a while before he pulled away gently. "All is forgiven?"

She smiled. "We could have started with that."

He rolled his eyes. "Like that would have been fun."

"They've made great progress, huh?" Haldt commented as he moved from the other side of the ship. Chiyo and Kaiden paused to study Nexus Academy. Many buildings were still under repair, but the rubble had been cleared and all the pathways were restored. The buildings that were in decent shape had already been fixed and were currently undergoing cleaning and repainting. He even identified a few new buildings that hadn't been there during his tenure over the last few years.

"You came to see if any of your stuff is still here, right?" Haldt asked. "They are holding everything they've recovered in the armory."

Chiyo nodded. "Thank you, Haldt, we'll head there now and—"

"I'll check that later," Kaiden interrupted and moved to the stairs off the landing pad. "I need to do something else first."

"What's that?" the security officer asked and looked at Chiyo, who shrugged.

"Pay my respects," the ace responded calmly. Her eyes widened and she rushed down the stairs to follow him.

Kaiden opened the door to the dojo. It had been cleaned but not organized and a large hole in the ceiling still needed to be repaired. Chiyo entered with him and surveyed what had once been Kaiden's training ground and what might as well have been Wolfson's abode.

"Are you okay?" she asked and rested a hand on his back as he took it all in.

"I'll be better soon. I haven't had a chance to do this since he..." The words trailed off and he glanced at where Wolfson's desk had been as a small smile formed. "Look at that."

She complied and saw numerous small items—guns, flowers, bottles of liquor, medals, eyepatches, and a small glowing orb in the middle that illuminated a memorial to the fallen sergeant.

"This bauble is probably from Laurie," Kaiden said,

knelt to poke the orb, and glanced at a bottle. "Firewater. Sasha and Wolfson used to drink this together." He caught a glint in the evening light and stretched tentatively to pick up an ornate Sauren spear. "Even Raza dropped by."

Chiyo knelt beside him and took his hand. He nodded gratefully as he replaced the spear. He brought his case forward, opened it, and removed his helmet from the battle. The visor was partially cracked and pieces had been lost in the fight with Merrick. "I put in a few good shots for you, Wolfson," he said quietly and studied the helmet one last time. "Thank you for everything."

Chief appeared above them and illuminated the memorial to give it an ethereal light. *"I honestly thought he would kill you the first time he dragged you away to this place."* The EI chuckled. *"It probably turned out to be one of the best things to happen to ya."*

"No kidding." The ace laughed and wiped his sleeve over his damp eyes. "God, I got angry at times but never felt like quitting, though. I didn't want to give him the satisfaction."

"Do you think he would have been satisfied if you had left?" Chiyo asked.

He shook his head. "Hell no, he would probably have dragged me back. It took a while, but I eventually realized he was looking out for me, in his way. And I never questioned his abilities as a soldier." He placed his helmet in front of the orb and bowed his head for a moment before he released it and stood. "In fact, he drilled something into my head even in the early days, something I've heard for a long time but that took even longer to click."

"What was that?" she asked. Chief continued to hover as they faced each other.

Kaiden smiled and rested his forehead against hers. "I told it to you during the first year, remember?"

Her eyes fluttered for a moment as she thought hard before she leaned back and looked at him. "Never settle?"

The ace nodded and held her close. "Yeah, and I will never settle."

EPILOGUE

"Way to go, dumbass. They're wrapping up!" Chief growled quietly in Kaiden's head.

"Why are you whispering?" he asked as he snuck through the upper levels of the recently rebuilt auditorium and tried to find a seat. "It's not like anyone can hear you."

"I'm trying to be civil, at least. Sasha is speaking." The ace finally found a seat next to Cameron and removed his tablet.

"I've waited for you all ceremony, man," he whispered. "Where you been?"

"I lost track of time talking to Haldt about the ship," he explained in a hushed tone. "I'd say sorry, but I'm already buying the drinks later so what more can I do?"

Before the bounty hunter could respond, Izzy leaned closer. "Quiet, guys. Sasha is looking this way."

Kaiden and Cameron focused on the front of the auditorium. While the man didn't make it obvious, the chancellor's eyes lingered in his direction. He hadn't lost his marksman's eye at all.

403

"And as we end today's celebration, the beginning of your graduation, I want everyone here to remember what you have not only gained over your years of training but also what we unfortunately lost over this last year," Sasha said, his voice solemn. "Let us take a moment of silence for those who cannot be with us now. These are our friends and fellow soldiers whom we lost during the war."

The entire auditorium stood and holoscreens appeared to display the images of the fallen. Some bowed their heads while others watched the images and names scroll, Kaiden among them. When the list reached those with last names beginning with 'W,' he bowed his head and closed his eyes as he drew a deep breath.

"Remember the fallen, but live for their sacrifice," the chancellor stated, and everyone remained standing as they once again looked at the stage. "And should any of you find yourself among them, know that we will always hold you dear." The man stood tall and his gaze drifted across the graduating class. "Your final year should never have been like this. But you survived, you all fought back, and you never gave in. You are the most prepared class in the Academy's history and know that everything you have trained for has paid off. You have the proof."

"Damn straight," Kaiden whispered and nodded.

"Today marks the end of your time here at Nexus, but you are always welcome back. We wish to see you, and know that we will also continue to train your future comrades and the defenders of our planet and galaxy." Sasha held one hand behind his back and saluted with the other. "We will strive to move forward. Thank you for your service and congratulations on your victory!"

Some saluted in return but most lost themselves in the moment, held their arms up, and yelled in happiness and celebration. Friends shook hands, embraced, and laughed with one another. Warm, triumphant music began to play over the speakers. It was hard to find a large orchestra even a couple of months after the war, but the holograms displayed bright flashes to mimic fireworks, and videos of moments and scenes throughout the years of the graduating class still provided a sense of joy and closure to the event.

Kaiden turned to his friends. Cameron, although he was ever the cynic, still offered his hand and a smile. He shook it and responded with a grin. The group gathered and Chiyo hugged him, Genos and Jaxon gave him a Tsuna salute that he returned, and Luke and Marlo threw massive arms around his shoulders. The heavies held tears back as the others laughed and congratulated each other.

Their new lives would begin soon, but first, they had a moment of a brief celebration.

"Another round everyone?" Julio asked and placed four large glasses of beer on the counter. Two each were eagerly snatched by Luke and Marlo.

"What the hell, guys? Hand one over," Cameron demanded.

Luke proceeded to down one while Marlo chuckled. "I'm sure there's more on tap. Ask them, Cam."

The bounty hunter grumbled and held his hand up to

beckon to one of the bartenders as Julio was busy fixing more drinks.

"Thanks for hosting this, Julio," Kaiden said and sipped his whiskey. "I'm glad you were able to get this place up and running so quickly."

"It wasn't an issue." The barkeep chuckled. "I made a good number of creds during the war and had enough to spare to get extra hands after I finished running supplies."

"Sasha wished to pass on his thanks for your work," Chiyo told him.

The man nodded. "It was better than sitting around with a thumb up my ass. And it was nice to get back into the field and know I could still do it."

"What's my tab up to so far?" Kaiden asked and checked his tablet.

Julio waved him off. "Don't worry about it, my friend. I got it."

He frowned at the barkeep. "For everyone?"

"I still got the creds. Besides, everyone deserves a chance to unwind after everything that happened. I can provide that moment, at least."

"Well, it's appreciated." The ace chuckled and raised his glass.

"Think of it as a going-away present," Julio quipped with a shrug. "So, do you know what you'll do now that you've graduated?"

"Yeah. I'll start my own merc company," he revealed. "I'm still ironing out all the details, but I've sent the forms in to have it recognized."

"Ah, you ain't running an outlaw company?" his friend asked and slid a few glasses down the bar.

Kaiden frowned and shook his head. "Are you kidding me? Even if I ran like that, after everything the Horde pulled, the galaxy is hunting all the other outlaw mercs. I'm very sure that if there was even a whiff of the idea, Sasha himself would put a stop to it."

Julio chuckled. "Where is the new chancellor? We keep mentioning him but I haven't seen him since all the chaos died down."

"He spent some time in recovery before he began his official tenure as chancellor of Nexus," Chiyo replied. "He's worked almost constantly since he recuperated."

"He said he wanted to see me when we got back," the ace added and tapped his finger on the bar.

"Really? Did he tell you what for?" she asked.

He shook his head. "I guess I'll find out when I get there, but I told him it would probably be a while."

"We invited him to join us, as well as Professor Laurie, but both declined," Amber added.

"It seems like both simply want things to get back in order as soon as possible," Cyra noted.

"Shouldn't you help the professor?" Indre asked. "Getting the lab in working order again will be a hell of a project."

Cyra shrugged. "I offered to stick around but he said I should enjoy myself as I probably wouldn't have another chance before the new year started. When I pressed the issue, he said he wanted time to himself."

"It probably means he is doing what we are, only in private," Kaiden commented and drained his glass.

"I don't think so," she responded. "Since we've returned

to the Academy, he's been less...eccentric? Let's go with that."

"Haven't you checked in with him, Kaiden?" Chiyo asked.

He thought about it for a moment. "I saw him in person on the first day he came back and spoke to him a couple of times over comms and video after that. I guess he has been more chilled than normal, come to think of it. I thought it was because he was too swamped with repairs and organization to let his mind wander."

"Does anyone need a refill?" Julio asked and slid more drinks down the bar.

"Fill her up!" Mack shouted and held his large stein up.

"I will imbibe more, elder Julio!" Genos called from a few seats down.

"He still hasn't dropped that elder business, eh?" Julio muttered and poured a pink liquid into a glass. Kaiden looked at it and glanced at the Tsuna's almost empty glass, which also held remnants of the bright drink.

"Are you still drinking poison, Genos?" he asked. He pushed his empty glass forward for another bartender to take.

"No, I was careful this time and elder Julio was kind enough to show me Tsuna-appropriate drinks on the menu."

The ace looked at the glass on the bar, opened a holoscreen in it to look at the menu, and noticed a small section of about a dozen drinks listed as Tsuna specialties. "Are you branching out, Julio?"

The barkeep shrugged. "I didn't have many non-human customers. After your buddy's mishap the last time, I decided it was smart to add a few drinks that didn't have the potential to poison any new clients. They might sue."

Kaiden looked at a table of Tsuna and humans who talked and laughed together. Each of the Tsuna held their unique concoctions. "That was probably smart."

A noticeably loud bang from behind him overwhelmed the chatter in the air and he turned his attention to about twenty people who walked in together. They were all dressed in designer versions of streetwear with punk and slummer cuts and looked familiar, but he couldn't put his finger on why.

Julio looked up wryly. "Well, ain't this appropriate," he muttered and his gaze darted from them to the ace before he leaned closer and gestured to the new arrivals. "I can tell you at least think you know them but have a little trouble recalling from where."

Kaiden nodded and leaned against the bar. "I do, but how do you—" He stared at Julio's amused smile for a moment before he focused on the group again and his eyes widened. "No way!"

"What is it, mate?" Flynn asked. Amber, Izzy, Silas, and his other friends turned their attention to either him or the newcomers. He laughed and slapped a hand against Julio's shoulder. "I thought you threw them out and barred them from coming back."

"I did," he stated and straightened as he folded his arms. "What the hell are you doing here?" he demanded and drew the attention of the slummers and their posse.

"Do you still hold a grudge, old man?" the one with blue spikes snapped. Kaiden wracked his brains. They all had idiotic names, but he'd run into a number of those over the years. Which one was it?

He pointed at the leader. "Caesar?"

"Czar, idiot!" he retorted but when he caught sight of the ace, his eyes widened. "Wait...no fucking way!"

"That was my response, kinda." A bartender returned with a new glass of whiskey. Kaiden took a sip, stood, and studied Czar and his now larger group. "I see you've made new friends since the last time."

The man was a little hesitant now, but with the eyes of his lackeys on him, he straightened and took a couple of steps toward him. "I have a real gang going now."

"Do ya? What's the name?" he asked and an amused smirk crossed his face.

"Rain City Royals," the man replied and a trace confidence bolstered his tone.

"Good God," the ace muttered and ran a hand down his face. "I thought you said gang, not Esports team."

"Oh, shut the hell up!" Czar demanded. A larger man—Moxy if he remembered correctly—stepped to his leader's side. "Where the hell have you been since that fight? I looked for you for months to tear your ass up for your insults."

"Only the insults? I would've been more pissed off about the concussions myself." Kaiden chuckled and Flynn, Cameron, and a few others behind him echoed his amusement.

A few more in Czar's gang stepped forward and some drew weapons such as knives and hammers. "Do you wanna repeat that? Me and all my boys will happily respond in kind," Czar threatened and brandished a blade as well. "Do you think you can take us all on?"

Kaiden drained his drink quickly and placed the glass on the counter. "Probably, but I don't think I'll have to." His friends nodded as they stood from their chairs and moved to his side. Czar and the group backed away a little, but a loud pop behind them gave them pause. They turned to see the doors to the Emerald Lounge had locked themselves and their gazes drifted to Julio, who put a tablet down as his smile grew wider.

"As for where I've been, that would be Nexus academy," Kaiden said calmly. More and more people from the tables and booths all around the two floors of the lounge stood. Some leaned over the railings above, others descended the stairs, and a few approached the now wide-eyed slummers. "In fact, everyone here has been there and you're interrupting our graduation ceremony."

The gang now gathered closer together as Nexus graduates approached from all sides. "S-Sorry about t-that," Czar stammered.

"Ah, don't worry about it." Kaiden waved a hand. "I'm cool with it. The others might still be pissed, though."

"Nah, only drunk." Luke laughed and swirled a drink in a large glass. "I need a good workout to sober up."

"You know what? Same," Silas agreed and cracked his knuckles.

The ace ran a hand through his hair. "Well, I don't want to feel left out now. Do you wanna help us, Caesar?" he asked with a wicked smile.

Czar had no chance to respond as Kaiden charged,

followed by his friends and essentially the entire lounge. The Rain City Royalty members uttered cries of fear as the Nexus graduates continued their celebrations in their own way.

Laurie looked out of the chancellor's office window to where the moon only now peeked out from amongst the clouds. "It's a beautiful night." He sighed and glanced at the table, where Sasha scrolled through messages on his tablet. Three glasses rested on the surface, one in front of each chair. "It's a shame to be cooped up while it is so pleasant. Are you sure you don't want to take a moment to go out and check the island?"

"I did rounds this morning," Sasha replied and continued to scroll through his messages list. "Everything is going well and the additions to your lab might be completed a couple of weeks earlier than expected."

The professor nodded and crossed the room slowly. At first, he intended to sit before he took a few steps around and stood behind his companion. "You've been hidden here ever since the room was completed. Before then, you worked constantly inside one of the temp buildings."

"There is much to be done. With the start date pushed back for the year, we'll have to adjust schedules and classes for the new arrivals so our entire calendar doesn't change," Sasha explained and glanced over his shoulder. "Besides, I told you I was able to get out earlier."

"It's still considered work, Sasha," Laurie grumbled, moved to his chair, and sat. He crossed one leg over the other and leaned back. "It will probably be some time before he comes, you know."

"I don't want to risk missing him," the chancellor retorted and focused on his tablet.

"You could always send a message that you are stepping out," he told him. "But...I get it and honestly, it is kind of amusing."

"What's that?" the other man asked. Although he didn't look up, he did stop reading.

"You've always been a good teacher and good military leader, but part of your method was not getting too close to a student or soldier," Laurie explained quietly. "Kaiden has been a unique trial for you, hasn't he? For once, you'll have to let go of a protégé and have no way to know when you'll see them again. It's rather adorable in a way."

Sasha lowered his tablet again and stared at him. The professor awaited his response with an amused smile, but the other man simply shrugged. "You're right, and I wouldn't change that."

He raised his brow in surprise. "It's rather direct coming from you," he commented and his grin widened. "I like it. You should try it more often."

Before the chancellor could respond, a knock at the door prompted them to share an expectant glance. "Already?" Laurie asked.

"I'm not expecting anyone else," Sasha reminded him and turned to the door. "Come in."

It slid open to reveal Kaiden, with tousled hair and a weary grin on his face. He stretched his arms as he walked to the table. "Hey, Sasha—and Laurie? Cyra said you stayed behind for personal time."

"I had a couple of projects I wanted to wrap up for the day before I visited our chancellor." He patted the armrest of the chair between the two faculty members. "Come on, dear Kaiden, have a seat."

"I appreciate it." The ace sighed as he sat. "It turned out to be more of an exciting night than I had originally thought it would be."

"Did something happen?" Sasha asked as he retrieved a blue bottle and removed the cap.

"We ran into some old friends and things got… Well, let's stick with exciting. I had to leave the bar in a hurry to avoid potential issues that could have stopped me from departing tomorrow."

"Old friends? Is it anyone I would know?" the professor asked.

Kaiden shook his head while Sasha poured liquid from the bottle into the glasses on the table. "Nah, but Sasha might remember them. I was surprised to see them myself." When the chancellor finished pouring, he screwed the cap on again. The ace peered at the glass, picked it up, and observed the clear liquid. "Vodka?" he asked. "I thought you were more into whiskey."

"This is a particular occasion," the chancellor said, put the bottle down, and picked his glass up. Laurie followed suit.

They toasted one another and the ace drained the glass in one swallow. His eyes widened and he almost spat it out, but not out of taste or the burn of the alcohol. His surprise was due to its familiarity. "What is this? I've had it before."

"I would think Wolfson would have had you try it on at

least a couple of occasions," Sasha said and set his glass down.

"Wolfson?" Kaiden looked at his glass. "Is this Firewater?"

"It was a favorite of his." Laurie sighed and leaned back with his glass pressed against his chest. What remained of the contents swirled around the bottom. "I always found it a little too dry, but it would have been his turn this year to choose the beverage."

"I don't understand." The ace looked at the two men in turn. "What's going on?"

"This was something of a ritual of ours," the chancellor explained and took another sip. "Before a new year would start, the three of us would get together, go over the plans, and make preparations before the Academy opened."

Kaiden looked at his glass. "So...am I Wolfson in this case?"

"You are, Kaiden dear boy." The professor snorted, finished his drink, and gestured to Sasha to pass the bottle. "This will be our first year without him, something we will have to deal with from here on."

"But given that you were his student—more than that really..." The chancellor handed Laurie the bottle before he looked at the ceiling. "I noticed a change in him when he started training you. Wolfson had grown...not dour, not content..."

"His fire was leveling out," Laurie suggested and poured vodka into his glass until it was a little over half-full. He placed the bottle in front of Kaiden. "He would get his work done and train a while, but he was getting comfortable. And while that sounds good, it annoyed the hell out of him."

Sasha nodded. "When he took you under his wing, that fire, as Laurie calls it, it sparked again."

"It made him almost pleasant to be around after a couple of years," the other man muttered and sipped his vodka.

The chancellor ran a hand through his hair and focused on Kaiden. "With him gone and you leaving, we felt that... well, this would be a proper send-off to both of you."

The ace nodded, took the bottle, and filled his glass again. "I appreciate the sentiment, but do you really think I can live up to him?"

"Possibly." Laurie shrugged. "It all depends if you want to do that."

"Shouldn't I?" he asked and handed the bottle to Sasha. "I mean, being his protégé and all?"

"I don't think Wolfson wanted an apprentice to continue his legacy," the chancellor stated and rested a hand on his shoulder. "He only wanted to make sure you were ready to accomplish whatever you wanted to do and be who you wanted to be."

"He...wouldn't be a bad man to mold yourself after," Laurie confessed and put his glass down. He looked at the ace. "But I doubt he would want you to simply be a copycat."

"That's true enough." Kaiden chuckled and nodded at Sasha when he removed his hand. "Thanks," he said and raised a toast to them both with his glass. "Even when I'm out in the great beyond, I'll be sure to remember this."

Laurie ran his arm across his eyes before he straightened and stretched. "This will be your first time beyond this system. Are you ready for that? Especially for such a prolonged period."

"Yeah, we're heading to Abisalo first so Genos can take care of something, then we'll meet Magellan." He looked at Sasha. "He said he has a few missions he's set aside to get us started."

"Do you have a ship?" the chancellor asked.

"It would be quite a problem if I didn't," he responded, leaned back, and swirled his drink. "Haldt said he would get one for me but I haven't seen it yet. He's bringing it in the morning."

"I should take a look at it," Laurie offered, "to see if it needs any last-minute tinkering."

"Genos and Chiyo will examine it as well," he replied and took a sip. "You can go over it with them."

The three of them chatted into the night before Kaiden finally headed out and left the island for the hotel room he shared with Chiyo. He took one last look at the Academy and realized it was probably the last time he would see it under moonlight in a long while.

"Ugh, good Lord," Kaiden muttered and rubbed his eyes.

"Are there problems, friend Kaiden?" Genos asked. "Shouldn't you be excited? This is the day we begin our expedition."

"I'm not entirely sure that's what we should call it," Chiyo said and ran a hand over Kaiden's back. "Was it the smartest idea to go out drinking the night before?"

"It was the last time we'd see everyone for a long time," the ace replied and grunted with annoyance as the carrier bounced along the road to Nexus Academy. "Besides, ya'll drank too."

"Moderately," she countered. "As you can see, we're fine."

"Yeah, yeah." Kaiden grimaced and shielded his eyes with his arms. "I should have had Haldt meet us at the hotel."

"Hmm, that would have been unwise," the Tsuna noted. "Current rules for incoming vessels bar anything larger than personal transport. Having Haldt drop the ship off at the hotel would have been problematic."

"It's only wishful thinking, Genos." The ace sighed and shifted in his seat. As a distraction, he took his tablet out and looked through his messages. They included well wishes from guys like Julio and the gang leaders but nothing from his friends. "Do you think they are all still asleep?"

Chiyo looked at the device and shrugged. "I did ask if you wanted to go and meet up with them."

"They deserve their rest and we got in our goodbyes yesterday, I guess," he said, but a part of him was a little wistful when he thought about the friends he probably wouldn't see in person for quite some time.

"We're almost at the gates," Genos said, stood, and retrieved his luggage from the compartment above. "It's time."

"It is, isn't it?" Kaiden chuckled and smiled as he and Chiyo stood to retrieve their gear.

"You are sure you had the time correct?" the engineer asked as the trio frowned at an empty landing pad. Waves crashed against the pier of the Academy and left a nice cool feeling. Kaiden felt his face redden and avoided looking at his friends.

"And the right destination?" Chiyo added before she withdrew her tablet from her bag and typed something.

"I can read," Kaiden muttered before he sighed, put his luggage down, and slid his hands into his jacket. "You know, I kind of hoped our last day on-world would be a little more grand and less a comedy of errors, but some things stay the same around here, huh?"

"It would be exactly that if it wasn't deliberate," she responded and looked at him with a secretive smile.

"What do you mean?" he asked and she turned the tablet so he could see a message she had just sent out on the screen. *Come down, he's ready.*

He raised an eyebrow at her in query. "Uh...do you wanna explain?" She pointed up in response and he looked skyward as a familiar dropship soared into view.

"Is that Haldt?" Kaiden held an arm in front of his eyes as the vessel drew closer and kicked wind up. "Is that—"

The dropship was Wolfson's, which Haldt had used through the war, but it seemed to have been recently cleaned and upgraded. When it landed, the doors opened immediately and all his friends funneled out, together with Laurie and Sasha.

"Did you plan this?" he asked Chiyo as the newcomers

looked at them from the landing pad and gestured for the three to join them.

"I wanted something a little grand too." She smiled and took his hand. "Let's go say goodbye one last time."

They hurried up the stairs. Haldt was the last to exit the ship and he smiled broadly. "Hey, Kaiden. Are you surprised?"

"Definitely." He looked at the ship. "So you weren't getting a new ship?"

The security officer shook his head. "Nah, this beauty still has many missions to complete before it's anywhere near retirement. I only fitted her out for prolonged travel." He looked at the vessel and continued to smile, although his expression was a little smug.

"Are you sure?" Kaiden asked. "You're taking his position so shouldn't you keep it close?"

"I won't leave campus that much for a while so it wouldn't get any use," Haldt explained. "Besides, he wanted you to have it."

The ace's eyes widened and when he looked at Sasha and Laurie, both nodded. "He didn't leave much in the way of an official will," the chancellor stated. "But he had a list and your name was marked next to the ship."

"I helped with the redesigns," Laurie said and his gaze slid over the vessel. "But Wolfson did have an eye for ships. I kept it as close to the original as I could."

Kaiden nodded and swallowed around the tightness in his throat. "Thank you."

"Are you sure you don't wanna stick around a while longer, mate?" Flynn asked. "The rest of us won't start our careers for another couple of months so we could have a little more time as a group."

"It is tempting, man." He sighed and looked at the gathering of friends and colleagues he had gained over the years. "But I think if I stick around any longer, I ain't gonna want to leave. It'll only be more of a pain to head out. Besides, I already have missions waiting."

"Then we wish you the best," Julius told him with a solemn expression.

"You'll kick ass out there, buddy!" Luke hollered and shook his hand enthusiastically. The others all offered their good wishes to the trio, and Jaxon handed a box to his fellow Tsuna after a few quiet words had been exchanged. Finally, the group backed away and waved as Kaiden, Genos, and Chiyo stepped onboard. The engineer immediately moved to the pilot's seat.

"Don't you wanna take a look around first, Genos?" Kaiden asked.

"I don't think the professor would appreciate me second-guessing his work," Genos responded and placed the box on the co-pilot's chair. "And I trust him enough to begin our flight without a look…at least until we gain some distance."

The ace laughed as the door to the ship closed and the vessel elevated to hover before it ascended slowly. He and Chiyo looked out the window and waved before their pilot activated the thrusters and moved them into the stratosphere.

"It feels real now, huh?" he said thoughtfully and wandered into the pilot bay. Carefully, he moved the box

Genos had placed in the co-pilot's seat and sat in what was now a very familiar place.

"Indeed, I must say it is nice to be able to pilot a ship in a more casual fashion," the engineer responded cheerfully.

Kaiden studied the simple metallic box. It was light-blue with an ornate symbol on top that looked like a replica of Abisalo. "What is this, Genos?"

"Something kin Jaxon asked me to return once we reach Abisalo." Genos checked the monitors.

"What's inside?" he asked and placed it to the side.

"Something of great importance," his friend responded cryptically.

"And you're not gonna tell me?" He tried to sound like the new leader of their little team, which he was even though it felt odd for a moment.

"That wouldn't be much fun, would it?" Genos reasoned and darted him an amused glance. "Besides, it means you will be less likely to take us on detours if you remain curious."

Kaiden shook his head. "You can be quite devious, you know that?"

"I do." The Tsuna made no further comment so left no opening for him to push.

"I already have the clearance to use the warp gates, thanks to Sasha," Chiyo told them as she slid into one of the two seats behind her friends. "They were a little wary to allow non-military and corporate ships through. I had to send them our new ship's identification number so they could approve it for us."

"We're a corporation now," the ace pointed out.

"We're a mercenary company and only registered as

such," she countered. "Until we complete our first ranked mission, we are not officially licensed and merely labeled as one."

He ran a hand through his hair before he rubbed it in annoyance. "Really? Shit."

"Fortunately, I do not believe we will need to worry about that while we are on my planet," Genos assured them and glanced at a passing ship as they finally left Earth and glided into the stars. "At least in theory."

"Theory? Is something going on?" Kaiden asked and frowned at the numerous ships now orbiting the planet.

"It shouldn't concern us, hopefully," the Tsuna told him. Chiyo leaned over his shoulder to show him an image on her tablet. She pointed to the left and their pilot changed course toward a warp gate.

"So you ain't gonna tell me what's going down or what's in the box?" he asked.

"I think not," Genos responded cheekily. "Isn't this new life already exciting, friends?"

"Cute, Genos," he snarked.

"I know you've been through a warp gate before, Genos," the infiltrator said as they drew closer to the gate. She looked at the ace. "What about you?"

"Sure, in the Animus," he told her.

"Only in the Animus?" Genos asked. "This will be your first time in reality?"

He nodded as Chiyo strapped herself in behind him. "Yeah, is that a big deal?"

His friends exchanged a glance and both grinned. "Well, you should know that reality is often more intense than a simulation, even one in the Animus."

"I have no doubt." He chuckled and Chief appeared in the air as the team approached the gate, where a purple light flooded the interior of the ring. The ship's speed increased, and a glance at a monitor showed a feed of the ships and planet they were leaving behind. He looked away and to his partner and friends. "And I say I'm more than ready for it."

The vessel entered the gate and vanished into the light. Kaiden left all that he knew and headed out into the unknown. He reminded himself there was more fun to be had out there, after all.

THE END

Kaiden and friends are now available in audio at Amazon, Audible and iTunes. Check out book one, INITIATE, performed by Scott Aiello.

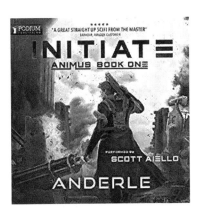

Check out book one at Amazon

(Books two - seven are also available in audio, with more coming soon.)

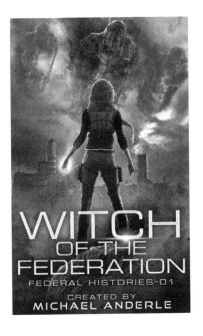

Available now at Amazon and through Kindle Unlimited

The future has amazing technology. Our alien allies have magic. Together, we are building a training system to teach the best of humanity to go to the stars.

But the training is monumentally expensive.

Stephanie Morgana is a genius, she just doesn't *know it.*

The Artificial Intelligence which runs the Virtual World is charged with testing Stephanie, a task it has never performed before.

The Earth and their allies, may never be the same again.

Will Stephanie pass the test and be moved to the advanced preparatory schools, or will the system miss her? Will the AI be able to judge a human's potential in an area where it has no existing test data to compare?

Available now at Amazon and through Kindle Unlimited

AUTHOR NOTES - MICHAEL

JUNE 14, 2020

This marks the end of the very first set of books for the Animus series and Kaiden and the team.

It's both exhilarating and sad.

As an author, even a collaborative author who doesn't have to write most of the words, it feels good to complete a series.

These characters are like friends I have talked to, listened to, and cried over as they fought and gave up their lives to tell this story.

But I couldn't be prouder of the way Joshua worked his way through these stories with me.

A fair number of times, new collaborators don't know how to work with me as the more successful author, and occasionally, I will encourage them to push back or ask if they want something to work a little differently.

My son had NO problem with that. It's almost like he has known me his entire life, and me being 'Michael Anderle best-selling Sci-Fi Author' didn't bug him in the least. Perhaps because it didn't.

Don't get me wrong, he cared enough to ask my opinion, and if he felt he was being too pushy, he would step back and ask – but I didn't have to worry he was wowed by anything, either.

In the end, I was someone he knew.

We both grew from this experience, and I already look forward to our next collaboration, which has been in the works for a couple of months now. Joshua took from our efforts with *Animus* to locate the areas of challenge and seek to address them early.

WHY WOLFSON?

I hate when characters I love die. However, when you have a battle (war) this large, to believe only third-tier characters would pass away is highly unrealistic.

Joshua and I talked about Wolfson passing, and I knew it was going to happen. But damned if it doesn't STILL hurt when I read through this book mentioning him, and the final scene when Kaiden sits in Wolfson's place to drink to the future.

That is the mark of both a great writer and character who can make you feel.

I'm not a drinker, so I don't know what it is like to throw back a liquor that's so potent it makes you cough, but for Wolfson, I might try it just once.

THE FUTURE OF THIS UNIVERSE

Joshua and I have talked about what's next, and the short answer is nothing, for now.

We have left the characters open to take the next path, and I kinda feel like we will come back around at some point and find out where they go.

But for now, with twelve books down and a need to

visit another world, we are going to allow Kaiden, Chiyo, and Genos a chance to fly out and start their business and their future. They have graduated, and they deserve a chance to do something without us looking over their shoulders.

For now.

If you like this kind of story, we have more for you, and more coming from us in the future.

Stay tuned!

(For fun, you can try *Witch of the Federation, Too Young to Die*, or if you would like something completely different try *The Unbelievable Mr. Brownstone*.)

Diary June 14 – 20, 2020

So, Las Vegas is a little weird right now. You have pockets of people who are very Covid-19-aware around the valley area, and then you have the casinos. Some of the casinos are very Covid aware and more stringent, and others aren't.

No casino (that I've been to) mandates wearing a mask.

The Station Casinos shoot that temperature gauge at you when you enter their establishment but are pretty open after that.

Caesar's Hotel and Casino (for this latest weekend) was packed with people, and they try to encourage social distancing, but occasionally people get a little close together—and by occasionally, I mean all of Friday night.

I can't speak to Saturday or Saturday night since I didn't get to continue playing. My budget was used up, so I worked and slept most of Saturday, catching up from some mixed up sleep during the week.

I'm at the Green Valley Hotel and Casino. Sitting in the food court, I can see at least twelve people playing on the casino floor. The mask to no-mask ratio seems to be about even, except for the person who has a mask, but is smoking, so the mask is pulled down.

I'm going to count that as a no-mask.

Here in the food court, the mask ratio is about one person with a mask to twenty without one.

We are fifteen feet from the slot machines.

I get why those of us in the food court have no masks (and there is no difference when I go to regular restaurants. Once a person sits down at a table, the masks come off almost immediately.)

I think I will be about done with these updates starting next week. Enough of my diary entries have dealt with Covid-19 and Las Vegas, it's time to just…talk about other stuff.

Like books, maybe?

Sometimes, it's hard to remember what readers want to hear about in our (author and publisher) lives. I eat, sleep, and breathe publishing and stories at this point in my career, and what's normal to me (and seems like would be boring to you) is probably not.

As always, THANK YOU for reading our stories. We would not be able to create the wonderful stories without readers like you supporting us!

Ad Aeternitatem,

Michael Anderle

Printed in Poland
by Amazon Fulfillment
Poland Sp. z o.o., Wrocław

60554116R00263